One Night

By Allie Everhart

One Night
By Allie Everhart

Copyright © 2017 Allie Everhart
All rights reserved.
Published by Waltham Publishing, LLC
Cover Design by Okay Creations
ISBN: 978-1-942781-08-0

CHAPTER ONE

May

AMBER

"Where are you going?" I yell over the music as Megan takes off with some guy.

"I'll meet up with you later!" she yells back, laughing as she stumbles on her heels. We've been at this party less than ten minutes and she's already tipsy. She swigged down two cups of spiked fruit punch which is all it takes for someone as tiny as her to get drunk.

"Amber!" she yells, stumbling back to me. "Todd said he'd take me home later so don't wait around for me."

"Megan, you just met the guy. You sure you can trust him?"

"Todd?" She laughs and waves her hand around. "He's totally harmless. And I didn't just meet him. I met him last week at Shooter's. He's bartending there this summer." She's bouncing up and down to the music. She always gets hyper when she's drunk.

"So he goes to school here?" I ask, looking behind her to see him. He's standing a few feet away, checking his phone.

"Yeah, he's a junior. Pre-law." She checks to make sure he's still there, then whips back to me. "I gotta go."

"So you're just leaving me here? What happened to girls' night? You said we were coming here to drink and dance."

She pouts her glossy pink lips. "I know. I'm sorry. But I didn't know Todd would be here."

I'm pretty sure she did. Out of all the parties we could've gone to, she kept insisting on going to this one, which isn't even at our college. It's on the other side of Chicago at Townsend College, a small liberal arts school I hadn't even heard of until just last week when Megan told me about this party. She said a band would be playing but I'm not seeing any signs of a band. There's no stage. No musicians. We're in a frat house off campus in a living room that's been cleared of furniture and is currently packed with wall-to-wall people. Club music is blasting from speakers, one of which is right next to my head.

"Where's the band?" I yell so she can hear me.

"What band?" she yells back as she moves to the music.

"Yeah, that's what I thought."

"What?" She leans closer. "I can't hear you."

"Never mind. You better get back to Todd. Just be careful, okay? You don't know him that well."

"I'll be fine. Have fun tonight!" She gives me a quick hug, then runs off into Todd's waiting arms. They kiss and he grabs her ass as she grinds against him. I bet they'll be having sex by the end of the night, or maybe in a few minutes the way they're going at it.

Megan's a free spirit. Wild and crazy and up for anything. We became friends a few months ago when we were on a project together for marketing. We're not close friends but just friends who go out now and then. She's not someone I'd share my deepest, innermost secrets to because she can't keep a secret to save her life. Last March I told her I liked this guy in our class and the next day he came up to me and told me he has a girlfriend. Megan had told him what I said! I was mortified. She said she was only trying to help because I hadn't been on a date in a month but her 'help' backfired and left me feeling

2

embarrassed around the guy for the rest of the semester. Thank God school is out for the summer so I don't have to see him.

I should've known Megan would take off with some guy the minute we got here. Now I'm stuck at this party not knowing anyone. But it's Friday night and I just finished a week of finals so I don't want to go back to my apartment. I want to be out having fun.

I gulp down some of my spiked fruit punch. It's way too sweet and whatever they spiked it with doesn't mix well with the fruity taste of the punch.

"Hey," a voice says from behind me.

I look over and see a blond guy walking toward me. He's tall and thin, wearing a smile that says he's looking for sex and wants to know if I'm interested. Maybe it's presumptuous to assume all that from a simple smile but after attending two years of college and a ton of parties, I've seen that smile many times on many guys and I know what it means.

"How's it going?" he asks, his eyes lowering to my breasts before returning to my face.

"Good," I say. "How about you?"

Instead of answering, he holds his hand out. "I'm Alex."

"Amber." I shake his hand. It's cold and clammy and his fingers are long and skinny and feel awkward wrapped around mine. I won't date a guy if his hand doesn't fit right in mine. Maybe that's crazy, but would you really want to date a guy you can't hold hands with? Or if you do hold hands with him, would you want it to feel awkward?

I've had this debate with Megan and she's told me that nobody holds hands anymore, except for old people and little kids. She said she never holds hands with a guy, but that's because she skips straight to the sex. There's no time for handholding. Her hands are too busy doing other things.

As for me? I like holding a guy's hand. I think it's romantic. If you do it in public, it shows people you're a couple. If you do it in private, it says you can't help but touch the person even if you're just sitting together watching TV.

3

"Need another drink?" Alex asks, pointing to my cup, which is still half full.

"No thanks. I'm good. So you go to school at Townsend?"

"Yeah. I'm a senior, or I will be in the fall." He finishes his drink.

"What's your major?"

"Business," he says, seeming completely uninterested in the topic. He wants sex, not someone to talk to. "You sure you don't want another drink?"

He wants me to drink up and get drunk so we can move this along.

"I still have some left," I say, holding up the cup.

He nods, and his eyes go to my breasts again. I'm wearing a sleeveless button-up blouse and the silky fabric clings to my chest. It's tucked into my short skirt, which Alex has taken note of, his eyes now skimming down my legs.

He's smiling, so obviously he likes what he sees but I'm not feeling the same way. I'm not feeling anything for him. Not even the tiniest spark. It's not like there's anything wrong with him. He has a good-looking face, bright blond hair, and pale blue eyes. I'm sure plenty of girls find him attractive, but not me. I'm not into blonds, despite being one myself. Maybe that's why I don't like them. I want something different. I tend to go for guys with dark hair and dark eyes, so this guy? Not at all my type. Add in the skinny fingers and the fact that he won't stop leering at me and wants to get me drunk, and I feel the sudden need to get away from him.

"I need to find my friend," I tell him. "But I'll see ya around." I walk off and he doesn't bother to follow me. He knows he wasn't getting any.

Glancing back at the dance floor, I see Megan and Todd grinding against each other to the slow pulsing beat of the music. I'm surprised they haven't found a room by now. When Megan likes a guy, she moves fast. A few weeks ago I went to a club with her and she hooked up with a guy ten minutes after meeting him. I admit he was hot, but hooking up after knowing him for ten minutes? That's crazy.

And yet, I was oddly envious of it because it's so unlike anything I would ever do. A one-night stand? Never had one and probably never will. Although...I'm not completely opposed to the idea.

I've never told anyone this, not even my best friend, Kira, who lives back in Michigan, but the truth is, I've fantasized about having a one-night stand. Not the kind where I'm so drunk I can't remember it the next day. And not the kind that's instigated by some overly aggressive guy like Alex who doesn't care who he's with as long as he gets sex. No. My fantasy is that I meet a guy I instantly connect with and have major chemistry with and we do it without any thought or reservations. We act on pure instinct, like those scenes in the movies where two people meet and have such a strong attraction to each other that they throw caution to the wind and act on their urges.

Unfortunately, I'm not good at throwing caution to the wind. There's always this part of me holding me back, telling me not to do it. I fight that part of me and yet it always seems to win out.

Maybe that's why I keep hanging out with Megan. I'm hoping her free spirit will rub off on me. So far it hasn't, but I recently promised myself that before the summer ends, I'll do at least one thing that's outside my comfort zone.

This promise was inspired a few weeks ago by a girl in my speech class. She talked about seizing the day, going after what you want. I'm sure the rest of the class thought the speech was cheesy and a total cliché but I actually found it inspiring. Although I'm very rational and realistic in my everyday life, I also have a dreamy, head-in-the-clouds side, so that girl's speech ignited a spark in me, inspiring me to go for it. To do something I've always wanted to do without letting my rational side stop me.

"Amber?" a girl says from beside me. I turn and see it's Reese, a girl I worked with last March at the women's business expo downtown. We were both volunteers at a booth for an organization that promotes women in marketing. We're both marketing majors but at different colleges.

"Reese." I smile, happy to see someone I know. "How have you been?"

"Great! How about you?"

"Good. Just finished a week of finals so I'm exhausted."

"Yeah, me too. You heading home for the summer?"

"No, I'm staying here and working and taking a couple classes."

She glances behind her. "Well, I just wanted to say hi. I'm here with my boyfriend so I should probably get back to him."

"Yeah, okay. See ya later." I was hoping she'd stick around so we could talk.

"Sorry," a guy says as he bumps into me, trying to squeeze through the crowd.

People keep bumping into me. I should go stand somewhere else but there aren't any open spaces. Looking to my left I spot Alex with a girl. He's still got that looking-for-sex smile and so does she. Well, there you go. A match is made. There's someone for everyone, at least for a night.

Maybe I should leave. The only two people I know here are hanging out with their guys and I'm feeling awkward standing here by myself.

As I contemplate this, my eyes wander to the front door.

And that's when I see him.

Tall. Dark hair. Dark eyes. A strong jaw and pronounced cheekbones that give him that pretty boy, model look. Like a rich, prep school boy. He steps into the room, his eyes scanning the crowd. His eyes are brooding. Mysterious. Hot.

Thump, thump. Thump, thump. That's my heart, beating so loud it's thumping in my eardrums. I don't know who this guy is but he's got my heart shifted into overdrive.

I can't look away. There's something about him. Is it his face? His eyes?

Oh no, he just saw me. He saw me staring at him! And now he's staring back! This is so embarrassing and yet I can't look away. His eyes are piercing through me, like they're willing mine to stay connected to his. He takes a step toward me, his lips slightly parted, almost like he's saying something to me.

Do I know this guy? Does he know *me*? And if not, why do I feel this odd connection to him? And why is my heart beating so freaking fast?

Our eyes remain locked as he makes his way over to me. When he finally reaches me, I'm unable to say anything. I just keep staring at him. Those brooding eyes. Those lips. He has perfect lips. And his jaw. It's strong, angular, with a thin layer of scruff.

"What's your name?" he asks. I love his voice. It's smooth. Deep. Sexy.

I pause, suddenly unable to remember my name. What the hell? What's my damn name?

"Amber," I blurt out. "My name is Amber." I'm so breathless my words come out in almost a whisper. I finally break my gaze from his and look down, embarrassed that I'm acting so strange.

"Amber," he says, not like he's confirming what he heard but more like he's saying my name aloud to himself. And when he said it, I could feel his breath on my face. That's how close we're standing.

I swallow and close my eyes for a moment, trying to make sense of this, trying to get myself together, because what's happening right now? It's surreal.

I feel his hand under my chin as he slowly lifts my face back to his. I open my eyes and see him watching me. Whatever this is I'm feeling, he's feeling it too. I can sense it. There's this incredibly strong attraction between us that makes absolutely no logical sense. This can't be real, can it? Am I drunk? I only had a few sips of punch. I don't feel drunk.

Yet I feel an intense urge to kiss this guy. A complete stranger.

As if he read my mind, his hand gently cups the side of my face and he leans down and kisses me. His soft, warm lips press gently against mine and a shiver of pleasurable sensations ripple through me from head to toe.

The feeling takes me by surprise and I tense up. He notices and lets me go.

He backs away, his dark brown eyes returning to mine. He looks regretful for what he did. Actually, not regretful, but more like he knew he shouldn't have done that, but isn't sorry that he did. He went with his gut. Followed his urges. Did what felt right in the moment.

I wish I could be like that. But who says I can't? Nobody, except me. I'm the only one standing in my way.

Seize the day. Seize the moment. The words from that girl's speech yell at me inside my head. This is my chance. This is my opportunity to do that one bold thing that's outside my comfort zone. To do what I want. To act on my instincts.

The decision is made. I'm doing this.

CHAPTER TWO

AMBER

The guy, who still remains nameless, is looking at me, waiting for me to make the next move. A move that would either end this or continue down a path I've never been on before.

I grab the guy's shirt and yank him toward me and kiss him back. And then it's like something unlocked inside both of us and caution didn't just get thrown to the wind. It got blown up, disintegrated, in the fiery hot passion between us.

We're no longer at a party with people everywhere and loud music pumping all around us. We're in our own world, lost in whatever spell we're under that makes us oblivious to anything but each other.

Somehow, some way, we make it up the stairs, our mouths intermingled in a heated frenzy of lips and tongues colliding, hands grasping for each other. We find ourselves alone in the hall and he backs me up against a wall.

"I'm Dylan," he says, breathing hard and fast.

I nod, like I don't care. I DO care, but right now, his name is not what I'm focused on. It's his lips that have my attention as they slide across my cheek. I feel his warm breath over my ear and a shiver of pleasure courses through me.

My hands are all over him. Running through his soft thick hair. Gripping his strong shoulders. Bracing against his hard chest. I grab a fistful of his t-shirt and yank him closer. He presses his body to mine, pinning me to the wall. Through his jeans, I can feel the hard length of him and I instinctively rub against it, my hips circling. He groans in response as his mouth returns to mine, his hand slipping around to grip my ass, keeping me held tightly against him.

As good as this feels, my rational side is rising up, reminding me I barely know this guy. Do I really want to do this? He could have a disease. Or be mentally unstable. A serial killer. An ex-con.

But if I go with my gut, it's telling me Dylan is a good guy. In fact, I feel oddly safe with him. There's no explanation why other than a feeling. I never trust my feelings, but right now? I'm choosing to go with my gut.

I break from his lips and turn my head and look at the open door that's to my left. Then I look back at Dylan.

He knows exactly what it means, what I want. He backs away just enough to take my hand. My heart swells because our hands are a perfect fit. An absolute perfect fit! His hand is warm, his hold strong, as he tugs me down the hall to the open room. We go inside and he closes the door. He backs me up against it as his hand goes to the side of my face, gazing at me.

"You really want to do this?" he asks, his eyes searching mine. "It's up to you."

I take a breath. "I want to."

"Are you sure?"

"Positive." I smile.

He smiles back. It's the first time I've seen him smile, and it just confirms my decision to go forward with this. His smile isn't the fake, sleazy smile that Alex had earlier. It's a genuine smile. Warm. Kind. But also incredibly sexy.

He kisses me and we return to the place we were at before; a wild frenzy of pure uncontrolled passion. Clothes get tossed aside, he grabs a condom, we make it to the bed, his body lowers over mine, and then...it's magic. Pure magic. I know it sounds over-the-top but it's the only way to describe it. You know that expression fits like a glove? Yeah, well, he fits me like a glove. And the way he moves, he hits just the right spot, over and over again until I'm swimming in a sea of pure bliss. Lost in a level of pleasure I didn't even know was possible.

When it's over, he collapses at my side, breathing hard, his chest covered in sweat.

"Holy shit," he mutters.

He means it in a good way. He was groaning and moaning right along with me so I know it was just as amazing for him.

"I'll be right back," he says, getting up and going to the bathroom to dispose of the condom. Thank goodness he had one. If he didn't, we would've had to stop ourselves, which would've been nearly impossible.

While he's in there, I quickly put on my skirt and blouse, then wait there on the bed. I'm not sure what to do now. What's the protocol? Do we just go back to the party as if nothing happened?

Dylan walks out of the bathroom and goes to the bedroom door.

I sit up. "Are you leaving?"

He turns to me, smiling. "You really think I'd walk out the door like this?"

Noticing he's still naked, I smile back. "Guess not."

"I just wanted to lock the door."

"Oh. Okay." I lie back on the bed. So I guess we're staying, but why? Does he want to do it again? Is it still a one-night stand if you do it more than once? I should've consulted Megan about this. "Maybe we shouldn't be in here. Do you even know whose room this is?"

"Kevin's. I know him from school." Dylan turns the bedside light on and goes to the closet and takes a blanket from the top shelf. It gives me an opportunity to check out his naked body. He's lean with muscles, but not too muscular. I don't like overly muscular guys. I prefer more of a lean, fit body, which is what Dylan has.

"You go to Townsend?" I ask.

"Yeah. Just finished my junior year."

So he's a year older than me. I'm 20, almost 21, and should've just finished my sophomore year but I take classes every summer, so credit-wise, I'm classified as a junior. By December I'll be a senior, and hopefully I'll graduate by the end of next summer, a year early.

Dylan puts his jeans on but leaves his t-shirt off, tossing it over the bedside lamp, leaving a soft glow in the room. Then he lies beside me and puts the blanket over us. So I guess we're going to cuddle? Or talk? I don't know what we're doing, but I'm glad he's not leaving. I'm not ready to say goodbye to him.

"You sure Kevin's not going to mind that we're on his bed?" I ask.

"He knows people come here and use it. That's what happens when you're hosting a party. Kevin's not even here tonight. He had to work the graveyard shift. He's a security guard at one of those gated communities." He turns onto his side and smiles. "So..."

I flip to face him and smile back. "Yeah?"

"What we just did? Pretty fucking amazing."

"I thought so too."

We gaze at each other, that pull, that connection, still so strong between us that it doesn't seem real. I feel this familiarity, like I know him, and yet I've never met him before.

"I don't usually do that," I blurt out.

"I don't either," he says.

"You don't?" I ask, surprised. I assumed a guy as hot as him would do stuff like this all the time.

"I've never hooked up with a girl right after meeting her." He smiles a little. "But don't tell anyone that. My friend thinks I do this all the time and if he found out I didn't, he'd give me shit about it."

"You mean Kevin?"

He laughs a little. "No. Kevin and I aren't that good of friends. I was talking about Van, my roommate. We've been friends since we were kids. We're both from Chicago and ended

12

up staying here and going to the same college. We live in a house a few blocks away. We have a band."

"You're in a band?" I sit up a little. "What do you play?"

"Guitar. And I'm the lead singer."

He's the lead singer in a band? And he's this hot? He must have girls constantly wanting to date him.

"And you've never done this?" I ask, now doubting his comment.

"No. I've had plenty of opportunities. I just chose not to take them."

"Then why now? Why tonight?"

He pauses, gazing at me as his hand lifts to the side of my face, resting behind my ear. "There was just something about you. I saw you across the room and...I don't know how to describe it. It was like there was this pull...something drawing me to you. You're gorgeous, so obviously there was that but there was something else." He sees me staring at him and chuckles. "I sound crazy, don't I?"

I lightly shake my head. "No. Not at all. I felt the same way."

"I kind of thought you did. This is going to sound even crazier but I could tell you were feeling the same way. It's almost like I could feel it. That's why I kissed you. I know I shouldn't have done that but it's like I couldn't stop myself. And then once I did I—"

"Had to do it again," I say, finishing his thought. "Because it was like no kiss you'd ever had before. You had to do it again to make sure it was real."

"Exactly," he says as he leans toward me.

"It was perfect," I whisper, closing my eyes as I feel his warm breath over my mouth.

"More than perfect," he whispers back, his lips brushing over mine.

I suck in a breath, my whole body awakening as he kisses me. His hand cups the side of my head, then gently places it on the pillow as I lie back on the bed. He remains on his side, his hand moving down to my waist. He holds it there as he takes the kiss deeper, his tongue moving slow and deep in my mouth, mimicking the way his hips moved earlier when he was inside me. Then his hand moves to the top of my blouse and begins slowly unbuttoning it.

He reaches the last button, then slides the fabric aside and I feel his warm hand brush over my skin. He stops suddenly. "You okay?"

I open my eyes and see him looking at me with concern. His eyes are so expressive. So honest. Revealing so much.

"I'm fine." I half smile. "Why?"

"You're shaking," he says, gazing down at my chest, his finger moving slowly up the center.

He's right. I'm trembling, not from fear, but from arousal. His touch has every nerve in my body responding.

"It's you," I say, closing my eyes again. "When you touch me."

His hand halts its movement. "You want me to stop?"

"No." I arch into his hand. "Don't stop. I like it." I smile. "I want more."

He leans down and kisses me and I feel his hand at my shoulder, slowly sliding my bra strap down. His lips trail down to my breast as his hand slides up my thigh under my skirt.

My eyes are closed, head tipped back, my breaths ragged as he touches me, making me want him again. Once just wasn't enough.

"Amber," I hear him say.

I open my eyes and look at him. "What?"

"Let's get out of here. Let's go back to my place. It's just a few blocks away."

"I'd rather stay here," I say, pulling his face back to mine and kissing him. "I don't want to stop."

I feel him smile against my lips. "Then we'll stay here."

We do it again and it's just as magical. Pure bliss. Like there's something in the air, a full moon, or something else that's making this night unlike anything I'll ever experience again.

Some would say I'm being overly dramatic but it's perfectly normal for me. I'm a hopeless romantic, emphasis on the hopeless. I want the fairy tale love story. Meeting someone at a bar is not my idea of a fairy tale. I want something more interesting than that. A story that's worth telling over and over again. An unexpected meeting. Fate intervening. Love at first sight. That type of thing.

And when I date someone, I want romance. Real romance, not the modern day romance that's fast and hurried and impersonal. For instance, texting? Emails? Social media? All are perfectly fine modes of communication but none of them are romantic. When it comes to love, I'm old-fashioned. I want letters. Handwritten letters on nice paper with a good quality pen. And if I go out with a guy, I want him to hold my hand, open doors for me, be a gentleman.

This is why I'm hopeless, because no man is ever going to write me letters and most guys my age aren't gentlemen, but I can still dream. After all, sometimes the universe surprises you, like tonight. Whatever's happening tonight is completely unexpected, unable to be explained. There's some cosmic force at work, causing everything to come together perfectly and make this night pure magic.

"What are you thinking about?" Dylan asks as I lie in his arms under the blanket.

"Letters," I say.

He chuckles. "Letters? What do you mean?"

"You know. Letters. You get a pen and paper and write down your thoughts."

"Yeah." He chuckles again and gently rubs my arm. "I know what letters are. What about them?"

"It's what I want. Handwritten letters like people used to write."

"And who do you want to write you?"

"The man I fall in love with," I say simply.

He pauses, then says, "So will the letters be written before or after you're in love with him?"

"Hmm. That's a good question." I ponder it a moment, then say, "It doesn't matter. No man will ever write me letters. It's more of a wish. A fairy tale. Did I mention I'm a hopeless romantic? I don't usually admit that because it's kind of embarrassing."

"There's nothing wrong with being a hopeless romantic. I write love songs, so I guess in a way I'm one too."

I lift my head from his chest. "You write songs?"

"Yeah, but I never finish them. Van writes most of the songs for the band." He runs his fingers through the length of my hair, his gentle tugging feeling like a really good head massage. "So what else is in this fairy tale of yours?"

I lie my head back down on his chest. "I want a gentleman. A guy who opens doors and sends flowers and goes on picnics and calls instead of texts. I prefer a phone call over a text. Why don't people call each other anymore?"

"You can't find a guy who does those things?"

"No. I'm pretty sure he doesn't exist, at least not in our age group."

"I'd call you."

"You say that, but eventually, you'd resort to texting. Everyone does. It's just our generation. It's how we grew up."

"I call people all the time. I still text a lot, but I agree that sometimes it's better to call. And if a girl wanted me to call her instead of text, I'd do it. And for the record, I always open doors for girls. I've also sent flowers. I can't say I've arranged for a picnic but I'm sure I could figure it out. As for the letters, I've never actually written one but I'd be willing to try."

Why is he saying this? Is he thinking this is going to last for more than one night? That we're going to start dating?

No. I don't want that. I don't want to date him. This was supposed to be a one-night stand. The one crazy thing I did to prove to myself I can be spontaneous. Seize the day. Seize the moment. That's all this was supposed to be.

And it ended up being beyond my wildest dreams. Not to be a broken record, but I'll say it again. Tonight was perfect.

Everything about it. Seeing him across a crowded room. That kiss we shared before I even knew his name. Our hot make-out session in the hall, then our even hotter make-out session in this room. And the sex? Fireworks. Explosions. The type of sex you think doesn't exist until you actually have it.

Tonight was a dream. A fantasy. A chance occurrence that can never be replicated. I'll be thinking about this night for the rest of my life. I'll store it in my memory and go back to it years from now. Dylan will be the handsome stranger I saw across a crowded room and instantly connected with to the point that we couldn't control our urges.

If I were to date Dylan, he'd no longer be the handsome stranger. Tonight wouldn't be a magical encounter, but just sex in a frat house. And if Dylan and I became a couple and then broke up, my memory of tonight would be ruined. Tainted. I'd see it in a totally different light. That may sound crazy but it's true. When your opinion of someone changes, your memories of them do as well. What used to be good becomes not so good, or even bad. You remember it differently.

I don't want to remember tonight differently. I want to remember it the way I do now. As a hot, sexy, perfect night with an extremely handsome stranger.

"You still there?" Dylan asks since I haven't said anything.

"Yeah." I push out of his arms and sit up. "I should go."

"Go?" He sits up as well. "Why would you go?"

"I have things to do."

"It's one in the morning. What do you have to do at one in the morning?"

"Take the dog out?" I cringe because that was probably the least convincing lie ever told.

"Amber," he says, holding my hand. "What's wrong? What did I do to make you want to leave?"

"You didn't. I just..." I take a breath. "I'm just not looking to get into a relationship right now."

"It doesn't have to be a relationship. We can start slow. As slow as you want. I just want to see you again."

I can't do it. I want to, but I can't. I won't. Tonight was one of those once-in-a-lifetime experiences and I'm not going to risk ruining the memory of it by dating Dylan. I don't have the best track record with relationships, probably because I expect too much. And then there's the fact that Dylan is the lead singer in a band so likely doesn't date a girl very long before moving on to the next.

Whatever the reason, our relationship would eventually end and then this night would mean nothing, or worse, it would become a memory I'd want to forget.

He tugs on my hand. "Come on. Lie down."

"I have to go."

"Please. Just stay with me. Just a little longer."

Against my better judgment, I lie down and he holds me in his arms.

"So tell me about yourself," he says.

I panic, not wanting him to know about me. If he does, he'll track me down and insist we go out.

"There's not much to say."

"I'm sure you could come up with something. I know nothing about you other than your name. Are you in college?"

Shit. What do I say?

"Um...no, not anymore. I just graduated." I hate lying, but in this case, I feel like I have to. "And I already have a job lined up. It's in New York. I'm moving this week."

The words come out of my mouth so fast I'm sure he'll know I'm lying. Plus, my rapid pulse is making me sound breathless, another sign I'm not telling the truth. I'm such a horrible liar.

"You're moving?" he asks, lifting my face up to his.

He actually believes me? Then I guess I'll go with it.

"I got the job a few weeks ago."

"In New York City?"

"Yeah. It'll be a big change, but I'm looking forward to it."

"Shit," he mutters, looking disappointed. "I mean, congratulations. That's great, but I was really hoping we could...well, I guess it doesn't matter, unless...would you try dating long distance?"

"I don't think so. That never seems to work."

"We could at least call each other. Stay in touch. Maybe the job won't pan out and you'll end up back in Chicago."

He's so desperate to make this work. To at least try. And for just a moment, I'm tempted to do it, but then I change my mind. He's in a band. And he's hot. I'm sure girls are lining up to be with him. I can't imagine a relationship with him lasting more than a few weeks. And when it ends, the memory of tonight will no longer be magical, but tainted by our breakup.

"Dylan, I'm sorry, but I can't. It just won't work."

"At least take my number. If you change your mind, call me."

I nod, but I won't be calling him. This was supposed to be one night so that's all it's going to be.

"Even though you're leaving, I still want to know about you," he says. "So what's your major?"

"Can we talk later?" I ask. "I'm really tired and I could use a little nap."

"Sure." He looks into my eyes. "As long as you don't go."

"I won't."

He kisses me, just once, then lies on his back. I rest my head against his chest and he holds me in his arms. It's heaven. Sheer perfection. And just confirms that this night needs to remain a memory and nothing more than that.

A night I will never forget.

CHAPTER THREE

DYLAN

"Dylan," I hear someone say. "Get your ass out of my bed."

I open my eyes and see Kevin at his closet, taking a t-shirt off the hanger.

"What time is it?" I ask.

"Six. I just got off work. I'm freaking tired. I need to get some sleep so get the hell off my bed."

Noticing Amber isn't beside me, I bolt up. "Where is she?"

"Who?" Kevin sighs. "Shit. Did you fuck some girl in my bed?"

I get up and race to the bathroom. She's not there.

"Why is everyone always using my room?" Kevin asks as he walks past me into the bathroom. "There are plenty of other rooms in this house."

"Did you tell her to leave?" I ask.

He takes his work shirt off. "Close the door. I gotta shower."

"Did you see her leave or not?"

He yawns. "Dude, I didn't see any girl. When I got here you were alone. She obviously took off."

"Shit!" I race back to the bed, frantically searching the nightstand to see if she left me a note. But there's nothing there. No note. No number. Nothing. I check my phone just in case she put her number in it, but it's not there.

I don't even know her last name. I can't even look her up. Shit!

"Was this one of your groupies?" Kevin asks, coming back in the room to get his phone from his desk.

"No. She didn't know I was in a band. She didn't even know who I was."

The band I'm in is just a local band but we play a lot so we're pretty well known around Chicago. We get a lot of attention from girls, especially because of Austin, who plays lead guitar. He's the youngest of the Wheeler brothers, and every girl wants to date a Wheeler. Austin's the only single one left so girls come to our concerts just to see if he'll go out with them.

"Maybe she was just pretending she didn't know you so you'd sleep with her," Kevin says as he swipes through his phone. "Everyone knows you stay away from the groupies."

"You sure you didn't see her leaving? Blond hair. Petite. Wearing a white blouse and a short black skirt. Freaking gorgeous."

He looks up from his phone and motions to his bed. "You didn't do anything kinky, did you? Because if you did, you're washing all my shit."

"There was nothing kinky. We didn't even touch the sheets. Now did you see her or not?"

"No. I already told you, she wasn't here."

"You didn't see her downstairs?"

He shrugs. "There's people down there but I didn't notice who. They're passed out from last night."

I race to the door and say to Kevin, "See ya later."

"Hey, what about my bed?" I hear him yelling after me. "Get your ass back here and wash this shit!"

Hurrying down to the main level, I search the living room but all I find are bodies passed out from last night. Some on the sofa. Some on the floor. But no Amber.

Next I go to the kitchen. Dave is there, his head in the fridge, reaching to get something. Dave and I had product management class together last semester.

"Dave," I say getting his attention.

My voice startled him and he bumps his head on the fridge as he stands up. "Shit." He shuts the fridge door while rubbing the back of his head. "What the hell? Can't you knock or something?

I go up to him. "Did you see a girl leaving here this morning? Blond hair, blue eyes, wearing a white shirt and black skirt? Super hot."

"Nope." He picks up the orange juice container from the counter and takes several big gulps, his throat moving as he swallows it down.

"Are you sure you didn't see her? Did you see *anyone* leaving here this morning?"

He finishes the orange juice, then tosses the container in the trash. "I didn't see anyone. I just woke up. I passed out on the pool table last night. My back's killing me." He cringes as he tries to straighten his back.

"I gotta go. I'll see ya later." I head for the door.

"When are you guys playing next?"

"Tonight. At the bar on Fifth and Ash." I hurry out of there. Dave's a talker and I don't have time to chat.

When I get outside, I search the street for her car but I don't even know what kind of car she drives. Maybe she doesn't have a car. Maybe she took the bus or came with a friend. *A friend.* Maybe that's why she left. Because her friend was leaving.

How am I ever going to find her? She says she's leaving for New York today. She can't leave. Not yet. I need to find her first and convince her to try to make this work. I'm not a fan of long-distance relationships, but I'm willing to try. Anything to keep this girl in my life.

Last night was...indescribable. Unlike anything I've ever experienced. I've never felt so strongly about someone that quickly. It was like there was some kind of spell on us, drawing us to each other and igniting a spark that lit a massive fire that just kept burning. I've never moved that fast with a girl and yet it didn't feel wrong. Everything about last night felt right. Like it was meant to be. Fate.

I wasn't kidding when I told Amber I'm somewhat of a romantic. I've never actually told anyone that, and even last night, I tried to make light of it. But the truth is, I have a romantic side. I secretly write love songs that will never see the light of day but that let me pour my heart out in notes and lyrics. That's why I never finish a song. If I did, I might actually have to perform it, and doing so is putting too much of myself out there and that's just not me. I like to keep that side of me hidden, reserved only for the right person. And I think that person is Amber.

Just thinking about her draws up all kinds of emotion. Powerful, real emotion that I shouldn't be feeling for someone I met just a few hours ago. But my romantic side believes in fate. In love at first sight. In soulmates. So it's entirely possible that all those elements came together last night when they brought me to Amber.

I wasn't even going to go to the party. Van and I were planning to go to a movie, but then he met a girl when we were out having dinner at the brewery down the street and he ended up going back to her place. So I decided to check out the frat party that Dave had invited me to earlier in the week. I'd planned to stay maybe an hour or two and then leave to go work on my music. But then I saw her. And I couldn't leave.

"Where you been?" Van asks as I walk in the house. We rent a house just down from campus. It's small and shitty and smells like stale beer but it's our own little slice of heaven, away from our families, who both live in town. There's no way I could live at home and neither could Van. We need our freedom.

"I went to that party," I tell him. "The one Dave invited us to."

"How was it?" He shoves a handful of peanuts in his mouth as he leans back in our fake leather recliner.

I smile. "Freaking awesome. Might've been the best night of my life."

"Shit, really? Did you have a threesome?"

Of course that's where his mind goes. Van's mind is always on sex, the kinkier the better.

"It wasn't a threesome. But there was this girl." I imagine her in my head. Golden blond hair. Bright blue eyes. And lips that were begging to be kissed.

"Yeah?" Van says. "So? What about her? Was she hot?"

"She was more than hot. She was alluring. Seductive. Like she had me under her spell. I saw her across the room and I was instantly drawn to her."

Van laughs. "Is this for one of your songs or are you for real right now?"

"Never mind," I say, wondering why I ever talk to Van about girls. With him, it's always about sex. He doesn't get romance, or fate, or instant connections.

"So did you fuck her?" he asks.

"Not that it's any of your business, but yeah. We went upstairs. Used Kevin's room."

Van bursts out laughing. "Kevin's gonna kick your ass. You know how much he hates it when people use his room." Van points his finger at me. "Just wait. Kev's gonna make you wash his sheets. I used his room once and he made me wash almost everything in there. He didn't trust that I limited myself to the bed." Van smiles. "And he was right. Jewel and I used every square inch of that room."

"I don't even want to know," I say, plopping down on our ratty plaid couch.

Van loves to share his sex stories, half of which I'm sure are made up.

"You hooking up with her later?" he asks. "Or was it just a one-time thing?"

"I wanted it to be more than one time but she took off. I woke up this morning and she was gone."

"And she didn't leave her number?"

"No. I don't even know her last name. I know almost nothing about her."

He shrugs. "Then I guess it was just for a night. No worries. We'll find you someone else tonight."

"I don't want someone else. I want Amber."

"Did you give her your number? Maybe she'll call you later."

"I didn't have a chance to give her my number. She took off while I was asleep. She didn't even leave a note."

"Man, you must've really sucked last night." He pops another handful of peanuts in his mouth. "I wouldn't be too worried about it. We all have our off nights."

"I didn't have performance issues, idiot. I was on last night. Firing on all cylinders. The sex was the best I've ever had, and based on her reaction to it, I think she'd say the same."

"Then why would she just leave like that? Without telling you goodbye or leaving her number?"

"Because she's not staying here. She's moving to New York today for a job."

"No shit?" He rubs his salt-covered fingers over his jeans. "So she just wanted to get some action before she goes?"

"I don't think either one of us planned on that happening. When I got to the party, she was standing on the side of the room, looking bored, not like she was on the hunt for a guy to have sex with."

"You sure about that? Maybe she was one of our band groupies."

"She didn't know about the band until I told her." I pause. "I just realized I didn't even tell her the name of it."

The name of our band is Vandyl, a combination of our names. Austin wasn't included because we didn't know him back when we named the band.

"And you don't know her last name?" Van asks.

25

She never mentioned it and I didn't tell her mine.

"Then I guess you won't be seeing her again."

But I have to see her again. I have to know if we can recreate what we did last night. And even if we can't, I still want to see her again. You don't feel that kind of pull, that kind of bond, with a person every day. This was one of those once-in-a-lifetime moments. And after experiencing something that powerful, that amazing, I'm not just going to give up trying to find the person I shared it with.

I have to find her. She's moving to New York, but even if I have to search for every Amber in that entire city, I'll do it. Because I have to see that girl again.

CHAPTER FOUR

AMBER

"Whatcha lookin' at?" Holly asks as she plops down beside me at the small table in the back of the restaurant. We're both on break after a long and really busy lunch shift.

"Nothing," I say, hiding my phone screen from her.

"Doesn't look like nothing," she says, smiling, as she leans around me in an attempt to try to see my phone. "Is it a text from a guy?"

"No. I was just looking something up."

She sighs and sits back in her chair. "You never have any good guy stories. After all the ones I've told you, you'd think you could at least return the favor now and then."

I don't respond, although I'm dying to tell her my guy story. The one I've been reliving every day since that night. It's been a month since it happened and I still haven't told anyone, not even Kira, because I know whoever I tell will say I'm crazy for running off like I did, and I don't want to hear it.

I've already yelled at myself enough about it. I keep thinking I should've stayed there that night, talked to Dylan, and at least explained why I didn't want to see him again. But that's not what I did and now it's too late. I'm sure he's moved on with someone else. And thinking about that makes me feel even worse. Even though I barely knew him, imagining him with someone else makes my stomach twist, my chest ache.

"God, I'm tired," Holly says, resting her head on the table. "Did everyone in Chicago decide to eat here for lunch today?"

"I know," I say, still looking at my phone. "It was the busiest I've ever seen it. Is something going on downtown?"

"Who knows?" she mumbles, her eyes now closed. "All I know is that I need sleep or I'm not going to be able to make it through the dinner shift."

"Why don't you go lie down in the break room?"

"Because The Asshole's in there." She opens one eye to me. "With Tara."

Holly used to date The Asshole, also known as Ian, the bartender. Everyone warned her he slept around but she fell for his charms and ended up sleeping with him, then got dumped the next day.

I glance up from my phone. "They're not, um..."

"No." She sits up. "They know they'd be fired if they did it in there. Rumor has it someone got fired for just kissing in the break room."

"Really?" I shrug. "Guess it makes sense. Kissing tends to lead to other things."

She sits up, suddenly full of energy, her eyes wide. "When's the last time you kissed someone?"

"I don't know. I can't remember." It's a total lie. I remember it perfectly. Every second. Every detail.

"It's been that long?" she asks. "I don't believe you. Come on. Tell me."

"So you can go tell everyone here? No way."

"You know I can keep a secret. Now come on. Tell me."

Actually, I *don't* know if she can keep a secret. We've only worked together a few weeks. It's just a summer job. I also take two classes. It gives me an excuse not to go home to Michigan. Every summer I stay here and take classes to avoid going home. Of course, that's not what I tell my family. They think I'm just in a hurry to graduate.

"Fine," I say, knowing she won't let this go until I tell her. "It was a month ago. Right after finals ended. I met him at a party."

"Who was he?" she asks eagerly. "Anyone I know?"

"You don't know him. He doesn't work here."

"That doesn't mean I wouldn't know him." She leans back in her chair, lifting her foot up on it and resting her arms on her bent knee. "I know a lot of guys. What's his name?"

"Dylan," I say, then wish I'd said a different name. I should've made up a fake name in the off chance that she actually does know him.

"Dylan," she repeats, tapping her finger on her chin as she thinks. "You're right. I don't know any Dylans. So what happened? You just made out at the party and that was it?"

"Um...yeah. That was it." I focus back on my phone. His name is still in the search box. I've been looking up every Dylan in Chicago since I left that night. I'm not even sure why. It's not like I'm ever going to find him. I don't even know his last name. And even if I did find him, I wouldn't date him. It was one night. That's it. And yet I keep searching for Dylans.

She grabs my arm, her foot landing back on the floor as she leans over to me. "You totally did it with him, didn't you?"

"What?" I feign surprise. "No! I'd just met him that night."

"Yeah, but you slept with him. I can tell. I have a knack for these things."

"What things?"

"Sensing when someone had sex. Like The Asshole." She motions to the bar, where Ian is now drying glasses, back from his break. "The night after we hooked up, I looked at him and knew he'd had sex with someone else earlier that day."

"Just a few hours after being with you?" I ask, shocked that Ian would do that. I know he sleeps around but I didn't know he'd be with two girls in less than twenty-four hours.

"Yep," she says, popping the 'p' for emphasis as she glares at Ian. "He denied it of course, but the girl came in to see him that night and I asked her and sure enough, they'd been together that morning. Asshole," she mumbles, giving him the death stare.

He notices her staring and smiles. "Hey, Hol," he calls out. "Want to go for another round? I could pencil you in for tonight."

"In your dreams," she yells back, then rolls her eyes as she turns back to me. "How could you let me sleep with him? You're supposed to be my friend."

"I didn't know you liked him. I had no idea you'd end up sleeping with him."

"I DON'T like him." She shoots him another death stare. "But he's hot and I'm weak, and that particular night, I was hormonal. And needy. And obviously not thinking straight. Anyway." She looks back at me, smiling. "Tell me about your night with Dylan."

Do I tell her? It would feel awesome to tell someone. Keeping this a secret has been nearly impossible. I've almost told Kira about a million times but then decided against it. I don't want her being disappointed in me for having a one-night stand. I always swore to her I'd never do that. Not that she'd judge me for it, but still. It's not something I'm particularly proud of.

"Amber?" Holly waves her hand in front of my face. "You awake over there?"

"Yeah. Sorry, I'm tired from the lunch rush."

She checks her watch. "We have five minutes. Tell me what happened."

I sigh. "Okay, but if I tell you this, it goes in the vault. You can't tell anyone. Not just people here but anyone."

"Got it." She nods, emphatically. "My lips are sealed. Go ahead."

"I was at this party, and right after we got there, my friend took off with some guy. I was left standing around, bored. Then I looked over and saw him coming in the door. And then...I don't know what happened. It doesn't make sense, but our eyes met and he came over to me and then he kissed me."

She scrunches her face up. "Without saying anything?"

"He asked my name. That was it. I know it sounds weird or creepy or whatever, but it wasn't like that at all. There was something familiar about him, almost like I knew him."

"But you didn't? You'd never met him before?"

"No. Never."

"Huh." She rests her arms on the table. "So you kissed and then you did introductions or what?"

"No. We kind of skipped the talking stage and moved right to...you know."

"Sex?" She says it so loud that Ian looks over.

"You change your mind about tonight?" he yells, then snickers to himself.

She doesn't look at him as she gives him the finger. "So let me get this straight," she says. "You had sex with a guy without even knowing his name."

"He told me his name when we got upstairs." I lower my voice. "Before we did it."

Just talking about this, my heart is racing, heat rising inside me. That was the hottest experience of my life. Not just the sex, but the moments leading up to it. I've never been so turned on.

"Oh my God, that is SO unlike you." Her voice rises in pitch. "I can't believe you did that!"

"I can't either. I still can't. But the odd thing is, I don't feel bad about it. Or regret it. At the time, it felt like the right thing to do. Like I said, there was something familiar about him."

She grabs my wrist. "Maybe he's your soulmate! Like you know how they say souls who are a match can recognize each other right away? Maybe that's what happened."

Like me, Holly is a hopeless romantic, which is why I told her this. I knew she'd understand, but I also know she'll tell me to go find Dylan, which I can't do. My hopeless romantic side ends whenever it hits reality. And the reality is, what happened that night with Dylan is not something that could be sustained. The passion. The connection we felt. The communication without words. In the real world, none of that exists. Whatever we experienced that night wouldn't last more than a day, if that.

"We're not soulmates," I tell her. "It was just one of those strange things that can't be explained."

"So what happened? You guys went out and it didn't work? Did he have a girlfriend? Or are you still dating him? Wait—have you been dating him this whole time and you didn't tell me?"

"No. I haven't seen him since that night. That's all it was. One night. Nothing more."

"He didn't call you?" She huffs and slumps back in her chair. "What an ass. Why are there so many assholes in the world?" She glances at the bar. "And why do we keep falling for them?"

"I didn't give him my number," I say. "The next morning I left without saying goodbye."

Her eyes shoot back to me. "Why? Was the sex that bad?"

"No, it was great. Best I've ever had. I just didn't want to get involved with him."

"Why not?"

"Because that night was perfect and I want to remember it that way. If I'd dated him, we'd probably be broken up by now and I'd be left hurt and alone and that night would be ruined. I'd rather just keep it a memory. What happened that night was something that will never happen again and I don't want to ruin it."

"Hmm." She drums her fingers on the table. "I kind of get what you're saying."

"You do?" I ask, surprised, because I thought for sure she'd say I'm crazy. Even *I* think my reasoning is a little crazy and yet I haven't changed my mind about Dylan. If I ever find him, I'm still not going to date him.

"Last year I dated this guy and we had the absolute best first date. Like the kind you see in movies. I mean, seriously, it was so perfect that part of me was convinced he was my future husband."

"And then what happened?"

32

"Found out he had a girlfriend. Apparently they were on a *break*." She puts air quotes around the word 'break'. "After I found out, that first date didn't seem so great after all. I started dissecting it, picking it apart, and by the time I was done, I'd decided it was the worst date ever."

"Yes! Exactly!" I say, elated that someone actually gets my somewhat-crazy reasoning. "If I had dated Dylan, the same thing could've happened to me. Things wouldn't have worked out and the memory of my perfect night would be ruined."

"But still...aren't you curious if things *might've* worked out? I mean, I didn't have a soulmate connection with The Cheating Dumbass. That's what I call him. He's not worthy of a name. Just like The Asshole." Her eyes flit to the bar, then back to me. "If I'd had that kind of connection, I'd have to know more about the guy. I'd have to at least see him once more, or call him, to see if I still felt that connection."

I've thought about that. About meeting with Dylan just once to see if I still felt that way about him. But I don't have his number or last name so it'll never happen, which is probably for the best.

"I'd rather have it just be a memory," I tell her. I check my phone and see that our break is over. "We have to go, but remember, you can't tell anyone about this. It goes in the vault."

"Got it. It's in the vault." She stands up. "Looks like someone just got seated at your table."

"Seriously?" I get up and see two men in suits sitting at table eight. "It's two-thirty. Who eats lunch at two-thirty?"

"It's probably a business meeting. Maybe they're just getting drinks."

"They have menus. They're getting lunch."

"The young guy's kinda cute, in a nerdy, nice-guy type of way."

"Then maybe *you* should wait on them. I'll switch tables with you."

"I don't like guys like that."

"Why not? You said he looked nice."

She looks at me. "And when have I ever dated a nice guy? I go for bad boys. The badder the better."

"Which is why you keep ending up getting hurt by guys like Ian. You should try a nice guy." I nod in his direction. "The guy at table eight may be your soulmate."

She laughs. "Yeah. I don't think so. Get to work." She takes off, leaving me there. I straighten up and smooth my long blond hair, which is in a sleek, low ponytail, and walk over to table eight.

"Hi, I'm Amber," I say, putting on a big smile. "Are you gentlemen here for lunch?"

"Yes," the older man snaps while perusing the menu. He's probably seventy, with white hair and bushy white eyebrows. "I'll have the Caesar salad, light on the croutons." He slams his menu shut and shoves it at me.

"Would you rather just have the croutons on the side so you can add them yourself?" I ask in a sugary sweet tone. I've found that smiling and acting overly sweet gets me better tips, especially with old people.

"Then it wouldn't be a Caesar salad, now would it?" he shoots back.

"Got it," I say, keeping the smile going. "Light on the croutons. And for you?" I ask the younger guy. Holly was right. He *is* cute, but not at all nerdy. I don't know why she said that, other than the fact that he's wearing a suit, but a suit doesn't make someone a nerd.

"I'll have the turkey club," he says, smiling. "No modifications needed." He glances at the old man, who's too busy with his phone to notice the young guy's comment.

"Dammit!" the old man says. "Griffin didn't get the contract right." He stands up, his eyes on his phone. "I need to deal with this." He walks off and goes outside.

"Anything else?" I ask the young guy. "Drinks?"

"He'll have a scotch," he says, pointing to the now empty chair across from him. "I'll have an iced tea."

"Sounds good. I'll be right back with your drinks." I go to the kitchen, put the order in, and return to the table with the scotch and iced tea. The old man is still outside.

"So what's your name?" the young guy asks.

"Amber."

"I'm Matt." He smiles. "Do you go to school around here?"

"Yeah. Katswick College. It's small. You probably never heard of it."

"I've heard of it. I went to a party there last year. I graduated from the University of Chicago in May. Got a job as a project manager. Allen is my mentor." He rolls his eyes.

I laugh. "The old guy?"

"Yeah. This is our first mentoring session. As you can probably tell, he's not too pleased to have to mentor someone, especially someone my age. He pretty much hates anyone under the age of fifty."

"So not the best job?"

He shrugs. "The job's not bad. Just my mentor. But I'll survive." He backs his chair up, turning to face me. "I don't usually do this, but would you ever want to get coffee sometime?"

He's asking me out? This is the first time this has happened. Most of our customers are older businessmen so I never considered that I might get asked out at work.

"Oh, um, I don't know," I say, not sure if I want to agree to it. Matt is cute but I'm not feeling any sparks. Then again, I don't usually feel sparks when I meet someone. Except for Dylan.

"Do you have a boyfriend?" he asks. "Sorry, I should've asked you that first."

"I don't have a boyfriend. It's just that you took me by surprise. I wasn't expecting you to ask me out."

"I'll tell you what." He pulls a business card from his suit jacket. "I'll give you my card and if you ever want to meet for coffee, just let me know. It's on me, and you can pick the place."

I take the card. "Thanks! I'll think about it." I put the card in my pocket. "Need anything else before your food comes out?"

"No. I think we're good." He glances outside. "Allen's coming back." We watch as the old man swings open the door so hard it hits the wall. "Looks like this is going to be a stressful lunch."

"Good luck," I whisper, then I sneak away before the old man gets back.

"So?" Holly asks when I return to the kitchen. "What happened?"

"What do you mean?"

"That guy. Nerdy, nice guy. Did he ask you out? I saw him give you his card."

"Yeah, he asked me out."

"I knew it! I had this feeling he'd ask you out. So what'd you say?"

"I told him I'd think about it."

"You don't like him?"

"He's not bad. I just wasn't feeling any sparks. But that doesn't mean I won't go out with him. He wants to have coffee."

"So you're going to meet him for coffee?"

I pause to consider it. "Actually, yeah, I think I will."

She shrugs. "You can, but if you're not feeling any sparks, there's really no point in going out with him."

"That's not true. Just because I don't feel anything right now doesn't mean I never will."

"If it's not there in the beginning, it'll never be there, so why waste your time with this guy?"

"I don't know. He seems nice and I feel like I should at least get to know him."

"Suit yourself," she says walking off. "But if I were you, I'd ditch nerdy nice guy and find Dylan." She turns back and winks at me. "See if the sparks are still there."

I know the sparks would be there. That's not even a question. But eventually those sparks would die out and then what? We'd break up, ruining the memory of that perfect night we had. I'm not willing to risk it. As much as I want to see him again, Dylan will remain a memory. A mystery. A fantasy.

Matt is real life. The type of guy I should be with. A nice guy with a decent job who seems mature and responsible and would make a good husband someday. Not that I'm looking for a husband right now, but eventually I'll want that and when I do, I'll seek out someone like Matt. Guys like Dylan do not make good boyfriends, or husbands. That initial flame of passion or attraction or whatever it is, burns bright in the beginning but then fizzles out, leaving you bitter and angry and wondering why you ever married that person. At least that's what happened with my parents, and I'm determined not to repeat the pattern.

But that doesn't mean I don't still believe in romance. Love at first sight. Soulmates. Instant connections. I believe all that exists. It just doesn't last. And I don't want to be disappointed when it's over. Or crushed from the loss of it.

So guys like Matt? They're perfect. Nice. Dependable. And don't mess with your emotions.

I take out his business card. I think I might call him. Not this week but maybe later. Maybe once I've convinced myself I'm over Dylan. Because I'm still not over him.

CHAPTER FIVE

DYLAN

I've been working on this song for weeks and it's finally ready but I'm not sure I want to share it with Van and Austin. They'll give me shit for it because for one, I've never finished a song, and two, it's a ballad, which I've always told them I don't like.

"Hey," Austin says, appearing in the basement where we practice.

Van leans back on the beat-up plaid couch that's sitting against the wall. "Did you just come from the gym?" He sniffs the air. "Because something stinks."

"It's not me. I showered at the gym. It's this basement." Austin takes a sniff of air. "It smells like something died down here."

I set my guitar down. "I said the same thing." I turn to Van. "Why the hell does it smell so bad?"

"Why you asking me? I don't smell. I showered like an hour ago."

I walk over to him. "The smell is worse over here. It's gotta be the couch."

This house came with the furniture and since it's been rented out by countless college students over the years, who knows what it's been exposed to? I try not to think about that whenever I sit on the furniture.

Van sniffs the air again, then sniffs the cushion next to him and reaches under it and pulls out a sandwich. He smiles as

38

he holds it up. "So that's where it went. I couldn't find it the other day. I assumed I ate it but I was still hungry so I couldn't figure it out."

"That's disgusting," Austin says, noticing the hairs sticking to the bread. "What is it? Salami?"

"Yep." Van gets up to toss it in the trash.

"Upstairs," I tell him. "Put it in the trash can in the garage."

Van rolls his eyes as he walks up the stairs. I swear, if Van lived by himself the whole place would smell like rotten sandwiches.

"So how's it going?" Austin asks, taking his guitar out of the case. "Do anything interesting today?"

"Not really. Work was boring, as usual." I work at a record store, which sounded cool when I took the job but it's so freaking boring. Records are supposed to be making a comeback but I'm not sure if that's true. Nobody ever comes in to buy records so I just stand around looking through albums. It seems like the perfect job for a musician, and it is, until you do it all day, every day, and have flipped through every stack of records at least a dozen times.

"Why don't you find something else?" Austin asks.

"Because it's easy. And the pay is decent."

"You could be a waiter. You'd make more money."

"Can't. I tried it and I sucked. I'm not good at any kind of foodservice. I couldn't even work the coffee cart on campus. They fired me after the first day. The record store is boring but at least I'm good at it. And I only have to work there until classes start. That's only a month away. Anyway, how about you? How's work?"

"Good. I'm on a new job with Nash. Started it yesterday."

Van comes bounding down the stairs. "Shit, it stinks down here."

"You didn't notice that before?" I ask.

39

He shrugs. "Guess I was used to it." He goes over to his drums, taking a seat on the stool. "So what are we starting with?"

Austin looks at me to answer. As lead singer, I decide on our set list. I take their input if they have any, but they usually don't. Van and Austin just like to play. They don't care what order we do the songs.

"We're going to try a new one." I'm nervous just saying it, my pulse racing. I poured my heart and soul into that song and I'm afraid to share it with anyone.

"New what?" Van asks, tapping his drumstick on his knee.

"A new song."

"You finished it?" Van asks. I thought he was talking to me but his eyes are on Austin. I'd forgotten Austin was writing a song.

"No," he says. "I decided I didn't like it so I stopped working on it."

"It's mine," I blurt out, wanting to get this over with. I know they're going to be idiots about it so I just want to hurry through all that so we can move on and play the song.

"You shittin' me?" Van asks. "You actually finished a song? Like actually finished it?"

"Yeah. I've been working on it for a while and it's finally done. I'm not saying we're gonna perform it. I just wanted to hear how it sounds."

"What's it about?" Austin asks.

"A girl." I shoot them both a look. "And before you say anything, I'm telling you now, I don't want to hear shit from either one of you. You've both written songs about girls. And our fans love those songs."

Austin and Van both stare at me. My fast talking and defensive tone has them even more curious.

Austin speaks first. "So is this about a specific girl or just a girl in general?"

This is why I didn't want to tell them about the song. I knew they'd ask who the girl is.

The song is about a one-night stand and how the girl ran off before the guy could find out who she was. It's a sad, soulful song that expresses how I felt when I woke up and found that Amber was gone.

"It has to be a girl he was with," Van says to Austin. "Dylan never finishes a song, so the fact that he did means he was inspired." He chuckles. "Let me guess. The redhead from that team project you had to do last year?"

"No. It wasn't her." Although I did date her for a week. We went out a few times and that was it. There wasn't anything wrong with her. We just didn't click.

"You spent a lot of late nights with her," Van says. "And you always said you wanted to do a redhead."

I look at him funny. "I never said that. YOU did."

He laughs. "That's right, I did. But I meant a true redhead. That chick from your class dyed her hair. That doesn't count."

"It wasn't her. Now can we just play the song?" I take the music out and hand them each a copy.

My stomach twists as I see them reading the lyrics. Damn, this is hard. Harder than I thought it would be. If it's this hard to share the song with my two closest friends, there's no way I could actually perform it in public.

"This is really good," Austin says. "I like the lyrics." He smiles at me. "But a ballad? That's the last thing I ever thought you'd write."

His comment proves how much I try to hide my romantic side. I don't want them knowing it's there, or knowing anything about my dating life. I don't like sharing that stuff. Pick any other topic and I'll talk to them about it, but girls? I like to keep that private.

"Yeah, I know," I say. "It's not really my style but it seemed to fit the lyrics."

"Is this Lyndsay?" Van asks, holding up the music.

Last March, I told Van I slept with this girl, Lyndsay, that I met at a party. I told him it was a one-night stand, but the truth is, I just made out with her. We didn't have sex.

When I told Amber I'd never done that before, I wasn't lying. Amber was my one and only one-night stand. But I was hoping it would be more than that. So much more.

It's been two months and I can't stop thinking about her. I think about her all day when I'm bored out of my mind at the record store. I think about her when I wake up in the middle of the night. I think about her when I'm performing, wishing she was out there in the crowd.

She's all I think about it and yet I can't find her. I've spent hours, weeks, months, searching online for every Amber in New York City, but so far I've come up with nothing. I considered going there, in the hopes that maybe I'd run into her in some kind of fateful encounter. If it was fate that brought us together the first time, maybe it would intervene once again.

"Was it Lyndsay or not?" Van asks, since I never answered.

"No. It wasn't Lyndsay."

"Then who is it?" He taps his drumstick on his leg, then stops suddenly and points it at me. "That girl!"

"What girl?" I ask, although I'm sure he's figured it out. I didn't tell him much about Amber but he knows I slept with her and he knows I searched for her after that night. And since he lives with me, he saw how depressed I was when I couldn't find her. That lasted about a week and then I went back to being myself so Van wouldn't give me shit about being that upset over a girl. But the truth is, I'm still upset that she's gone. How could she just leave like that? After the night we spent together, she should've at least left me her phone number.

"What girl?" Austin asks.

"That one he met at the frat party after finals week," Van says. "Anna."

"Amber," I say, correcting him.

"The girl who took off without leaving her number?" Austin asks.

"Yeah," I mumble, not wanting to talk about it.

"You still can't find her?" he asks.

42

"No. But she's in a city with eight million people, and a lot of people are named Amber."

"I don't know why you're still looking for her," Van says. "You got girls lining up to be with you. Just forget about her."

"I'm NOT looking for her," I say harshly.

"Yeah, right." Van chuckles. "Every time you're using your computer, you're doing searches for Amber."

"What the hell? Are you spying on me?"

He shrugs. "Just glancing at it when I walk by. I'm always hoping you're looking at porn so I can sneak a peek but instead it's always searches for that girl."

"She really got to you, huh?" Austin says. "That was like two months ago. Almost three. And you're still trying to find her?"

"She's gone, man," Van says. "Just let her go. But we'll keep the song. I have a feeling it's gonna be good. Let's try it." He turns to his drums, his foot tapping, ready to start.

At least they didn't ridicule me too badly. I was expecting much worse, especially from Van. He writes most of our songs and a lot of them are about the girls he's dated. I always give him shit about his love song lyrics so now is the time for him to give it back. He went easy on me just now but I'm sure I haven't heard the end of it. He'll be giving me a hard time about this for weeks.

We play the song and I make some adjustments and we play it again. And then once more just to make sure we're in sync.

"That's really good," Austin says when we're done. "I don't usually like ballads but I actually like this one. And the lyrics? Girls are gonna go crazy. They'll be coming to our shows just to hear that song."

"We're not performing it," I say, going to get my bottle of water.

Austin laughs a little. "Why wouldn't we perform it? Isn't that why you wrote it?"

"No. I wrote it because I had to. It was in my head and I had to get it out. It was a creative exercise. That's it."

"Bullshit," Van says. "You wrote it hoping she'd hear it."

Van knows me way too well. Makes sense. We've been friends forever. But sometimes the fact that he knows me so well is annoying.

"That's not why I wrote it," I lie. "How would she even hear it? She lives in New York now."

"Someone could record it and put it online," Austin says. "Our fans do that all the time."

"And she'd just happen to stumble upon it online?" I shake my head. "Not gonna happen."

Although it's not like I haven't considered that. Van is right. I wrote this song hoping I'd have the guts to perform it, and then hoping Amber might hear it. I know it's a long shot but stranger things have happened, like the night we were brought together. If two strangers can connect that fast, that powerfully, then it's possible Amber could hear my song. And if she did, maybe she'd call me or text me or reach out in some way and tell me she wants to continue where we left off. To see where this could go.

"Let's play it on Saturday," Van says.

"No," I blurt out. "It's not ready."

"Why not?" Austin asks. "It sounded good to me."

"I'm just...I'm not ready. I just wanted to hear how it sounds. I'm not ready to perform it."

Van beats on his drums. "Then let's play something else." He starts playing the intro for one of our songs. A breakup song with a heavy beat and darker sound. Austin joins in on lead guitar and I follow on bass, then vocals.

I get into the music, like I always do, but my mind keeps going back to Amber. Playing that song brought me back to that night. That's the thing about music. It makes you feel stuff. Makes you remember. Takes you back to whatever memory you associate with that song.

I wrote that song after being with Amber, and even if I never see her again it will always be our song. It will always bring me back to those few hours we shared together.

One Night. That's the name of the song.

And that may be all that Amber and I ever have.

CHAPTER SIX

August

AMBER

"I just got into town," Kira says, lying back on the couch. "Do we really have to go out tonight?"

Kira moved here last week. She'll be going to my college, and although we both just turned 21, she'll only be a freshman because she took time off after getting injured at a gymnastics meet. It was a really bad injury that ended her gymnastics career. Ever since it happened she's been sad and depressed and never goes out. Her parents are hoping moving here, living with me, and going to college will make her feel better but so far, it's not working.

I stand over her, my hands on my hips. "First of all, you didn't just get into town. You've been in Chicago for a week. And every night you have an excuse for why you can't go out. Now it's Saturday, and we're not sitting at home on a Saturday night."

"It's not *we* staying home, just *me*. You can still go out. I'd just rather stay here."

I sit beside her. "What's your deal with going out? We used to go out all the time."

"That was in high school. I'm not a big partier anymore."

"This isn't a party. It's a bar. With music. We'll listen to the band, have a couple drinks, then come home. It'll be good for—" I stop, realizing I sound more like her mom than her friend. "I mean, it'll be fun. You'll have fun. I know you will. Now come on. Let's go get ready."

"If I'm going, I'm wearing this. I'm not changing."

Kira doesn't like to dress up. If she could live in her workout clothes she would. Tonight she has on an old pair of jeans and a baggy t-shirt.

"Jeans and a t-shirt?" I say. "That's not going out clothes. Let's go to my room. You can wear something of mine."

"Amber, really, I don't want to get all dressed up. If I'm going, I'm going to hear the music, not find a guy, so it doesn't matter what I wear."

I smile. "You never know. You *might* find a guy."

She sighs. "For the last time, I don't want a guy. I need to stay focused." She pauses. "On school. I need to stay focused on school."

"School doesn't start for a week, which means you have a whole week to date someone."

"Yeah, a week-long relationship. That'll be great."

"Actually, it could be. Sometimes you connect with someone right away. You don't always need that long to—" My phone dings with a text from Matt, telling me he's here. I started dating Matt soon after I met him at the restaurant that day. We went for coffee and have been dating ever since. "Shit. Matt's downstairs. I have to finish getting ready. Can you let him in?"

"And there's another reason why I shouldn't be going out with you tonight. I'll be a third wheel on your date."

"Matt doesn't care. In fact, when I told him you were coming along, he thought it was a good idea." I head to my room. "When he gets here, tell him I'll only be a few minutes."

"More like a half hour," she yells at me.

"Ten minutes, max," I yell back.

Matt's always either right on time or early. After dating me for over a month, he should know I'm never ready on time. I'm always getting sidetracked with a million other things. Tonight I was sidetracked with Kira, trying to convince her to go out with Matt and me. She can't keep sitting in this apartment every night, feeling sorry for herself. I know she's still mourning the loss of her gymnastics career but it's been over a year since the accident and hiding out in our apartment isn't going to help her feel better.

When Matt suggested going to this concert tonight, I immediately thought of Kira. She loves live music so if I ever had a chance of getting her out of the apartment, this was it. All day I've been asking her to go, and she refused, but despite her resistance, I wasn't taking no for an answer.

Matt's totally cool with her going along. He's such a nice guy. He still works at that job he doesn't like but that mean old geezer, Allen, isn't his mentor anymore, which has made the job more tolerable. Matt also works at a men's suit shop to make extra cash to help pay off his student loans. Yesterday, the lead singer of Vandyl came in to buy a suit. While Matt was helping him find one, the guy mentioned his band had a concert tonight and told Matt he should stop by the bar and hear them play.

I don't follow local bands but I've heard of Vandyl so I assume they're halfway decent. And it's something to do that I know Kira will like.

Searching through my closet, I can't decide what to wear. Unlike Kira, I like to dress up when I go out. Tonight I feel like wearing a dress. A short sexy dress since we're going to a bar. Maybe the sleeveless black one I bought on sale a few weeks ago and haven't worn yet. Shuffling through my hangers to find it, I stop when I see the blouse. The one I was wearing that night last May. The night I met Dylan.

I take it out and hold it up, heat rising inside me as the memories from that night fill my head. I can still see his face, looking at me from across the room. I can still see his eyes after we kissed. They were filled with desire, but also something else. That connection between us that I still can't explain.

I remember that night like it just happened. I relive it all the time. I can hear his voice asking me if I really wanted to do what we were about to do. I'd had my doubts just moments before, but by the time he asked me, I was all in. I wanted him and he wanted me.

Looking at the blouse, I remember how I practically ripped the buttons trying to get it off as Dylan and I stumbled into the bedroom, racing to get to the bed. Then later, after we'd done it, we both got dressed and he laid beside me. He kissed me as his hand slowly undid the top button of the blouse.

I close my eyes, remembering how it felt, his lips on mine, his fingers brushing against my skin as he continued to slowly undo the buttons.

A shiver skitters through me as my arousal builds. I can practically feel his body pressing against mine. I can hear his voice whispering in my ear.

My eyes remain closed, the blouse falling to the floor as I get lost in the memory of that night. The way Dylan touched me, his hands caressing my body. The way it felt when he—

Music blares from the living room and I'm startled back to reality. Back to the present. My eyes pop open and I hear talking. It's a commerical. Kira must've turned on the TV.

I quickly grab my blouse from the floor and shove it in the back of my closet, right next to the skirt I wore that night. I haven't worn either of them since. I haven't even washed them. I couldn't. They still have the slight hint of Dylan's cologne, which rubbed off on my clothes that night.

What is wrong with me? I shouldn't be thinking about that night. Or about Dylan. I should be thinking about Matt and the date we're about to go on.

Why can't I get Dylan out of my head? I have a boyfriend now. A nice, caring boyfriend who treats me well, and yet I'm still thinking about some guy I had a one-night stand with. I try not to. I swear, I do. But then something will remind me of him, like that blouse, and my mind goes back to that night.

I should throw out that blouse, and the skirt. Maybe that would help me forget that night. Shoving the hangers aside, I reach to the back of the closet and grab the blouse again. I hold it up, knowing I should toss it but unable to do it.

I can't get rid of it. I should, but I can't. Not yet.

I hang it back where it was then shove my other clothes in place, hiding the blouse and the skirt from view. That's good enough for now.

Searching for the black dress, I finally find it and hold it up in front of the mirror. It's short and fitted. Matt will love it. He loves it when I dress sexy. Only problem is, wearing this will make him want to do things. Things I'm not ready to do.

Matt and I haven't had sex yet. Whenever he tries, I shut him down, telling him I'm not ready. But I don't know why I'm not ready. I've dated him for over a month. We've gone out a lot. Talked a lot. Gotten to know each other. He's a great guy and I'm attracted to him. I'm just not feeling that spark when we're together. I keep thinking I'll feel it at some point but so far I haven't.

Part of me blames Dylan for that. The way he made me feel that night was unlike anything I've ever experienced. It was magical. Perfect. And because of that, it messed me up and now I expect to feel that way with Matt, even though I know it's not realistic.

I need to force myself to stop thinking about Dylan and that night and return to reality where nice guys like Matt should be enough. More than enough. I need to be happy with Matt and stop putting off sex with him and just do it. Who knows? Maybe the sex will be great.

I hear the channels changing on the TV out in the living room. Kira and Matt are probably out of things to talk about and getting bored. I check the clock. I've been in here for fifteen minutes and I'm still not dressed and haven't done my hair.

I change into the dress then go in the bathroom to fix my hair. After another fifteen minutes, I'm ready. As I walk out to the living room, Matt sees me and smiles.

"You look great," Matt says as he gets up from his chair.

"Thanks!" I go over and give him a quick kiss. "Ready to go?"

Kira gets up from the couch. "I think I'll change my shirt."

"Okay." I smile, happy that she's agreed to wear something else. "We'll wait."

Matt sighs, in a joking way. "Is this going to be another half hour?"

"No, I'll be quick." Kira hurries down the hall to her room. Minutes later, she returns, wearing a fitted black t-shirt and different jeans. It's not great but it's way better than what she had on before. "Okay, I'm ready."

"See?" Matt says to me. "It's possible to get ready fast." He gives me a kiss.

"Maybe, but don't get your hopes up." I loop my arm around his and we head to the door.

We take Matt's car and when we get to the bar, Matt drops Kira and me off at the door, then goes to park. He knows the heels I'm wearing hurt my feet and he didn't want me to have to walk too far. He's so considerate.

When we get inside the bar, Matt pays the cover charge for all three of us. It's another considerate gesture that makes me feel guilty for even thinking about Dylan earlier.

"It's freezing in here," I say, shivering as the air conditioner blows ice cold air out of the vent right above me.

Matt puts his arm around me. "You want to go back and get a sweater or something?"

"Could we? I know it's a pain to go all the way back but—"

"It's not a big deal." He kisses me. "I'll go get the car."

"Matt, wait." I turn to Kira. "Kira, could you stay here and get us a table?"

"Sure. Go ahead."

I give her a hug. "Thanks! We won't be long, I swear."

Matt and I go back outside.

"Wait here," he says. "I'll get the car."

"I'm fine. I can walk."

"But your shoes." He points to my black high heels.

"I'll be okay. It's not that far."

He holds my hand as we walk to the car, then opens my door for me. Before I can get in, he pulls me in for a kiss. Like always, it's a nice kiss. There's just no sparks.

Why are there no sparks? I like Matt. I'm attracted to him. We get along great.

Damn Dylan. It's his fault. If it weren't for that night, I wouldn't have these high expectations. I'd feel sparks with Matt and everything would be great.

"You look really hot tonight," Matt says as we're driving back to my apartment. We're at a stop light and he reaches over and rubs his hand over my bare knee and smiles. "Maybe tonight's the night."

He wants sex. I knew it. I knew this dress would make him want sex. Or maybe it's just the fact that he's waited so long. By now we should've done it, and I would have if I weren't still thinking about Dylan. I'm worried if I have sex with Matt I'll be imagining Dylan while we're doing it, which isn't fair to Matt. But I can't get Dylan out of my head so what do I do? I can't put this off forever.

When I don't respond, Matt takes his hand off my knee and says, "Sorry, Amber. I wasn't trying to push you. I can wait as long as you need."

I nod and give him a smile. "Thanks. You're a really great boyfriend."

Back at my apartment, Matt waits in the car while I run up and get a sweater. Then we return to the bar.

Matt goes to get drinks while I meet up with Kira, who's sitting at a round table toward the back of the bar. It's a long ways from the stage but the place is packed so we're lucky we got a table at all.

"Sorry we took so long," I say to Kira, raising my voice to be heard above the sound of guitar strings coming from the speakers behind us. "Sounds like the band's warming up." I glance at the stage but can't see anything because girls are lined up in front of it. "Matt's getting drinks. What do you want?"

"Rum and Coke."

"Okay, I'll be right back."

I find Matt at the bar. "Kira wants a Rum and Coke."

"Got it." He tells the bartender and we wait for our drinks. I take Kira's and mine and we go back to the table.

"Here you go." I hand Kira her drink and sit down beside her. "They still haven't started?" I lean forward, trying to see the stage, but even more girls have lined up in front of it, blocking my view.

Matt sits next to me as a loud tapping sound comes over the speakers.

"Sounds like they're having issues with the mic," he says.

I turn to Kira. "Thanks for getting the table."

"I almost didn't get it. It was one of the last open tables and some guys took it before I got over here."

"Then how'd you get it?"

"This other guy asked them to leave so I could have the table."

I smile. "Some guy did that for you? So where is this guy?"

"I don't know. He took off."

"Kira!" I swat her arm. "That guy was hitting on you! Why'd you let him leave?"

"He wasn't hitting on me. He was just getting me a table."

I turn to Matt. "Was that guy flirting or not?"

"He was flirting," he says before taking a swig of his drink.

I look back at Kira. "See? I told you. So then what happened?"

"He sat down and we talked for a few minutes and then he left."

"What did you talk about?"

"Chicago. I told him I just moved here and he offered to show me around."

I grab her arm. "He asked you out? And what did you say?"

"I told him I didn't need him to show me around because my best friend already offered to do it." She smiles, knowing she's driving me crazy. I've been wanting her to go on a date for over a year but she refuses to even consider the idea. She keeps saying she doesn't want a boyfriend right now and that's fine but I think it'd be good for her to at least start dating again. It'd get her out of the apartment and maybe get her mind off gymnastics for at least an hour or two.

I toss my hands in the air. "Why did you tell him that?"

"Maybe she didn't like him," Matt says.

"She totally liked him," I say to Matt. "Look at her. She's blushing."

"I'm not blushing." Kira holds up her drink. "It's the alcohol. Always makes my cheeks pink."

"That's true. I forgot. So is Matt right? You didn't like him?"

"I liked him," she says. "He seemed nice. And he got me the table."

"But he's not your type," I say, trying to force her to give me an actual reason why she won't give this guy a chance. "You don't like how he looks. Is he too scrawny? You hate scrawny guys."

"He's not scrawny. He's tall. And really muscular."

A loud voice comes over the speaker. "Just an update for everyone. We're having an issue with the mic but we're getting a new one. The band will start shortly."

"So what's the deal?" I ask Kira. "Why won't you go out with him?"

"What's his name?" Matt asks.

I look at him, confused. "What difference does that make?"

"Sometimes girls are turned off by a name."

"That's not true." I turn to Kira. "Is it?"

"It could be true, but in this case it's not. I like his name."

"So what is it?"

"Austin. He didn't tell me his last name."

"You mean the guy in the band?" Matt asks Kira.

"What guy in the band?"

"The lead guitarist's name is Austin."

"Oh, um, no. It must be a different Austin. This guy didn't say he was in the band."

I turn to Matt. "Do you know what the Austin in the band looks like?"

"Yeah. So do you. He's that guy you and every other girl are always drooling over."

"You mean Austin Wheeler?"

"Yeah. The guy with all the muscles. I wonder how many hours a day he has to work out to look like that." Matt takes a swig of his drink.

"Okay, wait." I shake my head back and forth as I try to figure this out. "So Austin Wheeler's part of Vandyl? No, that's not right. He's in a different band but I can't remember the name."

"No, it's this one," Matt says. "I told you that the other night when I was telling you about the lead singer coming into the store."

I pause a moment, trying to remember what he told me that night. We were on the phone and I was working on my laptop while he talked so I didn't hear everything he said. I don't remember him mentioning Austin Wheeler but I know who Austin is. Everyone in Chicago does, especially girls. He's tall, has a great smile, and a body that's pure muscle.

Austin's the youngest of the Wheeler brothers. His three older brothers are also super hot. His brother, Jake, was even named Chicago's most eligible bachelor but he lost that title when he got a girlfriend. All the brothers have girlfriends, except for Austin, but practically every girl in Chicago wants to date him.

I whip back around to Kira. "Are you telling me that Austin Wheeler asked you out?"

"It's not him. He's not in the band."

"Tall?" I ask. "All muscle? Short dark hair? Gorgeous blue eyes? Around our age?"

"Austin!" a girl yells from up by the stage. She's right in front of the band, jumping around like a lunatic. She leans over to say something to her friend and I get a glimpse of the guy in front of her. It's Austin, standing there with a guitar, talking to some other guy as he messes with the mic.

I point at the stage. "Did you see him?"

"Yeah," Kira says. "That's him."

"Oh my God, are you serious?" I slam my hand on the table. "Austin Wheeler asked you out and you turned him down? You know how many girls are dying to go out with him? He's like the hottest guy in Chicago!"

"Hey," Matt says from behind me. "I'm right here."

I turn back and kiss him. "You're hot too."

"Yeah, thanks," he says, rolling his eyes and smiling.

"You are." I kiss him again. "I'm just trying to make a point here for Kira." I turn back to her. "Austin doesn't ask girls out. He doesn't have to, because girls ask HIM out. So the fact that he asked you out is a huge deal."

"Well, it doesn't matter. I don't go out with liars. He should've told me he was in the band."

The sound of a guitar rings through the speakers and Austin says, "Ready to rock this joint?"

Girls scream all at once and the ones up front are reaching out toward the guys in the band.

"For those who don't know," Austin says, "we're Vandyl. I'm Austin and I play lead guitar." Girls scream his name. "The guy on the drums is Van." More girls scream, this time for Van. "And our lead singer and bass player is Dylan." More screams as they yell Dylan's name.

Dylan. Of course. Just what I need right now. Another reminder of the night I'm trying so hard to forget. Is the universe trying to make this harder on me? Couldn't the guy's name be Bob or Joe or Curt? Anything would be better than Dylan, especially after I had that memory tonight. I'm still hot from that memory. I can't stop thinking about it.

"Ready boys?" Austin says.

The guys start playing and the crowd starts singing along. I can't see the band because the girls by the stage are dancing in front of it. I look over at Kira. She looks upset.

"Hey." I nudge her. "You all right?"

"Yeah, I'm fine."

"He's good, isn't he?" I ask, referring to Austin.

"I guess."

I smile and start moving to the music. These guys *are* really good. Now I get why this band is so popular. The music is good and the band members are hot, although I only saw Austin, but he's hot enough for the other two.

Matt's knee nudges mine under the table. I turn and see him smiling at me. He has a nice smile. He's a good-looking guy. I need to stop waiting to have sex with him and just do it.

He leans over to me and we kiss.

"Want another drink?" he asks, holding up his empty glass. "I'm going to get another."

"I'm good but let me ask Kira." I turn to her. "Want another drink? Matt's going back to the bar."

"No, I'm good."

"You sure?" Matt asks, getting up from his chair.

"Yeah. One's enough."

He takes off for the bar.

Looking back at Kira, I see her moving her head around trying to see Austin through the crowd of girls gathered by the stage.

I smile. "So what do you think? Hot, isn't he?"

"Who? Matt?"

"No! Austin."

"Yeah, he's hot. But I'm still not going out with him. And besides, they're all hot. Maybe I'll go out with the lead singer instead."

I turn to check him out. Just as I look, the girls lining the stage move enough where I can finally see him.

I freeze, my breath catching in my throat. No. It can't be. He's not part of Vandyl. The band he's in is...he never told me. He never told me the name.

My eyes are glued to him. That chiseled jaw. That dark brown hair. Those brooding eyes.

I grip the table, feeling like I might pass out. "Oh my God."

"What?" Kira leans toward me. "What's wrong?"

"I know him."

"Know who?"

"The lead singer." I rush the words out, feeling like I can't breathe.

"Dylan?"

"Yes! When they said Dylan, I didn't know it was THAT Dylan!" I look back at the bar where Matt is standing. He can't know about Dylan. And I can't let Dylan see me here.

"We have to go," I blurt out.

"Go? Go where?"

"Anywhere. We just have to get out of here."

"Why?"

"Because Dylan's here!" I yell at her. I didn't mean to yell but I'm panicking right now.

"I don't get it. How do you know him?"

I glance at Dylan, then back at Kira. "I slept with him."

"You what? When?"

"Last May. At a party."

"You never said you were dating anyone last May."

"We weren't dating."

"You had a one-night stand?" she asks, practically yelling over the music.

"Shh!" I check that Matt is still at the bar. "I'll tell you about it later. For now, we have to get out of here." I shove my chair back. "Unless you want to stay. I could come pick you up later."

"No. Let's go."

We meet up with Matt at the bar. He's still waiting in line to get drinks.

"I'm not feeling well." I tug on his arm. "We have to go."

"You're sick?" He looks confused because I was fine just minutes ago.

"It's my stomach. It came on really fast. I need to get home."

"Yeah, of course." He puts his arm around me and the three of us leave the bar. "Wait here. I'll be back in a minute."

He takes off, practically running to the car.

"Okay, explain yourself," Kira says as we wait by the building.

"Not here. Wait until we get home."

Matt's car pulls up and he gets out and opens the door for me. I feel bad making us leave and I feel even worse lying about it, but what was I supposed to tell him? That we left because I just saw the guy I had my first and only one-night stand with? The guy I can't stop thinking about? The guy who's the reason Matt and I still haven't had sex? The guy Matt waited on at the suit store who's the reason we're even here tonight? I can't tell him that. For one, it'd take all night to explain it, and two, it's best if he doesn't know. He doesn't need to. Dylan and I are over. It was one night. And now it's over.

When we get to my apartment, I tell Matt I need to rest. He insists on staying with me but I talk him out of it, telling him I really don't want him around me when I'm feeling like I might get sick at any moment.

Once he's gone, I stand by the door in shock, still not believing this happened. How did I not know Dylan was part of Vandyl? Last May, I tried looking him up online but I didn't know his last name so I didn't get very far. I should've researched local bands. If I had, I would've seen his photo with Vandyl and known he was part of it and never gone to the concert tonight.

"Since when do you have one-night stands?" Kira asks as she sits on the couch.

"I don't."

"You just said you did."

"Yes, but it was just one time and I'll never do it again."

"Then why'd you do it?"

I sigh, not wanting to tell her but knowing she won't give up until I do. "I was taking this speech class last spring, and this girl gave a speech about the psychology of fear and how the things you fear are often the things you really want to do. But you don't admit to it because you don't want the pressure of actually having to do it."

"Are you saying you secretly always wanted to have a one-night stand?"

"Yes. I mean, no, not really." I go sit next to her. "It was more like, I've always had this fantasy of meeting a guy who I have instant chemistry with, and then just acting on my desires and doing it. You know, like in the movies, when people meet and instantly want to rip each other's clothes off? That pure, undeniable passion that can't be controlled?"

"And you had that with Dylan?"

"Yes." I close my eyes, the memory replaying in my head. "I was at a house party just a few blocks from his campus. He came in the front door and I saw him across the room and our eyes locked, and it was like we just knew. He came over to me and asked my name. I could barely breathe my heart was beating so fast. That's how much I was attracted to him. And even though he's super hot, it was more than his looks. It was something else drawing me to him. He felt it too. He was looking at me the same way I was looking at him. And he was breathing just as hard as I was. Then, out of the blue, he kissed me."

"After you just met him?"

"I know, it's crazy. I didn't even know his name and he kissed me. But just once, and then he backed away, like he shouldn't have done it, but he didn't apologize. And I didn't want him to. I wanted more. So I grabbed his shirt and yanked him toward me and kissed him back. And then it's like we both knew there was no going back. We had to finish this."

"So you knew nothing about the guy, but you still had sex with him."

"I know it wasn't the best decision, but I kept hearing that girl's speech in my head, telling me to do something different. Something completely out of my comfort zone. Something I always wanted to do but was too afraid to."

"And you didn't question it? Like not at all?"

"Of course I did! You know me. I'm always cautious when it comes to that stuff. That's why I'm dating Matt. He's the safe choice. Nice. Dependable. Predictable."

"Okay, so you kissed him and then what? You went in a room?"

"We went upstairs, not sure what was going to happen. That's when I started questioning it, more out of safety concerns than anything else. But there was something about this guy. I felt safe with him. I'm not even sure why. It was just a gut feeling. Anyway, we ended up finding an open room and then he asked if I really wanted to do what we were about to do. He had this torn look on his face, like he wanted to but felt like he shouldn't. It made me want to do it all the more. I told him yes and then neither one of us hesitated from that point forward. Clothes went flying, and then the magic happened."

She laughs. "Magic? Seriously?"

I grab hold of her arm and look her in the eye. "Total magic. I'm not kidding. It was absolute perfection. Hot. Frantic. Pure passion. I'd never experienced anything like it."

She laughs again. "So it was good?"

"Good?" I let go of her and fall back on the couch, staring up at the ceiling. "Good doesn't even begin to describe it. And unlike most guys, he didn't run off when we were done. In fact, he didn't want me to leave so we just stayed there in that room, and that's when he started to tell me more about himself but I told him I didn't want to know. That it was just a one-time thing and that I'd just graduated and was moving to New York the next day."

"You lied to him?"

"I had to. I didn't want him trying to date me."

"Why not?" She yanks on my arm, forcing me to sit up. "You meet a guy you have instant chemistry with, you have amazing sex, and then you decide you never want to see him again?"

"Yes," I say simply.

She rolls her eyes. "You make no sense. This is just like when we had that homemade ice cream at the fair and then you refused to eat it again. I still don't understand that."

"Because it's never as good as the first time. I explained this to you a million times. When you experience pure perfection, like that ice cream, or sex with Dylan, experiencing it again will just ruin it. The second time is never as good as the first, and it just gets worse from there."

She shakes her head. "You're completely crazy."

"I'm not. You just haven't experienced what I'm talking about so you can't relate."

"Actually I can," she mutters. "And I'd do anything to experience it again."

She's talking about gymnastics and how she'll never compete again.

"Kira, I'm sorry."

I keep quiet to see if she wants to talk about it.

She leans back on the couch. "So you lied and told Dylan you were moving away and that you'd never see him again."

"Yes, but he didn't accept that. He wanted to see me again, or at least talk on the phone, but I wouldn't give him my number. I wanted him to remain a mystery. It was more romantic that way."

"Romantic? Never talking to him again is romantic? That's the worst happy ending I've ever heard."

"You don't understand. That night WAS our happy ending. It's something we'll always remember. At least *I* will. Dylan probably forgot about it. I'm sure he has one-night stands all the time."

"Now that you know who he is, you really don't want to see him again?"

"No. It would ruin the memory. Did you see how many girls were up there screaming his name? I don't want to remember him that way, with other girls hanging all over him. I want to remember him with *me*. Just the two of us, and the night we spent together."

"You spent the whole night with him?"

"Most of it. We fell asleep, and just as the sun was coming up, I snuck out."

"You left without saying goodbye? That's kind of mean."

"It's not mean. It's every guy's dream. He got sex and never has to see me again."

"But it sounds like he really *wanted* to see you again."

"He was probably just saying that to be nice." I shrug. "Doesn't matter. I'm not going to see him again. Besides, I've moved on. I have Matt now."

And it's true. I have Matt, a great guy who deserves a better girlfriend than one who keeps thinking about some other guy. From now on, I'm going to be that girlfriend. I'm going to stop thinking about Dylan and focus on Matt.

The problem is, seeing Dylan tonight only made me want him more.

CHAPTER SEVEN

October

AMBER

"I'm sorry, but this just isn't working," I say to Matt, my voice shaking because I feel so bad about breaking up with him. He's been a great boyfriend. Taking me out to dinner. Buying me flowers. Calling when he says he will. But there's still no spark. No chemistry.

I've tried to create that chemistry. Candlelit dinners at my apartment. Sexy lingerie. Even a few bedroom toys. But nothing has worked. He just doesn't excite me. I still blame Dylan for that. After experiencing what I felt with Dylan, I can't help but compare that to my experience with Matt, which doesn't even come close to what I felt with Dylan. Now I'm worried it won't just be Matt, but that every guy I date won't compare to Dylan. My night with him might've ruined me for anyone else.

Matt sighs. "I get what you're saying. We're good as friends but...it seems like you're never really there when we're...you know, intimate."

"Yeah." I glance down at my hands. "I'm sorry about that. I really am. I tried, I just..."

"Amber." He puts his hand on mine. "You don't have to be sorry. If it's not there, it's not there. There's nothing wrong with that."

He's so understanding, so sweet, that I feel even worse about this.

I look up at him. "I still really like you. I know it's a total cliché to say we could still be friends, but I wish we could. I'm going to miss talking to you."

"Cliché or not, we can still be friends, at least until you find someone else and he tells you we can't be friends anymore."

I smile at him. "Or until *you* find someone. You'll probably find someone before I do."

"Probably not. I work so much I don't have time to go out and meet people."

We're quiet for a moment and all I can think about is Dylan. Whenever I imagine myself with someone else, it's always him.

"Can I ask you for some advice?" I shouldn't tell him this but the fact that I want to just shows how much I value his friendship and his opinion.

"Sure. Go ahead."

I realize how insensitive it would be for me to bring this up now, after just breaking up with him, so I say, "Forget it. It's not the right time."

"Amber, just say it. We're friends, remember?"

"I know, but I feel like it's the wrong time to bring this up."

"Is this about some other guy?" he asks cautiously.

"Yes," I say with a sigh.

He sits back. "Go ahead. I'm all ears. But if I ever meet another girl, you owe me girl advice." He laughs a little.

"Deal."

Matt's such a nice person. I wish it could've worked out between us.

"So do I know this guy?" he asks.

"Um, kind of. He came to your suit store."

"You mean Dylan?" Matt asks, as if it's the first person he thought of.

"Yeah, how'd you know?"

He shrugs. "It was just a guess. I hate to admit this but when I met him, I kind of thought you two would make a good match."

"Why?"

"I can't really explain it. It was more of a feeling. Like when I was talking to him, he kind of reminded me of you."

"How so?"

"He's intense but also laid back. Does make that sense?"

"Yeah. I'm intense about things I'm passionate about and laid back about the stuff that doesn't really matter."

"Exactly. Dylan's the same way. When he talks about his music he's intense, but ask him about a suit and he doesn't really care. He told me to pick whatever I thought was best."

"Why didn't you ever tell me that?"

"Because I didn't want him stealing my girl." He looks down, then back up. "I know he's friends with Austin and Amber so I wondered if maybe you and him had hung out sometime."

"No. Never. Matt, I never cheated on you. I didn't even consider it. I hope you didn't think I—"

"I didn't think you did anything with him. I just thought maybe you'd hung out with him."

I shake my head. "I haven't. Not since before I met you."

"So before you met me, did you two date?"

"No. We um...we spent a night together. It happened at a party last May. Looking back, I can't believe I did that. It's completely unlike me, but I did, and it turned out to be..." I pause. "I shouldn't be talking to you about this. I'm sorry, Matt. Just forget I even said it."

"Amber, I can't give you advice if you don't tell me anything."

"I know, but this is weird. Talking about some other guy with you? It seems wrong."

"Eventually you'll have to talk about some other girl with me, so then we'll be even." He smiles and nudges my arm.

"Come on. Tell me what happened. You spent a night together and then what?"

"I panicked. That night was so great that I wanted to keep it as it was. A perfect night that I would remember forever. So I snuck out the next morning and never talked to him again."

"You didn't leave a phone number?"

"No. And I never gave him my last name. I told him I didn't want more than that night."

"Is that what he wanted too?"

"No. He wanted to keep seeing me but I told him I was moving to New York the next day. Like I said, I totally panicked. I didn't want anything to ruin that night."

"I don't get it. How would dating him ruin that night?"

"I was worried that if I dated him and it didn't work out, that the night we had together would've changed. I wouldn't remember it the same. I know that may sound totally stupid and completely irrational but there's this part of me that wants to believe in things like fate and destiny and true love. I know none of that probably exists in real life but I swear, that night, I felt it. I felt like all those things existed for those few brief hours and I didn't want to do anything that would take those feelings away. So I left."

"Why do you think that stuff doesn't exist? If you felt it that night, then there's your proof that it *does* exist."

"That night wasn't real. I don't know what was going on but I knew it would never happen again, which is why I wanted to preserve it as this perfect memory that I could keep forever. Untarnished by any other memories I had of Dylan. That's why I never talked to him again."

"And now you miss him."

I sigh, dropping my head in my hands. "Yes. Which doesn't make sense because I don't even know him. I mean, I know him through what Kira and Austin tell me but I don't personally know him."

Kira started dating Austin not long after she met him that night at the bar. Since he's good friends with Dylan, I made her promise not to tell Austin about Dylan and me. I still didn't want him knowing I was in town, Besides, I assumed he'd forgotten all about me. But then later I found out he'd written me a song. Kira was at a bar to hear Austin play and Dylan sang *One Night*. It's a song about the night we spent together. Kira found the song online and played it for me and that's when I realized Dylan felt the same way about me as I did about him. I've listened to that song a million times since then, and it brings tears to my eyes every time.

"Do you think he misses you too?" Matt asks.

I nod. "He wrote me a song, and in the lyrics, he said he wants to see me again."

"So what's stopping you?"

"Well, for one, he has a girlfriend."

"Are they serious?"

"I'm not sure but I know they've been dating for a while."

"What else is stopping you?"

"If I decide to contact him, I want to take things slow. I don't want to rush into anything, but I don't know if he'd be willing to do that."

"By slow, what do you mean?"

"I want romance. Gestures. Phone calls. Letters."

"Letters? Like handwritten letters?"

I laugh. "I know it sounds ridiculous but if Dylan really is the guy I'm supposed to be with and that night we had together really was fate or destiny, then this is the story I want for us. The slow build. The type of romance you read about in books or see in movies. I'm not sure it exists, but my whole life I've dreamed it was possible and I feel like this is my only chance to test if it's true. I've never felt this way about someone." I cringe. "Sorry, I shouldn't have said that."

"Don't worry about it. Like I said, I knew there was something missing in our relationship. And now I know what it was. You didn't feel that spark, that connection, with me, that you felt with Dylan. Don't feel bad about that, Amber. You can't force yourself to feel something that isn't there, so don't feel guilty about it."

"I still feel guilty," I say, looking down. "We were together for months. I shouldn't have waited this long to tell you how I felt but I really was trying to feel differently. I thought if I just gave it more time."

"So what are you going to do about Dylan?"

"I'm not sure. That's why I wanted your advice. But asking you this is so inappropriate I can't believe I even considered it. I'm sorry, Matt."

"Stop apologizing." He nudges my leg. "We're friends, right? So this is my advice."

I look up at him. "Yeah?"

"I think you should go to Dylan and tell him how you feel."

"I'm too embarrassed, and ashamed for running off like that."

"Then write him a letter."

"I've thought about doing that but I'm worried I'll scare him off."

"Why would that scare him off?"

"Because that night we were together, I told him I'd write letters to the man I loved."

"So by writing him a letter, you're telling him you love him?"

"Well, not really, but he could interpret it that way."

"Do you love him?"

I laugh. "I met him one night. You can't fall in love that fast."

"Love at first sight?" His mouth curves up. "I haven't experienced it myself but I've heard it can happen."

I'm not going to admit it to Matt, but I did feel like that's what happened with Dylan. Like it was love at first sight. Why else would I have felt so strongly about him? And continued to feel that way even now, all these months later?

"There's another reason why I'm afraid to contact him," I say.

"What is it?"

"I lied to him. He didn't know I was here in Chicago. Until just recently, he thought I was living in New York."

"Kira didn't tell him you're her roommate?"

"I told her not to. And I asked her not to tell Austin either."

"So Austin had no idea you're the same Amber that Dylan was with that night?"

"No, but he found out a couple weeks ago. Austin came over to see Kira after she hurt her leg. She was asleep in her room so Austin and I hung out in the living room, talking. I thanked him for not telling Dylan about me, assuming Kira told him. The two of them are so close that I thought for sure she'd told him who I was, but it turns out she hadn't. As soon as Austin found out, he went and told Dylan."

"And Dylan didn't call you after that? Or try to see you?"

"No. Why *would* he? After what I did, I'm sure he wants nothing to do with me. Besides, he has a girlfriend now."

"Did Austin say Dylan was mad at you?"

"No, but I'm sure he is. He has every right to be. I knew he was looking for me and I never even tried to contact him. Now that he knows the truth, I want to talk to him and at least apologize, but I'm afraid he won't even listen to me."

"Do you want to see him again?"

"I've wanted to see him ever since I found out he was looking for me. I just haven't been able to make myself do it. Plus, I was with you, and I really *was* trying to make it work between us."

"I know you were," he says in a kind, understanding tone. "But you can't force what's not there."

I nod again.

"Amber, if you really think this guy might be the one, you have to take the risk. Even if you're afraid, even if you think he'll reject you, you have to at least try. If you don't, you'll always regret it."

He's right. I can't keep putting this off. I'm almost a hundred percent certain Dylan wants nothing to do with me, but we both need some kind of closure, or maybe just *I* do. Dylan's with someone else now, and he's probably happy with her, happy to no longer be looking for the girl who lied to him and left him with no answers. I'd like to think Dylan still has feelings for me, but Austin told Kira that Dylan didn't have much of a reaction when he found out I've been here in town the whole time. And as I told Matt, Dylan hasn't tried to contact me. That tells me he's moved on. He wants nothing to do with me.

But I still want to talk to him. Tell him I'm sorry. Tell him I never wanted to hurt him.

I want to tell him even more than that. I want to tell him how I feel and how that night was the best night of my life. Even if he never wants to see me again, I want him to know how much that night meant to me. How it changed me, and made me believe that maybe fate and true love really do exist, even if just for a fleeting moment.

Since that night, I've wondered if maybe it *could* be more than just a fleeting moment. What if that night...and all those feelings I felt...were real? What if Dylan really is the guy for me? What if it actually worked out between us?

There's this part of me that wants to find out. It's that part of me that was there that night, telling me to go with my gut and be with Dylan. It's still there, nagging at me to see if there could be more than a night between us.

I have to find out. I can't keep wondering.

So I guess I'm going to do this. But if I'm doing it, I'm going all out. If Dylan really is the guy for me, and that night wasn't just some strange cosmic force making us feel that way, then let the universe prove it.

I want the love story. The romance. Old-fashioned romance with letters and gestures. If Dylan doesn't go along with it, then I'll know it was never meant to be.

"What do you think?" Matt asks. "Did you make a decision?"

"Yeah." I take a deep breath and let it out. "I'm going to write him a letter."

CHAPTER EIGHT

DYLAN

"I'm gonna grab a beer. You sure you don't want anything?" I ask, but both Kira and Austin are too busy making out on my couch to notice.

"No, we need to get going," Austin says as I walk past him.

From the kitchen I can hear Kira quietly talking to Austin. I know she's talking about me. She's been worried about me ever since Austin told me Amber has been in town this whole time, living with Kira. When I found out, I could've been mad at Kira but I understand why she kept it from me. She was just being a friend to Amber, who asked her not to tell me.

Austin didn't know about Amber until the night that he told me. It was a few weeks ago on a Friday night. Van and I were hanging out on the couch, watching a movie and drinking beer. Austin called and said he was on his way over. He sounded really upset. Turns out he'd had a huge fight with Kira. When he got to the house, he told us all about it. There were a lot of reasons why they were fighting but I didn't think they involved me until he looked directly at me and said, *"She didn't tell me something. Something she should've told me as soon as she found out you and I are friends. And definitely after she heard your song."*

"What does his song have to do with it?" Van asked.

Austin's eyes locked on mine. "Kira's roommate, and best friend, is Amber."

The room went silent. I was sure I'd heard him wrong. There was no way Amber was Kira's roommate. No freaking way. But Austin wouldn't lie about that. He knows how hard I tried to find her. All the hours I spent searching for her online. He wouldn't tell me he'd found her unless he had.

Van had no clue what was going on, his eyes moving between Austin and me. "I don't get it. We already know her friend's name is Amber. You've talked about her."

"He means MY Amber," I muttered, setting my beer bottle down on the coffee table.

"No shit?" Van jumped to the edge of the couch, spilling some of his beer. "Her roommate is THE Amber? I thought she moved to New York."

"It was a lie," Austin said. "Amber told Dylan she was moving to New York because she didn't want him to try to go out with her."

"Why?" I said under my breath, talking more to myself than to Austin. "Why wouldn't she want to go out with me? I thought we..."

I didn't finish my thought, but in my head, my thoughts were circling, wondering why she would do this. That night we shared...it was perfect. Why wouldn't she want to see me again?

"Van, can you give us a minute?" I heard Austin say.

"But I want to hear this."

"Then Dylan can tell you later."

I glanced at Van. "Go."

"I thought we were friends."

"We are," Austin said, "but sometimes your comments aren't very helpful."

"Whatever." He took his beer and went in the kitchen.

I felt bad telling Van to leave but he tends to make a joke out of everything and I wasn't in the mood. Not in the least. I was pissed. Confused. Shocked.

"So Kira just told you this?" I asked. "Why now?"

"Kira didn't tell me. Amber did. Amber thought I knew and when she found out I didn't, she'd already said too much. So she told me."

"And she said she never wanted to see me again?" I leaned forward and stared at the floor, trying to filter through all the thoughts going through my head. "So that night meant nothing to her. It was just a one-night stand. And she must've hated it if she made up some elaborate story to make sure she'd never have to talk to me again."

"No. Dylan, that's not it at all. It's the opposite. I know this sounds crazy and I still don't understand it, but Amber told me she didn't want to see you again because she didn't want to ruin the memory of that night. She didn't want to date you, then have it not work out, and have it change how she remembers that night. Like I said, I don't understand it. Those were her words, not mine."

"What did she say about that night?"

"That it was the best night of her life."

I was so shocked by his answer that I dropped the beer bottle I was holding. "She really said that?"

"Those were her exact words."

"Then why did she leave? Why did she make up that story? You're saying she's been living here in Chicago this whole time?"

"Yeah. She lived here all last summer."

"And you said she's a junior?"

"Yeah, but she's almost a senior because she takes summer classes. She grew up in Michigan with Kira. They were both gymnasts until Amber got into cheerleading in high school and quit gymnastics. I told you all this, right?"

"Everything but the gymnastics and cheerleading. I didn't know she did that stuff. Makes sense. She had a killer body." I rubbed my head because it was aching from trying to figure this out. "Why couldn't she just tell me this? I mean, I don't understand the whole ruining a memory thing, but she still could've told me that. At least it would've been an explanation and I wouldn't have had to spend months searching for her."

"I told her all that. For what it's worth, she said she never meant to hurt you. She assumed you'd forgotten all about that night, until she heard your song. When she heard it, she still didn't want to talk to you. She was dating someone else. She's still dating him, but I don't know why. The two of them have zero chemistry. You know, maybe that's why she's dating him. Maybe she's purposely dating someone she has no chemistry with because it keeps her from getting too close to him."

"Why wouldn't she want to get close to him?"

75

"Because she's still hung up on you. I could tell by the way she talked about you. Maybe she's dating a guy like Matt because she's not ready to give her heart to someone else. She's not ready to let you go."

"There's nothing to let go. We're not together."

I don't remember what Austin said after that. My mind kept tuning in and out. But before he left, he asked me a question. A question I've thought about a lot the past two weeks.

"Do you still want her? Even after knowing what she did?"

"I don't know," I said, because I really didn't. Finding this out was a huge shock, something I never expected. *"I'd have to think about it,"* I told him. *"But the answer doesn't matter. We're obviously never going to be together."*

Austin left after that and I got drunk off my ass, then fell asleep. I didn't handle the news well and still haven't. Ever since I found out, I've been moping around, drinking more than I should, and slacking off on my classes. Guess I'm depressed, but I don't know why. All these months later, I should be over Amber, especially since she has no interest in continuing what we started last May.

I thought that night was special. I thought we shared something that was a hell of a lot deeper than just than sex. I thought we shared a connection, a bond, that most people would be lucky to find after a lifetime of looking, and yet for Amber and me, it was handed to us without even asking. Like a gift from the universe. And then she just threw it away.

What has she been doing all these months? Has she even thought about me? I could ask Kira but I haven't because I'm trying to forget about Amber and move on with my life. But no matter what I do, I can't forget her or that night we spent together.

My phone rings as I'm taking a sip of my beer. It's Allison, my so-called girlfriend. We've been going out for over a month and I call her my girlfriend but we've never actually gone on a date. I've tried to take her out, but every time I go to pick her up, we end up having sex and never make it out of her apartment. So we basically use each other for sex. And she likes telling people she's dating the lead singer of Vandyl. Those are the only reasons we're together. Oh, and there's also the fact that she reminds me of Amber, not in her personality but with her blond hair and hot body.

I met Allison last September after I'd pretty much given up on ever finding Amber. I'd spent all summer searching for her online, looking up every Amber I could find who lived in New York and was around Amber's age. By the time school started, my life got busier and I couldn't spend as much time searching.

The day I decided to end the search was the day I met Allison. I was at a party and saw this girl. She had her back turned to me and when I saw her long blond hair, the same shade as Amber's, I thought I'd finally found the girl I'd been searching for. I rushed over to her, but when she turned around it wasn't Amber. It was Allison.

Allison immediately recognized me as the lead singer of Vandyl and started flirting with me, then touching me, kissing me. We ended up back at her place. I hadn't had sex since Amber, which is the longest I'd gone without it since I first started doing it at the age of 16, and yet I didn't want to do it with Allison. For some reason, I felt a loyalty to Amber, like we belonged to each other, and I couldn't betray her by being with someone else. But as Allison continued to kiss me and touch me and led me to her bed, I realized how stupid it was to keep waiting for Amber. So I did it, but when I had sex with Allison, it was Amber I was imagining. I still do.

"Hey," I say, answering the call.

"Hey, babe, what are you doing?"

"Just hanging out, having a beer." I hear music blaring in the background. "Are you at a party?"

"Yeah, but it's boring. I'm gonna come over and see you. I'll be there in a few minutes."

"I don't know. I'm kind of wiped out from classes this week. Why don't you just come over tomorrow?"

"Because I need you *now*. And I'm busy tomorrow."

I'm taking that to mean she'll be with some other guy. I've recently suspected that she's been seeing someone else. My depressed attitude since finding out about Amber has angered Allison. She doesn't know why I'm depressed but she has no patience for it. She's head cheerleader for the football team at my college and could have any guy she wants so she's not going to stick around if I continue to act depressed or turn down her sexual offers.

"Then come over," I tell her, figuring I could use her company. We haven't had sex since last weekend, which was the last time I saw her.

I return to the living room, where Kira and Austin are kissing. "You guys can go. Allison just called me. She's coming over."

Austin groans under his breath. He hates Allison. He hasn't actually come out and said that but he's made comments about how she's using me. But I'm using her too so he really shouldn't judge her for that.

There's a knock on the door.

"Shit, that was fast," I say, going to get the door. But when I open it no one's there. I look left and right, trying to see through the darkness. "Anyone there?" I step outside and my foot slips on something. It's an envelope. I pick it up and go back inside. "That's weird," I say, closing the door.

"Where's Allison?" Austin asks.

"I don't know. She's not out there, and her car's not there."

"Then who knocked on the door?" Kira asks.

"Whoever left this behind." I hold up the envelope. It's a regular business-size envelope made of thick beige paper. My name is written on the front but there's no stamp and no return address.

"What is it?" Austin asks.

"Hell if I no but it can't be good. Who drops off an envelope late at night?" I sit down on the recliner, staring at the envelope and my name, written in fancy cursive using thick black ink. For a moment I think maybe it's from Amber. She said she'd write letters. She said letters were romantic.

"Are you gonna open it?" Austin asks.

"Whoever wrote this has good handwriting." I show them the writing on the front. "Check this out. It's like calligraphy, or whatever they call that scripty type."

"Wait a minute." Kira steps up to get a closer look at it. "That looks like..."

"What?" Austin asks her. "It looks like what?"

"Nothing," she says. "You should open it," she says to me.

From her reaction, I'm starting to think my earlier thought was true. Could it really be from Amber? Does Kira know about the letters? Did Amber tell her?

My heart beats faster, knowing it's possible that the letter I'm holding is from the girl I've wanted since she left my side six months ago. The girl I think about and dream about and spent months searching for.

There's no way it's from her. But what if it is?

CHAPTER NINE

DYLAN

I rip open the envelope and pull out a piece of paper. It's folded in thirds, and as I unfold it, I see there's writing on both sides. It's the same handwriting that was on the envelope.

"What is it?" Austin asks.

"A letter," I say, smiling when I flip it over and see her name. She ended the letter with *Love, Amber.*

Holy shit! It's really from her. But why now? Why did she wait so long?

"A letter?" Austin says. "Who the hell writes letters anymore?"

I hear Kira whisper, "Let him read it."

I tune them out as I focus on the letter. Turning it back to the front, I read the first page, devouring each word.

It reads,

Dearest Dylan,

Let me start by saying I'm very sorry for leaving without saying goodbye, and I'm sorry I haven't spoken to you since. I wanted to, but I was afraid. Afraid that you'd be mad at me for leaving the way I did, but even more afraid that we could never replicate what we felt that night should we ever try to date.

I don't know if you remember me telling you this that night, but I never do things like that. I only did because I felt something for you. Something strong that I couldn't explain. And it was more than just physical. There was something else between us but I didn't trust that it was real. I still don't.

But I want to find out.

My eyes linger on those last words at the bottom of the page, my heart pounding with excitement, anticipation, a newfound energy that I haven't felt in months. Is she saying she wants to try this? Try being together? I flip the page and continue reading as fast as I can.

I know you're with someone else now and I don't want to harm that relationship. I just wanted to tell you I'm sorry and that I still think about you, and always will.

I'm not asking for your forgiveness because I know I don't deserve it. I hurt you, and for that I am sorry. I completely understand if you never want to speak to me again. But if your current relationship doesn't work out, and if you think there's any chance you might want to see where this could go, then I want to try.

For months I've stayed away, not wanting to ruin the memory of that perfect night. But now I'm willing to risk it for a chance with you. A chance to make even more memories, ones just as good, if not better, than that night. I've never stopped thinking about you and the night we spent together.

But if we do this, I want to take it slow. I want the romance. The love story. The letters. You may think I'm crazy and maybe I am, but it's what I want. If we do this, I don't want to mess it up. And if it lasts, I want a story. A story we can tell for years to come.

I'm leaving it up to you, Dylan. If and when you're ready, write me back. Tell me how you feel. What you want. And I promise, this time, I won't leave you without answers.

I want this, Dylan. The question is...do you?
Love, Amber

My eyes shift from the letter to the floor as I think about what I just read. She wants this. She wants ME. After all these months, I was starting to think I was the only one who felt something that night. I thought I was the only one who wanted more. The only one who wanted to see what could happen if we let ourselves go there. And now I find out she feels the same way.

81

She wrote me a letter. She said she'd write letters to the guy she loved. Does that mean what I think it means? If so, I feel the same way. If I told anyone that, they'd say it's not possible to feel that way after just meeting someone, but I wouldn't expect people to understand. It's something you have to experience to believe.

Kira says something quietly in the background, then I hear Austin's voice but I'm not listening, my attention focused on the piece of paper in my hand.

"She said she'd write letters," I mutter to myself. "She said if she ever found him, she'd write him letters. She said it's romantic." I let out a laugh. "The girl is fucking crazy. And yet..."

I burst from my chair and run to my bedroom. I have to write her back. Right now. She has to know how I feel. She has to know I want this just as much as she does.

After searching my desk and every drawer in my room, I can't find any paper, at least not any decent paper. I need good paper. I remember Amber telling me that night how important the paper is, and the pen. She said the pen and paper can be almost as romantic as the words written.

The girl has her head in the clouds and yet I love that about her. I love that she's dreamy and romantic. I love that she has these ridiculous dating rules and that she's only applied them to me. I guess I can't say for sure if it's only me but I know she didn't do those things with Matt, the guy she used to date. I assume they broke up or she wouldn't have wrote me the letter. When I used to hear Kira talk about Amber and Matt, it sounded like they dated like any other couple. There were no letters. No old-fashioned romance. Was it because Amber didn't see a future with Matt? Does doing this mean she sees a future with me?

Racing back to the living room, I search the side table next to the couch. There's no paper, and the only pens are cheap ones that barely write. Next I go to the kitchen, searching every drawer, only to find scratch paper and more cheap pens.

I hurry back to living room. "We don't have any paper." I run my hand through my hair. "Shit."

"What do you need paper for?" Austin asks.

"For his letter," Kira answers. So she knows about the letters. I assumed she did, given that Amber is her best friend. "Can you use notebook paper?" Kira asks me. "I'm sure you have some of that."

"No." I shake my head. "It has to be real paper. Nice paper. Like old-fashioned paper."

"Old-fashioned paper?" Austin asks as I search the side table once more. "What the fuck you talking about?"

The doorbell rings and I stare at it, wondering if it's her. But she wouldn't just show up here. She wants me to make the next move.

The bell rings again and I hear Allison's voice, "Dylan, hurry your ass up. It's cold out here."

I race over to the door and fling it open. Allison's there, wearing a trench coat, which means she's in a hurry for sex. She always shows up in that coat when she wants a quickie. From past experience, I know that under the coat is a bra and panties, probably black, her favorite color.

As I stand here looking at her, I'm realizing how shitty this arrangement is. She doesn't give a damn about me and never has. I've called her, asked her out, tried to get to know her, but all she wants from me is sex. It's meaningless and emotionless and I'm tired of it. I'm tired of her and I'm tired of feeling shitty when I'm with her.

"Hey." I block the door so she can't come in. "Tonight's off. Actually, we're done."

"What?" she asks, a shocked look on her face.

"We're done. I don't want to do this anymore."

She huffs. "Are you drunk?"

"I've had some beers, but no, I'm not drunk. I'm just not interested."

"Every guy's interested in this." She opens her trench coat, showing off her black push-up bra and matching panties. I admit, she's hot, but even so, she doesn't excite me the way Amber does. No girl has ever excited me that much.

"What are THEY doing here?" Allison asks, closing her coat as she notices Austin and Kira behind me.

"We were just hanging out," I say. "Now could you leave? I have things to do."

She huffs again. "Fine. I was cheating on you anyway."

"Yeah, I figured you were. Have a good life, Allison." I shut the door, not feeling even the tiniest shred of regret or sadness or guilt over breaking up with her.

"Well, we're going to head out," Kira says, walking up to me.

"Don't tell her it's coming," I say, referring to the letter I'm going to write.

"I won't." She hugs me, then turns back to Austin. "You ready?"

"Yeah." He seems confused by what happened tonight. I'll explain it to him later. He gives me a wave. "Talk tomorrow?"

"Yeah, I'll call ya."

As they leave out the front door, I go in the kitchen and find my keys and wallet and hurry out to my car. As I'm backing out of the driveway, I'm forced to stop, blocked by Austin's pickup.

I beep at him and he rolls down the window and yells, "Where you going?"

"To the store. I gotta get paper."

"It's after midnight. Nothing's open."

"The drugstore's open twenty-four hours. Now get your big-ass truck out of the way."

He backs up onto the street and I continue out of the driveway and speed down to the drugstore. I hope they have what I need.

Thank God Van's out of town. If he saw me right now, racing to find paper and a pen to write a letter, he'd give me shit about it from now until the end of time.

At the drugstore, I find the office supply section but the only type of paper they have is printer paper. Does anyone even sell paper to write on anymore? Maybe they don't. Nobody writes letters so there's nobody to buy that stuff.

"Need some help?" a girl asks as she sees me frantically searching the shelves.

I move some folders aside. "Um, no, I don't think you have what I'm looking for."

"Dylan?" The girl steps closer to me as I continue to search the shelves. "It's Macy."

I was crouched down, searching the bottom shelf, but I stand up and turn to face her. "Macy. How's it going?"

Macy and I dated for a month my junior year. It was nothing serious but she took the break-up hard. After I ended things, she stalked me on campus for two months until I started dating someone else.

"I'm good." She leans her shoulder against the shelf in front of me and I notice she's wearing a navy shirt with the store logo on it. I didn't know she worked here. Then again, I don't come here that often. "I went to your concert last week. I love that song you wrote. *One Night?* It's like my favorite song ever."

"Thanks. A lot of people seem to like it." I glance to the right and jingle my keys in my hand, hoping she'll get that I'm in a hurry.

"Who was it about?" she asks.

Girls ask me this all the time and I always give them the same answer. "It wasn't about anyone. It was just a song."

She pouts. "Come on. You can tell me. We're friends. I wouldn't tell anyone."

We're not friends. And Macy loves to spread gossip. That was one of the reasons I broke up with her.

"Sorry, but there's nothing to tell. I didn't write it based on anyone I know." I get my phone out and check the time. "Macy, I can't really talk right now. I'm in a hurry."

"Where you going? To a party?"

"No, I just have stuff to do. Homework."

I should've gone with the party lie. It's more believable than homework. Anyone who knows me knows I don't do homework on Friday nights.

She turns toward the shelf. "So what are you looking for? Printer paper?"

I was really hoping she would leave, but given that she works here, maybe she could help.

"I was trying to find a different kind of paper," I tell her. "Like the kind you'd write a letter on? You know what I'm talking about?"

"A letter?" She scrunches up her face. "Who writes letters?"

"My grandmother," I say, adding a smile to better sell my story. "She writes me letters and I told her I'd write back but I didn't have the right kind of paper."

"Aww." She tilts her head. "That's so sweet you write to your grandmother. See? This is why I liked you so much, Dylan. It's too bad things didn't work out for us." She goes to touch my arm but I take a step back before she can.

"So anyway, do you guys sell that kind of paper?"

She straightens up. "No, but we have cards. Why don't you get her a card?"

"Because a card's not a letter. It needs to be a letter."

"You can write in a card. Just get one of those cards that are blank inside."

"You sure that's all you have? You don't have any paper in the back room or anything?"

"No. What's out is out. Follow me." She walks off. "I'll show you the cards."

I guess a card will have to do. Or maybe I should wait until tomorrow when more stores are open.

Macy stops at the card section. "You should get her one with flowers. Grandmas like flowers." She picks out a card and hands it to me. "How about this one?"

It has pink roses on it and would be fine for a grandma but not for Amber. She needs something more modern and artistic. She may be old-fashioned when it comes to romance but she's modern when it comes to other things, like her hair and clothes. She seems to have good style, at least based on what little time I spent with her.

I hand Macy the card back. "I don't think she'd like that one. I'll keep looking."

She puts the card back and starts scanning the other ones.

"Macy, you don't need to help me. I'm good."

"I don't mind. I don't have anything else to do. It's really slow this time of night."

"I'd really just kind of like to look by myself, if that's okay."

"Oh." She seems hurt. "Okay."

That's another reason why I broke up with her. She always took everything the wrong way, assuming I was rejecting her if I didn't go along with everything she said.

She finally leaves and I search the card rack and find one that looks like a watercolor print with bright swirling colors. It's not great but it'll have to do. I forgot to get a pen so I return to the office supply area but all the pens are crappy ones like I have at home. I find a thin black marker and buy that instead.

Back at the house, I sit at the kitchen table and try to figure out what to write. It's almost one in the morning and I should be tired from a week of classes in which I had two tests and a paper due, but right now I feel wide awake, on a high from the thought of seeing Amber again. I wonder when I'll see her. I know she wants to take it slow but we can't just write letters forever.

My Dearest Amber, I write, being overly dramatic, hoping it'll make her laugh. Am I supposed to be funny or serious? Can I be both? I have no idea how to write a letter. I've never actually written one. Or does email count? If so, I'm not very good at writing emails so I'll probably suck even more at letters.

I continue. *Thank you for the letter. I appreciate your honesty and hold no ill will toward you regarding what happened after that night.*

Ill will? Who talks like that? Writing this old-fashioned letter is making my thoughts come out like an old man. But Amber said she wanted a gentleman so maybe she'll think my formal words are gentleman-like.

I look back at her letter to address the comments she made.

As for my relationship status, I'm currently single. I recently parted ways with the girl I was seeing. She wasn't the right girl for me. The right girl, the girl I want, is you, and has been since the night we met.

Shit, that's too much. Too over-the-top. Even though it's true, it might scare her off. I go to erase it but then realize I can't. I could cross it out but that would look sloppy and ruin the mood. I decide to just leave it. If I want this girl, I can't hold back. I have to let her know how I feel.

I want this, Amber. I want to try and see where this could go. I've never experienced anything like that night and I want to experience it again. I know you think that's not possible but I think it is. I think we could be even better than that night. And as for the romance and taking it slow, I don't think you're crazy. Okay, maybe a little crazy, but I'll do whatever it takes to see you again. When can we meet? I'm here all weekend so give me a call. I really want to see you. Get to know you. And continue our story.

Love Always, Dylan

I fold up the letter, stuff it in the envelope, and lick it closed before I change my mind about what I wrote. I'm thinking I might've said too much. I don't usually expose that much of myself this early in a relationship, but the fact that I did shows how much closer I feel to Amber than other girls I've been with.

A half hour later, I've delivered the letter to Amber's apartment and am back at the house. I can't sleep so I go downstairs and play *One Night* on my guitar, thinking of that night. Thinking of Amber. And hoping that one night will lead to so much more.

CHAPTER TEN

AMBER

"He wrote me a letter!" I squeal as I wave it in the air. It's Saturday morning and as I was walking to the kitchen, I saw something wedged under the door.

Kira runs up to me. "Who are you talking about? Who wrote you a letter?"

"Dylan!" I look at her. "You were there last night. You know I left him a letter. Why are you pretending you didn't?"

She shrugs. "I wanted it to be a surprise."

"So you knew he was writing me back?"

"Yeah. Your letter got there just as Austin and I were getting ready to leave."

"And?" I grab the sleeve of her oversized sweatshirt. "What was his reaction?"

"He was shocked. He got all intense as he read the letter, and then he burst from his chair and started searching for paper so he could write you back. But he couldn't find the right kind of paper so he took off to buy some."

"That late at night?"

She smiles. "I told you he still likes you. He *more* than likes you. He's crazy about you. He said it couldn't be just any paper. It had to be good paper. Old-fashioned paper."

"He really said that?"

"Yeah. Why?"

"Because that's what I told him. I said it had to be written on nice paper. I can't believe he remembered. That was so long ago."

"But that doesn't look like paper." She points to the envelope. "It looks like a card."

"He probably couldn't find stationary paper. They only sell it at specialty stores."

"Are you going to open it?"

I stare at it in my hand. "Um, yeah."

"What's wrong?"

"I'm afraid to read it. What if he turns me down? He has to, right? I mean he has a girlfriend. He can't—"

"He doesn't have a girlfriend. He broke up with her last night, right after he got your letter."

"He broke up with her? But they've been dating for months."

"I think it was only a month, maybe two, but it wasn't anything serious. Now hurry up and open it."

I go over to the couch and sit down, then carefully unseal the envelope and take out the card. On the front is a colorful design, like an abstract watercolor. Opening the card, I see Dylan's letter. It's written with a thin black marker. It makes me smile knowing he wrote it with a marker instead of a regular pen, in an attempt to mimic my calligraphy pen.

My plan was to read it slowly, savoring each word, but instead, I read it quickly, once, and then again.

"So?" Kira says from the chair that's next to the couch. I didn't even know she was sitting there. "What's it say?"

"That he wants to do this. He wants to try going out. He's even willing to take it slow and do the whole romance thing."

"Amber, that's great! I think you guys will be perfect together."

"I think so too," I say, my voice trailing off as I imagine myself with Dylan. I've dreamed about this for months and now it's actually going to happen.

"You should see your face right now," Kira says. "I've never seen you smile that wide the entire time we've been friends."

"It's because I'm so relieved he's not mad at me."

And because I'm so happy he wants to be with me. After all this time, I was sure he'd given up on me.

"What are you going to do now?"

"Write him another letter." I shoot up from the couch, taking his card with me.

"Why don't you just call him? I gave you his number."

"It's too soon for that. Letters first, then phone calls, then an actual date."

"Do you really want to do that? Aren't you dying to see him?"

"Yes, but if we see each other, we might end up doing what we did last time. We need to slow down and get to know each other. That night we met, I told him almost nothing about me, not even my last name, and he didn't tell me much about him either. We need to make sure that we like each other on more than just a physical level."

"You can still do that and see each other. You can get to know each other by dating."

"Yeah, but then it's just like every other relationship. I want ours to be special. Something I'll always remember."

She sighs. "You and your romantic ideals. You're nuts, you know that?"

"I have to write him back. I'll see you later." I run to my room, shut the door, and sit down at my desk. With my calligraphy pen in hand, I write *Dear Dylan* at the top of the sheet of paper.

What should I tell him? He knows almost nothing about me. Should I just list off facts about myself? Like my major? Or my favorite foods? Or should I tell him something more personal?

My phone rings and for the briefest second I think it's him calling and grab my phone to answer it, desperate to hear his voice. But then I see it's my sister calling. I have two sisters back in Michigan. Leah is 25 and lives in an apartment about an hour away from my parents and works as a paralegal at a law firm. She's saving up to go to law school. My younger sister, Brittany, is 16 and a sophomore in high school. Like me, she's in a million activities; cheerleading, show choir, track, soccer. Anything to get her out of the house.

"Hey, Britt, what's up?" I ask, setting my pen down.

"I'm going to the gym soon. I was just calling to say hi. And to um...see if you'd come home for Thanksgiving."

Her voice got quiet at the last part because she knows it's a sensitive topic. Since starting college, I've avoided Thanksgiving, saying it's too far to go home for such a short time. But my sisters know that's not the reason. The truth is I can't take listening to our parents fight. It makes me feel anxious and sick to my stomach, to the point that I can't even eat the turkey dinner my mom prepares, which is too bad because she's a good cook. The food is always great at Thanksgiving but the constant bickering at the table makes me lose my appetite. It starts out as a few hostile comments, then gets worse as the meal continues. By dessert, my dad is out of his chair shouting at my mom and she's either crying or shouting back.

I don't know how or when it got this bad between them but every year it gets worse. They say they still love each other. But shouting? Screaming? Sleeping in separate rooms? How is that love?

"I really need you here this year," Britt says. "Leah isn't coming."

"Why not?"

"Because she doesn't want to be here. She said if *you* don't have to come, she shouldn't have to either."

"I'm a long ways away. That's why I'm not coming. Leah's only an hour away. She should be there."

"Kira's coming home. Why can't you ride home with her?"

"She's flying home. Austin bought her a ticket."

"Mom and Dad would buy you a ticket. Please? I don't want to be the only one at the table with them."

I sigh. "Can you invite one of your friends over? Mom and Dad are less likely to fight if someone they don't know is there."

"I guess I could do that. There's this new guy at school I've kind of been hanging out with. His parents are divorced and they let him do his own thing. I bet he'd be able to come over."

"Who is this guy?" I ask in my protective big sister voice. Britt's really pretty, with long blond hair, perfect skin, a great body. Because of that, every guy in her high school wants to date her. She's had boyfriends, but nothing serious, and I worry that someday soon some guy will try to take advantage of her sweet, trusting ways. I keep warning her about guys but I'm not sure she listens to me.

"His name is Lark. He moved here from Virginia."

"Lark? What kind of name is that?"

"I like it. I think it's cool."

"Are you dating this guy?" I ask.

"No, we're just friends."

Based on her defensive tone, I don't believe her.

"Britt. Are you dating him or not?"

She pauses, knowing I can tell when she's lying. "Okay, we're kind of dating but not really."

"What does that mean?"

"We hang out and we've kissed a few times, but it's nothing serious."

"Are you planning to do more than kiss him?"

"I don't know. Maybe."

"Britt, don't do it. You're too young. Wait until you're older."

"Like you did?" she asks sarcastically.

I had a serious boyfriend at her age so she thinks I had sex back then, which I did, but I never told her that. She just assumes I did.

"Just don't do it, okay? You'll regret it. But go ahead and bring him to dinner. It'll give Dad someone else to focus his anger on." I smile as I picture my dad glaring at this Lark guy, wanting to kill him. My dad is super protective of us. He's hated each and every one of our boyfriends.

"I don't want Dad fighting with Lark."

"He won't. He'll just shoot questions at him and give him the death stare. If Lark survives, then maybe he's not so bad."

"He's not bad. He's really nice. I think you'd like him. Oh, crap, I'm late. I told Stacy I'd meet her at the gym in five minutes. I gotta go."

"Britt, I'm sorry I can't be there at Thanksgiving, but I promise I'll be there at Christmas."

"You better, or I'm coming to Chicago. I'll call you later." She hangs up.

I'm dreading Christmas. I dread it every year. Winter break lasts three weeks and I can barely stand being at home that long. I don't know how Britt survives living there. My parents are worse now than they were when I was still living at home. I've talked to my mom about this and told her she needs to stop fighting with Dad, especially in front of Britt, but my parents can't help themselves. Whenever they're around each other, they fight.

The sad thing is, they used to be the perfect couple. They fell in love in college, got married after they graduated, and got along great. But then, when I was in junior high, they started growing apart, avoiding each other, sleeping in separate rooms. I don't know what happened, but their marriage fell apart and just keeps getting worse.

This is why I don't believe things like soulmates and destiny exist in real life. I want to believe in that stuff, and I used to, until my parents turned against each other. I used to look up to them, wanting a relationship just like theirs someday. But their happy, blissful state didn't last and now they hate each other.

Will that happen to Dylan and me? Or whoever I end up with? And if so, then why am I pursuing this thing with Dylan?

Picking up my pen again, I look down at his name on the paper and remember the night we shared. The way he looked at me, the gentle way he touched me, the way he held me protectively in his arms. There was something there. Something between us that is too real to ignore.

And that's my answer. That's why I'm doing this. I want to feel that way again, even if it's just for a short while. When it ends, it'll just prove my point that those feelings don't last. And then, years later, my realistic side will win out, quieting my dreamy romantic side, and I'll marry someone like Matt, a nice guy I feel no sparks for. Because if it's not that great to begin with, then it won't be as big a loss when our relationship crumbles apart like my parents' did. It seems like a sensible approach, and yet it's also really sad. But that's life. It doesn't play out like the movies, with true loves and soulmates and happily ever afters.

Holding my pen over the paper, I feel my romantic side taking over again. I remember what it felt like to be with Dylan and feel hopeful, like maybe I'm not doomed to turn out like my parents. It scares me to pursue a relationship with someone I feel so strongly for, fearing it won't end well, but it also makes me believe in love again. And I like that feeling. I crave it.

I return to my letter, deciding to go the facts route rather than the more personal route.

Dear Dylan,

Since you don't know much about me, here are some of the basics. I'm a marketing major at Katswick College with a minor in communications. I should be a junior, but credit-wise I'm almost a senior because I take classes every summer instead of going home to Michigan. I used to be a gymnast, like Kira, but I quit when I was in high school. I'm in a million clubs and activities. I have a really hard time relaxing. I guess I'm just wired that way. Even when I'm home, I'm always doing something. Cleaning. Organizing. Making lists. It's another crazy thing you should know about me.

This letter is boring. I don't want to bore him but facts are boring. Maybe I'll add something more personal.

I'm really happy you wrote back. Like extremely happy. In fact, Kira said she'd never seen me smile that much in all the years she's known me.

Damn. That's giving too much away. I don't want to scare him off, telling him how much I like him. But I can't erase the ink and I don't want to start over. And maybe he'll like that I was that honest, that vulnerable. I owe him that level of honesty after leaving him hanging all those months.

As for seeing each other, I think we should wait. I'd like to keep writing letters, at least for a while.

I look forward to your next letter.

Love,

Amber

Okay, that was a really bad letter, but I'll make sure the next one is better. I seal it up in an envelope and run back out to the living room. Kira is on the couch eating cereal and watching TV.

"Is Austin coming over?" I ask.

"Yeah, in like an hour."

"Can you have him give this to Dylan?" I hand her the letter. "Vandyl plays tonight, right?"

"Yeah. I'm going to hear them play. Why don't you come with me?"

"I can't. I have to keep my distance from Dylan."

"Amber, come on." She sets her cereal bowl on the coffee table. "This is stupid. I mean, I think the letter thing is sweet and romantic and all that, but you've wanted to be with Dylan since last May so just go be with him. You can still write letters but—"

"No. It has to be this way. Just give him the letter, okay?"

"Okay, but I think you should just go deliver it in person."

"I couldn't even if I wanted to. I have to go meet Liza for coffee, then I have to go to work. I probably won't see you until tomorrow."

"I'm staying with Austin tonight so I probably won't get back here until tomorrow afternoon."

As she talks, I'm already halfway to the bathroom, hurrying to get ready. With my mind consumed with Dylan, I totally forgot I had this meeting with Liza. She's a nurse at the hospital where I'm trying to get an internship.

I met Liza through Kira, who knows her because of Austin. Liza's sister, Ivy, is dating Jake Wheeler, Austin's older brother. Last week, Kira and I met Austin and his three brothers at a bar for drinks. His brothers' girlfriends were there and all us girls started talking, and Ivy mentioned her sister, Liza, worked at the hospital where I had just applied for this internship. She gave me Liza's number and that led to today's meeting.

"Liza?" I ask, when I see her sitting at a table by the window. Ivy showed me her picture so I knew what she looked like.

She stands up and smiles. "Amber. Nice to meet you."

"Nice to meet you too." We both sit down. "Thanks for doing this. I'll try to be quick. I don't want to take up too much of your Saturday."

"Don't worry about it. I'm not in any hurry. So Ivy said you want to know more about the hospital?"

"Yeah. I applied for three internships for the spring semester. If I'm lucky enough to get more than one offer, I'll have to make a decision so I'm trying to get more information about each place."

"Well, I think you'd really like working at the hospital. I've only worked there since last summer but so far I really like it."

"You work on the children's floor, right?"

"I do. It's sad to work with sick kids, but it's also really fun. The kids have such a great attitude that sometimes it's hard to believe they're sick. Did Donna tell you about the holiday fundraiser?"

Donna is the woman I'd be working for if I got the internship. She's head of the corporate communications department which handles all the marketing, communications, and event planning for the hospital, including fundraisers. The holiday fundraiser is to raise money for the children's cancer unit.

"She mentioned it during my interview. She said anyone's welcome to help, even if we don't end up getting the internship."

"Are you going to do it? You'd get paid, and it's a really fun event."

"I told her to sign me up. I just need to let my manager at the restaurant know."

I never quit my restaurant job from last summer. The tips are good and I'm able to have flexible hours. I only work when they need someone to fill in, which isn't very often.

"So what do you want to know?" Liza asks.

"Let me grab us some drinks before we start. What would you like?"

"Caramel machiatto." She gets her wallet out.

I wave it away. "It's on me."

After I get our drinks, we sit and talk for over an hour, not just about the hospital but other stuff. Liza's fun and easy to talk to. I already feel like she's a friend. Before I leave, we make plans to go out again.

Back at my apartment, I change clothes and get ready for work. I'm going to be a horrible waitress today. I'm completely distracted, wondering if Dylan got my letter and if he'll write me back.

On my way to my car, I stop at the mailbox. There's a letter inside from the hospital. I rip it open and smile when I see the first line.

We're happy to inform you you've been chosen as an intern for the spring semester.

The letter goes on to give details about the holiday fundraiser, saying that if I want to, I could start next week, helping with the marketing and promotion of the event. I get out my phone and email Donna to tell her I'm excited about the job and would be happy to start next week. Out of all internships I applied for, the hospital was my first choice and Liza just convinced me I made the right decision.

So at least my career is on track. Now if I could just figure out my love life.

CHAPTER ELEVEN

AMBER

"Too early," I moan, fumbling to turn off my alarm. It's Sunday and I forgot to turn my alarm off last night. I hit the button, silencing it, but five minutes later it goes off again.

"Fine, I'll get up," I say to the alarm, too awake to fall back asleep. I'll have to take a nap later. My mind's awake but my body is exhausted from work yesterday. There was a convention downtown so the restaurant was busy from the time I got there to the time I left. I even missed one of my breaks, but I made out big on tips. It's the most I've ever made in one shift.

I go to the kitchen to make coffee, but first stop and check the front door for a letter. I know it's too soon to get one, but I still check. Vandyl performed last night so Dylan probably didn't get home until two or three in the morning. It's just after eight now so I'm sure he's asleep. Maybe he won't write back for a few days, or a week. The wait is killing me. I want to hear from him again.

After a quick breakfast, I take a long hot shower, then put on yoga pants and a soft, oversized t-shirt. I'm going for comfort because I have to spend the day working on a paper, then studying for a test.

Around ten, there's a knock on the door. Who would show up here on a Sunday morning? Maybe someone went to the wrong apartment.

"Who is it?" I yell as I walk to the door.

"Special delivery," a deep voice answers.

Special delivery? What does that mean? I check the peephole, my body freezing up when I see that it's Dylan. What is he doing here? He's supposed to write me, not show up at my door! I'm not ready to see him. I'm a mess. A sloppy mess, wearing a baggy t-shirt with my hair in a ponytail and no makeup on.

"Amber, I know you're in there," he says in his regular voice. He was faking his voice earlier, pretending to be a delivery guy. "Would you open the door, please?"

"I'm kind of busy right now."

"I need to give you something."

"Just leave it at the door."

"I can't. I have to give it to you in person."

My heart's beating so fast I can barely breathe. I deeply inhale, trying to calm down but it doesn't work. My heart knows Dylan is just a few feet away and it really wants to see him.

"Amber," he says.

"Yeah, okay." I open the door and see him there in dark jeans, a black t-shirt, and black leather jacket. His hair is tousled like he didn't bother to style it this morning. And he hasn't shaved so his sharp jawline is covered in scruff. He's even hotter than when I saw him in May.

"Hey." He gives me that same sexy smile he gave me at the party that night. The one that led us to a bedroom. "This is for you." He hands me the envelope. His letter. It's in a regular envelope this time instead of a card envelope. He must've found stationary paper.

"Thanks." I feel like my mouth isn't working, or my brain, as I stare at the guy I've been dreaming about for six months.

He's staring back, but seems calmer than me. I'm practically shaking. Why am I so nervous?

"So...can I come in?" He laughs a little.

"Oh, um, I um..." My brain still isn't working. I can't even form words or sentences. What is he doing here? The thought leaves my mouth. "What are you doing here?" I step aside to let him in.

"I told you, I had to give you something." He still has that smile as he comes into my apartment and closes the door.

I hold up the envelope. "You already gave it to me."

"I could've just left that at your door. That's not what I came here to give you."

"I don't understand."

He steps up to me and his hand cups my cheek, his eyes moving over my face. "You're even more beautiful than I remembered." He leans in and my heart starts pumping so fast I feel lightheaded. His lips press softly against mine, and just that small movement, that barely-there kiss, is enough to feel those sparks again.

He remains close, his breath hovering over my mouth. I grab his shirt and yank him closer, just like I did that night.

He kisses me again, and I part my lips, wanting more. His tongue moves over mine and I nearly melt to the ground, held up only by Dylan's arm which is now around my waist.

His kiss, and the way he holds me, is just liked I remembered. Like I'm home. Back at a familiar place that shouldn't feel familiar at all because I barely know this guy and yet being with him feels so right. He doesn't feel like a stranger. He never has.

The door swings open. "Oh, shit." I hear a guy say.

Dylan and I turn and see Kira and Austin at the door, staring at us.

"Sorry!" Kira says, stumbling back into Austin. "We'll leave. We're leaving right now." She turns to Austin and shoves him out the door.

"You don't have to leave," I say, but they're already gone. That's just great. Now I'm going to have to explain this to Kira. Except I don't even know how to explain it. I don't know what's going on here.

Dylan still has his arms around me and that big grin on his face. "I knew it wouldn't change."

"What?" And then I realize he means the kiss, and the chemistry between us.

"It was even better than last time."

"I know," I say, my shoulders slumping.

"Is that a bad thing?"

"No. It's good. But it's going to make this difficult." I bite my lip.

The action draws his attention to my mouth and he slowly leans down and draws my lip from between my teeth and kisses me.

"We can't do this," I whisper, even though my body disagrees as it relishes the effect his kisses have on it. "We have to slow down."

He backs up enough to see my face. "Why? I know you feel the same way I do. I can feel it."

"Which is why we need to stay apart, at least until we get to know each other."

"Amber, we can have both. We can get to know each other *and* do this. People do it all the time."

"Yes, and it confuses things, and takes the romance out of the relationship. It becomes all about sex and nothing else."

"So what are you saying?"

"That we need to keep our distance while we take time to get to know each other. That's what the letters are for."

"We can still do the letters but..." He glances to the side, seeming frustrated.

"I knew this wouldn't work. You said you'd try but you're already giving up after just a day."

"I'm not giving up. I just...I just don't know why we can't see each other."

"Because whenever we're together, this happens." I feel my face heating up. "I can't control myself around you."

"So don't." His voice is soft, his head lowering to the side of my neck, his lips grazing my skin. "Just let us be together."

My resolve is weakening, my body craving him. Even his scent, fresh and masculine, is intoxicating, making me want to give in.

"Dylan, I can't do this."

He stops and backs away. "Do what? Us?" He sounds panicked.

"No, I meant sex. I don't want us having sex. I was serious when I said I wanted to take this slow. I know it seems meaningless now that we've already done it, but it's important to me. I want us to take this slow. So will you do it?"

He ponders it. "What about kissing? Is that off the table because I don't know if I can agree to that."

"No kissing," I say it seriously but crack a smile. "Okay, maybe the occasional kiss, but only in a public place. Otherwise, we risk something happening."

"So you're saying I can see you? Like go out on actual dates?"

"Not yet. For now, we stick with writing letters."

"Speaking of letters," he says, "I got yours last night. It was kind of lame."

"Lame?" I push him back but he keeps me held against him. "It wasn't lame."

"It wasn't romantic. And isn't that the whole purpose of writing letters?"

"It WAS romantic," I say, but he's right. It wasn't romantic.

"It was like reading a resume, or a bio. It was just a listing of facts."

"Fine." I roll my eyes. "I'll do better next time."

"I expected more from you, especially since you call yourself a romantic." He smiles.

"Yeah, got it." I smile back. "I'll be sure to be more romantic."

"And maybe draw some hearts. Spray the paper with your perfume."

I laugh. "Okay, now you're just making fun of me."

"Hey, you need to go all out. No holding back. I sprayed mine with cologne."

"You did?"

"I'm obviously better at this than you."

I huff. "I can't believe you just said that."

"If you'd like me to stop talking, just kiss me. Works every time."

"Yeah, you're funny." He really is. I'd forgotten how funny he is.

"So no kiss?"

"We're not in a public place."

"We could go out in the hall."

As much as I'd love to kiss him again, I know where it'll lead and I really do want to slow things down.

"No kissing," I say.

"Then I guess I'll keep talking. Since I didn't include any facts in my letter, I'll just tell you them. Like you, I'm also a marketing major, but I'm graduating in May. Not sure what I'm going to do for a job yet but I'd like to leave Chicago. I've been here my whole life and would like to try something different. You already know I'm in a band so I'll skip that part."

"Wait. What about your song?"

"What song?"

"*One Night.*"

"That's *our* song, not mine. What about it?"

Our song. My heart skipped a little when he said it. He already considers us a couple.

"When did you write it?" I ask.

"The day after you left. The lyrics just came to me and I had to write them down. I added the music later."

"I love that song." I look down. "Even though it makes me sad."

"It shouldn't make you sad. I got what I wanted. I found you."

"But not until months later. I'm really sorry about that, Dylan. What I put you through. It was wrong of me."

"Then why'd you do it?" His hand goes under my chin, lifting my face up. "Tell me why you did it."

"You already know. I didn't want to risk ruining the memory of that night."

"You sure it's not more than that?"

His eyes are searching my face. He knows there's more to the story, but I'm not telling him what that is because I'm not even sure myself.

"I just didn't want anything interfering with how I remembered that night," I say, going with my original story, which is still true. "And if we dated and broke up, I might not feel the same way about it."

"But you changed your mind. Why?"

I look in his eyes. "Because I missed you."

"I missed you too," he says softly.

As our eyes lock, I feel that connection again, that familiarity I don't understand but that's kept me thinking about Dylan all these months.

"Let's go somewhere," he says. "Get coffee. Breakfast. Whatever you want."

"We said no dating. Not yet."

"It's not a date. It's an interview."

"What?"

"You said we don't know each other, which is true. But I refuse to write boring letters detailing all the facts about myself. Because I gotta tell you, I've read one of those letters and it about put me to sleep."

I roll my eyes, smiling. "Yeah, got it."

"So if you want to know about me, you need to go out with me, even if it's just for coffee."

"Hmm. I guess you're right." I glance at my books spread out on the kitchen table. "But I really need to study. And I have to write a paper."

"I have *two* papers due this week and a test on Monday, but I won't be able to think straight if I don't spend at least an hour with you today."

I feel exactly the same way. Since the moment I dropped off that letter, I haven't been able to think about anything but him.

"Then I guess we don't have a choice. Our grades depend on it."

He smiles. "Whatever you need to tell yourself." He backs away and takes my hand. "Let's go."

"I'm a mess. I have to go change."

He looks me up and down. "You don't have to change. You look great."

"I look like I just rolled out of bed. I at least need to put on a different shirt and fix my hair."

"Then hurry up. I'll wait right here."

Back in my room, I rip my shirt off and search for the right top and consider changing out of my yoga pants. This isn't a date but I still want to look decent. I'm being seen with Dylan, lead singer for one of the hottest bands in Chicago, who I'm sure gets a lot of attention from other girls. I know he does because I've seen them pawing him at his concerts when I've watched them online. Girls are always putting their hands all over him, flashing their breasts at him. The same thing happens to Austin. Kira says it doesn't bother her but I know it does. I know she hates it. She's just learned to accept it, which I guess I'll have to do too if I want a relationship with Dylan.

I never thought I'd date someone in a band. Just like I never thought I'd have a one-night stand. Or find someone who sends sparks flying whenever he kisses me. This is a year of firsts for me.

"Amber?" Dylan knocks on my door.

He startles me and I quickly cross my arms over myself, covering up my naked chest.

"What are you doing?" I ask through the door.

"Telling you to hurry up."

"I AM hurrying."

"You've been in there for almost ten minutes. What's taking so long?"

"I'm trying to find a shirt."

"Want me to help?"

"No!" I yell. If he comes in my bedroom, we'll be having sex before we can stop ourselves. That kiss left me with an aching need for more, a longing to be with him like we were that night. "Don't come in!"

"I will if you don't hurry up. You've got one minute."

"One minute? That's not enough time." I frantically search through my clothes. Coffee on Sunday. What do you wear for coffee on Sunday? It should be casual but not too casual. Maybe I should go with jeans instead of yoga pants.

"Thirty seconds," he says.

Shit. I rip my yoga pants off and try to find the right pair of jeans. I want them tight, but not too tight. Something that makes my butt look good.

"Time's up." He opens the door and sees me standing by my closet wearing only a pair of skimpy pink panties. "Shit," he mutters, his eyes drinking me in, his mouth slightly parted.

I swallow, unable to move. If I even attempt to, I'll end up running into his arms, kissing those perfect lips, pressing myself into that perfect body of his.

And so I stay where I'm at, the air heavy with heat, lust, desire.

"You should leave," I say, somehow managing to speak.

His neck moves as he swallows. "Yeah. I'll um...wait by the door."

I slowly nod, and watch as he turns and leaves, closing the door behind him.

Exhaling the breath I was holding, I try to regain my composure. He saw me naked. He has before, but this was different. We weren't in the heat of passion, our bodies melded together. This was from a distance, and he looked at me, all of me, with a look so hot I could feel his desire. I still feel it, burning up the room, intensifying that aching need between my thighs.

I've got to get out of here before I do something I regret. If I'm serious about Dylan and seeing where this could go, we can't be having sex. It'll just confuse me and how I feel about him.

No longer caring which pair of jeans I wear, I grab the top one on the pile and yank them on, then quickly put on a bra since I wasn't wearing one and pull on a thin pink sweater. I wear a lot of pink. I'm a girly girl. It goes with my romantic side.

Hurrying to the bathroom, I put on some blush and mascara then brush out my hair and put it back in a ponytail.

"Okay, I'm ready," I say, meeting up with Dylan, who's standing by the front door, checking his phone.

He looks up and smiles, slipping his phone in his coat pocket. "You look nice."

"Thanks."

"Although you looked nice in the bedroom too. You could've just stayed like that."

He's got that heated look in his eyes again and it's taking everything in me not to give in to him.

"Yeah, that probably wouldn't be appropriate for a coffee shop," I say as I open the front door. "And by the way, next time I'll be locking my door. You shouldn't have barged in like that."

He catches me as I walk out the door, his arm going around my waist. "Are you mad that I did?" His eyes go to mine. Dark. Intense. Expressing how much he wants me. I want him too. So bad.

"No," I say, being completely honest.

"I didn't think so." He lets me go, but takes my hand as I lock the door.

As we hold hands, I'm reminded of that night, and how perfectly our hands fit together. They're still a perfect fit, making me think there really is some element of fate at work. A force that brought us together, knowing we're a perfect match. But does that really exist? It can't. There can't be a match for everyone. With all the people in the world, they'd never find each other.

"Do you usually take a long time to get ready?" Dylan asks as we're walking down the street. I assume he's going to the coffee shop on the corner.

"I guess I do, at least by guy standards."

"How long are we talking here? Like an hour?"

"An hour's a bit much. More like forty-five minutes. But it depends on the day."

"What takes so long? You don't need makeup and you look hot in whatever you wear."

I smile. "Thanks, but I disagree. And I like getting dressed up. Putting makeup on. Doing my hair. I'm girly that way. Probably because I grew up with two sisters."

"Younger or older?"

"One younger, one older. How about you?"

"A brother. Younger."

"And you said your family lives here in Chicago?"

"Not in the city. They're way out in the suburbs. I don't know if it's even considered the Chicago metro area. With traffic, it can take almost an hour to get there."

"Do you go home much?"

"Not really. Between school and the band I don't have much time to go home." He opens the door to the coffee shop for me. "Let me guess," he says as we walk up to the counter. "Some kind of latte?"

"Yeah. Mocha, made with whole milk. I'm not a skim milk kind of girl."

"Got it." He goes up and orders it for me, along with a black coffee for himself. "And an apple danish and cranberry muffin," he says to the girl. She rings him up, then we wait at the other end of the counter.

"You like cranberry muffins?" I ask.

"That's for you. The danish is for me."

"How do you know I like cranberry muffins?"

He gently squeezes my hand, which he held as soon as he finished paying. "I might've asked Kira a few questions about your likes and dislikes."

"Why didn't you just ask me?"

"Because you wouldn't talk to me, and as I said before, I didn't want our letters to become an exchange of biographical information."

"Order up for Dylan," a guy behind the counter says. We take our coffees and food and find a table by the window.

"What else did Kira tell you?" I ask.

"Not much. A few food preferences and your favorite type of flower. She also said that you used to kick ass in gymnastics. That you were even better than her."

"That's not true." I glance out the window. "She's exaggerating. She's the one who went to nationals."

"She said you would've gone too if you hadn't quit. So why'd you quit?"

"I just wanted to do other things."

"Because gymnastics wasn't important to you anymore?"

"It was, but..." I don't finish the thought.

"What?" He puts his hand over mine, stopping me before I peel the wrapper from my muffin. "What were you going to say?"

"Nothing."

"Amber." He pauses until I look at him. "I know you're not telling me the whole story here. So what is it? Why'd you quit gymnastics?"

"There's no other story. I told you, I wanted to do other things. I got into cheerleading, which took a lot of my time, and then I joined some clubs and did some volunteer work and I just didn't have time to keep up with gymnastics."

"And?" His eyes bore into me, urging me for the truth, the other reason I quit.

But I'm not telling him. I never even told Kira, and she's my best friend. The truth is, I quit because I thought it was tearing my family apart. I thought it was the reason my parents

111

weren't getting along. Gymnastics used to consume my life, and the life of my entire family. My parents were constantly taking me to practice and meets and competitions out of town, which took time away from them being a couple. They couldn't have date nights. They had no alone time. And all my training was expensive. It put a strain on their finances and they started fighting about money.

By high school, I realized I had to quit before things got even worse. But it didn't do any good. They fought even more. So I can't say for sure I was the reason for their relationship problems, but if it was even a possibility, I had to end my gymnastics career.

"You ever regret quitting?" Dylan asks.

"Sometimes, when I see a competition on TV. Or when I watch the Olympics. Kira and I both dreamed of going to the Olympics. But dreams change and now here we are." I force out a smile and pull my hand from his and peel the wrapper from my muffin.

"So now what's your dream?" he asks, sitting back in his chair.

"I don't know. I haven't decided. How about you?"

"Not sure. I kind of just take things day by day and see what happens. In a way, I kind of feel like I'm already living my dream. I always wanted to be in a band and I have been for years now." He picks up his coffee and takes a drink. "You ever going to come hear us play?"

"I've heard you play," I say, tearing off a chunk of muffin. "I went to one of your concerts back in August."

"That was months ago. I think it's time you come hear us play again." He smiles. "I'm your boyfriend. You've gotta come hear me play at least few times."

I smile back. "You're not my boyfriend. We're not even dating."

"We write each other love letters. Well, at least *I* do."

"Hey, I—"

"I'm just saying. I'm pretty sure the guidelines of an old-fashioned romance would say that writing love letters signifies a relationship, or a courtship if we're using old-fashioned terms. That would mean I'm your boyfriend, or beau, if we're continuing with the old-fashioned terminology."

"Then what does make *me*? In old-fashioned terms?"

"Hmm. I'm not sure what the equivalent for beau is. Sweetheart? Darling? Kitten?"

I laugh. "Definitely not Kitten. I'd feel like I should be walking around in a cat suit."

His eyebrows rise. "I'd actually like to see that."

I point at him. "Stop it. Wholesome thoughts only. Got it?"

He takes the hand I was pointing with and holds it in his, leaning across the table. "You can't control my thoughts. I can think whatever I want. Imagine you wearing all kinds of things. Or nothing at all."

He's going to kill me with his flirting. Kill any resolve I had to stay away from him.

Clearing my throat, I say, "So going back to names, I think girlfriend will do. Or just friend. Either one works."

"I think I'll go with sweetheart. It fits you."

"Why does it fit me?"

"It's classy. A little old-fashioned yet still in style. And it says a lot with just one word. It doesn't need explanation."

I'm trying to figure out what that means. I think he's complimenting me, saying I'm classy and a mix of modern and old-fashioned. But what does he mean when he says it doesn't need explanation? Is he referring to the fact that he knows what I'm thinking without me saying it? If so, that's true.

So I guess sweetheart *does* fit me.

How did this happen? I wasn't even supposed to see him today, maybe not even for weeks. And yet now I'm having coffee with him and we've given each other names. And kissed.

God, that kiss. I want to do it again. And so much more.

CHAPTER TWELVE

DYLAN

"Ready to go?" I ask.

Amber and I have been sitting at this coffee shop for an hour and I'd love to stay but I have to work on a paper that's due tomorrow that I haven't even started.

"Oh, um, yeah." Amber quickly gets up. I think she wanted to stay. She says she wants us to spend time apart but I know she doesn't mean it. Her reluctance to leave just proved it.

As we walk back to her apartment, hand in hand, she points to the cars parked on the street. "Which one is yours?"

It's odd that we've declared ourselves boyfriend and girlfriend, and had sex, and yet she doesn't even know what kind of car I drive. Our relationship is not traditional, to say the least, and yet I love it. I love whatever this is we're doing. It's not the typical romance. It's different and strange and quirky and unexpected.

"It's that one," I say, pointing to the silver Prius. "It was my dad's back when he decided to be environmentally conscious. But after a few months he decided being comfortable was more important than going green. He's 6'5 so didn't really fit in it, so I got the car."

"But you're also tall."

"I'm 6'2 so I fit in it better than he does. I'd like a larger car but this one is new so I can't complain. I used to have an old pick-up. It was my grandfather's. He had a farm in Wisconsin so he always drove trucks. When he moved to a retirement home he gave me his truck, but it was a piece of shit and broke down all the time. So what do you drive?"

"I have a Ford Focus. It was my mom's. She got a new car so I got her old one. But it's only five years old so fairly new."

We're at her apartment building now and stop in front of it.

"You don't have to walk me upstairs," she says.

"It's the gentlemanly thing to do. Old fashioned romance, remember?"

She smiles. "Then let's go."

She turns to head to the door but I keep hold of her hand, stopping her. "Wait."

"What?"

"Come here." I tug on her hand until she turns back around, then I step closer to her and wrap my arms around her waist.

"What are you doing?" she asks.

I nod toward some people walking by. "We're in public."

"Yeah? So?"

I lean down and kiss her, and not a short goodbye kiss, but a real kiss. Slow and drawn out and expressing what I feel for her, which is more than I should feel for a girl after knowing her for such a short time and yet I still do. My feelings for Amber are more than I've felt for girls I've dated for months. But why? Why do I feel this way? Was it the sex? Did that one night mess with my head, making me think I love this girl after knowing her for just a few hours? That can't be it. I've had sex plenty of times and never felt this way.

Someone's car alarm goes off and I force myself to back away.

"You weren't supposed to do that," Amber says in a soft, breathy voice.

"You said I could if we're in public."

"But I didn't mean—"

"No changing the rules now. If we're in public, I can kiss you. That's what you said."

"Fine, but it doesn't matter because we're not going out like this again. We're going back to the letters. You said you'd try it so that's we're going to do. No texts. No emails. Just letters. You broke the rules today by coming here but we're going to get this back on track."

I just smile at her, then wrap my hand around hers and lead her inside. We go up the elevator and when we're at her door, I say, "I didn't break the rules."

"What are you talking about?"

"By showing up here, I didn't break the rules of our arrangement."

"Yes you did. You were supposed to just write letters."

"And do romantic gestures. That's what you said. And today was a romantic gesture. I showed up at your apartment unannounced. I surprised you. Surprises are romantic gestures."

"Oh." She looks perplexed. "Well, that's not really what I meant."

"You can't define romantic gestures. They're different for everyone. And to me, surprising you like this was a romantic gesture, as was buying your favorite muffin."

"But what if I didn't want the muffin? Speaking hypothetically, because I kind of did want the muffin."

"If you didn't want it, that's fine. You didn't have to eat it, but that doesn't mean I can't buy it for you. A gesture is meant to convey a feeling for someone, an affection, and whether or not that's reciprocated or wanted or appreciated isn't the point of the gesture."

"Did you look up the definition of gesture? Because you seem to know a lot about them."

"Not really. I'm kind of learning as I go. This is all new to me. I've never had all these dating rules before."

"I know it seems strange but I warned you I was a little crazy when it comes to romance. And given the way we met, I just feel like we need to step back and start again. I don't want us to just be about sex. I want more."

"So do I." I kiss her cheek. "I have to go. I'll call you—I mean, I look forward to your next letter."

She smiles. "I'll put extra time into it."

"I hope so," I say, walking to the elevator, "because if it's like the last one, I'll fall asleep before I even finish reading it."

The stunned look on her face is the last thing I see before stepping into the elevator. It's fun giving her shit about that letter. She knows it was crap and I could tell she was embarrassed by it. I can't wait to see what she writes me next to make up for it.

***

When I get home, Van is on the couch in the living room watching TV. He must've just got back. He took a road trip to Kansas City this weekend to see a band that he likes. I didn't feel like going so he went with a buddy of his from class. Van's a music major but doesn't know what he's going to do with his degree. He doesn't like to plan ahead or set goals. He likes to just live his life and see what happens.

"How was the trip?" I ask as I hang my coat on the hook behind the door.

"Damn car broke on the way home." Van lifts his legs up on the coffee table. "I knew we should've taken mine. Jason's car is a piece of shit. We ended up stuck on the freeway just outside Kansas City."

"So what'd you do?"

"Had it towed. Jason's still down there, waiting for it to be fixed. I rented a car to get home."

"Was the concert any good?"

"It was great. And afterward Jason and I went to a bar and met some girls." He smiles. "Had a good time. Speaking of girls, I heard you dumped Allison."

"You talked to Austin?"

"Yeah. He said Allison showed up in a trench coat and nothing else. Why'd you dump her, man? That girl gave you sex whenever you wanted. And she's hot." He shakes his head.

"Damn, she's hot. If she hadn't been with you, I'd do her in a heartbeat. So why'd you dump her?"

"Austin didn't tell you?"

"No. Why? What happened?"

"I finally heard from Amber."

"No shit?" He sets his feet down on the floor and sits up. "She called you?"

"No, she came over and dropped off a letter. I didn't see her. The letter was left at the door."

"Letter? Who writes letters?"

"She does. She thinks they're romantic. It's a long story. Anyway, the letter said she wants to try going out, except we're not actually going out. We're writing letters."

"Writing letters? What the fuck you talking about?"

I can't explain this to him. He won't understand. He's not into romance. He'll take a girl to dinner or the movies or to hear a concert, but those are just dates, not romance, at least not what I would consider romance.

"Just forget it," I tell him. "You wouldn't understand." I go in the kitchen and open the fridge to see if we have any food. That apple danish I had at the coffee shop did nothing to kill my appetite. I'm starving.

Van bursts through the kitchen door and sits at the table, his long legs stretched out in front of him. "So let me get this straight. You've wanted this girl since you met her. You wrote a song about her. You searched for her for months. You finally find her and find out she's interested, but you're not dating her. You're just writing letters."

"Pretty much." I shut the fridge and turn to him. "You want to go get something to eat?"

"I just ate, but if you order a pizza I'll have a slice."

"Pizza. That sounds good." I get my phone out and order an extra large.

"Sit your ass down," Van says, "and tell me what's going on with this girl."

"There's nothing to tell." I take the seat across from him. "We're taking it slow. She thinks letters are romantic so we're writing letters."

"That's completely stupid."

"It's not stupid. It's different. Just because nobody does it anymore doesn't make it stupid."

"Why are you agreeing to this? This girl left you hanging for months. She treated you like shit. She should just be happy you're talking to her, not making you write some dumbass letters."

"She didn't treat me like shit. She just wasn't ready to continue what we started. And we were both dating other people. Now we're not."

"Still doesn't give her the right to make you do whatever she says."

"I don't mind the letters. In fact, I kind of like writing them."

"So what do you write?"

"Like I'm really going to tell you?" I shake my head.

"What'd she write in *her* letter?"

"Again, I'm not telling you."

"Have you seen her since the night she left the letter?"

"Yeah. I was just at her apartment. She got mad at me for just showing up but she got over it pretty quick." I laugh a little as I think of her reaction when I kissed her. She couldn't even stand up. I had to hold her. And the way she looked at me when I walked in on her when she wasn't dressed? She couldn't hide how much she wanted it. I felt the same way. If I'd actually gone into her room, we would've done it. No question. But she said she wanted to take things slow so I left.

"Meaning what?" Van asks. "You guys had sex?"

"No, but we could have. She wanted to. She just wouldn't let herself do it."

"Why?"

"Because she doesn't want our relationship to just be about sex. She wants us to get to know each other. I mean, shit,

119

I didn't even know her last name until a few weeks ago, when Austin told me."

"But you can't go out with her? Then how are you supposed to get to know her?"

"I'm going to *find* ways to go out with her. I don't know how yet but I'll figure it out."

"I know you like this girl, but this is stupid. She's making you work way too hard. You should get back with Allison. Sex whenever you want it. No strings. And she's freaking hot."

"She was also cheating on me."

"When'd you find this out?"

"Friday night. She told me after I broke up with her but I'd suspected she was for weeks."

"Shit. Sorry, man."

I shrug. "It doesn't matter. I'd planned to break up with her anyway. Every time I was with her, all I could think about was Amber."

"So you showed up at her door today? And then what happened?"

"We went out for coffee. Talked."

"That's it?"

"We kissed. We didn't do more than that, but shit, I wanted to. I accidentally walked into her room when she was changing and..." My voice trails off as I remember how she looked, standing there in just a pair of pink panties. Her body is smoking hot. She still has the body of an athlete, lean and toned. Flat abs. A tight ass.

"Dylan."

"What?" I look at Van.

"What'd she look like? I've asked you three times now."

"She's hot. Hottest girl I've ever seen. She used to be a gymnast so she has the body of an athlete. Tight. Toned."

"Like Kira."

"I guess, but I don't really look at Kira that way. Unlike you, I don't check out my friend's girl."

120

"Like you've never looked at Kira? Seriously?" He huffs. "Whatever."

"Yeah, she has a good body but she's more muscular than I like. That's why Austin likes her. I like a girl who's softer, but still lean. That's Amber. She's freaking perfect."

"Even better than when you were with her in May?"

"I didn't get a good look at her back then. The room was dark and after we did it she was lying next to me so I didn't really see much of her. But today? I saw plenty, and damn, she's seriously got the best body I've ever seen."

"Tell her to send you pics so I can see."

I reach over and smack him. "You're not seeing my girl. Don't even think about her that way. Get your own girl."

He smiles. "Sienna called me last night. She wants to get back together."

Sienna is a girl he dated last year for a few weeks. She's a massage therapist who also tells fortunes and reads tarot cards.

"You sure you want to go out with her again?" I ask. "She's kind of scary with all that mystical crap."

"That's just a side job for extra cash. She doesn't really believe in that shit. And she gives me massages." He laughs. "With happy endings."

"If that's what you want, then go for it."

He gets his phone out. "I'm gonna call her right now. See if she'll come over tonight."

The doorbell rings. "That's the pizza."

After loading up on pizza, I get to work on my paper and a few hours later it's done. It's not the greatest paper ever written but it's good enough. That's been my attitude about all my classes this semester. It's my senior year and at this point, I really don't care about getting all A's, especially in classes I don't care about, like sociology, which is what the paper is for. I was supposed to take this class freshman year but didn't and kept putting it off until now. But I have no interest in it so I skip a lot of the classes.

I'm interested in my other classes, my marketing classes, but I still don't put forth the effort I did in past years. Instead, I've been putting my energy into finding a job for after I graduate. Of course, every job I'm interested in expects you to have some experience so I've been applying for internships for the spring semester. I really wanted to get one at this start-up web company downtown but found out last week that they gave it to someone else. My next top pick for an internship was at a company that makes sports equipment, but they hired some guy who's graduating in December. The other ones I applied for I'm not really interested in but I can't be picky. I need the experience. I'll take what I can get.

"Mail," Van says, dropping it on the kitchen table where I'm sitting with my laptop.

"Guess I forgot to get it yesterday." I glance at the stack of envelopes. The one on top is from a hospital I interviewed with for an internship. I'm not interested in health care marketing, but like I said, I can't be picky. If I get it, I'm taking it.

I rip open the envelope and take out the sheet of paper. The first line reads, *We are pleased to offer you an internship for the spring semester.*

"Got an internship," I say holding the letter up to Van, who's standing at the open fridge.

"Did you drink my beer?"

"No." I pause to think. "Maybe I did. I don't know. Who cares? Did you hear me? I got an internship."

"Yeah? So? Where is it?"

"The hospital, which is the last place I wanted to work but at least it pays and gives me experience."

I finish reading the letter. It says I can start next week if I want to help out with the holiday fundraiser. Why not? It'll give me extra cash as well as the experience I need.

"That girl wrote you a letter," Van says, shoving some chips in his mouth. "It's in the stack."

Sorting through the mail, I find a cream colored envelope with her fancy handwriting. She couldn't have mailed it. She must've dropped it off. Why didn't she knock on the door? She could've at least said hello before leaving. She's going to drive me crazy with this letters only thing. I want to be able to talk to her, and I definitely want to see her.

"You gonna open it?" Van asks as he sees me staring at it.

"Yeah, but not in front of you." I get up, the letter in my hand.

"You can stay there. I'm leaving to go buy some beer. You want anything?"

"No, I'm good."

As he goes out the back door, I sit down and open the envelope and take out the sheet of paper. I smell something. A hint of perfume. I bring the paper to my nose and inhale. It's a sweet, flowery smell. Girly. Romantic. Just like Amber.

Here's what she wrote.

My dearest Dylan,

It was a pleasure seeing you today. Although your unexpected visit took me by surprise, I appreciated the gesture. And the cranberry muffin.

But...I do think we need time apart. As we both know, being together without "being together" is nearly impossible and makes it hard to take things slow. So for now, let's stick with letters, and maybe I'll call you to discuss the biographical information that's not suitable for letters.

That was the unromantic part of the letter. Here's the romantic part.

I find your eyes bewitching. Beguiling. Perhaps that's why I'm so drawn to you. You beguile me with your eyes. They're the color of chocolate, dark chocolate, the kind that's supposed to be good for you. I like dark chocolate. I also like milk chocolate. I basically like any kind of chocolate.

I'm getting off track. Back to the romance. I love your eyes. I'd like to see them again but it'll have to wait. We need to take time to let our romance blossom, to become a beautiful flower that won't wilt over time but will remain strong, even in the strongest wind and times of drought.

For now, I'll simply dream of your dark chocolate eyes, and the soulful look they give me whenever we're together.

Love, Amber

I'm smiling as I read it. It seems that she decided to go the humorous route. From our brief encounters, I can tell she's not comfortable expressing her feelings, despite claiming to be a romantic. But I think she's serious when she says she likes my eyes. She's always staring at them. I like her eyes too. I'll have to write about them in my next letter.

As I told Van, I have no problem writing these letters but I am annoyed she won't let me see her. It's true our attraction makes it hard not to act on our impulses when we're together, but that shouldn't matter. After all those months apart, we need to see each other, even if it's just for coffee.

Fate brought us together, first at the party, then through Austin and Kira. If that's not a sign we should be together, I don't know what is. But maybe Amber needs yet another sign.

But how many times can fate intervene?

CHAPTER THIRTEEN

AMBER

I've read his letter over and over again and yet here I am, reading it once more. That's the great thing about letters. Unlike texts and emails, letters can sit in your drawer forever, to be read whenever you want.

Dear Amber,

I think you're beautiful. Did I tell you that? I'm sure I have, but if not, I'm telling you again, this time on paper. I thought you were beautiful the moment I saw you. You caught my attention from across the room and I couldn't take my eyes off you. I still can't.

But it's more than just your beauty that drew me to you. It was something else. I don't really know what it was because it was something I've never felt before.

The way our relationship started out, you may think I'm only interested in you for that, but it's not true. I promise you, Amber, it's not. I've thought about you since the day you left, wanting to know more about you, wanting to date you, wondering where we'd be right now if you hadn't run out on me that night.

Part of me is still angry at you for that and doesn't fully understand why you did it. But none of that matters now because we have a second chance. A chance to see where that one night could lead.

Yours truly,

Dylan

P.S. - Do not let anyone see these letters! If you do, I might lose my man card. Seriously, Amber. This goes in the vault. For your eyes only.

I laugh at that last part. He didn't need to tell me that. I wouldn't show his letters to anyone, and I trust he wouldn't show anyone mine. I didn't pour my heart out in mine the way he did in his but that's because I'm not great about sharing my feelings.

"Amber?" I hear Kira yell. "Are you home?"

She's been gone all day. After walking in on Dylan and me, she stayed at Austin's place for the rest of the day.

"I'm here," I tell her, meeting her in the kitchen.

She turns toward me, a big wide grin on her face. "So?"

"So what?" I say, going past her to the fridge.

"What happened?" She grabs my arm, stopping me.

"He came over."

She looks around. "Is he still here? In your room?"

"He didn't go in my room. He wasn't here that long. He came by and brought me a letter and we went and had coffee down the street."

"And kissed." She can't stop grinning. She's wanted Dylan and me to get together ever since I told her about him last August.

"Yes. We kissed. But that's all we did."

"And? How was it? How was the kiss? As good as last time?"

"Better." I can't help but smile as I say it.

"Details." She pulls me to the table to sit down.

"There aren't any details. We kissed. That's it."

"Oh, please. That wasn't just any kiss. You're practically breathless just talking about it. And when Austin and I walked in and caught you guys, it took you forever to even notice we were there. That had to be some kiss for you to react like that."

"It was," I say, unable to stop the dreamy tone in my voice. "I don't even know how to describe it. I've never felt that way from a kiss."

"But it didn't go anywhere? You guys just left to get coffee?"

126

"I changed clothes first." I pause. "And Dylan saw me naked."

"What?" She leans toward. "You stripped for him?"

"No!" I laugh. "Kira, when I have ever stripped for a guy? Never. And I probably never will."

"Then how'd he see you naked?"

"He was telling me to hurry up and he opened my bedroom door and there I was, with no clothes. And the way he looked at me? It took everything in me not to do it. We wanted each other so bad."

"Then why didn't you do it?"

"Because we're supposed to be getting to know each other."

"There are many ways to get to know someone. Like getting to know him in your bed?" She smiles.

"Yeah, which messes with your judgment. Anyway, I told him he can't keep coming over here. We need distance."

"Meaning you're not going to see him?"

"Not yet. Not until we know each other better. But he's writing me letters. He writes the best letters. Better than mine. I'm so glad we're doing this letter writing thing. It lets me see a whole different side of him. I'm finding out he's really funny. But also sweet. Sensitive."

"You could find all that out by dating him too."

"But I wouldn't, because we'd spend all our time making out. We can't seem to control ourselves when we're around each other. This morning just proved that."

"You didn't do anything."

"But we could have. And almost did."

"How long are you going to keep this no-contact thing going?"

"Maybe until the end of the year?"

"That's like two months. That's crazy."

"But I'll be home for part of December so that doesn't really count."

"It's still too long. You should make it a week. Or two, max."

"Two weeks isn't long enough."

"Two weeks is plenty long enough. And in two weeks it'll be Thanksgiving break. You'll both be in town. You guys could hang out that week. Go for dinner. Meet for lunch. See a movie." She pauses, then cautiously asks, "Or um, do you think you'll go home?"

Kira keeps trying to talk me into going back to Michigan for Thanksgiving. She knows I don't want to be around my parents but she still thinks I should go, for my sister's sake.

"I'm not going," I tell her. "I'll be there at Christmas."

"You could have Thanksgiving at *my* house."

"Like my mom would allow that. If I'm there, I have to be home."

"Well, maybe your parents won't fight this time."

"They always fight and it gets worse every year. Besides, I don't mind being here. It's quiet and I can catch up on homework. Oh! Guess what? I got that internship I wanted."

"The one at the hospital?"

"Yeah. It doesn't officially start until January but I'm starting next week to help out with a holiday fundraiser they're doing. So that's another reason I need to stay here."

"They're not going to have you work on Thanksgiving weekend."

"Then I'll work at the restaurant."

"They're not open on Thanksgiving."

"Fine, whatever, but I'm not going home."

"Then you can hang out with Dylan that weekend. You'd have four whole days to get to know each other." She gives me an exaggerated wink.

I laugh. "I'm not going to survive dating him if you keep this up. You're way too eager for Dylan and me to get together."

"Because you guys are perfect for each other. And think how great it'll be if you guys are a couple. We're all best friends. We can double-date. Go on trips together. It'll be awesome!"

"You're getting ahead of yourself. Dylan and I barely know each other. It'll be a long time before I'll consider us a couple. I'm not even going to see him again for weeks."

"Which makes absolutely no sense." She goes around me and opens the freezer door. "I know you want this romantic dream or whatever, but not seeing him is crazy."

"Yeah, you've told me that like a million times."

"And I'm going to keep telling you until you finally agree to go out with him. On a date. Like a normal couple." She hands me a quart of ice cream. "Want some?"

"Sure. Do we have any sprinkles?"

"Ha!" She points her finger at me.

"What?"

"You only want sprinkles when you miss a guy, which just proves how much you miss Dylan, even though you just saw him this morning."

I roll my eyes. "That's ridiculous. I don't only want sprinkles when I miss a guy."

She puts her hands on her hips. "High school. Sophomore year. You were dating Cody and he went to Europe with his parents for two weeks. You came to my house everyday and went through an entire container of sprinkles in two weeks. You even ate them plain, like candy."

"Because I like sprinkles."

"Sorry, but it's more than that. You stopped eating them when Cody got back. And senior year? When you were dating Luke and he went to that football camp? The day he left you made us go to the store to get sprinkles."

"You're making this up. Eating sprinkles does not mean I miss a guy."

"Fine," she says as reaches in the cupboard and takes out a jar of colored sprinkles. She shakes it in front of me. "Then I'll just save these for myself."

"I just told you I wanted some, and NOT because I miss Dylan."

"Then just for fun, let's do a little experiment and see how long you can go without eating sprinkles."

"Your experiment is pointless because the two are not correlated."

She smiles and sets the sprinkles on the counter. "If you eat those, it's proof you miss Dylan and want to see him."

I sigh as I open the drawer to get the ice cream scoop. I hand it to her. "I changed my mind. I don't want ice cream. I have to go study." Then I walk off to my room.

"Go see Dylan," she calls after me. "He's just sitting at his house, waiting for you. *Pining* for you." I hear her laugh to herself.

Shutting the door to my room, my mind goes back to when I was in here earlier, when Dylan walked in on me. What if we'd given in to what we wanted? Would it really change our relationship going forward? Of course it would. I'd be crazy to think it wouldn't. We can't go back to doing what we did that night. We need to be friends first. Hold off on the physical part of our relationship until later. Which means I can't see him.

Kira was right. I *do* eat sprinkles when I miss a guy. I have no idea why. Whatever the reason, the fact that I want to eat that whole container of sprinkles right now shows how much I miss Dylan. But I can't see him. Seeing him would make it too tempting to do more than just kiss. So for now, I'll just wait for another letter.

***

The next day, I go to two classes in the morning and one at noon, then I scarf down a quick lunch as I drive to the elementary school to read to Emily. I volunteer for a program for kids who are struggling in school. Emily is seven and still can't read more than a few words. Her mom works two jobs and doesn't have time to read to her and her dad took off a few years ago and never came back.

Along with her teacher, I've been trying to help Emily learn to read but I'm not getting very far because she has a hard time focusing.

"You have a boyfriend?" she asks when we're halfway through the book. She's smiling, her legs swinging back and forth as she sits in the tiny chair.

I smile back at her. "You ask me this every time and the answer is always the same."

She shrugs. "I know but someday you'll say yes."

"Why do you care if I have a boyfriend?"

She tilts her head. "Because you're pretty and you should have a boyfriend."

I laugh a little and hold the book up. "Let's keep reading. Why don't you help me? What's this word?" I point to it.

Turning to me, she says, "If you had a boyfriend, what would he look like?"

"I wouldn't know until I met him."

"But what do you think he'd look like?"

I've lost her. She's distracted, and now I'll never get her interested in the book again, at least not today. Once she starts talking, she forgets all about the book. But I always stay and talk to her because I don't think she gets much attention at home.

"He'd probably have dark hair, brown eyes, and be taller than me." As I say it, I realize I just described Dylan. Then again, that description fits a lot of guys, but I was thinking about Dylan when I said it.

"Would he be a fireman?" she asks, her eyes wide.

The story we read last week was about a fireman and his dog so I'm guessing that's where she got the fireman reference.

"He probably wouldn't be a fireman. I don't know any firemen." Although imagining Dylan as a fireman is turning me on. Shit. I need to stop thinking about sexy fireman Dylan and focus on Emily. "Why don't we talk about something else?" I set the book down. "What'd you do last weekend?"

"Watched TV," she says, bouncing on her chair as her feet continue to swing back and forth. "If you had a boyfriend, would he be nice?"

"Well, I would hope so. Otherwise he wouldn't be my boyfriend."

"My mom's had boyfriends that aren't nice."

"Then she shouldn't date them. You should only date boys that are nice to you. Remember that, okay?"

She nods and looks at me as though I hold all the answers to anything she'd ever want to know. She reminds me of Brittany when she was younger. She'd always ask me tons of questions and believe everything I said.

"If a boy is nice," Emily says, "would he give you candy?"

"Maybe, but that doesn't mean he's nice. Anyone could give you candy, even people who aren't your friends. Like on Valentine's Day, all the kids in your class give you candy even though not all of them are your friends."

"Then how do you know if a boy is nice?"

"If he treats you well. Like if he talks to you when you need someone to talk to. Or if he helps you when you need help. Or if he tells you a joke when you're feeling sad."

"Then he's like a friend?" she asks.

"Yep. Your boyfriend should also be your friend. That's how they got the word 'boyfriend'. He's a boy who's also your friend."

Her eyes brighten. "I never thought about that."

The teacher appears at the door. "Emily, it's time to go. Say goodbye to Amber."

She hops off her chair and hugs me. "Bye, Amber."

"Bye. Have a good day."

She runs off. "Hope you get a boyfriend this week!"

I laugh as I gather my stuff and put it in my backpack. A boyfriend this week? Not going to happen. Despite Dylan's labeling of our status as boyfriend and girlfriend, or beau and sweetheart, I'm not considering us that yet. It's too soon.

Back at my apartment, I check my phone to make sure I didn't forget any meetings. It's easy to forget because I'm involved in a ton of campus activities and clubs, along with my volunteer jobs and my job at the restaurant. Adding the hospital job will make me even busier but it might lead to a job after graduation so I need to make it a priority.

Today's my first day and I'm feeling both nervous and excited. I've had many jobs over the years but this one actually pertains to my major so I feel like it's my first real job. Like I'm finally embarking on my career.

When I get there, Donna, my new boss, greets me as I come into her office. "Welcome to your first day," she says with a smile.

"Thanks!" I smile back. "I'm looking forward to getting started."

"Before you do anything," she says, "you'll need to get an ID badge and fill out some paperwork."

"Okay. Where do I go for that?"

"You'll go down one floor to Human Resources. I told them you're coming. They have the paperwork ready for you to sign."

"Then I guess I'll head down there."

"Wait," she says as I turn to leave. "The other intern will be here shortly. I'd like you two to go together. It'll give you a chance to get to know each other. You'll be working together a lot the next few weeks."

"I thought I was the only other intern starting early."

"You were, but then one of the other interns called and said he'd like to help out as well. He should be here any minute."

He? So I'm working with a guy? For some reason, I thought all the interns would be girls.

"There he is," Donna says, grinning at whoever's behind me.

I turn and see Dylan there. Wait—what? Dylan? Dylan's the other intern?

Donna goes around me and shakes his hand. "Welcome to your first day."

"Thanks," he says, his eyes going from her to me. He's better able to hide his surprise. I'm staring at him with what I'm sure is a shocked and confused look on my face and he's simply smiling, like seeing me here is the most normal thing in the world.

"Amber," he says, holding his hand out to me. "Good to see you again."

"Yeah." I shake his hand. The hand that fits perfectly around mine.

"You two know each other?" Donna asks.

"We do." Dylan looks back at her. "One of my good friends dates Amber's roommate."

"So you're just friends," she says, sounding relieved. "I thought you were going to say you were romantically involved, in which case this wouldn't work out. We don't allow people working in the same department to date. It's an HR rule, not mine, but I have to enforce it."

"Of course," Dylan says in a businesslike tone. "So where do we start?"

"I was just telling Amber that you need to go down to HR to fill out some paperback and get your ID badges."

"Sounds good. Ready, Amber?"

"Um, yeah. I'm ready." I follow him out the door and when we're in the hall, I whisper, "What are you doing here?"

"Working. I'm an intern."

I swat his arm. "Obviously, but why didn't you tell me?"

"I just found out. You won't let me talk to you and I didn't have time to write a letter so this is the first chance I've had to tell you." He punches the button on the elevator and we stand outside it, waiting.

"I never said you couldn't call me."

"You didn't? I thought you did." He shrugs. "Well, anyway, I wouldn't have had time to call. I had to write a paper yesterday."

"You could've told Austin. He would've told me." I keep my voice low because two doctors just walked up beside me.

"I didn't talk to Austin yesterday. He was with Kira all day. Oh, but I did get your letter. It was much better than the last one." He turns to me and smiles. "So my eyes are beguiling? Interesting choice of words."

The two doctors glance over at us and I step closer to Dylan and whisper, "Not here. Not now."

The elevator doors open and Dylan and I get in, moving to the back to leave room for the two doctors. When the doors close, I feel Dylan's hand wrap around mine. I look up and see that gorgeous smile of his and those beguiling eyes. Why did I write that? It's so embarrassing. Maybe we should stop writing letters. I'm not sure I want all my innermost thoughts preserved on paper forever, or for as long as Dylan keeps my letters. I'm guessing he'll keep them for a long time. He seems like the sentimental type.

The elevator doors open again and Dylan lets go of my hand as we move past the doctors and get off.

"It's to the left," he says as I start to go right.

"How do you know?" I ask.

"I've been here before. My dad had heart problems a few years ago. He was in the hospital a lot."

"What kind of heart problems?"

"He had a heart attack. Ended up having to have surgery and then he had to have another surgery a year later."

"Is he okay now?"

"He seems to be. But if he wasn't, he wouldn't tell me. My parents try to keep that stuff hidden from my brother and me. They don't want us to worry." He stops and motions me into the large office. "This is it."

We walk inside and a girl who looks like she just got out of college greets us. "Dylan and Amber?"

"That's us." Dylan gives her his signature smile and she smiles back, in a flirtatious way.

"Do I know you from somewhere?" she asks him.

"I don't think so," he says.

She keeps her eyes on him, then smiles even wider. "Vandyl! You're the lead singer, right?"

He nods. "That's me."

"You're working here now?" She's breathless, almost nervous, like she just met her teen idol.

"Just as an intern," he says. "A few hours a week."

"I can't believe we have a celebrity working here! Would you sign something for me?"

"Sure." He glances at me, then back at her.

Celebrity? He's not really a celebrity.

She hurries behind one of the desks and grabs a notebook and a pen. "Make it out to Julie."

He eyes her as he takes the pen. "Is that you?"

"What? Oh, um, yeah. Sorry. I forgot to introduce myself. I'm Julie Swanson. I handle all the new hires."

Dylan signs the notebook and hands it back to her with the pen.

She remains there, staring at Dylan, so I say, "We should probably get the paperwork done."

She snaps out of it. "Yes. Right this way."

She takes us to a small room where we have our photos taken for our ID badges. Then she takes us to another small room with a table and chairs. She hands us each a folder with the hospital name and logo on it.

"Just read over everything and if you have questions, let me know," she says. "Otherwise just fill out the forms and bring them to me when you're done."

She leaves, shutting the door behind her.

"Looks like you have a fan." I try to hide my jealousy as I take a seat at the table. Maybe it's too soon in our relationship to be jealous but seeing that girl flirt with Dylan really got to me.

"Do I?" he asks, sitting right next to me.

"Well, yeah, didn't you see how she was acting? She was practically drooling."

"I meant you." He scoots his chair closer to mine. "Are you a fan?"

I turn and see his face right in front of me. Those deep brown eyes. Those full lips.

"Um, yeah, I guess, although I haven't really heard you play." My heart's pounding being this close to him.

"I wasn't talking about the band. I meant, are you a fan of this?" He kisses me before I can stop him, not that I'd stop him. I couldn't even if I tried. I'm addicted to his kisses so pulling away from him right now is pretty much impossible. So I wait for him to pull away, which he does after a few seconds.

"You can't do that here," I tell him.

"Why not?" He turns back to his paperwork and picks up a pen.

"You heard Donna. She said we can't date. It's against the rules."

"So we'll be discreet." He scans the first sheet of paper, jots down his initials at the bottom, then flips to the next page.

I pick up the pen and look down at the stack of papers. "I told you not to kiss me."

"Unless we're in public. Which we are."

"We're not in public. We're in a room by ourselves."

"With people just outside the door. By definition, that means we're in public."

"That's not what it means. Other people have to be here in order for it to be public."

"I disagree." He sets his pen down, turns my face to his and kisses me. It's a bold, aggressive move and completely turns me on. "You know." He kisses me again. "I wasn't really looking forward to this internship, but now? I have a feeling I'm going to like it." He smiles and goes back to his paperwork.

How is he being so calm about this? I'm a nervous wreck. If we got caught, we could both get fired. And yet I find that kind of thrilling. Just like that night we met. I did something totally unlike me, totally unexpected. And it was thrilling. A rush. A feeling I craved to feel again.

So is that why I like Dylan so much? Does he bring out the bad girl in me? Or is it just *him* making me feel this way? Or us, whenever we're together? I don't know, but it's a feeling I can't get enough of.

CHAPTER FOURTEEN

DYLAN

After we fill out the paperwork and get our IDs, Amber and I leave the HR office and go back upstairs. She's been quiet ever since I kissed her, but I don't think she's mad at me for doing it. She was a willing participant in the kiss. I think she's just shocked that I'm here and afraid we'll get caught if I kiss her again.

But I'll definitely be kissing her again. I can't help myself. It's just what happens when I'm around her. And now, it sounds like I'll be around her a lot more.

Seeing her today made my freaking day. Not only does having her here mean this internship won't suck as much as I thought it would, but it also means I'll have an excuse to spend time with her at least a few times a week, maybe even every day.

I can't believe she's working here. Out of all the places in Chicago we could've interned at, we both end up here. The universe just keeps finding ways to bring us together and I couldn't be more thankful for that. There's just something about this girl that makes me want to be around her. Writing letters isn't enough. I need to see her. Be with her.

"This is where you'll sit when you're here," Donna says, pointing to two small desks that face each other, each set up with a computer and phone. "You'll share these with our part-timers who work mornings so if you notice someone else's things in the desk, just leave them there."

Amber and I take our seats. I gaze into her eyes and a smile creeps up her cheeks before she averts her eyes back to Donna.

"Is there a password for the computer?" Amber asks.

"Yes," Donna says. "But you'll need to create a new one just for yourself. The instructions are in the drawer. Once you log in, you'll find a spreadsheet with all of the vendors who have donated items for the silent auction. I need you two to split up the list and confirm with each vendor that they're still willing to donate that item. Since you only have a couple hours left here today, that should take up your time until you leave. If you have questions, just let me know."

"Got it," I tell her. "Thanks."

Once she's gone, I wake up my computer screen and set my password. Amber does the same, then we look across the desks at each other. It's going to be hard to work with her right across from me. I'll want to keep staring at her because she's gorgeous, and watching her trying to hide that smile that keeps sliding up her cheeks is both funny and sweet. She's doing all she can to remain professional and pretend we're just acquaintances, but so far her attempts aren't working too well.

"Do you want the first half of the list or the last?" Amber asks.

"I'll take the last." I scroll down the screen and find the first number. Before I pick up the phone I lean back in my chair and stretch, my legs extending under the desk until they brush against hers.

"Stop it," she whispers.

"What?" I ask innocently. "I'm just stretching. I went running this morning and my legs are tightening up."

"You run?"

"A few times a week. Do you?"

"I used to but I don't anymore. I try to go to the gym on campus but I'm usually too busy to make it there."

When we had coffee yesterday, Amber told me about all the stuff she's involved in. Clubs, activities, volunteer work. I don't know when she has time to sleep.

"Maybe you should cut back on some of your activities," I say.

"Maybe, although I wouldn't know what to do if I had free time."

"Spend it with me?"

"Shh," she says, glancing around to see if anyone heard. She picks up the phone. "We need to get these calls made."

We both start calling people on our lists. Two hours later, I've only reached half the business owners.

"So I guess I'll see you later," Amber says, putting on her coat. It's a little after five and two of the full-time workers have already left. Donna is still in her office with the door closed but she came out a few minutes ago, telling us we could leave and finish the list later this week.

"I'll walk you out." I pull on my jacket as we leave the office.

"So when are you working again?" Amber asks.

"Wednesday afternoon. How about you?"

"Same." She stops briefly and moves to the side to let a guy in a wheelchair go by. I stop as well, then we continue walking.

"And Friday morning?" I ask.

"Yeah."

"So Donna gave us the same schedule. That explains why she said I'd be working closely with the other intern." I glance at Amber. "It's kind of odd, isn't it?"

"What's odd?"

"You're trying to keep us apart and yet somehow we keep being brought back together. First your roommate ends up dating my friend, and now we end up with the same internship. Same hospital. Same department. Same hours."

She shakes her head. "It's not that unusual."

I turn and hold her arm, stopping her. "You don't find that odd?"

We're now at the door that leads to the parking garage. She looks back to see if anyone's trying to go past us, but right now we're alone in the narrow hallway.

"Okay, yeah, it's odd," she says, looking at me. "But it's also kind of scary."

"Why is it scary?"

"Because I don't understand it. Why do we keep finding ourselves together like this? Why did we find each other that night? I almost didn't even go to that party."

"Neither did I. Which just proves there's something else going on here."

"Like what?" she asks.

The door swings open and Amber and I both step back.

A young woman with blond hair comes through the door. She's wearing colorful scrubs that have cartoon characters printed on them.

"Amber." The woman stops in front of Amber and smiles. "Was today your first day?"

"Yeah. I'm just leaving. I'll be back on Wednesday."

"How do you like it?"

"It's good. Donna's really nice. I think it'll be a good experience."

"Are you the only intern?"

"No. Dylan's also working there." She motions to me. "You know Dylan, right?"

The girl looks at me, pausing a moment. "Austin's friend?"

"Yeah." I smile when I see her face, realizing I know her. Her sister, Ivy, dates Jake Wheeler, one of Austin's brothers. "I don't think we've ever met but I've seen you with your sister at some of our concerts. You're Liza, right? Ivy's sister?"

"Yeah." She smiles back. "And you're the lead singer of Vandyl."

"That's me."

"And you're working *here*?" She seems surprised.

I shrug. "Music is more of a hobby. My major is marketing. I graduate in May and needed some job experience."

"So you must know Amber because of Kira. Is that how you guys met?"

"Not exactly." I flash a grin at Amber.

"We met at a party," she blurts out. "Last May. But we didn't see each other again until just recently."

"Why didn't you tell me you were dating Dylan?" Liza asks Amber. "When we had coffee last Saturday you didn't even mention him."

"Oh, um, no, Dylan and I aren't going out." Amber sounds panicked. "We're just friends."

"Really?" She glances between us. "That's too bad. You guys make a cute couple."

I lower my voice and say to Liza, "Can you keep a secret?"

"Sure. What is it?"

I put my arm around Amber. "We actually *are* dating, but we have to hide it when we're at work. There's some rule that says people in the same department can't date."

Liza waves her hand around. "Forget that. Nobody follows that rule."

"Donna seemed really serious about it," Amber says, removing my arm from around her shoulder. "And I'm not willing to risk losing my job."

"Then I guess you'll have to sneak around." Liza smiles. "Hey, I gotta go. I'm working the night shift and if I don't hurry I'm going to be late."

"Yeah, go ahead," Amber says.

"See you guys later." She continues down the hall.

I open the door for Amber. "After you."

"Why did you tell her about us?"

"Why wouldn't I?" Putting my hand on her lower back, I lead her through the door into the garage. "She would've found out eventually. She's Ivy's sister. And Ivy's living with Jake. At some point Austin would mention us to Jake or Ivy and word would get back to Liza."

143

She stops when we reach her car. "Why would Austin be talking about us to his brother?"

"Because I'm one of Austin's closest friends and I know his family. If I'm dating someone, chances are he'll bring it up in conversation, especially since I'm dating his girlfriend's best friend. Why are you so worried about this? Liza wouldn't tell anyone."

"I guess you're right. I just don't want us getting in trouble."

"We won't." I lean against her car as she searches for her keys in her purse. "So where do you want to go for dinner?"

"Dinner?" She contemplates it for just a second, but then shakes her head. "No. I can't. I have things to do. I haven't been home all day."

"You have to eat, right?"

"Well, yeah, but..."

"Then let's go out. That way you won't have to make anything. It'll actually be faster to eat out then eat at home."

She smiles. "I doubt that. I usually heat up a frozen dinner. I can't cook, by the way. That's something you should know."

"I can't cook either, but it doesn't matter because I like eating out. So where do you want to go?"

"I didn't agree to it."

"Amber, don't fight me on this. It's just dinner. We're both tired. We're both hungry. Let's just stop somewhere on the way home. You like Zelliti's?"

"The spaghetti place?"

"It's fast so it won't take up your whole night. And from that grin on your face, I'm guessing you like their food."

"I do. Okay, then I'll guess I'll meet you there."

A half hour later, we're at a table waiting for our order. The place only serves spaghetti with like thirty different sauces.

"Enjoy," the waitress says, dropping off our plates. She doesn't bother to ask if we need anything else. This is no-frills dining. You order at the counter and get your own silverware and napkins.

"You always get marinara?" I ask Amber as she twirls spaghetti around her fork.

"Yeah, it's my favorite."

"You ever try one of the other sauces?"

"No. I go with what I like."

"How do you know you wouldn't like one of the others if you've never tried them?"

"I don't, but why bother trying them if I like this one?"

"Because you might like one of the other ones better." I hold out my fork, which I've loaded up with spaghetti and sauce. "Try it."

"I don't like sausage. It's always got that gristle in it that's hard to chew."

"Not this one. You might like it. Just try it."

She sighs, then leans forward and parts her lips just enough for me to slip the fork in her mouth, which for some reason I find arousing. I've never fed a girl anything but now I'm thinking this is something I should add to my repertoire.

She closes her eyes and chews, then smiles slightly as she opens her eyes. "It's good."

"Better than the marinara?"

"Hmm. Maybe."

"You want some more?"

She sets her fork down and leans forward again.

"Hold on." I get up and go to the other side of the booth and sit next to her.

"What are you doing?"

"I can't reach from that side." I slide my plate over and load up another forkful of spaghetti and hold it up to her.

"I can feed myself." She tries to take the fork from me but I don't let her have it.

"It's more fun this way." I chuckle when I see her cheeks turning pink. She's embarrassed because the older couple at the table next to ours is giving us strange looks.

"Dylan, go back to your seat," she says in a hushed tone.

"This IS my seat. Now have a taste." I hold my fork up.

She quickly takes a bite. "Yeah, it's good. Now go sit over there." She points to the other side of the booth.

"I like this side better," I say, going back to eating my spaghetti.

She picks up her fork. "This is totally breaking the rules. We shouldn't be out like this."

"Forget the rules. Obviously the universe wants us together so we might as well be together."

"I'm pretty sure the universe is not involved in this."

I stop eating and turn to her. "Do you really think that?"

She pauses, her eyes on her plate. "No."

"So stop fighting it and just go with it."

Turning to me, she says, "Okay, yes, I agree there's something going on here. Some cosmic force that keeps bringing us together, but that doesn't mean we can't take some time apart to get to know each other."

"I can't get to know you with just the letters. It's not enough. We need to see each other. Spend time together."

"We can't."

"Why not?" I set my fork down and turn to face her.

"Because we can't..." She drops her voice to a whisper. "We can't stop ourselves when we're together. Alone."

"We were alone together yesterday and we didn't do anything."

"We almost did."

"And if we had, and if we did going forward, what's the big deal? It's part of dating. It's normal."

"It complicates things. I want to get to know you without that interfering."

She's so frustrating. And stubborn. And yet I'll do most anything to see her again.

"Okay, how about this?" I say. "We make a rule that when we're alone together, there's no physical contact. We're just friends getting to know each other."

"And when we're not alone?"

I place my hand under her chin and lift her face up to mine and kiss her. Softly. Slowly. Then I back away.

"Was that supposed to be your answer?" she asks, sounding breathless.

I chuckle. "Yes." I pick my fork up and continue eating. "We'll stick with your original rule. And given that rule, I'm guessing a lot of our dates will be in public."

When I glance at her, I see her trying to fight a smile. "I haven't agreed to date you."

"You don't have to. We're already dating. You're my sweetheart, remember?" I lean over and kiss her cheek. "And I have to take my sweetheart on dates. I can't leave her sitting at home all alone."

"I'm not alone. I have Kira. And I'm almost never home. But..." She sighs. "I suppose we could go out now and then."

"Don't sound so excited about it." I nudge her side before taking a big bite of spaghetti.

"Dylan." She holds my arm before I scoop up more spaghetti. "It's not that I don't want to see you. I'm just worried our relationship won't have a chance if all we do is...you know...what we did that night."

"Which is why we'll keep things platonic when we're alone together. At least until you're ready to take things farther. Sound good?"

She nods. "Yeah."

I see her eyeing my plate. "You want to share the rest of this?"

"Could we?" she asks hesitantly.

I slide my plate between us. "Dig in. And next time we come here, I'm banning the marinara. You have to get this one or something else."

"It's a deal."

She scoots closer, our bodies touching as we share the plate of spaghetti. She could've just put some on her plate but instead she's eating off of mine. It's one of those things you'd

147

do after dating someone a long time, and yet this is technically only our second date. But something feels right about it. Like it'd be odd if we *didn't* share a plate.

After dinner, I walk her out to her car. "I'll follow you home."

"That's okay. I'll be fine. But thanks for offering."

"So I'll see you on Wednesday?"

"Yeah." She opens her car door. "So um, thanks for dinner."

"You're welcome." I step up to her, catching her eye and holding her gaze.

"I should go," she says, her eyes still on mine.

"I don't want you to."

"But...I have things to do."

"So do I. But I don't want to say goodbye. Not yet."

"Me either." She bites her lip.

My hand cups the back of her head and I pull her toward me and kiss her for a good long minute, then linger at her lips. "Let's go somewhere."

"Where?"

"You want to go to a movie?" I kiss her again but keep it short.

"We could, but I doubt we'd watch it."

"That's the point." I kiss her once more. "Why'd you think I suggested it?"

She laughs. "Let's just go get coffee."

"How about dessert?" I back away. "You like cupcakes?"

"Yeah. Why?"

"There's this bakery I grew up going to that's a few miles from here. They're the only bakery I know of that's open at night. They have all kinds of pastries but they're known for their cupcakes. My mom used to get them for us for birthdays."

"Okay, but you'll have to show me where to go."

"Why don't we just ride together? I'll take you back here later to get your car."

She agrees to it and we head to the bakery. I finally feel like we're on a date. We went to dinner, kissed, and now she's riding in my car on our way to get dessert.

Earlier today, I wondered if we'd ever go out on a date or if we'd just write letters forever. But now, hours later, we're going out, and she's agreed to go out with me again.

And it's all because of that internship. The one I didn't even want and never would've taken if I'd had another offer. That can't just be a coincidence. It has to be something else. A sign from the universe, saying Amber and I should be together.

CHAPTER FIFTEEN

AMBER

It's Saturday morning and I've seen Dylan for four of the past five days. My commitment to only write letters and not actually see him lasted about a day. To be fair, I'm sure I could've kept it going longer if it weren't for the internship.

You'd think working with him would be enough, but no. It just makes me want to see him even more. Looking across the desk at him for two or three hours a day is like looking at a bowl of candy you're not allowed to eat. Dylan feels the same way. By the time our shift is up, we're both dying for a taste of that candy. We race to our cars, drive to the nearest restaurant, hide away in a booth, and make out while we wait for our food.

We really need to stop doing that. For one, it makes the waitress uncomfortable and whoever else can see us in the booth. And two, if we keep this up, we'll be moving past kissing and onto other things. That almost happened last night. He was dropping me off at my apartment and we were in his car and things started happening. Hands under clothes, going places they shouldn't be going. I had to force myself to stop. Dylan seemed frustrated, but he wasn't mad. He understands why I don't want to rush this. I just hope he's willing to wait longer. He has girls constantly coming up to him, so if he wanted a girl who'd do more than kiss, there are plenty of girls he could choose from.

My phone rings as I walk in my bedroom. I just showered, my hair sopping wet and a towel wrapped around me.

"Hello?" I say, answering without checking who it is.

"Hey, what are you doing?"

It's Dylan, using that upbeat, casual tone of his that always seems to lighten my mood. Not that I was in a bad mood, but Dylan always seems to make even my good mood a little brighter.

"I just got out of the shower."

"Can I come over?"

"Right now? I thought we said we'd meet for lunch."

"We did, but I was in the area so I thought I'd stop by."

I smile. "Why were you in the area?"

"Not sure. I was driving around and my car just took me here. Maybe because it wanted to see you."

"Your car wanted to see me?"

"It's highly influenced by its owner. Now will you let me in?"

"You're already here? Like at my door?"

"Yeah, and you need to let me in. There's an old lady out here walking her cat on a leash and she's about to come over and talk to me."

"That's Mrs. Klanton. If she starts talking to you, you'll be there all day."

"Then what are you waiting for? Hurry up. She's like ten feet away."

I laugh as I run to the door. When I open it, I see him standing there in navy track pants and a white, long sleeve t-shirt. It's one of those fitness shirts that fits tight to his body, clinging to the muscles in his arms and chest.

"Why are you dressed like that?" I ask, not that I'm complaining. He looks really hot. I've never seen him in workout clothes.

"Are you gonna let me inside?" He glances down the hall.

"Oh. Yeah." I peek down the hall and see Mrs. Klanton watching us as she pretends to search for something in her purse. She loves to gossip about her neighbors. Seeing Dylan here will give her something new to talk about.

I shut the door and my towel nearly comes loose. I quickly grab it and realize I'm not dressed.

"Do you always answer the door like that?" Dylan asks, a big grin on his face. "Or is this just for me?"

"I told you I just got out of the shower. And then you made me get the door and I didn't have time to put anything on." I'm getting really turned on, being this close to Dylan, wearing nothing but a towel. I'm surprised he hasn't come up to me and tried to take it off, but instead he's standing a few feet away. "So what's the real reason you came over?"

"I thought I'd see if you want to go for a run. I thought maybe we could do a few loops around the neighborhood. Or around the college. I've never been on the Katswick campus."

"You want me to run with you?"

"Yeah. Why?"

"I haven't been running in like a year."

"If you're too out of shape to run, we could walk."

I huff. "I'm not out of shape. Do I look out of shape to you?" I hold my arms out and my towel drops to the floor. "Shit!" I quickly grab it and cover myself.

The room goes silent. Dylan's eyes are still on my body and I see his throat move as he swallows.

His eyes slowly rise to my face. "So...back to the run. Yes or no?"

That's it? He's not going to try anything? He just saw me naked, completely naked, no panties this time. Given how much we want each other, I thought he'd at least attempt to make a move. But he's following the rules, pretending we're just friends whenever we're alone.

"Sure, I'll go on a run," I say. "I'll be ready in a few minutes. You can watch TV if you want."

I turn to go to my room.

"Amber."

"What?" I turn back and he's right in front of me.

"I'm not rejecting you." He places his hand on my shoulder and runs it down my arm, causing goosebumps to rise up on my skin. "You know how much I want you, but you told me—"

"I know. And I appreciate that you listened. You're being a gentleman and I respect that."

"Don't give me too much credit. The part of me that's not a gentleman is thinking very dirty thoughts right now." His eyes lock on mine as his hand moves slowly along the top of my towel, pausing at the part I've folded over to hold it in place. "You could always change your mind."

I hesitate, thinking how much I want to change my mind. But I can't. We've only been going out a week, and although I've gotten to know him, I want to know more, and I don't want sex clouding my judgment.

"I think it's best if we don't."

He takes his hand away. "Go ahead and get dressed. I'll wait here."

Back in my room, I race to my closet to find something to wear. We need to get out of the apartment before we do something we shouldn't. I hurry and change into black yoga pants, a long sleeve t-shirt, and zip-up hoodie. Then I race to the bathroom, dry my hair, and gather it into a ponytail.

"Aren't we going to freeze out there?" I ask as I come back to the living room.

"It's not that cold. It's in the fifties but feels warmer with the sun."

"Okay, then I'm ready."

I grab some gloves, just in case my hands get cold, then we go outside and take off toward campus, which is about a mile from my apartment. When we get there, I take him to the path that Kira always runs on. It's a two-mile loop that goes along the perimeter of campus.

"You doing okay?" Dylan asks.

"Yeah. How about you?"

"Good, but why don't we take a break?"

We stop next to a bench and stretch our legs.

153

"For someone who doesn't work out much," he says, "you're in really good shape. I was going pretty fast and you still kept up."

"I walk a lot on campus and I'm a fast walker. And all of those years of gymnastics paid off. I'm still in good shape from that."

"Why don't you show me what you can do?"

"What do you mean?"

He motions to the lawn behind us. "Show me some of your gymnastics."

"That was a long time ago. I don't do that stuff anymore."

"But I'm sure you still know how. Come on. I want to see you do something."

I check to make sure no one's coming down the path. I go behind the bench, stretch a little, then get a running start and do a series of forward flips, adding a twist in the air for the last one.

"Holy shit, that's amazing," he says.

I laugh. "It's really not. That was like gymnastics 101. I can do a lot better than that."

"Can you show me?"

"I don't know. The ground is really hard. I don't want to fall and get hurt."

"Yeah, of course. Sorry, I wasn't thinking about that. Come sit down."

It *would* be kind of fun to do a routine for him. I wonder if I could still do it.

"Hold on. I'm going to try."

"Amber, no. I don't want you getting hurt."

"I won't." I get in position, pause a moment to get my mind in the game, then do a routine I used to do for a warmup. It's not my hardest routine but it was always one of my favorites.

When I'm done I glance over at Dylan and see him staring at me like he can't believe I just did that. He lifts his hands and slowly claps.

"You liked it?"

"That was fucking amazing."

I walk back over to him. "I used to do that routine all the time. I know it so well I could do it in my sleep."

"I didn't know you were that good. Why the hell you'd stop? You could've gone to the Olympics."

"Believe me, I'm not that good. But I could've made it to nationals."

"Then why didn't you?"

"All the training took up too much time. I didn't have time for anything else." I check my phone. "We should head back. I need to get home and write out invitations."

"For what?"

"My entrepreneur club. We're having a holiday party in early December."

"Can't you just email the invitations?"

"I could, but it seems nicer to hand write them and send them out."

"Or." He pulls me into him. "You could forget all that, email them, and spend the rest of the day with me."

"I also need to organize a luncheon for my Women in Marketing group. I need to call around and get a location and make a reservation and—"

He stops me with a kiss. And then another. "Spend the day with me."

"I can't. I have too much to do."

"Just let it go. The world won't end if you don't do those things."

"But people are counting on me."

He pulls back, keeping his arms around my waist. "Do you like doing those things? Belonging to all those groups?"

I sigh. "I don't know. I think I do."

"Amber, if you don't like doing that stuff, don't do it."

"It does get to be a lot sometimes, especially with classes and my job and now this internship."

"Then stop doing so much. Quit some of your activities."

"I don't know. I'll have to think about it."

"So how about today? Can I have you for the day?"

I smile. "How about half a day? We'll run back and then go have lunch."

"Not good enough. I need the whole day. Next week is Thanksgiving and you'll be gone for four days. Or are you leaving on Wednesday?"

"I'm not leaving. I'm staying here."

"You're not going home?"

"It's too far for just a few days."

"But Kira's going."

"Only because she's homesick. She's never been away from home this long."

"So what are do you doing for Thanksgiving?"

"I'll catch up on homework, sleep, watch TV."

He looks at me a moment, then lets me go and takes his phone out.

"What are you doing?"

He calls someone and holds the phone to his ear. "Mom. Question. Can I bring a guest to dinner on Thursday?"

"Dylan, no," I whisper. "I'm not going there."

"Yeah, okay. Talk to you later." He puts his phone away. "Ready to head back?"

"I'm not going to your house for Thanksgiving."

"Did I ask you to?"

"No," I say, confused. "But then why'd you call your mom just now?"

"I had to get her okay."

"Okay for what?"

"Let's head back. I need to go home and shower and then I'll pick you up for lunch."

"Wait, I didn't agree to spend the day with you."

"But you agreed to lunch. So we'll start there and see how it goes. You're still coming to hear us tonight, right?"

"I'm not sure." I look over at some guys as they jog past us. They're really slow, barely moving.

"Why aren't you sure?" Dylan asks. "Don't you want to hear the band?"

When I look back at him, I see the hurt look on his face. "Of course I do. I just...I don't really want to see girls hanging all over you."

"They won't be hanging all over me. Sometimes they ask me to sign something but that's it."

"Dylan, I've seen your concerts online. Girls are practically throwing themselves at you. They throw themselves at you wherever we go. Kira says I'll get used to it but I don't know if I will. I know it upsets her when girls do that to Austin. She just doesn't tell him how much it bothers her."

He brings me to the bench to sit down. "Okay, first of all, I don't get near the attention that Austin does. And when I do, I make it clear I'm not interested. I told you, I don't date band groupies."

"Still, it's hard to watch them pawing you while you're on stage."

"Amber you know I'd never do anything with them. Or any girl. I have a girlfriend, and she's the only one I'm interested in." He smiles. "And I want to spend the day with her. If I have to, I'll even help her write those damn invitations so she won't have an excuse not to see me."

"I wouldn't make you do that." I stand up. "Let's go. Maybe on the way back, you'll talk me into emailing the invitations."

And he does. By the time we get back to my apartment, he's got me agreeing to set aside my to-do list for the day and hang out with him instead. He goes home to clean up, then we go to lunch, then a movie, then have an early dinner. At six, he leaves to go back to his place.

***

"You ready?" Kira yells from her room. It's Saturday night and we're getting ready to go to the bar where Vandyl is playing.

"I just need to grab my phone." I run to the kitchen where I have it plugged in.

"What's this?" Kira appears, holding an envelope. I can see the writing on the front. It's in Dylan's handwriting.

"Where'd you get that?" I ask, taking it from her.

"It was on the floor. It must've fallen off the table. Is it from Dylan?"

"Yeah, but I didn't see him leave it."

"He must've set it down when you weren't looking."

I take the letter to the living room and plop down on the couch.

"Amber we have to go," I hear Kira say. "We're already late."

"It'll just take a minute."

"You read his letters like ten times. It'll take more than a minute."

"I won't read it ten times."

As I open the envelope I wonder when Dylan even had time to write this. I was with him all day. He must've written it when he went home to shower before lunch. This past week, we've only exchanged letters once. I was starting to think maybe he'd given up writing them.

My Dearest Amber, he writes.

It's now been a week since you sent me the letter that reignited our relationship but it seems like much longer than that. Maybe because I've thought about you every single day since that night last May. For whatever reason, I had a feeling that wasn't the end for us. And it wasn't. It was only the beginning.

I know you didn't want us to see each other this past week but fate brought us together once again and I'm grateful it did. We already had our time apart. Six very long months. Now it's time to be together. Get to know each other. Become friends. And eventually more than that.

I'm in no rush to get to that point, the place we were at the night we met. There are parts of me that vehemently disagree with that, one part in particular, but he'll just have to wait.

I want this to work. I want it to be more than just a casual relationship that ends in a few weeks or a month. So if taking things slow will help us do that, then I'm all for it. But I can't go without seeing you.

I'll still write the letters because I know how much you like them, but they can't replace my time with you. I hope you feel the same.

Love, Dylan.

I *do* feel the same. Now that I've had a week with Dylan, going without seeing him seems impossible. He's right. The letters aren't enough. I love them, and I love reading them over and over again, but I also want to see him.

"What'd he say?" Kira asks, her coat on, indicating she's in a hurry to leave.

"I can't tell you. I'll be right back." I run to my room, deposit the letter in my drawer and meet Kira at the front door.

"Why can't you tell me?" She hands me my coat.

"He asked me not to." I laugh as I shrug my coat on. "He said he'd lose his man card if I ever told anyone what's in those letters."

"So he writes you lovey dovey stuff." We go out in the hall and she locks the door.

"Well, yeah, they're love letters. They're supposed to be romantic."

"I can't imagine Dylan writing that. He doesn't seem like the romantic type."

"He is. He just tries to hide it."

I think that side of him only comes out when he's with me. At least I hope that's true. I don't want to think about him being that way with someone else.

As we're driving to the bar, Kira asks, "You going to be okay tonight?"

"No." I keep my eyes on the road. "But there's nothing I can do about it. He's the lead singer. He's hot. And girls love him."

"But you know he'd never do anything with them, right?"

"He said he wouldn't, but I've only known him a week so I guess I can't really be sure about that."

"He wouldn't cheat on you. Dylan's so crazy about you, I can't imagine him even *looking* at another girl."

"Is this it?" I point to the bar.

"Yeah, that's it."

"It doesn't even have a sign."

"You came in on the back side. The sign is in the front. Just drive around."

The front of the bar is packed with cars, some lined up by the door, letting people off, and the rest parked in the lot.

"There's no place to park," I tell Kira as we circle the lot. "Is it always like this when they play?"

"Usually. You know how popular they are."

"Yeah, but I didn't think it'd be standing room only."

"They'll save us some seats. Just park in back. If we tell the owner we're with the band, he'll let us park there."

"You sure?"

"It's a perk of dating guys in the band," she says as I park next to Austin's truck.

Getting out of the car, I spot someone coming out of the bar. It's Austin.

"Hey." He smiles and waves us over. "Just come in this way."

Kira runs up to him and kisses him. "Packed house again."

"Yeah, it's great. The bar owner has already booked us again for next month." He looks at me. "Hey, Amber. Dylan's in the back room if you want to go say hi." He chuckles. "He's kind of nervous having you here tonight."

"Why would he be nervous?"

"He's never played for you before, except for that time last August, but he didn't know you were in the audience back then."

"He doesn't need to be nervous."

"Go see him and calm him down."

Austin holds the door open and Kira and I go inside. There's a room off to the left, which I assume is where Austin told me to go. I can't ask him because he took off with Kira.

I go in the room and see Dylan pacing the floor, taking deep breaths.

"You all right?"

He smiles. "Hey. What are you doing back here?"

"There wasn't any parking out front so I parked in the back and ran into Austin. He said you were nervous about tonight?"

"A little."

"Because of me?"

He comes up to me, wrapping his arms around my waist. "I want you to like it."

"You know I'll like it. I've heard you play before and I told you how good you guys sound."

"You heard a recording online. You haven't heard us play live."

"It'll be even better live. So stop worrying."

He lowers his mouth to mine and kisses me. "I'm already feeling more relaxed. Let's just keep doing this until I have to go."

"I need to go get my seat."

"We already saved you seats. You can wait back here until we start."

"But don't you need to practice before you go on?"

"No. I need to do this." He presses his lips to mine.

"Dylan!" some girl yells.

I turn my head and see the girl stomping up to Dylan, her hands on her hips. She's gorgeous. Tall and thin with bright blond hair and blue eyes. She's wearing a short red dress and spiked heels and her skin is a perfect golden brown, like she has a standing appointment at the tanning salon.

"What the hell are you doing?" the girl shouts at Dylan. "We have one argument and now you're cheating on me?"

This must be Allison, his ex-girlfriend. Or by the way she's acting, his *crazy* ex-girlfriend.

CHAPTER SIXTEEN

DYLAN

Just what I need. Allison barging in while I'm trying to be alone with Amber. And right before I have to go on stage. Allison always had horrible timing.

"I'm not cheating on you," I tell Allison. "You and I broke up over a week ago. And actually, you were the one cheating on *me*. You admitted it, remember?"

She huffs. "Only because I was mad at you for trying to break up with me. I didn't actually cheat."

"That's not the rumor on campus."

"There IS no rumor."

"Several people have confirmed you were with Tyrone."

"We kissed. One time. But only because we were drunk after a football game."

Tyrone is a running back and has had his eyes on Allison for months. He even asked me once at a party if I'd mind sharing. I almost punched him but he's lot a bigger than me and I didn't feel like ending up in the hospital over it. Now if he'd asked me if I'd share Amber, I would've punched him without even the slightest hesitation.

"Kissing counts as cheating," I tell her. "Allison, I'm not going to stand here and debate this with you. I have to go on in like five minutes and I'd like to spend that time with my girlfriend."

Allison whips her head back and glares at Amber. "HER? She's not your girlfriend. I am!"

"No. You're not. You never were. You were just a girl I..." I don't finish the statement, knowing how bad it sounds. There's no denying it. I used Allison just like she used me. I'm not proud of it and it's not something I normally do, but I was at a bad place when I met her. I still wanted Amber. She was all I could think about, but I couldn't find her and I assumed I never would.

Allison points to Amber. "Get her out of here so we can talk."

"There's nothing to talk about. We're done. We've both moved on. I'm with Amber and you're with Tyrone."

"I am NOT with Tyrone. I'm with YOU, and if you don't admit it, I'll go out there on stage right now and announce that you cheated on me. You think your fans will like that?"

One of the bouncers appears at the door. "Everything okay in here?"

He must've heard Allison screaming. Her shrill tone could probably be heard all the way to the front of the bar.

"I want her to leave," I say, pointing to Allison. "But she refuses."

He walks over to her and takes her arm. "Come on. Let's go."

She yanks her arm back. "I'm not going anywhere!"

"I don't want her here," I say to the bouncer. "Not just in this room, but in the bar."

"No problem," the bouncer says. "Miss, you need to leave."

"I have every right to be here," she spits out. "Dylan is my boyfriend. We're just having a fight."

"She's lying," I tell him. "She's not my girlfriend. My girlfriend's right over there." I motion to Amber, whose standing off to the side, looking uncomfortable.

"You leave on your own," the bouncer says to Allison, "or I'll be carrying you out."

"If you lay a hand on me I'll call the police!" she yells.

He stares down at her, a menacing stare that matches his menacing look; tall, wide, bald head, his body covered in tats.

"I'm not going to ask you again," he says.

She storms off and I hear the back door open, then slam shut.

The bouncer smiles at me. "Need anything else?"

"No, I'm good. Thanks."

"Have a good show," he says as he leaves.

"You really dated that girl?" Amber asks.

"Unfortunately, yes. For longer than I should have."

"She seems crazy."

"She is. But hopefully she'll leave me alone now."

"I should go." Amber hurries to the door.

"Wait." I catch up to her, grasping her arm. "What's wrong?"

"Nothing. I just need to get to my seat."

"Are you mad about Allison?"

"No. But it *is* a little annoying that you have girls attacking you before you even get on stage."

"That only happened because Allison's crazy and wants me back. And she only wants me back because I'm in the band. There's nothing going on between her and me. It's over." I slide my hand down Amber's arm and press my lips to hers. "All I want is you. So whatever happens tonight, remember that. You're it. There's no one else."

She nods, then kisses my cheek. "Have a good show."

She walks off and I let her go. I don't have time to convince her I'm not interested in other girls. After a week of being together, and months of me trying to find her, I thought she'd know she's the only one I want, but I guess she needs more time before she believes that.

"Hey." Austin appears. "You ready?"

"Yeah. Let's go. Is Van already out there?"

"No, he's making out with some girl. He said he'll be out there in a minute."

"What girl?"

164

"Just some girl he met when he was setting up the equipment earlier." Austin looks behind me. "Where's Amber?"

"She went to go find her seat."

"Did something happen? I heard yelling."

"Allison showed up, claiming we were still together. When I told her I was with Amber, she went crazy and started screaming at me. I had to get the bouncer to throw her out."

"Like out of the bar?"

"Yeah. He told her she had to leave."

He laughs. "She must've been pissed."

"She was, but what the hell was I supposed to do? If she'd stayed, she would've made a scene."

"So about the set tonight. Are we still playing *One Night?*"

"Yeah. Why wouldn't we?"

"I'm just worried you might look at Amber when you're singing it. And if you do, everyone will know it's about her."

"Then I won't look at her."

"You may do it without realizing it."

I sigh. "We're singing it. The fans love it. They expect us to play it."

He shrugs. "I just wanted to give you the option."

When Van, Austin, and I step out onto the small stage, I spot Amber off to the right, sitting next to Kira. She smiles at me and I relax, any nervousness I felt now gone. I don't know why I was nervous. I've been doing this for years and I already know Amber likes our music. There was no reason to be nervous.

The night goes great. We play awesome. The place is packed. And Amber is here, singing along and even getting up and dancing to a couple songs.

We save *One Night* for last. That nervous feeling returns and I realize this was the reason I was nervous earlier. This song. The song I wrote about Amber. It's the only song I've ever written and actually performed and it always makes me emotional. I always imagine Amber when I sing it, and now she's here and I'm not sure how I'll react. Austin warned me about this and I probably should've listened to him and not performed the song.

But it's too late now. The fans are chanting "One Night", begging me to sing it, and Austin has already started playing the intro.

Forcing my gaze away from Amber, I sing the first line, then close my eyes as my fingers strum the guitar. I get lost in the lyrics, like I always do with this song.

Saw you across the room...That face, those eyes...couldn't find the words, but no words were needed...I knew you were it...I went to you, you smiled...and I was gone...yours...forever...still on my mind, in my dreams.

The people in the bar sing along with the chorus. *One night. But it was more than that. One night. But I'll never forget. One night. And you were gone. One night. And I want you back.*

It isn't until the very end of the song that I open my eyes and look over at Amber.

One night, I sing in a low breathy tone. I slow down and draw out the last line, *And I want you back.*

My eyes are still on Amber but nobody notices. They're too busy yelling and clapping and chanting our names. Girls rush the stage like they always do at the end of the night, and I lose sight of Amber. I want to rush over to her and ask her what she thought but I can't ditch my fans or I wouldn't have any left.

After fifteen minutes of taking pictures with fans and signing autographs, we make our way to the back room. Kira and Amber are already there.

Amber runs up to me. "That was awesome!"

"Thanks." I kiss her.

She leans up and whispers in my ear, "You made me cry."

I take her out into the hall. "Why were you crying?"

"That song. Even though I've heard it hundreds of times, that's the first time I've heard you sing it live and it just got to me. Dylan, I'm so sorry I left like that. I feel so bad."

"It's all in the past." I smooth her hair and smile. "And hey, it made for a good song, right?"

She laughs. "Yeah, it did. A fan favorite."

"I wanted to look at you when I sang it but I thought you'd be mad if I did."

"Why would I be mad?"

"Because people would know it's about you. And I wasn't sure you'd be okay with that, given what we did that night."

"Oh. Yeah. I wasn't even thinking about that. That song is so beautiful and about so much more than...sex."

"Because that *night* was so much more. I tried to capture that in the lyrics. How I felt about you. How I couldn't stop thinking about you when you were gone."

She wipes her eyes. "You're going to make me cry again."

"Don't cry." I kiss her. "Like I said, it's all in the past."

"You guys coming?" Austin says as he walks out of the room with Kira on his arm.

"Where are we going?" Amber asks.

"We always go out to eat after we perform," I tell her. "Well, not always, but usually. We'll drop your car off and you can ride with me."

"Want to go the place on Highland?" Austin asks.

"Yeah, that works. What about Van?"

"He's staying here to pack up."

"What about the girl?"

"She has a boyfriend. He showed up halfway through our show."

"That sucks." I peek my head in the room and see Van on the phone. He's probably finding someone else to hook up with later tonight.

"I think I'll just go home," Amber says. "I'm not really hungry and I can't be out all night."

"Tomorrow's Sunday. You can sleep in."

"Not really. I have to catch up on all the work I didn't get done because my boyfriend kept me busy all day."

I love hearing her call me her boyfriend. It never gets tiring.

167

"Your boyfriend insists you come with him for greasy burgers and fries at an all-night diner." I give her a kiss. "Come on. I don't want to be stuck alone with these two." I point at Austin and Kira who are making out right in front of us.

Amber laughs. "I'm used to it. They're like this at my apartment all the time."

"Still. Come with us. Please?"

"Okay. But I'll just follow you there. I don't need to drop off my car."

I lean down to her ear. "Unless you want to stay with me tonight." Remaining by her ear, I wait for her to respond. When she doesn't, I say, "We don't have to do anything. I just want to be next to you."

"It wouldn't work," she whispers. "It's too tempting."

"Try it and see."

"Not tonight."

I stand up straight. "I had to at least ask."

"We're heading out," Austin says, taking off with Kira. "We'll see you there."

"Yeah, see ya."

"Van." I get his attention from the door. He's still on the phone but I give him a wave and say, "We're heading out. Thanks for packing up."

He nods and continues talking to whoever's on the phone.

At the diner, Amber and I have burgers and split a big basket of fries. Kira and Austin, the health nuts, order turkey burgers and don't eat the bun. Those two are made for each other. Nobody else I know eats like them, and anyone else they dated would be annoyed by their strict diets. It's a good thing they found each other.

After we eat, Kira and Austin go back to his place for the night. I follow Amber to her apartment, wanting to make sure she gets back there safely. I walk her to her door and kiss her, because technically the hallway is considered a public space, even though nobody else is around.

"I think I'm going to write a new song," I say.

"Oh, yeah? What is it?"

I turn her slightly, leaning her against the door. "It's called *One Week*."

She tilts her head, looking up at me. "What's it about?"

"You." I kiss her. "And me." I kiss her again. "And the week we spent together."

"Last week?" She smiles. "We didn't really do much."

"No. But we were finally together. That's all that matters." I position my mouth by her ear and softly sing, *One week. I was with her. One week. Couldn't get enough of her. One week. And she was mine. One week. I have her back.* I stop singing and quietly say, "And I hope she never leaves again."

Her neck moves as she swallows and I turn to see her face. Her eyes are wet, but she's smiling. "That was beautiful."

I chuckle. "And I didn't even practice it."

"You need to finish it. It'll be another hit."

"Maybe I'll just write it for us. Other people don't need to hear it."

"Dylan, no. You need to write it, and perform it. Girls will love it."

"I told you, I only care about one girl. And if you like it? That's good enough."

"You need to let others hear it. You sound so good singing it. I love your voice. Did you take lessons? Or how did you learn to sing like that?"

"I just sang along to my guitar. I never took singing lessons. Just guitar lessons, and when I'd practice, I'd sing along."

"You're really talented. You should go on one of those shows. Those singing competitions on TV."

"I don't think I'm good enough for that. I think I have a better shot at a job in marketing."

"Will you sing it again? One more time?" She rests her head back on the wall and closes her eyes.

One week. I was with her. One week. Couldn't get enough of her. I sing softly so I don't wake up her neighbors, and when I'm done, we kiss once more and then I leave.

When I get home, I write the song, the entire thing in less than ten minutes. The music and lyrics flow faster than I can get them down, but when I finally do, I go to the basement and play the song from start to finish.

Amber's right. It's gonna be another hit. Another favorite with the fans. But as I told her, none of that matters. The only thing I care about is as the song says...I have her back.

CHAPTER SEVENTEEN

AMBER

I have so much to do," I say to Kira as I sort through the stack of folders on the kitchen table.

"Is it homework or other stuff?"

"Both, but most of it's for the clubs I belong to. The holiday time is the worst. From now until Christmas break, there are parties and mixers and luncheons and dinners. And I not only have to attend them but also plan them." I sigh. "I should've stayed home last weekend."

She sits next to me. "You did what you should've done, and that's spend time with Dylan. And don't try to say you didn't have fun because I haven't seen you that happy in years."

"I DID have fun. And I love spending time with him, but now I have to pay for it."

It's Monday morning and I have class in an hour but I've been working at the kitchen table since five a.m. Yesterday, I was supposed to stay home and get stuff done, but in the morning, Dylan called and I wanted to see him. I had to. I couldn't even go a whole day without seeing him. So I went to his apartment and surprised him. He was more than surprised. More like shocked, given my insistence on not seeing each other.

I tried to make up some excuse about why I had to go over there, saying I wanted to know how his song was coming along, but he could see right through my lame reasoning. So I just admitted I went there to see him. Why hide it? He knows how much I like him.

We went out for brunch, which was all we were going to do, but then of course we couldn't say goodbye and ended up spending the entire day together. He dropped me off at ten last night and now I'm trying to catch up on my to-do list, which didn't get touched last weekend.

"Don't you ever get tired of this?" Kira asks, picking up one of my folders and dropping it back in the pile.

"Sometimes I do, but you know me. I go crazy when I'm not busy."

"You weren't busy last weekend. And as far as I know, you didn't go crazy."

"What are you talking about? I was busy."

"Not doing work. Watching TV with Dylan? Going running with him? Going out to eat? I hate to tell you this, but that's called relaxing." She leans toward me. "You, Amber Moore, relaxed for an entire weekend." She sits back again. "Might be the first time that's ever happened."

I pause to think. "Oh my God, you're right. I did nothing for two whole days. I was lazy. I've never been lazy."

"You weren't lazy. Lazy and relaxed are two different things. And you needed to relax. You've been running nonstop since I moved here last August. I don't know how you do it, but you need to stop, or at least slow down. It's not good for you to never relax."

"This coming from someone who works out hours a day."

"Yeah, but I work out with Austin. It's something we both like to do. It's another way for us to spend time together. That's what you and Dylan need to do. You need to find activities you can do together."

"I can't spend every minute with him. We're already interning together. That should be enough."

"But you're not really together when you're working."

My laptop pings, bringing my focus back to the invites I was sending out. "Kira, I can't talk right now. I have to finish this before class."

"And I have to head to the gym." She stands up and goes over to the counter. "Found this under the door." She hands me an envelope.

"How'd he have time to write a letter? And drop it off?"

"Guess he makes time for things that are important." She smiles and walks away. She's hinting I should make time for Dylan, and it's not that I don't want to. My schedule just doesn't allow it. That doesn't mean he's not important to me.

The envelope is square and inside I find a piece of heavy cardstock. On it, he's written the following.

Dear Amber,

The Mickelson Family requests your presence at Thanksgiving dinner this Thursday, to be served at two in the afternoon. The dinner will feature such favorites as Roasted Turkey, Apple-Sage Stuffing (Grandma Mickelson's secret recipe, God rest her soul), Creamy Mashed Potatoes (made by yours truly), Cranberry Sauce (from a can because nobody ever eats it but you have to have it), Green Bean Casserole (my dad's specialty), and Pumpkin Pie (the kind you buy in the freezer section but my mom always pretends she made it).

The meal will last approximately one hour because my grandpa's dentures never stay in place and it takes him forever to eat. But in that hour, you'll be entertained by my dad's lame jokes, my mom repeatedly asking you if the turkey was too dry, and my little brother making fart noises but telling everyone it was his chair squeaking. And if that's not enough, you'll have me there, and as you know, I'm always entertaining. I might even break out in song.

Your RSVP is requested by tonight. Dana Mickelson (my mom), needs to know if she'll be setting an extra place at the table. She takes her place settings very seriously. It's one of the few times of the year she actually decorates the table.

Have I enticed you yet? If not, I'll add that I really want you to come.

Love, Dylan

"I can't go," I say to myself.

"Can't go where?" Kira asks. I turn and see her behind me, adjusting her ponytail.

"To dinner at Dylan's house."

"He invited you to dinner?"

"Yeah, but I'm not going."

"Why not? As far as I know, he's not the greatest cook but it's nice of him to try."

"He's not the one making dinner, and it's not at the house he rents. It's at his actual house, the one he grew up in. His parents' house."

She comes around in front me. "He's taking you to meet his parents? Wow, this is serious."

"I know. And it's not just any dinner. It's Thanksgiving dinner. He even gave me an invitation." I hold it up. "He wants an answer by tonight."

"And you're going to tell him no?"

"Well, yeah, obviously. I've dated him for a week. I can't go home with him for Thanksgiving."

"Why not? It's just dinner. And his family lives in town. You can go for a few hours and leave."

"Kira." I set the invitation down. "This is Thanksgiving dinner. That's a huge deal. And his whole family will be there, including his grandfather. If I go, they'll assume Dylan and I are serious."

"You two ARE serious."

"After a week? I don't think so."

She sits beside me. "Amber, don't lie to yourself. You know you and Dylan aren't the typical couple. It's not like you just met. You've been thinking about him since you met him last May. And he spent all that time searching for you."

"Yeah, but we've still only been dating for a week. It's too soon for me to meet his family."

"Dylan doesn't seem to think so. And it's not like you have anything else to do. If you don't go on Thursday, you'll just be sitting here watching TV, eating cereal for dinner."

"I won't be eating cereal. I have at least three frozen dinners just waiting to be eaten."

"Or...you could have a homemade turkey dinner at your boyfriend's house. Come on, Amber. It's just dinner. You're not announcing your engagement."

"I might as well be. Showing up for Thanksgiving is serious, Kira. You admitted it just a minute ago and now you're acting like it's no big deal."

"Because I thought about it and decided it's not that big a deal. If you were flying home with him to attend Thanksgiving, then yeah, his family might read something into that, but since they live in town, it'll be seen as more of a polite gesture on Dylan's part. You weren't able to go home to Michigan so Dylan invited you over. College students do that all the time. They can't go home and end up spending the holiday with whatever friend lives close by."

"I guess, but I'm more than just a friend."

"They don't have to know that. If you really don't want his family to know the truth, you and Dylan could say you're just friends."

"I suppose we could do that."

"There you go." She stands up. "Problem solved. I gotta get going. See you tonight for dinner?"

"Maybe. I have to work at the hospital until five and then I might have dinner with Dylan."

"Tell him yes. I don't want you sitting here alone again on Thanksgiving. It's depressing."

She leaves and I look at the invitation again. Part of me really does want to go, but going means fast forwarding our relationship to a place I'm not ready for. I'm not supposed to meet Dylan's family. Not yet. Not until I know where this is going, and right now, I have no idea where we're headed. My feelings for him are intense, and I still don't trust that they're real. It all goes back to that night. That magical, hot, perfect night. It messed with my emotions, made me feel things I've never felt. I was on a high, and with Dylan back in my life, I feel like I'm on it again. Back living in the clouds, but knowing full well that at any moment, it could all end and I could come crashing back down to Earth. I've seen it happen with my parents and I don't want it happening to me. It's that fear that makes me afraid to be with Dylan.

"Got a boyfriend yet?" Emily asks as I turn the page on the book we're reading. I just started and she's already distracted.

"Emily, come on. We need to finish the book. We didn't even finish the one we read last week."

"Because it was boring." She folds her arms over the table and lays her head on them.

"Then you pick the book," I tell her. "Next week you bring whatever you want me to read."

"Can't you just tell me a story instead?"

"The book is a story but you won't let me read it."

She pops upright again, her eyes wide with excitement. "Tell me about a pretty princess and how she meets a boy on a horse and finds out he's a prince and they fall in love and live happily ever after."

Why do we keep telling these stories to girls? Princesses meeting their prince? Living these fairy tale lives? I bought into all that back when I was Emily's age and part of me still believes it. It's not like I'm waiting around for a prince but I still believe in the fairy tale. But why? Was I so brainwashed by these stories as a kid that it makes me still believe that stuff?

"You know those stories aren't real, right?"

She shrugs. "Maybe they are." She smiles really wide. "My daddy was a prince. He had to leave to fight the bad guys."

Does she really think that? Did her mom tell her that? Or did she just make it up? Either way, I'm not going to break her heart and tell her her dad is a loser who took off. If she'd rather believe he's a prince, then so be it.

"Let's finish the story." I point to the book. "What does this say?"

She sighs, annoyed that I'm making her read. "The. Ma...man. Ssss..."

"Said," I say slowly.

"Said. To. The. Li..." She bounces in her chair, frustration on her face.

"You're almost there. Just sound it out."

"I don't want to." She pouts.

"But you almost had it."

"I said I don't want to!" She jumps up and runs out of the room.

I pushed her too far but that was the most she's ever read and I wanted her to keep going. Getting up to go find her, I stop when she runs back into the room.

"I'm sorry," she says, hugging my legs. She's short for her age, and tiny. She looks more like a five-year-old than a seven-year-old. "Please come back."

"Come back? What do you mean?"

"I got mad and now you won't come back."

I bend down to her level. "I'll come back. I promise."

She frowns and looks at the floor. "Daddy didn't come back. Mommy got mad and he didn't come back."

So that's what happened. Her parents fought and her dad took off and never came back. And she made up that story about him to make herself feel better.

I hug her. "I'm sorry your daddy left. But you need to know that getting mad doesn't mean people will leave you and not come back. Just because your daddy did doesn't mean everyone else will." I let her go. "I'll be back next week, just like always, okay?"

She nods, then smiles. "This week is Thanksgiving!"

"That's right. It's Thursday. Are you gonna have turkey?"

She nods again. "And stuffing and mashed potatoes."

"Sounds yummy." I hear the door open and see the teacher standing there. "Looks like our time is up. I'll see you next week."

"Bye!" She runs off.

My mind is still on Emily when I arrive at the hospital. I've been reading to her for months now and she still struggles with even the simplest words.

"Good afternoon, Amber," Dylan says as I take my seat across from him. "How have you been?" He's so serious I want to laugh, but I don't because we share this room with three full-time workers, who are currently all sitting at their desks. One of them, Mary, an uptight old lady, is always watching us, like we're kids that need babysitting.

"Fine," I say, keeping my eyes on my computer as I take my coat off and hide my purse in the drawer. I caught a glimpse of Dylan when I walked in and he's looking especially hot today. If I look over at him, I may never look away. "How about you? Did you have a good weekend?"

"I did. Spent it with my girlfriend."

"Oh yeah? What's she like?" I type my password in, unlocking the screen.

"She's gorgeous. Most gorgeous girl I've ever seen."

"So you just like her for her looks?" I scroll through the list of attendees for the fundraiser. We're sending reminder emails out today, confirming the details of the event.

"She's also funny," Dylan says. "Intelligent. Talented. She's a kick-ass gymnast. You should see this girl flipping in the air. She could've been in the Olympics. She's also a hard worker, although I keep telling her to work less. With her schedule, I barely have time to see her."

"She shouldn't spend all her time with you. She needs other interests."

"I agree, but there has to be some balance. You know what they say, all work and no play."

"So are you seeing her tonight?"

"I'd like to, but I have a feeling she'll tell me no."

"I bet she'd say yes." I type on the keyboard, but I'm not actually typing anything. I'm just trying to look busy because nosy Mary has her eyes on me.

"I don't know about that." Dylan's also pretending to type, or maybe he's really typing. I can't tell. "She keeps telling me how busy she is."

"Guess you'll never know unless you ask." I glance up at him and our eyes lock. His are dark, heated, and causing a shiver of pleasure to run down my core.

"Donna asked me to get some supplies from downstairs," he says. "Would you mind helping?"

"No, I don't mind." I glance back at Mary and catch her staring. She quickly looks back at her computer.

Dylan and I go out in the hall.

"Where are you going?" I ask as he takes off down the hall.

"To get supplies."

"What? We're really getting supplies?"

"Yeah. What'd you think we were doing?"

"Um, nothing. Never mind."

Last week we snuck downstairs and found a quiet hallway and he kissed me. I thought maybe we were going to do the same thing today, but I guess not.

"It's right here," he says, opening the door of a room that actually does say 'supply closet'. We go inside and I see that it's not filled with office supplies, but cleaning supplies.

He shuts the door and locks it.

"What are you—"

His mouth covers mine as he pulls me against him, his other hand tangling in my hair. It isn't a slow, gentle, hello kiss, but a hot, sexy, I-want-you kiss. And even though I know we shouldn't be doing this, I can't make myself tell him to stop. Because I don't want to stop. This is thrilling, exciting, and so unexpected. He had me convinced we were going to find supplies.

I'm so aroused, I don't even consider stopping his hand as it unbuttons my blouse and pops open the clasp on the front of my bra. He breaks from the kiss and slides his lips down my neck as his hand shoves my bra aside and cups my breast, rolling my nipple between his thumb and forefinger. Pleasure ripples through me. I'm addicted, wanting more. His mouth lowers to my breast as his hand goes under my skirt, right where I want it.

I moan out his name, a little too loud, and hear him chuckle.

"Quiet," he demands but in a kidding tone.

"I can't," I whisper, my head falling back as his hand moves faster under my skirt. "Unless you stop what you're doing."

"You want me to stop?" His hand stills, leaving me aching, throbbing.

"No. Please. Don't stop."

He chuckles again, and moments later, he finishes what he started, leaving me completely spent, my legs struggling to hold me, my chest glistening with sweat.

"Fuck, that was hot," he says as he kisses me. His hand is still under my skirt but now on my ass, supporting me, keeping me pressed against him. Feeling his erection, I instinctively grind my hips into him.

"Amber," he moans.

My heart is thundering in my chest, fearing we'll get caught. And yet I love the feeling. It's a rush, and makes me feel alive. Like when I used to do gymnastics. When I'd do a really tough routine, one that pushed my skill level to the max, I'd always get a rush. And when it was over, I craved to do it again.

"We can't do this," Dylan says, but he's still kissing me, still gripping my ass. "Not here. Unless..." He presses into me. "Unless you really want to. I'm not against the idea. I just..."

"You're right. We can't. I'm not really thinking clearly right now."

He smiles. "And why is that?"

I laugh. "You know why." I finally get control of my brain and push him back. "We have to get out of here." I quickly button my blouse and notice him watching me. "Did you plan this?"

"Getting you off in the supply closet?" He smiles. "Not really. I mean, it wasn't my initial thought. I walked past here earlier and saw the janitor getting supplies. And then you got here and I was looking across the desk at you and suddenly all kinds of dirty thoughts ran through my head, of us, in this closet." He shrugs. "What can I say? I'm a guy. I think about sex every six minutes."

"Every six minutes? Seriously?"

"Not sure. I've never timed it. The number came from a show I was watching on men's health. Apparently there's research to support the claim."

"How do guys get anything done?" I tuck my shirt in. "Okay I think I'm ready."

"You're not buttoned right." He points to the middle of my shirt where the fabric is bunched up.

"Crap." I quickly yank my shirt out from my skirt and start fixing the buttons.

He leans against the door. "How often do girls think about sex?"

"I don't know. I don't think there's any statistics on that."

"What about you?" He comes up to me and buttons the last button. "How often?"

"I have no idea. Depends on the day."

"How about today?" He tucks my shirt in, his hands slipping under the waistband of my skirt. I'm already feeling aroused again. "How often did you think about it today?"

His eyes are on mine and I can't seem to look away. "A few times."

"What's a few?"

"I don't know. I didn't count."

"More than normal?"

"A lot more."

Since dating Dylan, I feel like I think about sex constantly. And after what he just did to me, I'll be thinking about it even more.

Instead of continuing his line of questioning, he just gives me his sexy smile.

"Ready to go?"

I take a deep breath. "Yeah."

"You go first. Tell me if anyone's out there."

He opens the door and I go out in the hall. Nobody's there so I open the door a crack and say, "Coast is clear."

He comes out, acting completely casual, as if nothing happened.

I turn to him. "What about the supplies? People are going to ask why we didn't come back with anything."

"We'll tell them they were out of whatever we needed."

"What did we need?"

"Paper? Staples? I don't know. I'll make something up."

"This is so bad," I whisper as we walk back. "They're totally going to know."

"Only if you give us away."

"ME? What about YOU?"

"I can keep a secret. You're still blushing. You need to stop that."

"I can't control it."

"Then we'll have to come up with an excuse for why you're blushing. We'll tell them you tripped. In front of a group of doctors. Who were really hot." He laughs.

"Yeah. Real funny. Let's just go in there and not say anything. We don't need to explain where we were. We work for Donna, not them."

And yet when we get back in the room, I feel like we have to explain ourselves because I can tell that nosy Mary is suspicious of us. As soon as we walked in, she was eyeing us, and now, ten minutes later, she keeps looking over here.

Dylan and I shouldn't have done that. But damn, it was fun.

CHAPTER EIGHTEEN

DYLAN

"You've gotta come on Thursday," I say to Amber as we sit at our favorite booth at Patty's Pizza Palace. We've only been here twice so I guess the booth couldn't technically be considered a favorite, but I'm officially naming it that because it's private, tucked way in the back, allowing us to make out all we want without people bothering us.

"I'd feel weird being there," Amber says, picking up a slice of pizza, the cheese strings hanging down. She swipes them up and takes a bite. I like that she doesn't get all uptight when eating in front of me. I've been out with girls who will only eat pizza with a knife and fork, fearing the mess it might make if they picked it up.

"Why would you feel weird? Because you think it's too soon?" I assume she's worried about that. I'm worried about it too. I never bring girls home to meet my family but I don't want Amber sitting home alone on Thanksgiving, eating some shitty frozen dinner.

"Exactly." She wipes her mouth with her napkin. "It's too soon."

"Then we'll tell them we met last May. It's the truth and it'll make it less weird that I invited you to dinner."

"You can't tell your family how we met! Are you kidding?" She tries to swat at me but I catch her hand and kiss it, then lean in to kiss her lips.

"I won't tell them *how* we met, or at least what we did when we met. I'll just say I met you at a party and we've been friends ever since."

"So you won't tell them we're dating." She turns back to her pizza. "I was thinking the same thing. It'd be better if we told them we're just friends."

"My mom already knows we're dating." I pick up my glass of pop and take a swig.

"You told her?"

"She assumed we were. She could tell by the way I talked about you. My mom's very perceptive. She picks up on things, especially with her kids. When I was living at home, I never got away with anything. She always knew if I was lying. Same with my little brother."

"Does she know how long we've been dating?"

"No. I ended the call before she could ask. But she'll ask on Thursday so be prepared with an answer." I take a bite of my pizza.

"ME? You should be the one answering questions, not me."

"I just told you she can tell when I'm lying, so if we decide to tell them we've been dating for months, and I'm the one who tells them, my mom will know it's not true. She doesn't know you so you've got a better chance of selling the lie."

"Is that what we're telling them? That we've been dating for months?"

"It's up to you. Tell them whatever you want. I don't care." I take another drink of my pop, then turn to her. "You do realize that you just agreed to go on Thursday."

"No I didn't."

"This whole time, you've been talking as if you're going. I'm taking that to mean you're going." I get my phone out and text my mom, then show Amber the text, which reads, *Amber's coming on Thursday.*

Her jaw drops, then snaps shut. "Dylan! Why did you do that?"

"Because you want to come. And I want you there."

She sighs. "I never agreed to it."

"You really want to sit at home all alone when you could be eating a delicious homemade turkey dinner and be entertained by my family? I told you about my brother making fart noises at the table, right?"

I laugh. "Yes."

"My grandpa does it too, except his aren't just noise. They're real, so you better hope you're not seated next to him."

She laughs again. "I can't wait to meet him."

I kiss her. "And I can't wait for them to meet you. They're gonna love you."

It's the first and only time I've ever wanted my family to meet a girl I'm dating. I'm actually excited about it. I want to show her off. Show everyone how great she is.

***

The next day, Austin stops over to hear the new song I wrote.

"Holy shit, that's awesome," he says.

"You really like it or are you just saying that?"

"You know I always tell you the truth. I think it's great, and you know I normally don't like ballads, so that's saying a lot. Did Van hear it yet?"

"Yeah. He liked it. Thinks we should add it to our set list."

"Definitely. Girls are gonna go crazy over this."

"The thing is, I'm not sure if I want to perform it."

"Why not? It's a follow up to *One Night.* A conclusion to the story. This song's gonna be huge."

"I don't know if I want people hearing it. It's personal. I wrote it for Amber."

"Has she heard it?"

"Not yet. I wanted to see if you or Van thought it needed any changes before I played it for her."

"It doesn't need any changes. It's perfect. And nobody has to know it's about you and Amber. Unless..."

"Unless what?"

"Unless you want them to. You ever think of letting people know who the mystery girl in the song is?"

"No. I wouldn't do that to Amber. She doesn't want anyone knowing she had a one-night stand."

"The song's not even about that. You don't even say it in the lyrics."

I look at him. "It's called *One Night*. Everyone knows it's about a one-night stand."

"Fine, but it's nothing to be ashamed of. A lot of people have one-night stands. It's not like she's the only one who's ever done that."

"Yeah, but still. She doesn't want everyone knowing."

He nods. "I get where she's coming from. It's different for girls than for guys. Kira probably wouldn't want people knowing either."

"Did Kira tell you Amber agreed to come to Thanksgiving?"

"No. When did that happen?"

"Last night. Maybe she hasn't told Kira yet. I hope she doesn't change her mind. My mom's already excited about meeting her. She called me this morning to tell me. She also said to tell you it's been too long since you've been over there for dinner."

He smiles. "What's she need done?"

Austin works construction for a living. He and his brothers all work for their dad's construction company. Austin can fix most anything so my mom has Austin over to fix things around the house that my dad can't figure out. And in return, she makes him dinner.

"She said something about an outlet in the living room."

"Jake's better with electrical stuff than I am, but I'll check it out. If I can't fix it, I'll have Jake do it."

"Thanks, man. Sorry she asks you to do this shit. You know you could always tell her no."

"And miss out on her lasagna? I don't think so."

My mom makes awesome lasagna. Austin rarely eats carbs so the fact that he'll eat her lasagna is proof of how good it is.

"You worried about Amber meeting your family?"

"Not really. I already told her they're crazy."

He laughs. "No crazier than *my* family, although your grandpa's gas problems might scare her away."

"I already warned her about that."

"What about Owen?"

"Yep. Warned her about him too."

"And she still agreed to come over?" He laughs.

"Yeah, but she may never come back."

"I'm just kidding you, man. Your family's awesome. Speaking of family, I gotta go help Nash with some drywall."

"And I gotta get to class." I walk him to the door.

He steps outside, stopping to pick something up. "You guys are still doing this?" He holds up an envelope.

"Yeah." I take it from him. "She must've just dropped this off. It wasn't here earlier."

"Why are you still writing letters? You guys see each other all the time."

"Yeah, but she likes the letters so I just keep sending them."

"You're totally whipped," he says, walking away.

"Like you aren't?" I call back, but he's already in his truck.

I'm not whipped. If I didn't want to write the letters, I wouldn't do it. Okay, that's not entirely true. If the letters make Amber happy, I'll do it. I'll do most anything to make her happy.

***

It's Thanksgiving day and Amber and I are heading to my parents' house. Up until this morning, Amber kept trying to back out of coming to dinner, giving me a million excuses for why she couldn't be there. I told her if she didn't come, she'd have to let my mom know, which would disappointment my mom and my entire family, who are all excited to meet her. My little guilt trip worked.

"They really do live a long ways out," she says as we pass through yet another suburb. We've been driving for almost an hour, slowed down by all the cars trying to leave Chicago.

"We're almost there. It's the next subdivision."

"So let me make sure I've got this right. Your dad sells office equipment and your mom is a librarian at a grade school. And your little brother is in sixth grade and likes playing soccer and basketball."

I chuckle. "Yes, but you don't have to memorize everything about them. They're not going to quiz you."

She exhales a breath. "I'm nervous."

"You'll be fine." I reach over and hold her hand. "My family isn't intimidating."

"I'm still nervous."

"You've never had to meet the parents before?"

"Not since high school. As for people I dated in college, I never met their parents."

"Did you bring guys home to meet *your* parents?"

"I tried not to." She glances out the side window.

"Because your dad wanted to beat up any guy who dated you?" I ask in a kidding tone.

"It's not just that. It's also...never mind."

"What? What were you going to say? Something about your parents?"

"They just embarrass me. That's all."

"Embarrass you how? By telling funny stories about when you were a kid? If so, my parents do the same thing so be prepared to hear at least one of those stories today."

"Can't wait." She smiles at me. "I bet you got in a lot of trouble growing up."

I shrug a shoulder. "A few bank robberies. Grand theft auto. Nothing too serious."

She laughs. "I didn't know I was dating a criminal."

"It's all in the past. I'm reformed. Just a regular, law-abiding college student now." I point to my street. "Guess which house is mine."

She scans the street. "The one with the funny mailbox?"

"How'd you know?"

"Because it looks like a stack of books and your mom's a librarian."

I pull into the driveway. "She made that during her wood crafting stage, which didn't last long. That's the only project she finished."

"She did a good job on it. It looks like actual books. Does she do other crafts?"

"Not currently, at least not that I know of. But as I was telling you, she really gets into her Thanksgiving table decor so if you want to win her over, compliment her centerpiece."

As we get out of the car, the front door opens and my dad comes out, wearing gray trousers and one of his old man sweaters. I call them that because people haven't worn sweaters like that since the Eighties, when he was in high school. He swears they're still in fashion but my mom disagrees so he only wears them at home.

"You must be Amber," he says, smiling and holding out his hand.

"Yes." She shakes his hand. "Nice to meet you."

"Come inside. We're having some appetizers before the big meal."

"She didn't make those salmon puffs again, did she?" I ask my dad as we go in the house. When guests come over, my mom attempts to make fancy appetizers, which are usually not very good.

"She didn't have time," he says. "Just cheese and crackers and some of those little meatballs."

We go in the house, which is filled with the smell of turkey. My dad walks ahead, leading us to the kitchen where my mom is busy at the stove.

"Dana, our son is here with his girlfriend." He picks up a baby carrot from a tray and pops it in his mouth.

She stops stirring whatever she's making and hurries over to us. "Amber, right?" She smiles at her.

"Yes. Nice to meet you."

"Would you like something to drink? We have pop, water, coffee, tea."

"Nothing for now." Amber looks around at the kitchen, which is a mess. My mom doesn't clean up until after we eat so dirty pots and pans are scattered everywhere. "Do you need help with anything?"

"No, everything's almost done." She waves us away. "You two can go wait in the living room. Gramps is in there. He might be sleeping."

He's not sleeping. He's wide awake, yelling at a football game on TV. It's not even a new game, but one being replayed from a year ago.

"Damn idiot, can't even hold onto the ball!" He shakes his fist from his recliner.

"Gramps, that game is from last year," I tell him as Amber and I sit on the couch.

"Doesn't matter." He keeps his eyes on the game. "The boy still needs to learn how to catch a ball."

"I brought a guest," I say. "This is Amber. My girlfriend." As I say it, I realize that's the first time I've introduced her like that.

He nods at her, then looks back at the TV. "Did you see that play he just made?"

"He's not much for conversation unless it's about sports," I say to Amber.

She smiles. "It's okay."

"Dylan, catch!" my brother yells as he launches a football at me.

"Hey." I grab it before it hits Amber in the head. "Don't be throwing this in the house."

He lumbers over to us, rolling his eyes. "You sound just like Mom."

"You can't play ball in here. You almost hit Amber in the head."

"Hi," she says, offering him a wave.

190

"Are you his girlfriend?" He stops in front of her.

"Um, yeah." She always sounds unsure about it, even when I call her that when we're alone. It makes me wonder if she's second-guessing our relationship. She doesn't say she is but she's constantly reminding me she wants to take things slow.

My brother quickly loses interest in Amber and takes the football from me. "Dylan, let's go out back and play."

"Not today," I tell him. "We have a guest."

He huffs. "We can't play because of some girl?"

Amber quietly laughs, then says to me, "Go ahead. It's fine. I'll stay here with Gramps."

"Touchdown!" He leans forward and stomps his foot on the floor. "Damn idiot finally did something right!"

I hitch my thumb at Gramps. "I can't leave you with that."

She laughs again.

"Owen." My dad appears. "Get your coat on. We have to go to the store and get cranberry sauce."

"Why do I have to go?" he whines.

"Because I don't want you bothering your brother and his girlfriend. Now come on."

"Nobody's going to eat that stuff," I say to my dad.

"It's tradition. It has to be there, whether we eat it or not."

"I'll eat it," Amber says.

I turn to her. "You will?"

"Sure. I grew up eating it. At my house we have it every year and we actually finish the whole can."

"Well, there you go," my dad says. "It won't go to waste. See you kids soon."

He takes off with Owen.

"What else does your family have at Thanksgiving?" I ask Amber. "Besides canned cranberry sauce?"

"The usual. Turkey, stuffing, mashed potatoes."

"How many people come over?"

"This year it's just my parents and younger sister. Oh, and her boyfriend. That should be interesting."

"Penalty!" Gramps yells, throwing his hands up. "Can't you see that's a penalty?"

"Just ignore him," I tell Amber. "So what were you saying about your sister's boyfriend?"

"She claims he's just a friend but I'm pretty sure he's more than that. My dad hates any guy we date. This poor guy she's dating is going to be questioned to death before dinner even starts. He may not even make it to dinner. My dad may scare him off."

"Then why'd your sister invite him?"

"It was my idea. I thought it would keep my parents from..." She trails off, her eyes going to the TV.

"Keep your parents from what? Fighting?"

She looks back at me. "How'd you know I was going to say that?"

"You tense up whenever you talk about your parents so I assumed there was a story there. I figured either you didn't get along with them or they didn't get along with each other."

"I get along with them separately, but as a couple, all they do is fight and I don't like being around that." She tenses up, her face tight, her shoulders stiff.

I hold her hand. "You want to talk about it?"

She fakes a smile. "There's nothing to say. That's just how they are. So anyway, do you guys do anything else on Thanksgiving besides dinner?"

"Watch football." I give a sideways glance to Gramps.

"Interference!" he shouts, pounding his fist on the chair. "No wonder they lost this game!"

Amber startles every time he yells but I barely even notice. He's been this way for as long as I can remember..

"What about *your* family?" I ask Amber. "Do you guys do anything besides the big dinner?"

"My sisters and I used to go to the movies, just to get out of the house. I kind of miss our Thanksgiving movie tradition."

"Then let's go after we eat."

"Go where?"

"To the movies. There's a new theater just a few miles from here. It has like sixteen screens."

"What about watching football?"

"I can skip it. I'm not that into football. I catch a game now and then and that's good enough."

"But won't your parents be mad if you leave?"

"We don't have to leave right away. We'll have dinner, hang around for an hour, and leave." I get my phone out and find the theater. "Here. Pick what you want to see."

Two hours later, we've finished dinner and are having dessert, except for Gramps, who's still working on his turkey leg.

"Damn gristle," he mumbles to himself. He always blames the food for why he takes forever to eat, even though we all know it's because of his dentures, but he refuses to get new ones.

"So you never said how you met," my mom says as we're eating our pumpkin pie.

Amber chokes and coughs on her pie. She was hoping this topic wouldn't come up and now she's panicking.

I hand her a glass of water, then calmly say, "We met at a party."

"Oh." My mom pats her mouth with a napkin. "I guess I assumed Austin set you two up. Amber, isn't Austin's girlfriend your roommate?"

Amber's gulping down her water so I answer for her. "Yeah, Kira and Amber share an apartment. They grew up together back in Michigan. But I actually met Amber last May, before I knew Kira."

"And you're just now dating?"

Amber jumps in. "We didn't exchange numbers at the party. We lost track of each other and I didn't see him again until just recently."

Amber desperately wants to get off this topic. She's nervous, her foot tapping the floor under the table.

Luckily for her, the conversation is interrupted with a loud noise across the table coming from Owen. It's his fake fart noise. He's done it three times now and laughs every time.

"Owen." My mom gives him her warning look. "Stop it."

"What? It's the chair. I swear."

Amber's trying to hold in her laughter. She knows laughing will just encourage him. He loves an audience, especially someone new to entertain.

Just as I take my last bite of pumpkin pie, a real fart noise cuts through the silence in the room. It's long and drawn out and when I look at Gramps, I see him still gnawing on his turkey leg, as if nothing happened.

Owen bursts out laughing. "Wasn't me!" he yells.

"Dad," my dad says to his father. "Maybe you should excuse yourself."

"Why?" He smiles at Owen. "I can't help it if your damn chairs make noise."

Looking over at Amber, I can tell she's doing all she can to keep from laughing.

I lean over and whisper, "Sorry. My family's nuts."

"Well," my mother stands up, "anyone like more coffee?"

"I'll have some," my dad says.

"I'm fine," Amber says. "By the way, I love your centerpiece. Did you make it?"

"Yes, I made it last weekend."

"It's really beautiful. I like how you mixed the leaves with the mini pumpkins."

My mom's beaming. Her centerpiece, the crowning glory of her meal, has been recognized and appreciated by an outsider. This will make her day.

I can tell my mom likes Amber. My dad does too. They were smiling at her all through dinner and kept asking her questions. Then they'd smile at me, as if letting me know they approve. I don't need their approval but it's good to know they like her. Because I *more* than like her. I could see a real future with her.

CHAPTER NINETEEN

AMBER

This is how Thanksgiving should be. No parents screaming at each other. Just a family sitting around a table having a normal conversation. I haven't had a Thanksgiving like that since I was twelve. After that, my parents started bickering which eventually became what is now full blown fights, not just at Thanksgiving, but all the time.

All week I worried about coming to Dylan's house but it turned out to be good. I got a real turkey dinner, didn't have to sit in my apartment all alone, and was able to see a different side of Dylan. Unlike me, who would be a nervous wreck if he were around my family, Dylan's been completely relaxed, even when his brother made fart noises, which was hilarious, not just the noises themselves but the fact that no one reacted. And then when Gramps let one rip? They still didn't react. But I had tears in my eyes trying to hold back my laughter. Dylan's grandpa is too old to care about what anyone thinks so he just does whatever he wants.

"So, Amber, do you have any activities outside of class?" Dylan's dad asks as his mom refills his coffee.

Dylan chuckles. "We'll be here all day."

I explain. "I belong to a lot of clubs and organizations on campus. I also work at a restaurant, usually just one day a week. And I volunteer to read to kids. Well, just one. Her name is Emily. I go to her school every Monday."

Dylan's mom sets the coffee pot down. "Does she have trouble reading? Is that why she's part of this program?"

"Yes. She's in second grade but has trouble reading even simple words."

"Has she been tested for a learning disability?"

"I assume she has but I don't really know."

"If she hasn't, they need to test her. Her mother needs to tell them to. When Dylan was struggling, I had to push the school system to test him."

I look at Dylan. "You had problems reading?"

"I'm dyslexic," he says casually. "I thought I told you that."

"No. I didn't know."

"When he was first learning to read," his mom explains, "he used to get so frustrated that I knew something was wrong. Once he was diagnosed, his teachers were able to adapt their teaching methods, and things went a lot better after that. He had to work harder than the other children at school, but he did, and ended up getting mostly A's."

"Wow, that's great," I say to Dylan.

"Where's my pie?" Gramps barks from the end of the table, wiping his face with the napkin.

"Right here." Dylan slides the dessert plate down to him.

"Are we playing football?" Owen asks Dylan.

"No. Amber and I are going to a movie."

"Can I come?" Owen asks.

Dylan smiles. "No way. It's a date. No annoying little brothers allowed."

"I'm not annoying."

I nudge Dylan. "You guys can play some football before we go. I'll stay here and help your mom clean up."

"Oh, Amber, you don't need to do that," she says.

"I don't mind. My sisters and I always help my mom clean up. I'm used to it."

"Nonsense. The dishes can wait. Let's go to the living room and see if there's anything good on TV."

Owen jumps off his chair. "So we're going outside?"

Dylan nods at Gramps. "When we're done with dessert."

Owen sighs and sits back down. But it's not a long wait. The pie is easier to eat and Gramps wolfs it down in a matter of seconds.

While Dylan plays football with his brother and dad, I talk with his mom while Gramps snores in the recliner. Even though I just met Dylan's family, I feel comfortable around them. His family is great. And it was nice to finally have a peaceful Thanksgiving without all the fighting. I miss my family, but I don't miss the screaming matches at the dinner table.

Dylan and I leave a couple hours later and go to the theater. It's packed and we end up sitting near the front, right in the middle, with people all around us.

"I was hoping for some privacy," Dylan whispers in my ear.

I was too. I've wanted to kiss him all day but didn't want to around his family, and since I still have that rule about only kissing in public places, our options are limited. Maybe I should just forget that rule and we should go make out at his house or my apartment. Except I know where that will lead.

"Let's get out of here," he whispers.

"We just got here," I whisper back. "The movie just started."

"Do you really want to watch it? Or go do something else?" He catches my eye in the darkness.

I smile. "Let's go."

We hurry out of the theater and go back to his car. Once we're inside, we bump noses in our race to kiss.

"Sorry," I say, laughing a little.

"At least I know you want to do this as much as I do."

"I've been wanting to all day."

We kiss, our tongues tangling, our bodies heating up the otherwise cold car. We don't stop until a few minutes later, when someone gets in the car next to ours.

"Guess we should leave," Dylan says.

"Yeah." I sit back and put my seatbelt on.

"Where should we go?" He starts the engine and turns the heat on.

"I don't know. There's not much open today."

"How about your apartment?"

I pause, chewing on my lip.

He turns to me. "We won't do anything. I promise. Unless you've changed your mind."

Despite my body telling me to change my mind, I shake my head and say, "Not yet. It's too soon."

"Then we'll just watch TV. If I try anything, you can kick me out." He smiles. "What do you think?"

"Okay. We'll go to my apartment." On the way there, I say, "So why didn't you tell me you were dyslexic?"

"I thought I did, but I guess it never came up. It's not something I try to hide. I'm not ashamed of it or embarrassed by it. It just takes me a little longer to read than other people. But I do all right."

"Is it hard for you to write the letters? Because we don't have to do it. If I'd known about this, I never would've asked you to do it."

"It's not hard. It may take me a little longer than other people but it's always been that way for me so I'm used to it." We're at a stop light and he looks at me and smiles. "And I know how much you like the letters. It's part of our story, remember? The romantic tale of how we met?"

"Speaking of that, I can't believe you told your parents how we met."

"I didn't tell them how. I told them when."

"Yeah, but that made them wonder why we didn't talk again until just recently."

"And you explained why. So we're good." He checks his mirror as he merges on the freeway. "Going back to the dyslexia thing, if you think that little girl you read to might have it, or if she gets diagnosed with it, I'd be happy to meet with her. Sometimes it helps to know you're not the only one that

198

struggles with it. At least it did for me. My mom got me in a group that had other kids that struggled with reading problems and it made a big difference."

"You'd really do that? Talk to Emily?"

"Sure. If she wants me to. And if her mom's okay with it." I smile at him. "You're really sweet."

"Not always. I have a bad boy side." He says it like he's joking, but it's kind of true. When he's rocking it out in his band, dressed in all black, playing his guitar, he seems like a bad boy. And that night we met, when he saw me across the room and came over and kissed me without even telling me his name? That was bad. Very bad. And yet I loved it.

He was also bad when he did what he did to me in the cleaning closet at work. And yet I loved that too.

"I'm not afraid of your bad boy side," I tell him.

"Then I guess it needs to come out more. But not tonight. Tonight I've gotta summon my inner angel if I'm going to survive being at your apartment as your platonic friend."

I smile. "You could just go back to your place."

"Is that what you want?" He sounds disappointed.

"No. I want you to come over. I'll just throw on some baggy sweats and put my hair in a bun so that I'm so hideous you won't even want to get near me."

"Not possible." He squeezes my hand, which he's holding. "There's nothing you could do that would make me not want to be near you."

"See? You're being sweet again."

"Told you I was summoning my inner angel. No bad boy tonight. Only good."

It's what I asked for but part of me is a little disappointed bad boy Dylan can't come out and play. But he will eventually. We just need a little more time.

My phone rings and I answer when I see it's my little sister. "Hey, how was dinner?"

"Dad almost killed Lark."

Lark. I still can't get used to that name. It sounds like a type of bird.

"Why? What happened?"

"During dessert, we were talking about school and Lark said something about how I'm really good in art and then he put his arm around me and it totally set dad off. He told Lark to leave."

"So did he leave?"

"No. Mom told Dad he was overreacting and then..." She sighs.

"They got in a fight."

"Yes. With Lark there. It was so embarrassing. You told me they wouldn't fight in front of him."

"I didn't think they would. So what did you do?"

"I told Lark we're leaving."

"And did you?"

"We went outside but I didn't leave. If I did, it would've just made Mom and Dad fight even more. I apologized to Lark and then he left."

"Britt, I'm sorry. I figured Dad would question the guy but not tell him to leave. So have you talked to Lark since he left?"

"Yeah, and he was cool with everything. But I doubt he'll come over here again. Hey, Mom wants to say hi. I'm handing you over."

My mom's voice comes through the phone. "Hi, honey. How was dinner?"

"Good." I glance over at Dylan. "Dylan's family was really nice. And they made sure I left there completely stuffed."

"You'll have to give me their address. I'd like to send them a thank-you note."

"Mom, you don't have to do that. I already thanked them."

"I know, but as your mother I'd like to thank them for inviting you. It always upsets me when you're alone on Thanksgiving."

I wouldn't be alone if you and Dad would stop fighting. I'd be home, where I should be. I think that but I don't say it.

"So Britt said she had a friend over."

My mom sighs. "Yes, but your father overreacted when Lark put his arm around Britt. Scared the poor boy away, which I suppose was your father's intention but it wasn't called for. Lark seemed like a very nice young man. Speaking of young men, how are you and Dylan doing?"

"Fine."

"Is it getting serious?"

"No. We're just dating." I feel Dylan looking at me and change the subject. "So anything else new?"

"Not really. I have to put away all the leftovers and then I'm going to take a nap. What are you doing the rest of the night?"

"Dylan's coming over to watch TV."

"Do you two have plans for this weekend?"

"No. I have to catch up on homework."

"Honey, you need to relax. Just take this weekend off. Spend time with Dylan."

"I'll think about it. Well, I should go. Tell Dad I said hi."

"I will. Bye, honey."

"How's the family?" Dylan asks as I put my phone away.

"Good, although there was some drama at the dinner table. Apparently my dad doesn't like Lark, my sister's boyfriend."

"His name is Lark? Like the bird?"

"So it IS a bird. I knew it sounded like a bird but I wasn't sure if it was."

"Why doesn't your dad like him?"

"Because he touched my sister."

"Touched her how?" he asks cautiously.

"He put his arm around her so he basically touched her shoulders." I roll my eyes. "My dad yelled at him and told him to leave."

"Shit, that's harsh. Now I'm worried about meeting him."

"You probably won't meet him. I always go home. They don't come here."

"You don't think I'll ever meet him?"

What is he implying? That we'll be together in the future? I'd like for that to be true but I'm not sure I believe it. It's too soon to say. I still don't trust this will last. It started with a one-night stand. How many relationships start that way and end with the couple being together? None that I know of.

"Amber?" he says since I didn't answer him.

"Yeah. I don't know if you'll meet them. They probably won't come here until I graduate."

"Which you plan to do next summer. Are you saying we won't be together then?"

"Dylan, we've only dated for a couple weeks. It's too early to say what will happen. You graduate in May and may end up leaving Chicago for a job."

"Maybe I wouldn't take it. Not if it meant the end for us."

I look at him. He's totally serious. He really thinks we'll be together. But how could he think that? We're both graduating this year. Our futures are uncertain and could take us anywhere in the country.

"Dylan, you don't mean that. You know if you got the right job, you'd have to take it, wherever it is."

He just nods, and then gets quiet for the remaining few minutes it takes to get back to my apartment.

When we reach my door, he pulls me in for a kiss. A slow, deep kiss, his arm wrapped around me, keeping me close, his hand cupping the back of my head. It has my mind swimming with thoughts of doing more with him, repeating what we did last May. That was so great that I don't think we could replicate it, but with our intense chemistry, I bet we could come close.

"We're still in public," he says, smiling as he lets me go. "I might have to bring you out here every ten minutes just so we can do this."

I laugh. "We won't watch much TV if we do that." I open my door and we go inside. He helps me with my coat, then takes off his own while I go turn some lights on.

"You want something to drink?" I ask, going in the kitchen.

"Maybe a pop if you got it."

I grab a can for each of us and meet him on the couch. "Anything special you want to watch?" I take the remote from the coffee table and turn on the TV.

"You can pick. As long as it's not that home channel. My mom is obsessed with that channel. It was always on at our house growing up. Now I can't even watch it."

"But those shows are so good. Like the one where people search for houses. Or that one where they do room makeovers."

He lifts his brow. "Are you serious? You really want to watch that?"

He sounds so disappointed I have to laugh. "No. I'm not a big fan of that channel either. Those shows bore me, maybe because I don't own a house. Maybe when I'm older I'll find them interesting."

"I never will, homeowner or not."

"How about this?" I stop on Casablanca. "Do you like old movies?"

"If they're classics, I don't mind."

"I love old movies. I think they're romantic."

"Old-fashioned romance?" He smiles.

"Exactly. Back when people wrote letters. And men wore suits and hats and women wore dresses and gloves. There was just something romantic about those times. People weren't in such a rush. They took time to get to know each other. It wasn't all about sex."

He chuckles. "They weren't as innocent as you think they were."

"How do you know?"

"In one of my history classes, the professor was talking about it. He basically said people back then were almost as bad as they are now. They just weren't open about it."

"Then how would anyone know if that's true?"

"Historical documents on STD rates. Unplanned pregnancies. Journals people kept. Catalogs with sex toys. There's all kinds of evidence they weren't the prudish people we thought they were."

"They still had romance."

"Maybe, but they also had sex." He smiles. "Although getting through those corsets must've been a bitch for us guys."

I nudge his arm. "It prolonged the foreplay. That's a good thing."

"We've gotta stop talking about this. Foreplay? Sex? It's taking my mind places it shouldn't go. Talk about something else."

"Like what?"

"Anything. Just not sex."

I laugh it off, but the truth is, that short conversation got *me* aroused too. How did we even get on that topic? Are we trying to make this even harder on ourselves?

He stands up. "Let's go out in the hall."

I pull him back down. "You're funny."

"I'm serious. I have to kiss you. It's been like five minutes."

"You went all day without kissing me."

"Yeah and it sucked. Now come on. Let's go."

"I don't want to go out there. People might walk by and I don't want my neighbors watching us."

"All right." He sighs and leans back on the couch, his eyes on the movie.

My eyes are on *him*, taking in how hot he is with that strong jaw that compliments his pretty boy face, those deep brown eyes, that dark mussed up hair that looks like he just ran his hand through it. "I suppose if you uh..."

"If I what?" he asks, still watching the TV.

"If you wanted to give me a kiss—just a kiss, nothing more—it'd be okay."

He looks at me, at my lips, then my eyes. I prepare for him to kiss me, but then he says, "That's okay. Let's just watch the movie."

"Wait—what? You're turning me down?"

"You were right. Kissing could lead to other things. Things you don't want to do." He's trying not to smile because he knows his refusal to kiss me will drive me crazy. Now that he said no, I really want a kiss, even more than before. Damn him!

"I'm sure we can control ourselves," I say.

"I'm pretty sure we can't. Isn't that why you made the rule? Because you thought we couldn't stop once we started?"

"Yes, but..." I don't know how to explain my reasoning. Right now, I don't even care why I made those rules. I just want him to kiss me.

"This movie's kind of slow. You want to watch something else?"

"Sure." I sound frustrated because I am. Sexually frustrated, and it's all because I insist on these stupid rules. I'm about ready to ditch old-fashioned romance. If those people were doing it, why can't I?

Because I didn't want this to be about sex, that's why. I want us to be about more than that. If this relationship is going to have a chance, we can't base it on what we did last May.

But it's hard to resist temptation. And right now, I'm really tempted to relive that night. The heat. The passion. It's all I can think about.

CHAPTER TWENTY

DYLAN

She made the rules and I'm following them. But then she asked for a kiss. That wasn't in public. I said no, which was nearly impossible to do, but I wanted to see how she'd react. How strong her willpower is. I know it's not great because she didn't resist me that day in the hospital cleaning closet. Or later than week when I kissed her in the conference room while everyone was at lunch. Or when I led her behind a concrete pillar in the parking garage, backed her up against it, and kissed her until we heard a car driving up the ramp.

She always says we shouldn't do that stuff at work and yet she gets all turned on when we do. She's like the girls in her old-fashioned movies, who seem all prim and proper but then let their wild side out when nobody's looking.

I think I'm torturing her right now by not kissing her. She keeps smoothing the pillow she's holding on her lap, then tugging on the tassels, then smoothing, tugging, smoothing, tugging, to the point that if she keeps it up, that pillow's going to be destroyed by the end of the night.

"Why don't you give that pillow a break?" I ask after two of hours of her attacking it.

"What are you talking about?"

"That pillow." I point to it. "You've been beating on it for two hours straight. If you keep going, there's not going to be anything left of it."

She crinkles her nose in confusion. "I'm just holding it. Not beating on it."

"Why don't you just set it down?" I smile as I take it from her. "I'm just going to put it over here, where it's safe."

She swats at me. "You're being crazy."

"You know, some experts would say your obsessive handling of the pillow is a sign of sexual frustration."

She rolls her eyes. "I was not doing anything to the pillow. And I am not sexually frustrated."

"That's good. Because if you were, it'd be very difficult to sit next to me right now." I slide closer to her. "And it'd be very hard to say no if I did this." I cup the side of her face and lean in until I'm an inch from her mouth.

She lets out a soft breath, her eyes falling shut.

I kiss her, my lips barely touching hers. I've held out long enough. I couldn't take it anymore. I had to kiss her. That sexual frustration I was talking about? We're both suffering from it and it needs to be dealt with.

"More," she breathes.

I kiss her again and her lips part for me, and moments later, what was only going to be a kiss becomes more as I lie her down on the couch, my hand sliding up to her breast. And then it's like the floodgates break open. We kiss harder and faster, our hands yanking at each others clothes, trying to get them off. Soon my shirt is tossed aside and so is hers and I'm tugging the zipper down on her skirt.

"Dylan," she whispers, her eyes closed. "We said we wouldn't do this."

"You want to stop?" I ask, but in my head I'm begging her not to end this. I know we said we'd wait, but why? This doesn't feel wrong. Or too soon. It feels perfect. Right. Just like that night back in May.

"Keep going," she whispers.

I pick her up off the couch and go to her room, setting her on the bed. We're both breathing hard as we race to shed the rest of our clothes. She grabs a condom from her dresser and rips open the package and slides it on me while we kiss. And then I'm on her, inside her, and nothing has ever felt more right.

She's the one. Amber is the one. I felt it that first night we met and I've felt it ever since. I don't know why I feel this way about her. Why I feel so strongly that we belong together. I can't explain it. I just know that whenever I'm with her, it feels right.

Like now. The sex is freaking hot, but it's more than that. It's more than just physical. I feel like we're connecting on a deeper level. An emotional level. And the combination of what I feel, both physically and emotionally, is so powerful it's overwhelming. And addictive. We haven't even finished and I already want more. I crave her body. Her touch. The feel of her legs wrapped around me as I move in and out of her.

She cries out my name as she comes, her hands digging into my shoulders, her legs clenched tightly around me. The feel of her release causes my own release, and it's so strong I grip the sheet, my body jerking from the force of it until it finally comes to rest.

Lying over her, I kiss the smooth skin along her shoulder, inhaling the soft sweet scent of whatever perfume she wears. It's heaven and I just want to stay here, right here in this spot, for as long as possible.

"Dylan." Amber rubs her hand over my back, softly, lovingly, and I wonder if she feels as much for me as I feel for her. I don't want to say I love her, even inside my own head, but I feel like I do. I've never been in love so I don't know if that's what this is, but I feel like it might be.

"Can you move?" she asks.

"Yeah, sorry." I move onto my side. "Was I crushing you?"

"A little." She smiles. "I was starting to have trouble breathing."

"Sorry." I kiss her. "I'll move off sooner next time." I said 'next time' to see how she'd react. Was this just a one-time thing or are we going to continue this?

She doesn't respond, her eyes closed, like she's falling asleep. I get up and go to the bathroom and when I come back she's under the covers. I slide in beside her and she snuggles against my chest, her hand wrapping around me, her head on my shoulder, and we fall asleep.

We wake up a few hours later. I'm hard again and I can't hide it. I'm on my side, my arms wrapped around her, her body tucked into mine. Her smooth, naked ass is lined up with my crotch, positioned in just the right spot for me to slip inside her. But she's asleep, and even if she were awake, I don't know if she'd want to do it again. So I adjust my head on the pillow and try to go back to sleep.

As I close my eyes I feel her move, just slightly. Then I feel her ass press against me. Her hand reaches back and grips my thigh as she continues to circle her ass, making my cock twitch, as if begging if it can go where it wants to go. I'd like to help it get there but I don't want to assume anything so I keep it where it is and slide my hand up to her breast and caress it while kissing her shoulder. She pulls away as she reaches for the nightstand, then I feel her hand under the covers as she slips me the condom. I quickly roll it on, then resume where we were, my hand on her breast as I kiss the back of her neck. She softly moans, then slides up just enough to position herself over my tip. I slide it in, then grasp her hip and guide her the rest of the way, until I'm deep inside her. I keep her there a moment, then begin a slow rhythm of thrusts, wanting to prolong this because it feels so fucking good. I reach around and touch her breasts, tease her nipples, and feel myself getting even harder.

She's moaning, breathing heavy, pressing into me. So much for making this last. It's too much. I'm ready to burst. I lower my hand between her legs and when I feel she's almost there, I thrust faster and harder. Her body tenses up, and as I feel her come, I do as well.

Our bodies fold into each other as we catch our breath. I slip out of her and hold her closely against me. I'm completely relaxed, left in a content, happy state that makes me want to drift off to sleep.

But then I hear her talking. "Dylan."

"Yeah?"

"I don't think I can do this."

My heart takes off in a panic and I sit up, looking down at her face. "Do what?"

"This...this rule where we can't be together like this."

I let out a huge sigh of relief. "Shit, I thought you meant—"

"No." She turns to me and smiles. "Not that. I meant this. What we just did. I don't think I can go without it. When I'm with you, I can't help but want to be *with* you. Like this. I know it's not a good idea but..." She reaches up and moves the hair off my forehead. "You're hard to resist."

"Then don't." I lean down and kiss her. "Don't even try to resist. Let's just be together." I smooth her hair. "Amber, I know you're worried this is just about sex but it's not, at least to me it's not. I care about you. I want to be with you, and not just like this. I like spending time with you. Getting to know you. And I want to *keep* getting to know you, which means not just doing this but other things. Things that will help me learn more about you, and help you learn more about me. I want a relationship with you, Amber. And not one based on sex, but a real relationship. I've wanted that with you since the night we met."

She looks up at me. "I want that too."

"Then it's settled. No more rules. We can do what we want. Act on our urges." I kiss her. "And right now, my urge is to kiss every inch of you until you scream my name like you just did."

She smiles. "It won't happen again for a while. Maybe not until tomorrow. I can't have more than one or two in a day."

"Says who?"

"Me. I know my body."

I grin. "I'm taking that as a challenge."

She laughs. "It's not gonna happen. Two maybe, but not three."

"We'll see about that." I pat her hip. "Let's go."

"Where are we going?"

"I need to eat. I'm starving."

She turns and checks the clock. "It's three in the morning. Why don't we just go to sleep?"

"I'm too hungry to sleep. Sex always revs up my appetite. You got anything to eat or do you want to go find some twenty-four hour diner?"

"Let's stay here. I'm sure I have something."

We get out of bed and she puts on a robe and I pull on my jeans, leaving my shirt off. Her apartment is warm. She keeps it much hotter than I keep my house.

"Cereal?" she asks. We're in the kitchen now and she opens a cupboard, showing me her collection of cereal boxes.

"You got anything else? Cereal doesn't seem like enough."

"I have peanut butter. We could make sandwiches."

"Then we'll both smell like peanut butter. What else you got?" I open her fridge. "Eggs? You've got cheese and some ham. We could make omelets."

"We could, but I don't know how. I always burn eggs."

"I'll make them. Just need a skillet."

"Kira said you didn't know how to cook."

He takes the ingredients from the fridge. "Why were you and Kira talking about my cooking skills?"

"I'm not sure. I can't remember. As for me, I can't cook. I've tried and it almost never turns out."

"I can't really cook either but I can do basic stuff, like omelets, spaghetti, mac and cheese. And I can grill meat. We have a grill at the house."

"What about your roommate? Can he cook?"

"Van? God, no. And if he tried, I wouldn't eat anything he made. Cleanliness is not his thing. I've seen him drop a burger

211

on the carpet and pick it up and eat it. And the carpet at that house is disgusting. I don't even want to think about what's living in there." I find a bowl and crack the eggs. "You'll have to come over sometime and meet Van."

"I've met him. I met him at the bar when I went to hear you guys play."

"Yeah but you only met him for like a minute. You should come over and hang out when he's there so you can get to know him. He may offend you at first because he doesn't filter what he says, but if you can get past that, you'll see he's a really good guy." I turn on the stove and pour the eggs in the pan. "Shit, I did it wrong. I was going to make two omelets and now it's gonna be one. Or I could just scramble everything together."

"That works," she says, hopping up on the counter.

I go over and kiss her. "This has been a great day. And a great night."

"I agree." She kisses me back. "But tomorrow, or I guess it's morning, so later today, I need to get some work done."

"Does it really need to be done today?" I place my hands on the counter and lean in to kiss her neck. "Or could it wait?"

"Dylan, don't tempt me."

"Why? You need some time off and so do I. So let's spend the next three days together. Kira won't be back until Sunday night. We have the whole apartment to ourselves."

"I know, but I have so much to do."

"Like what?"

"Your eggs are going to burn." She points at the skillet.

"I have it on low. It won't burn. Now tell me what you have to get done that's so important."

"Just stuff for holiday parties for the groups I'm in."

"So not homework? This is all just volunteer stuff?"

"Yeah, but it's still important."

"More important than spending time with your boyfriend?" I kiss her. "The guy who makes you scrambled eggs? Makes you scream in pleasure?"

212

She smiles. "Okay, fine. I'll take the weekend off. But after that, it's back to work. No more excuses. And you can't come over here and tempt me."

"I'll just tempt you at work. I know how much you like it when we sneak around."

"I do not," she insists. "It stresses me out."

"In a good way." I run my hand up her thigh. "In a way that makes your heart race. Makes you aroused. Makes you want to do things you don't think you should be doing."

She tilts her head. "Maybe that's a tiny bit true. It does kind of turn me on." She smiles and runs her hand down my chest.

"You're making me hard again. You wanna forget the eggs and go do it?"

She glances down at my tented jeans. "You're ready to go again? Damn, you're a machine. A sex machine."

I chuckle. "I've never been called that, but okay." I press my lips to hers. "And this doesn't always happen. Only with you. So...food or sex?"

"Food first, sex second."

"Then I'll hurry with the food." I find a spatula in the drawer and go back to the skillet, turning the eggs. I add the ham and cheese, and a few minutes later we eat our early morning snack at the counter.

"I need a shower," I say, sliding my plate aside.

"Now? Don't you want to sleep?"

"After the shower." I stand up and help her off the barstool.

"But—"

I kiss her again. "I should probably mention that we're doing more than showering."

She smiles. "Oh."

The shower sex is something Amber's never done. I could tell because she acted like she didn't know what to do. So I took charge, which turned her on, and that, along with me thrusting into her as I held her against the shower wall, had her coming for the third time today. Something that's only happened to her with me. Just like the shower sex. She's only done it with me. I feel some pride in that.

Back in bed, we fall asleep. I wake up at ten and find Amber is gone. She's in the bathroom. I hear the sink running.

My phone rings and I see it's Austin calling. "Hey," I say, picking up. "How was Thanksgiving?"

"Good. We had a ton of food, even more than usual. I wish Kira had been able to come but she really wanted to see her family. When I talked to her yesterday, it sounded like she was having a good time."

"And she's coming back Sunday?"

"Yeah. I'm picking her up at the airport."

"What time do you guys think you'll be over here?"

"Why would we go over there? Am I forgetting something?"

Shit. I meant *here*, at Amber's apartment, but Austin doesn't know I'm over here so he assumes I meant my house. Can I tell him about Amber and me or is it a secret? We haven't talked about this but I don't know why it'd be a secret. Austin and Kira know we're dating.

"I meant the apartment," I say.

"You said 'here' like you're there right now."

"I am."

"Why are you there so early? You guys got plans for today?"

"I'm not sure. We haven't talked about it."

"So you just dropped by or what?"

"I've actually been here since last night."

"She let you spend the night? Did you sleep on the couch?"

Austin knows about Amber's rules. He just doesn't know we're no longer following them.

"We slept in her room. In her bed."

"No shit? What happened to her rule about you guys not being allowed to make out in the apartment?"

"That rule is gone." I chuckle to myself. "Long gone."

"So you finally did it."

"We didn't plan on it, but yeah."

"Well, good for you. It's about time."

"We've only dated a few weeks."

"Yeah, but in your heads it's like you've been dating since May. I know you thought about her every day, and according to Kira, Amber felt the same way. She couldn't stop thinking about you. So does Kira know?"

"Not yet, unless Amber called her. She's in the bathroom. I just woke up."

"I'll let you go. I just wanted to check in and see how Thanksgiving went. I guess I never asked. How was it?"

"Good. My family loved Amber. She fit right in. She didn't even freak out when Gramps let one rip at the table."

He laughs. "Good ol' Gramps. He cracks me up."

"I gotta go. I'll call you later."

"Yeah, bye."

Amber walks in, wearing a long t-shirt that hangs down to her thighs. "Were you talking to someone?"

"Yeah. Austin called. I told him about us. I hope that's okay. I didn't mean to but he kept asking me questions which led to me telling him I stayed over."

"I don't mind. He'd find out sooner or later. You want to use the bathroom? I'm done in there."

"Yeah." I get out of bed and go over to her. I give her a kiss and smile. "Morning."

She smiles back. "Good morning."

I walk out of her room to the bathroom, smiling the entire way. She makes me happy. Even when she's not around, I feel happy knowing she's mine.

CHAPTER TWENTY-ONE

AMBER

While Dylan's in the bathroom I call Kira. I hope she picks up. I have to tell her this and I don't want to wait.

"Hello?" she answers.

"Hey, it's me. What are you doing?"

"I'm at the mall with my mom. She's Christmas shopping for my brothers. The crowds are insane so I went to a coffee shop to get a break while she battles other moms at the toy store."

"Oh, yeah, it's Black Friday. I totally forgot. Can you talk or do you have to go meet up with your mom?"

"Are you kidding? I'm not getting anywhere near that store. The lines are out the door. I told her I'd wait here. So what's up? How was Thanksgiving at Dylan's house?"

"Great! I loved it. His family is hilarious, especially his grandpa."

"Did you leave after dinner?"

"No, we stayed for a few hours then went to a movie, but the theater was so crowded we decided to leave. We came back and watched TV."

"Are you guys doing anything today?"

"Yeah, but I don't know what."

"What time's he coming over?"

"He's already here. He, um, spent the night."

"Wait, does that mean what I think it means?"

I smile. "Yes."

"You broke your rule? Already?"

"I know. I'm so bad. I couldn't even make it two weeks. But there's just something about him. I can't resist him. I seriously can't. That's why I made the damn rule. And then he kissed me last night on the couch and that was it. The rule was out the window."

"And was it just as good as last May?"

"I think it might've been even better. It got better each time."

"Each time? You did it more than once?"

"Three times."

"Amber! You're gonna hurt yourself." She says it jokingly.

I laugh. "I'm fine. In fact, I'm ready to do it again."

"Just don't be doing it all over the furniture. I have to sit on that stuff, you know."

"Hey, I know for a fact you and Austin did it on the couch. I walked in on you guys, remember?"

"One time. And we never did it again."

"And the kitchen counter?"

"Okay, yeah, but I thoroughly cleaned it when we were done. I'll clean it again if it makes you feel better."

"Don't worry about it. I'm just kidding. And as for Dylan and me, we'll keep it in the bedroom." I pause. "And the shower."

"You did it in the shower?" she asks, her voice raised.

"Maybe. Why? Are you mad?"

"No. I'm shocked because you've never done it in the shower. It seems too...unconventional for you."

"What are you saying? I'm a prude?"

"No, but you do tend to live on the safe side, and I distinctly remember you saying shower sex was dangerous. Wet floors. Slippery tile."

"Yeah, well, I guess Dylan brings out my wild side because I wasn't even thinking about that."

"Did you like it?"

"Loved it. Last night was great. The sex. Falling asleep with Dylan. He even made us eggs at three in the morning."

"So you could refuel for more sex."

"Exactly."

She laughs. "I'm proud of you. You finally faced the fears you had about Dylan. Now you guys can act like a regular couple."

"We were a regular couple before," I insist.

"Not with your goofy rules. And all that talk about preserving the memory of your one-night stand."

"I'm still worried about that. I mean, right now that night still seems perfect, but if we break up, that might change."

"It won't change. And you guys won't break up. Why would you? You get along great and it sounds like you have amazing sex."

"True. Okay, fine. I'll try to stop worrying about the past and just focus on the future."

"Wow. I go away for a day and you're a whole new woman."

"Not exactly, but I do feel different. Meeting Dylan's family helped me get to know him even better. I really like him, for more than just his bedroom skills, although that alone would be a reason to keep him around."

She laughs. "I gotta go. My mom's here. With no shopping bags. I guess she gave up on waiting in line."

"Tell her I said hi. I'll talk to you later."

Dylan walks in, toweling off from his shower. "Talking to Kira?"

"Yeah," I say, admiring his naked body as he tosses his towel aside and comes up to me on the bed.

"Did you tell her about last night?"

"Not in detail, but yeah, she knows you stayed over."

"I thought you girls shared details." He lifts up my t-shirt and takes it off, causing my pulse to spike, already anticipating what he's about to do to me.

"Sometimes we share details." I lie back on the bed. "Not always."

"Let's keep the details between you and me."

I agree, but I can't get the words out because he's kissing me. He lowers himself over me and we do it again.

This has never happened to me before. I've never wanted it this much, with any guy, even when the relationship was new and fresh.

It must be Dylan. We have an attraction to each other that can't be matched by anyone else. It's another reason I was reluctant to date him. I knew if I did and we broke up, I'd always be comparing him to other guys and would never feel what I felt with him.

Later that day, we go to a movie and actually watch it this time now that we're not limited to making out only in public places. Then Dylan takes me to one of his favorite Mexican restaurants.

"This is the first time in years I've done nothing all day but relax," I say to Dylan as we're eating dinner.

"And you've still got two more days."

"I don't know if I can do it."

"I'm going to make sure you do. I'll lock you in the bedroom with me if I have to."

I smile. "That wouldn't be so bad."

"Let's hurry up and finish eating so we can go home."

"Dylan," I hear a girl say from behind me.

Dylan sighs. "Hey, Allison."

Allison. His ex.

"What are you doing here?" she asks. "Why didn't you go home for Thanksgiving?"

"I'm *from* here, remember? My family lives in the suburbs."

"Huh." She tips her head to the side. "I don't think you ever told me that."

"I did." He sounds annoyed. "You must've forgot."

"So what are you doing tonight?" She walks up to him, her back to me, pretending I'm not even there. "My girlfriends and I are going to a club. Why don't you come with us? It'll be like old times."

"You and I never went to a club."

She touches his arm. "I meant afterward. We'll go back to your place."

"I have a girlfriend, which you already know." He motions to me across the table. "This is Amber. Amber, this is Allison."

She stares at me, her eyes narrowing. "You really think you can steal him from me?"

"She didn't steal me," Dylan says to Allison. "I broke up with you."

"Yeah, because of her." She points her bony finger at me.

"It wasn't just because of her. It was because you and I didn't have a real relationship and I was tired of it."

Her hands go to her hips. "And yet you had no problem fucking me."

The people at the next table look over at us.

Dylan notices and lowers his voice. "Allison, get out of here. You're making a scene."

"You're seriously staying with HER? You've known her for what—a week? We have a history, Dylan. You owe it to me to get back together."

"I don't owe you anything. Now leave. I'm serious."

She glares at him, then turns to me, leaning over and getting in my face. "He said I was the best he ever had. You'll never be able to take my place." And then she storms off.

"Sorry," Dylan says, shaking his head. "She's freaking crazy."

"Then why'd you date her?"

"Because she—" He stops suddenly. "Never mind."

"She what? Just tell me."

He hesitates, then says, "Because she reminded me of you. Not in personality. In that respect you two are nothing alike. But when I first saw her, we were at a party and she had her back to me, and with her body and the blond hair, for a moment I thought it was you. I'd been searching for you all summer, and even though you told me you were in New York, I kept hoping that maybe you'd come back here to visit friends, or I don't know...just come back. So I raced up to her, thinking maybe it was possible, but then she turned around and I saw it wasn't you. But I wanted it to be so badly."

I reach over and hold his hand. I still feel guilty about what I put him through.

He continues. "Allison saw the excitement on my face when I thought it was you and she interpreted it to mean I wanted her. She knew me from the band and wanted to go out without knowing anything else about me. I was so disappointed it wasn't you that I decided it was time to give up looking. You were gone and weren't coming back. So I went out with her, and for some stupid reason, kept going out with her until you left me that letter."

He's never told me the story of Allison and him and how they met. Kira would've told me if I'd asked but I never did. Even before Dylan and I started dating, I didn't want to think about him with someone else. It was too hard. I still had feelings for him from the night we shared.

He rubs my hand. "Say something. You're too quiet. I feel like you're mad at me."

"I'm not mad. I have no reason to be. We weren't together when you were with her. Like you said, you thought I was gone."

"I know, but I still had feelings for you, so being with Allison always felt wrong. That's why I don't know why I kept going out with her."

"Because she was, uh...good at certain things?"

"Shit, I totally forgot she said that. Don't listen to her. I never said that. It's a total lie."

"Then why'd you keep dating her?"

"Because I was lonely. And because my relationship with her was shallow. Meaningless. I knew it would never be anything more than it was, and I was okay with that. I wasn't ready to open my heart to anyone else."

"I felt the same way."

"What do you mean?"

"With Matt, my ex. I dated him because I didn't feel much for him. Our relationship was more of a friendship than anything else. He wanted more but I couldn't give it to him. My heart just wasn't in it. He was just someone to do stuff with. I feel bad about it now, but at the time I didn't even know I was using him like that."

"You and Matt are still friends, right?" Dylan asks.

"Yeah, but I don't see him much anymore. He has a new girlfriend and it's going really well and I don't want to get in the way of that."

"I only met him that time at the suit store, but he seems like a nice guy."

"He is. He's really nice. He's just not for me."

He smiles. "But I am?"

"You are." I smile back. "Let's get out of here."

He drops some money on the table and we get up to leave. Allison sees us as we go, but I don't look at her and neither does Dylan.

On Saturday, Dylan and I go Christmas shopping together. I won't have time to do it later and Dylan wanted to get it over with because he doesn't like shopping. The mall is crowded so we find what we want and get out of there, then head back to my apartment and Dylan makes us dinner. It's just pasta and sauce with a salad but it's sweet that he offered to make it. Most guys I've dated wouldn't even attempt to cook for me.

Sunday, we savor our last few hours of having the apartment to ourselves. When Kira gets back, Dylan will head home and I'll tackle at least one item on my growing to-do list.

"This weekend went too fast," Dylan says as we lie in bed after another great round of sex. I'm going to miss the sex. With my crazy schedule starting up again tomorrow, there won't be as much time to be alone with him. Who knows when we'll do it again?

"It *did* go fast. I was just getting used to relaxing and now tomorrow it's back to school and work."

"We could sneak off to the cleaning closet again." He kisses my neck, then up to my lips.

"We can't. We'll get caught."

"We won't get caught."

"We might, and then we'll both be fired."

"Then we'll find another internship."

"But I like this one. And I like that I get to work with you." I lay my head on his chest.

He kisses my head. "Then we'll just have to be more careful when we sneak around."

"We shouldn't do that anymore. Now that we can do it here, we don't need to be fooling around at work. It's too risky."

"So you're saying you'll let me come over during the week?"

"Yeah. Why?"

"Because you're never here. Are you planning to cut back on some of your activities?"

"Maybe. I don't know yet."

"You gonna let me stay over? I'm sure Kira wouldn't mind, given that Austin practically lives here."

"Actually, they've been staying over at his place a lot. The past few weeks I've had the apartment to myself."

"Then I need to come over more."

"What about your place?"

"We can go there but it's not that clean and it kind of stinks thanks to Van leaving food everywhere. You want to go there tonight?"

"I guess we could. But I have to be back here by seven tomorrow."

"I'll set the alarm. I have class at eight."

Normally, I wouldn't spend this much time with a guy but with Dylan it's different. I want more time with him. These past few days have proved to me that Dylan is more than just a one-night stand. I knew that back in May. I felt it, but I didn't know what to do about those feelings because I never in a million years believed something like that would lead to a serious relationship. But it did. We haven't dated long but it already feels serious. Dylan is already talking about a future with me. I'm not quite at that point but I definitely want to keep dating him.

A door shuts and we hear voices.

"Sounds like they're home," Dylan says. He checks the clock. "It's only four. Why are they back so early?"

"It's not early." I sit up and find my t-shirt on the bed and slip it on. "Kira said she'd be back at three so this is late."

There's a knock on my bedroom door and I hear Kira. "You guys decent in there?"

"Yeah," Dylan calls back. "Come in."

"Dylan!" I whisper, scolding him, because we are *not* decent. He's naked under the covers and I'm wearing a t-shirt and nothing else.

Kira opens the door and walks in with Austin at her side.

Austin grins at us. "Couldn't get out of bed this morning? Late night?" He chuckles.

"Very late night," Dylan says, grinning back. "Barely got any sleep."

I hit his shoulder. "No details, remember?"

"I didn't give any details. I was just commenting about how much we slept."

I roll my eyes. Even though Kira and Austin know what we were doing, I'm still embarrassed talking about it.

"Maybe we should go," Kira says, sensing my embarrassment. "We just came in to ask if you guys wanted to go get some food. We didn't know you were um...still in bed."

"I could go for some food." Dylan looks at me. "What do you think?"

"Might as well. I doubt I'll get any work done today."

"It's still the weekend. No work allowed."

"He banned me from working," I tell Kira. "I went four whole days without doing anything."

"Oh, no, how did you survive?" she asks, being overly dramatic.

"Stop teasing me. You know how I get when I'm not busy."

"Sounds to me like you two were pretty busy," Austin jokes.

"I'd have to agree with that," Dylan says, smiling as he sits up in bed, his bare chest exposed. I notice Kira checking him out, but then she glances away. I do the same thing to Austin. He's a little too muscular for me but he's still really hot. And when he's shirtless, no girl could look away.

"Check out this shirt Austin gave me," Kira says, pointing to her gray t-shirt that has a drawing of a guitar on it. "Isn't it cool?"

"Yeah, I like it," Amber says. "Was it for an anniversary or something?"

"No, he just gave it to me." She kisses him. "He's sweet that way." She turns back to us. "We'll let you guys get ready. We're ready to go whenever you are."

"Hurry up. We're starving," Austin says.

Kira drags him out of the room. "You're always starving."

When the door is closed, Dylan hauls me into him and kisses me. "You sure you want to go to dinner with them? We could just stay here and do this."

"We've done a lot of this the past few days. I think it's time we get up."

He sighs. "If we must."

I sit up. "Come on. This will be our first double date. It'll be fun."

"Staying here is also fun."

"True, but I want to go out with our friends so let's get dressed." I get out of bed before he pulls me back down and tempts me again.

A half hour later, we're having burgers at a pub down the street, Kira and Austin on one side of the booth, Dylan and me on the other.

"So what'd you guys do all weekend?" Austin asks with a grin.

"Austin." Kira nudges his side.

"What?" He laughs. "I just wanted to know if they did anything fun?"

Dylan puts his arm around me. "We went to a couple movies," he says, not playing along with Austin's reference to our sex life. "Went out to eat."

"And tomorrow it's back to work," I say.

The conversation turns to work and school and then our food arrives. This is strange, being on a double date with Dylan as my date. Strange but good. For months, Kira and Austin went out with Matt and me and it never felt right. No matter how much I fought it, my mind kept thinking about Dylan, and it didn't help that Austin was his friend and talked about him all the time. Austin didn't know about Dylan and me back then so it's not like he knew that his comments about Dylan were affecting me, but they were. They only made me miss him more and wonder if I'd made the wrong decision that night.

Now Dylan and I are together and I couldn't be happier. I wish I'd done this sooner. All those months, I was so afraid to be with Dylan, thinking my feelings for him would never live up to that night. Afraid to be disappointed and wanting to just keep that night a memory. Thinking that if we ever dated, it'd only be about sex. But now, even after doing it, my concerns about our relationship only being physical are gone. I feel like we're about so much more than that. We have a lot in common. We have a similar sense of humor. And we complement each other well. He's laid back. I'm a workaholic. He has a wild side and I tend to be overly cautious. I could go on and on, but the bottom line is, I feel like that night was meant to be because it led us to each other.

CHAPTER TWENTY-TWO

AMBER

The next day, I go to Emily's school for our weekly reading session.

"You have a boyfriend," she sings, moving side to side in her seat.

As usual, she's distracted. I set the book down. "How do you know I have a boyfriend?"

She points to my face. "Because you have a big smile."

"Maybe I'm just happy."

"Because you have booooyfriend." She giggles and covers her mouth.

"Okay, you're right. I have a boyfriend. Now let's read the story." I pick up the book.

"What's he look like?"

There's no way she's going to concentrate on reading now. Our time's almost up so I decide to just talk to her.

"He's tall. Got dark hair. Dark eyes."

Her face lights up. "Like Prince Charming?"

I laugh. "Yeah, I guess. He also plays in a band. He plays guitar and he sings. He's really good. He even wrote a song about me."

"Wow," she says in a dreamy tone.

"Yeah, and he writes me letters."

She scrunches her face up. "All of them?"

"What do you mean?"

"My teacher makes us write the letters and I don't like it. I get to the D and want to be done."

It takes me a moment to figure out she's talking about the alphabet and learning to write letters. I forgot that kids her age probably don't even know what letters are since they've been replaced by texts and email.

"I didn't mean those kind of letters," I say. "Letters are a note you write someone to tell them something. Instead of talking to them or calling them on the phone or texting or emailing, you get a sheet of paper and a pen and you write them a note."

"What does it say?"

"Anything you want. It can say what you did today or how you feel about them or it could tell them to have a good day."

"Do only boys write them?"

"No. I write them too. We take turns writing to each other." As I say it, I realize I haven't written Dylan a letter in days. I'll have to write one. Even though we're officially dating, I'm still going to keep writing the letters and I hope he does too.

"What do you tell him? That he's cute and you loooove him?" She sings the words and then giggles.

"No, I haven't told him those things, although he IS cute."

"Do you love him?"

Do I? No. Of course not. We just started dating. So then why do I feel like I do?

"We haven't dated long enough for me to love him," I say, deciding it must be true. It's the only thing that makes logical sense.

"Are you gonna get married?"

"We have to be in love first before we think about that."

"Emily." A woman appears at the door. She's short, with petite features, dark hair, and big brown eyes. She looks just like Emily. Must be her mom. "We have to get going."

Emily stands up and hugs me. "I have to go."

Her mom walks up to us. "She has a dentist appointment." She smiles. "I'm Rhonda, Emily's mom. I'm guessing you're Amber?"

"Yeah. Nice to meet you." I stand up and shake her hand.

"She talks about you all the time."

"Amber has a boyfriend," Emily says to her mom. "They might get married but only if they're in love."

I laugh. "We just started dating," I tell her mom. "Marriage is a long ways off."

"But they should get married because he's Prince Charming and Amber's a princess."

"I am?"

She nods. "We both are." She looks at her mom. "I gotta go potty."

"Okay, go ahead. I'll wait here."

Emily runs off to the bathroom.

"So how's the reading going?" her mom asks. "Her teacher said she's still struggling."

"She is. She has trouble concentrating. She can't stay focused. I think it's because she's frustrated." I want to suggest Emily be tested for dyslexia but I don't know if it's my place to do so. But then I think of what Dylan's mom said about how much better Dylan did in school once he was diagnosed so I decide to just ask her. "Have you ever had Emily tested for dyslexia?"

"No. Why?" Rhonda's brows draw together and I can't tell if she's mad at me for suggesting it or concerned that her daughter has it.

"My boyfriend is dyslexic and his mom said he really struggled when he was first learning to read. He couldn't focus and he got easily frustrated, much like Emily. But once they figured out the issue, things were a lot better. His grades improved, and now it's like you wouldn't even know that he has it. In fact, I didn't know until just last week."

"I hadn't considered she might have a learning disability." Rhonda sounds concerned, not angry, so at least she's not mad at me for bringing it up. "I would've thought if she did have some kind of issue, her teachers would know."

"They might just think she has trouble concentrating or can't sit still long enough to read. I don't know. I was only suggesting that maybe you look into it. I could be completely off base but I've been working with Emily all semester and nothing has changed, so maybe this is why."

Rhonda nods. "I'm glad you said something. I hadn't even thought about that, but maybe that IS what's causing her to struggle. I'll talk to her teacher about it. So as for your boyfriend, how's he doing now? As an adult?"

"He's doing great. He's in college and he's in a band and writes his own music and lyrics. He said he has to work a little harder than other people but he's used to it now so he doesn't think anything of it. I mentioned Emily to him and he said if you find out she's dyslexic, he'd be happy to talk to her. Let her know she's not alone."

She smiles. "Sounds like a nice young man."

"Yeah, he is."

Emily comes running back in the room and up to her mom. She holds her hands up. "There's no towels."

"They must be out. We'll tell your teacher. For now, just wave your hands around until they're dry."

"Okay." She does a little dance as she waves her hands in the air.

"We'll see you later," her mom says.

"Yeah, bye."

I hope she's able to get Emily tested. She's such a sweet little girl and I know she wants to be able to read.

"I talked to Emily's mom," I say to Dylan when I get to work. He always arrives earlier than me because he comes straight from class and the hospital isn't that far from his campus.

"How'd it go?"

"Good. Her mom thought it was a good idea to get Emily tested. She's going to talk to her teacher." I sit at my desk and wake up the computer. "I told her about you. I hope that's okay."

"It's fine. I told you I'm not ashamed or embarrassed by it. I just learn differently than other people. It's not a big deal."

I smile at him. "Emily kept asking about you. She said she knew I had a boyfriend because I kept smiling. She calls you Prince Charming."

He chuckles. "I don't know if I'm that charming but I'll take the title. What did you tell her about me?"

"That you write me letters. She thought I meant that you write out the alphabet for me, like practicing your letters. She didn't know about the other type of letter so I had to explain it. Then she wanted to know what I wrote. She suggested I tell you you're cute and that I love you." I laugh, but am a little nervous I mentioned the love part.

"You should take her suggestion and write that in your next letter."

"I think I've already told you you're cute."

"I don't think you have. And even if you did, I'd like it in writing."

"Okay," I say, not addressing the love part of the letter. I don't think either one of us is ready to discuss that.

Nosy Mary walks up to our desks. "Donna is sick today so she asked me to supervise you two." She says it like she's our babysitter.

"I think we're good." Dylan gives her a big, wide smile. "Donna gave us enough work to keep us busy for the next few days."

"What are you working on?" she asks in a tone that says she's testing him to see if he's lying.

"We have to check in with everyone who's working on the event, including the in-house departments, like janitorial and foodservice. Would you like to see the spreadsheet of the people we need to contact?"

"No." She lifts her nose up in the air. "Just don't be causing any trouble."

231

Trouble? We're not kids. We're not going to cause trouble. Does she know about us sneaking around? Maybe she does. Maybe that's why she's acting so odd. But even so, why does she care?

"We'll be on our best behavior," Dylan replies, giving her another smile.

She walks back to her desk.

Later, we go down to the cafeteria to talk to the catering manager who's doing the desserts for the event.

When we're done and walking back, Dylan says, "Do you think Mary's following us? Or maybe she has cameras watching us."

I laugh. "I wouldn't put it past her. The woman is nuts. I don't know why she cares what we do. We're interns. It's not like we'll be working here forever. In a few months, she'll never have to see us again."

We're approaching the children's wing and I spot Liza by the nurses' desk. Since meeting for coffee, we've been talking on the phone and making plans for a girls' night with Ivy, her sister, and Kira. I didn't know Liza was working today. She usually works nights.

"Let's go say hi to Liza," I say to Dylan.

"You sure? I don't think Mary would approve of that," he says in a kidding tone.

"All the more reason to do it."

His hand brushes mine as we walk. "Listen to you, you little rebel."

"I'm just tired of her being so nosy. She needs to mind her own business."

I stop walking when I see a guy walk up to Liza. From his lab coat and stethoscope, I'm assuming he's one of the doctors. But he's young, probably just finished his residency. He's smiling at Liza, like really smiling, as if he's not asking her a work-related question.

"Wait," I say, holding back Dylan. "I think that guy's asking her out."

"The doctor?"

"Yeah. See how he's smiling and angling his body toward her? He's definitely asking her out."

"I think he's just talking to her."

"No, it's more than that. I can tell."

"So we're not going to go say hi?"

"Just wait a minute."

Liza nods and says something to the guy, then he walks away.

"Okay, let's go." I grab Dylan's sleeve and we walk up to Liza.

"Hey, guys," she says. "What are you doing here?"

"We're on our way back to the office. We were at the cafeteria for a meeting. So um..." I glance around to make sure he's gone. "Who's the guy?"

"Andrew. He goes by Drew. I mean, Dr. Hamilton."

"Did he ask you out?"

"Yeah. For dinner tonight."

"I told you," I say to Dylan. He just shrugs. I turn back to Liza. "Did he just start here? I've never seen him."

"Yeah, he's new. We went out last night. Tonight will be our second date."

"So you like him?"

"Yeah, but I'm a little worried about dating someone at work. I always said I wouldn't do that."

"What department does he work in?"

"Internal medicine, in the clinic on the other wing of the hospital."

"He's really hot."

"Hey!" Dylan pokes my arm.

"I'm just making a comment." I lean over to him and lower my voice. "You're way hotter."

Liza laughs. "Guys, I gotta go but it was good seeing you."

"Yeah, bye."

Dylan and I head back to the elevators. There's a long line of people waiting to get on, including some in wheelchairs.

233

"Let's take the stairs," he says.

I follow him into the empty stairwell and as soon as the door closes behind us, he grabs me around the waist and kisses me. I get that rush of adrenaline I get every time he does something like this when we're at work.

"Dylan stop," I say. "We'll get caught."

"I can't help it. I haven't kissed you since yesterday."

I kiss him back, losing any resolve I had to not do this. But then the door opens from the floor above and we break apart. From her clomping shoes, I know it's Mary. She always wears these black loafers that don't fit her feet right and make a lot of noise.

Dylan must also recognize her shoes because he loudly says, "We should ask Mary. She really knows what she's doing. We could learn a lot from her."

As we walk up the stairs, I try to hold in my laughter at his little show. We run right into Mary, who eyes us, suspiciously.

"Mary, we were just talking about you," Dylan says. "If you have some time, we'd like your input on the radio ads. We're working on those later this week."

"Certainly." She smiles at him. His compliments won her over. "I'll be back to the office in a few minutes."

"Sounds good."

She walks past us but then turns back. "You don't normally take the stairs."

How would she know that? Maybe she IS watching us.

"There was a big line at the elevator," Dylan says, "so we decided to take the stairs."

We continue up to the next floor and when we're back in the hallway, Dylan says, "That was close."

"Yeah, too close. I swear she's trying to get us fired."

"Just suck up to her. If we win her over, eventually she'll leave us alone." He smiles. "So can I come over tonight?"

"I have to work on a paper for class."

"Then I'll come over later, whenever you're done."

"Okay." I should've told him no so I can get to bed early, but I couldn't make myself do it. I want to be with Dylan.

***

The next few weeks, Dylan and I spend almost every night together. During the week we both have to do homework or study so it's usually late before he comes over. Weekends we have a little more time together but between studying for finals, all my activities, and his gigs with the band, we don't have as much time as we'd like. I'm hoping that'll change next semester. I'm dropping out of some of my campus clubs so that I'll have time for Dylan but also time to start job hunting. I'll graduate next August, which is still a ways off, but I want to start looking for jobs now to see what's out there.

"You'll call me, right?" Dylan asks as we stand by my car.

Finals are over and it's the first day of winter break. Kira and I are driving home to Michigan together.

"Of course I'll call you." I give him a hug. "I wouldn't go all that time without calling you."

"I meant from the road. I want you to check in so I know you're safe."

"I will. I promise."

"I'll give you your present when you get back."

"What is it?"

"You'll find out later."

I smile. "Now I'm dying to know."

"Then that'll be a reason for you to hurry back."

"I already want to hurry back. I'm going to miss you."

"I'll miss you too. Three weeks seems like forever." He kisses me. "Have a good time. And Merry Christmas."

"Merry Christmas."

We kiss goodbye until Kira beeps the horn.

"Okay, you guys," she yells from inside the car. "Stop kissing. We have to go."

"I'll see you soon," I say to Dylan.

My heart sinks as I get in the car, knowing I won't see him for weeks.

"You all right?" Kira asks as we're driving away.

"Yeah. It's just hard when you're used to being together all the time and then you're not."

"I know. Thanksgiving was tough when I went home for those few days, but now? Three whole weeks? It's going to seem like forever."

And it does. After just three days of being home, I'm going crazy wanting to see Dylan. We talk on the phone but it's not the same as seeing him in person.

My older sister, Leah, is home for the holidays so at least I have her and Britt to keep me busy so my mind isn't always wandering to Dylan. And I have Kira who lives just a couple miles away. I've been over to her house a few times to watch movies but her younger brothers can get really loud so we usually end up leaving and going for coffee or to the mall.

It's odd but my parents haven't fought since I got here. Britt said they didn't fight the week before either. Guess they're giving each other the silent treatment. I'm sure a fight will blow up at Christmas dinner, like it always does.

But two days later, which is Christmas day, we make it all the way through dessert without my parents even raising their voices. And they didn't fight when we opened presents this morning. Normally, my dad would yell at my mom for spending too much and my mom would yell at him for leaving wrapping paper and bows all over the floor.

As we finish our pie, Leah, Britt, and I keep looking at each other across the table like something's wrong. Why aren't our parents fighting? They always fight.

"Have you talked to Dylan yet?" my mom asks as she sips her coffee.

"Yeah, I talked to him this morning, remember? I told you how he got those goofy socks from his mom."

"Yes, that's right. And what did you get him?"

"Guitar picks. They're these special picks he really wanted."

Dylan loved my gift. He said it was the best gift he ever got.

"How about that little girl you read to?" my mom asks. "Did you get her anything?"

"Yeah, I got her a princess book. She's really into princesses."

Emily got tested a few weeks ago and it turns out she does have dyslexia. Her mom called and thanked me for suggesting Emily get tested but she should really thank Dylan's mom. I wouldn't have even suspected that was the problem if his mom hadn't brought it up.

"Okay, what's going on?" Britt asks, looking at my mom, then my dad.

My mom answers. "What do you mean?"

"Something's going on with you and Dad. You two are acting strange."

My mom sighs. "It's not the time."

"Not the time to what?" Leah asks, sounding nervous.

I feel nervous too. Something's definitely going on.

"Do you guys have something to tell us?" I ask my parents.

My mom fakes a smile. "We will tomorrow. Today is Christmas. Let's just enjoy our time together."

"Judy, just tell them," my dad says. "They know something's up and you're torturing them by making them wait."

"I'M torturing them?" She raises her voice. "It's always me, isn't it? Never you."

Here we go. Let the fight begin.

But instead, my father calmly says, "Your mother and I are getting divorced."

My sisters and I all stare at him, jaws dropped. We always knew it was possible, but after so many years of them fighting and not breaking up, we'd kind of given up on the idea that they'd ever divorce.

"You're divorcing?" Britt's eyes tear up, her lip quivering. She hates their fighting but I know she's not ready for them to divorce. Living here at home, this will mean big changes for her.

"We aren't selling the house," my mom says to Britt. "Your father is moving out but I'll stay here with you. He's getting a place across town. You can go visit him whenever you'd like."

"No!" She starts crying. "You can't break up!" She gets up and runs off to her room.

"I'll talk to her," Leah says, hurrying off to Britt's room.

I'm left there with my parents, feeling awkward, not sure what to say or what to think. Ever since they started growing apart and fighting all the time, I thought it'd be best if they divorced. But now that it's happening, I don't like it. I want them to stay together.

CHAPTER TWENTY-THREE

AMBER

My mom turns to my dad, glaring at him. "I told you we shouldn't have said anything until tomorrow."

"What difference would it make? They had to be told."

"Yes, but now you've ruined their Christmas."

"They knew this was coming. It's not a surprise."

"Still. I wanted them to have a nice Christmas." My mom covers her face with her hands and breaks down crying.

My dad sighs and gets up from the table. I assume he's going to comfort her but instead he just walks away. I guess when you're divorcing, you no longer care that the person you once loved is hurting, crying right in front of you.

"Mom." I race over to her, sitting beside her.

She hugs me. "I'm sorry, honey. I didn't want to tell you girls today. I didn't want it ruining your holiday."

"It's okay. Don't worry about it." I pull back. "When did you guys decide this?"

"A week ago. Your father had had enough so he went and found an apartment. He's been staying there all week. We just pretended he's been here in the house for Britt's sake. He'd come over early, before she woke up, so she wouldn't suspect anything. I suppose we could've told her, but she gets so excited about the holidays and we didn't want to ruin it for her. Plus we wanted to wait until all three of you were home so we could tell you together." She glances down the hall. "I need to go talk to her."

While she goes to Britt's room, I go in the kitchen and find my dad. He's cleaning up the mess from dinner, washing pots and pans.

"Need some help?" I ask.

My dad turns to me. "I wash, you dry?"

"Yeah." I stand next to him and pick up the dish towel. "So you and mom...why now?"

He shakes his head. "We just can't keep doing this. Your mother and I keep hurting each other and we can't seem to stop."

"Could you go to counseling?"

"We've been. We tried it years ago but it just didn't work."

"Oh." I didn't know they'd gone to counseling. They never told us. I take the saucepan from him and dry it. "So you wouldn't want to try again?"

He looks at me. "Honey, sometimes these things just aren't meant to be. You think they are in the beginning but then things change. People change. And you find you're no longer compatible."

"I don't understand that. If you love each other, then why can't you get through the changes together? What happened to for better or for worse?"

"Your mother and I have been stuck in the 'for worse' part for years now, and it hasn't gotten any better. That's a sign it's time to end things."

"But you love her, right?"

He sighs. "I honestly don't know anymore."

"How could you not know?" I throw the dish towel down. "She's your wife! The mother of your children!" I'm yelling now, anger and sadness rising up past the shock. "How can you not feel any kind of love for her?"

"Amber." He reaches for me but I turn away and storm down to my room. I yank my phone out and call Kira.

She picks up right away. "Merry Christmas!" she says in a cheery tone.

"It's not merry. It sucks." My breath is shaky, tears welling up in my eyes.

"Amber, what's wrong? Is it your parents? Are they fighting?"

"They're getting divorced. Apparently my dad's already moved out." I sniffle.

"You just found out?"

"Yeah, they told us on Christmas. Great timing, right? At least we finished dinner first."

"Amber, I'm so sorry. What can I do?"

"Can I come over? Would your parents mind? I know it's Christmas but—"

"Of course you can come over. My parents are watching a movie upstairs and my brothers are in the basement playing their new video games. I'm just hanging out in my room."

"I'll be there in a minute."

As I'm racing out of the house, I pass my dad and mumble, "Going to Kira's."

He doesn't try to stop me. He knows I don't want to be home right now. I'm sure my sisters don't either. Here we all thought we were having this blissful Christmas with no fighting but we should've known it was too good to be true.

Kira's waiting at the door when I get there. She gives me a hug. "Let's go in my room." We go in there and sit on her bed, facing each other. "So why now?"

"They'd just had enough." I stare down at her comforter, which is covered in pink and white hearts. Her mom let her pick it out when she was 16. Actually I'm the one who did. We went shopping together and when we saw this, Kira said it was too much pink but I loved it so I convinced her to get it. Back then, I loved anything that was pink and had hearts. I thought it was romantic. But now seeing those hearts is making feel sick.

"It makes sense," I say. "You know how much my parents fight. I just never thought they'd actually break up. And for some stupid reason, I don't want them to, even though I know it's probably for the best."

"Everyone wants their parents together. It's normal to be upset about them breaking up, even if it's for the best. It changes things and change is stressful."

"It's even worse for Britt. She'll have to live there while all these changes are going on. When she found out, she ran off to her room, crying. Leah and my mom were talking to her when I left."

"Have you told Dylan?"

"No. I'll call him later." I lean back against the headboard. "What I don't get is how they ended up at this place. My parents seemed so in love when I was a kid and now they hate each other. How does that even happen?"

"I don't know. I guess they just grew apart."

"But why? If you love someone, why do you grow apart? Why isn't love enough to keep people together?" My tone is desperate, expressing my intense need to make sense of this. Because I want to believe in love. I need to. The hopeless romantic in me needs to know that real love exists and can last, but right now, I'm doubting it. It seems fake, temporary, something we've been tricked to believe in because of romantic movies and books.

"Amber, your parents have been like this for years." Kira keeps her voice soft, cautious, not wanting to upset me even more.

"Yes, but I still believed there was a small part of them that still loved each other."

"Maybe they do, at least on some level. Just because they're getting divorced doesn't mean they don't care about each other."

"Trust me, they don't care about each other. My dad saw my mom crying at the table and he just got up and walked away. He didn't show any concern. Any emotion. He just walked away and left her there. How do you do that with someone you used to love enough to marry? To have children with? How do you even get to that point?"

She shrugs. "I really don't know. Everyone says marriage is hard and if you don't work on it, you risk falling out of love. Maybe that's what happened. They didn't work on it."

"Or maybe they didn't have time to," I say quietly.

"What do you mean?"

"Never mind." I pick up one of her pillows and hug it to my chest.

"Come on. Tell me what you meant."

"No. You'll just tell me it's not true, but I know it is. It at least contributed to it."

"What are you talking about?"

I don't respond.

"Amber, you know I won't give up until you tell me."

I sigh. "Gymnastics."

"What about it?"

"You know how much time it took. When we were younger our parents devoted their lives to gymnastics. They had no time for each other."

"That's not what led to your parents' divorce."

I huff. "See? I told you you wouldn't believe me."

"I'm just saying, their problems started a long time ago."

"Their problems started when I got really good at gymnastics and began training more. They were never home, never with each other, because one of them was always taking me to practice."

"My parents did the same thing and their marriage is fine."

"Because they found a way to get through it. My parents didn't."

"Wait." She scoots closer to me. "Is that the real reason you quit gymnastics? Because you thought it was making your parents fight?"

Instead of answering, I take a deep breath, looking down.

"You told me it was because you wanted to do other things. Be more involved in high school."

"All that was true." I look up at her. "But I also thought it would help make the fighting stop."

"But it didn't."

"No."

"So do you regret quitting?"

"Not really. I mean, I guess sometimes I do, but at the time, I really thought I was helping my family, and I think I did. When I quit gymnastics, my parents were able to spend more time with my sisters, which they needed, especially Britt. She spent most of her childhood being dragged to practice and meets, which wasn't fair to her. Anyway, it doesn't matter. It obviously didn't help enough for them to stay together."

"Did your parents explain to you guys why they were breaking up?"

"They couldn't because Britt ran off and then my mom went to talk to her. But when I was talking to my dad, he said he and my mom both changed and were no longer compatible. He acted like it wasn't a big deal but it IS a big deal. How can I ever have faith in love when I'm told it won't last? When I'm told love isn't enough? That it isn't enough to keep people together?"

"That's only true sometimes, not always. Lots of people stay together."

"And a lot of people divorce. I don't want to be one of those people, Kira."

"Meaning what? You're never going to fall in love?"

I don't want to admit to her that I feel like I'm already there. That I'm already falling in love with Dylan.

"Why bother falling in love when you know it's going to end?"

"Because being in love is part of being human. Amber, don't let this change how you feel about love and relationships. You've always believed in true love and soulmates and love stories. Don't give up on all that because of what happened to your parents."

"Why not? That stuff only exists in the movies. It's not real life."

"Sure it is. Maybe it doesn't happen to everyone but it still happens."

My phone rings. "It's my mom," I say to Kira. I answer the call. "Mom, I'm at Kira's. I'll be home later."

"Honey, come home. We need to deal with this as a family."

"There's nothing to deal with. You've made your decision. You and dad are breaking up our family." My voice cracks as I say it.

"We'll still be a family. Your father and I will do all we can to make this easier on you girls."

"It won't be easy, no matter what you do. Look what it's already done. Britt's crying in her room and I ran off to Kira's house."

"It'll take some time but we'll get through this. Something had to be done, Amber. Your father and I couldn't go on like we've been."

"Why couldn't you just try harder?"

"We did. For years. And nothing worked. Honey, come home and we'll talk about it."

"Not yet. I need to finish talking to Kira."

"Then finish up and come home. Bye, honey."

I hang up and say to Kira, "I'm supposed to go back there to talk about it. Like any of us wants to talk about this on Christmas. I don't want to talk about it at all. It's not like they're changing their minds so why bother?"

"Maybe you should just go back there for the sake of your sisters. Maybe you guys should just talk and leave your parents out of it for now. Like you said, the decision is made. Now it's about finding a way to accept it and move on."

But I don't want to accept it. Accepting it means accepting my parents no longer love each other. It means accepting the same thing could happen to me. I could fall in love, get married, have children, and somehow through all that, the love that started it all could disappear. And if that's the end result, then why bother? Why put yourself through that?

"Amber?" Kira wakes me from my thoughts.

I scoot off her bed. "I should go. I don't want to, but I can't hide out here forever, and as you said, my sisters need me." I give her a hug. "Thanks for being here."

"Always. Come over whenever you want. We could have a sleepover." She smiles. "Remember the blanket forts we used to make?"

I smile back. "Yeah, except I called them castles."

"You and your princess obsession. I somehow escaped that phase."

It's true. I was obsessed with the whole princess thing. Dreams of living in a castle, waiting for my prince to come take me away. But it was nothing more than a fairy tale. There are no princes in real life. Just guys who come into your life, say they love you, maybe even marry you, then leave you because their love for you didn't last.

On the short drive back to the house, Dylan calls.

"Merry Christmas!" he says when I answer.

"You already said that this morning." I park in the driveway and shut the car off.

"What's wrong?" I hear the concern in his voice, likely caused by my curt response.

"I'm sorry, Dylan. I didn't mean to respond like that. I'm just not feeling good right now."

"What happened?"

"My parents are getting a divorce."

"Shit. I'm sorry. When did you find out?"

"At Christmas dinner. My mom wanted to wait until tomorrow to tell us but then my dad just blurted it out."

"Where are you right now?" he asks because someone in the driveway next door just beeped their horn.

"I'm sitting in the car outside my house. I was over at Kira's and my mom called, telling me to come home. But I don't want to go in there. I don't want to talk about it, or think about it, or discuss it. I just want to pretend it isn't happening."

"Amber, I'm so sorry. I wish I was there with you. If you want, I could drive out there later this week. Or I'll leave tomorrow. Whatever you want."

"Thanks for offering but I need to spend time with my sisters. All three of us are in shock right now and we need to help each other get through this."

"So you had no idea this was coming?"

"I knew it was a possibility but I wasn't ready for it. And part of me thought it would never happen. My parents have been fighting for years, so why now? What made them take the next step and end things?"

"I don't know," he says quietly. "I'm just sorry it's happening. I wish I could do something to make this easier. To make you feel better."

He's so sweet, so caring. Even that night back in May, I got the feeling Dylan was a kind, considerate person, not just some guy trying to have sex with me. I still remember his face and the sound of his voice when he asked me if I really wanted to do it. There was genuine concern in his expression and tone, wanting to make sure I was the one making the decision, not him. And after it was over, he didn't run off, like some other guy would. Instead, he stayed there, holding me, talking to me, falling asleep with me.

"Dylan, I should go before my mom calls me again. Can we talk later?"

"Of course. Call me when you can."

"Okay, bye."

Back in the house, I find the living room is empty and the kitchen too. I check the garage and see my dad's car is gone. So he left. On Christmas. Probably went back to his apartment.

I go down to Britt's room. The door is open and my mom and sisters are all sitting on the bed. Their eyes are red, like they've been crying.

My mom gets up. "Amber." I walk over to her and she hugs me. "Come sit down."

"Mom," Britt says.

My mom lets me go and looks at Britt. "Yes, honey?"

"Can Leah, Amber, and me be alone? So we can talk?"

She nods. "Of course. I'll be in my room." She leaves, closing the door behind her.

I sit on the bed and hug both my sisters at once. "This sucks, you guys." As I say it, the tears I'd been holding back break free, which makes Leah and Britt cry and soon we're all sobbing messes, holding onto each other on the bed.

When our tears finally subside, we pull back and take some deep breaths.

"Well, now what do we do?" I ask, not knowing what else to say.

"I'm thinking of moving back home," Leah says. "To be with Britt."

I look at Leah, shocked she would even suggest that. Moving home is the absolute last thing she wants to do. When she was younger, she was always insecure, never having confidence she could do things. And now, she has a good job, her own apartment. She lives in a different city. She's finally proved to herself that she's strong and can make it on her own. She's been moving forward. Moving home would be taking a step back. A big step.

"Leah, no," I say. "Don't move home. Your life isn't here in this house anymore. You're doing great and you're happy. You can't move back."

"She's right," Britt says. "I don't want you doing this for me. I can get through this. I know I can."

"You can always call us," I tell Britt, "and if you need us to be here, we will. I promise. You tell me to be here, I'll drop everything and get in the car and start driving."

"And I'm just an hour away," Leah says. "If you want, I'll come home every weekend, or whenever you need me to."

Britt nods, her eyes tearing up again.

I hug her, then Leah. "I love you guys."

"We love you too," they say at the same time.

My sisters and I used to fight constantly, usually over sharing clothes or shoes. Those fights seem so stupid now. For one, because I'm older and more mature, but also because I love my sisters and need them in my life. I don't want to fight with them or grow apart from them. All three of us need each other, now more than ever.

Leah hops off the bed. "Let's get out of here."

"And go where?" I ask. "Nothing's open."

"Movie theaters are. So let's go. Why sit around here, moping and crying all day? We need to get out of here. And besides, we missed our Thanksgiving movie tradition." She smiles at me. "Except for Amber, who went without us and took her boyfriend."

I smile back. "That doesn't count. We didn't even stay for the movie."

"Because they wanted to hurry home so they could do it," Britt says, a smile creeping up her face.

"That's not why we left," I say, tossing a pillow at her. "We left because it was too crowded and we were stuck in the very front row."

"So what'd you guys do after you left?" Leah sits back down on the bed. "You never told us. Was Britt right? Did you guys do it?"

My face heats up. "Let's go. A movie sounds good. And let's get popcorn. The big bucket. We can each get our own."

"She totally did it," Leah says, nudging Britt.

"Totally." Britt smiles.

I didn't want to admit this to them, or talk about my love life at all, but it's getting their minds off Mom and Dad and making Britt smile, so what the hell?

"Okay, yeah, we did it," I admit. "He stayed at my place that night."

Britt's eyes widen. "Did you do it all night?"

I point at her. "You're way too young to know this stuff. Or talk about it."

"I'm 16, almost 17. My friends and I talk about this all the time. And I'm the only one who's not doing it."

"And you shouldn't," Leah says. "You're too young."

Britt rolls her eyes.

"So was that your first time with him?" Leah asks.

I never told them about my one-night stand and I'm not going to. They don't need to know.

"Yeah," I lie. "That was the first time. We didn't plan on it. It just happened." I look at Britt. "And we were careful. We used protection, which you should always do, even if you're on the pill."

"Seriously?" Britt rolls her eyes again. "Like I don't know this? They teach sex ed in like fourth grade now."

"I'm just reminding you," I tell her. "In the heat of the moment, it's easy to forget to use one. But don't. You have to be careful."

"How was it?" Leah grins. "The sex?"

"Good. And that's all I'm saying. I'm not telling you guys any more than that. It's private."

"Do you love him?" Britt asks.

I hesitate. "It's too soon to say."

"You've dated him for over a month," she says. "Wouldn't you know by now?"

I *do* know, but I'm not ready to admit it. And now, after finding out my parents are divorcing, I'm not even sure what love is. Maybe what I feel for Dylan isn't love, and if it is, I have zero faith it will last. We're too young. We haven't figured out what we want in life. We haven't known each other long enough.

I could come up with a million reasons why it can't be love that I feel for Dylan. And yet deep down, I know that it is.

CHAPTER TWENTY-FOUR

AMBER

"When I'm in love, I'll let you know," I tell them. "Now let's get out of here and go to the movies."

When we get there, we all agree romance movies of any kind are banned. The last thing we want to do is watch a story about some happy couple, then go home to parents who hate each other. But what I didn't realize until today is that it's surprisingly hard to find movies that don't involve some kind of love story. Action films, sci-fi, comedies. Almost all genres of movies include a love story. That left us choosing a cartoon, but then halfway through the movie the damn duck ends up falling in love. So you can't even escape love in a cartoon!

Later that night, I call Dylan. He left me messages all day but I didn't want to call him back when I was in a bad mood and feeling down on love. Unfortunately, I still feel that way but I can't avoid him forever.

"Hey," I say when he answers. "I'm sorry I took so long to get back to you."

"Don't worry about it. I know you got a lot going on. So how are you doing?"

"Not great. My dad took off earlier today and hasn't come back. I guess he's staying at his apartment. My sisters and I went to a movie and when we got home my mom was asleep in her room. I think she's depressed. We all are."

"God, I'm so sorry. You sure you don't want me to drive out there?"

"Dylan, that's sweet, but no. I need to spend time with my sisters. Britt's really struggling. I need to give her all my attention right now."

"I understand." He pauses. "I miss you."

"I miss you too."

I miss him so much it scares me. For years, I wanted to feel this way. To feel this deep connection with someone and want to be with him all the time. But now? I don't know what I want. I definitely don't want to go through what my mom is going through right now. Alone and sad and locked away in her room, probably crying herself to sleep. And my dad? Who knows what he's doing or how he's feeling. He hides his emotions but I know he, too, must be suffering.

When I was younger, I remember my dad coming home with little gifts for my mom. Sometimes it was flowers. Sometimes a box of candy. Once it was a purse that she really wanted but didn't buy because she thought it was too expensive. My dad surprised her with it for no reason at all. It wasn't a birthday or anniversary. He just wanted to make her happy. So how do they go from that to where they are now?

I could imagine Dylan doing all those things for me. Bringing me flowers and candy and buying me special gifts. In fact, he's already sent me flowers, several times, saying it was one of his romantic gestures. And he still writes me letters. Sweet, funny, beautiful letters that I keep tucked away in a shoebox and read over and over again.

He hasn't said it yet, but I think he loves me. Just like I love him. That should make me happy but instead it makes me panicked, thinking this happy state we're in now is the peak of our relationship and will soon begin a slow gradual decline until we fall out of love. Or maybe the decline won't begin right away. Maybe we'll keep dating and eventually move in together and then it will happen, and it'll happen so gradually that we won't even recognize it and be able to stop it.

I feel like that's what happened with my parents. Their love for each other just gradually went away without them even noticing. And now it's gone. Completely gone.

I hear Dylan's voice again. "Do you want to talk about this or are you sick of it? Because we can talk about something else."

"Something else. Please."

He knows me so well. He knows when I'm happy or sad or stressed or tired and he reacts accordingly, knowing what I need. It's like he could sense I was all talked out when it came to my parents and that I needed a break.

"So after Christmas dinner," Dylan says, "I suggested we go to a movie. Gramps didn't want to go but we made him. My mom insisted we see a family movie because she doesn't like my brother hearing curse words even though he hears them all the time at school. Anyway, we ended up seeing a cartoon."

I laugh. "We saw that one too. The one with the duck?"

"Yeah. The duck who fell in love with the rabbit. Cross-species romance. Very taboo in the animal kingdom. I told my mom that was way worse than a few curse words."

I laugh again. Only Dylan could make me laugh when I'm feeling so sad and depressed.

"And then," he continues, "near the end of the movie, Gramps had a coughing fit. He wouldn't stop so we had to get up and leave. My mom was freaking out, thinking Gramps was really sick or choking or something, but then we found out he was sucking on an atomic fireball."

"The candy?"

"Yeah, my brother got some in his Christmas stocking. He loves those things. Anyway, Gramps thought they were just cherry-flavored candies so he stuck a few in his pocket and started eating one during the show. It was so hot he had to spit it out but the fiery aftereffects had him coughing so hard he couldn't stop."

"He's never eaten a fireball?"

"Guess not. He's diabetic so he's not supposed to have candy but he always cheats and steals candy from people at the

253

retirement home. Anyway, going back to the movie, the coughing isn't even the worst part."

"What else happened?"

"Gramps was coughing so hard, he couldn't control his bodily functions."

"He wet his pants?"

"No. He farted, each time he coughed. God, it was so embarrassing. He was letting them rip as we were leaving the theater and everyone was staring at us."

Imagining this has me laughing so hard my stomach hurts. "Oh my God, that's hilarious."

"Not for the poor people he had to walk in front of to get out of our aisle. They got it right in the face."

"Please, stop," I say as I laugh. "I'm getting a side cramp from laughing so hard."

"Just a typical outing with the Mickelson family."

"That's classic. I love your family."

"Well, if you ever become one of us, at least now you'll know what to expect. You can't say I didn't warn you."

Become one of us? What is he saying? That we might get married someday? That's the only way I'd ever be part of his family.

I'm not ready to even think about marriage, especially now. In fact, I'm thinking I might never get married. What's the point? It only leads to heartache and disappointment and divorce.

"Dylan, I should go. It's late and I'm tired. Can I call you tomorrow?"

"You can call me whenever you want, day or night. You know that."

"Okay, then I'll talk to you tomorrow. Have a good night."

"Yeah, goodnight."

My tone turned cold at the end there. I didn't mean for it too but I started panicking when he hinted at marriage. Maybe I need to slow this down. Dylan and I are getting too serious, too fast. Even if I love him, I'm not ready to make any kind of commitment, especially after today, witnessing the end of my parents' marriage. Right now I feel like I may never be able to commit to anyone, which means I owe it to Dylan to at least slow things down until I can figure out what I want.

***

Over the next few days, my sisters and I busy ourselves with movies and shopping, anything to get us out of the house. Now that we know about the divorce, my dad's been packing up his stuff and my sisters and I don't want to be there to witness it. He has this week off, but my mom had to work, or maybe she chose to so she wouldn't have to be at home.

I've been talking to Dylan every day. It's the highlight of my day. He always finds a way to make me laugh. And he's been keeping me updated on the hospital fundraiser, which was last night. Since he's there in town, he kept working on it this week while I was gone. I'm calling him now to see how it went.

"Hey, it's me," I say when he answers. It's noon on Sunday and I wasn't sure if he'd be awake yet. I assumed he had a late night helping clean up after the event.

"Hey, you." I hear the smile in his voice. "How's it going?"

"The same. Not much new here. So how was the event last night?"

"Great! They raised a lot of money on the silent auction. I don't remember the exact amount but it was more than they thought they'd get."

"Did you dance?" I ask kiddingly, knowing he wouldn't dance without me there.

"And who would I dance with? My girlfriend's in Michigan."

"You still could've danced with someone. Like maybe Mary?"

He laughs. "Yeah, that'll be the day. She'd probably break my foot with those big clumpy shoes she wears."

"Did you see her there?"

"Yeah, but she didn't talk to me. But I talked to one of the former interns who was there. When I asked him about Mary,

255

he told me she's like that with everyone. She's just a cranky old lady who can't mind her own business."

"So it's not just us. That's good to know."

"Liza was there. She was with that doctor."

"Oh yeah? Before I left, she told me he'd asked her to the event but she hadn't agreed to it yet."

"I wish you'd been there. I know you couldn't, but I still missed having you with me. You still heading home next Sunday?"

"Yeah, unless Britt decides she needs me to stay longer."

"How's she doing?"

"About the same. I think she'll feel better once she's back in school with her friends. That'll help take her mind off of things."

"And how are *you* doing?" He asks because I've avoided talking about the divorce. I change the subject whenever the topic comes up.

"I'm doing okay."

"Amber, you know you can talk to me so why won't you?"

"I'm just not ready to. I never thought I'd feel this way if they broke up. I never thought I'd feel this sad. I always thought I'd be relieved, maybe even happy, because I'd no longer have to listen to them fight. But now it's almost worse because my parents won't even talk to each other. They walk past each other and won't even look at each other."

"I guess that's just their way of dealing with it."

"I guess. It's just weird." I sigh. "I don't want to talk about it. It's depressing. Talk about something else. Any new Grandpa stories?"

"He stole a candy bar at the retirement home. They called my dad. Made him come there and talk to the administrator about Gramps' candy theft problem. My dad said it was like he was being called into the principal's office. He said he got lectured to keep his father in line."

I laugh. "I don't think that's possible. Gramps seems like a free spirit."

"He is. He doesn't listen to anyone. Never has."

Dylan continues to tell me more stories and we stay on the phone for an hour. Afterward, I go to the kitchen to get a drink and find my mom sitting at the table with her laptop.

"What are you doing?" I ask, sitting across from her.

"Just looking some things up." She closes her laptop. "So how are you feeling?"

I shrug. "Not great, but I'm more worried about you. How are *you* feeling?"

"I'm not feeling much of anything, other than sadness for you girls. I've known this was coming so I've already been through the sadness and anger and loss and everything else you feel when a marriage ends. In some ways I'm relieved it's ending because I'm so tired of fighting with your father."

I look down, then back up at my mom. "Can I ask you something? And I really need an honest answer."

"Go ahead."

"What happened to you and Dad? How did you get to this point?"

"We grew apart. Became different people."

"But you loved each other. Can't love survive those things?"

"Not always. People change and sometimes that means they fall out of love."

"How can you fall out of love? That doesn't even make sense to me. If you're really in love, how does it just go away? How do you just turn your feelings off like that?"

"It doesn't happen all at once. It happens gradually, over time. Sometimes you don't even notice it's happened until it's too late."

I hesitate, my eyes dropping to the table. "Did I help cause it?"

My mom touches my arm. "Honey, how could you possibly cause it?"

"Because of gymnastics." My eyes lift to hers. "When I got really good, it took up all your time. And Dad's. And it was around that time that you guys started fighting."

"Amber, that had nothing to do with you. Did you really think it did?"

I nod and quietly say, "It's one of the reasons I quit."

"Oh, honey." She squeezes my hand. "I wish you'd talked to me before you did that. Your father and I thought you were just tired of it. You told us it was taking up too much of your time."

"It did, but it was also taking time from you and Dad. I thought maybe that's why you guys grew apart."

She sighs. "No. That wasn't it."

"Then what was it?"

"It was a lot of things. There wasn't a specific event that started it. Like I said, it was gradual. Your father and I both started working more. Our jobs became more demanding and we got tired and didn't have the time or energy to talk at night or go on dates or do anything other than sleep. Eventually we lost the connection we once had and started getting on each other's nerves. We were stressed and taking it out on each other, and once it started, it just kept getting worse. We got angry and resentful, and when that happens, it's hard to go back to a loving relationship."

"But you loved him a long time ago, right? I mean, when you first got married?"

She smiles. "I was so in love I couldn't think straight. I didn't know love like that existed until I met him."

"Was it love at first sight?" I ask, because I want to know if such a thing even exists.

"Your father said it was," she says with a smile, "but I'm not sure if I believe him."

"You don't believe in love at first sight?"

"Not really. I believe you can instantly feel something for someone, a familiarity, a connection. But I don't think it's love."

So maybe what Dylan and I felt last May wasn't love. Although we've never admitted it, I know we both felt like it might be. But it was probably like my mom said. A connection. A familiarity. Not love.

"But it wasn't long before we fell in love," she says. "And once we did, we spent every minute together." A distant, longing look comes over her face, as if she's wishing she were back in that time. Back when she loved my father. "We couldn't stand to be apart. I loved everything about him. And when we got married, I was so happy. It was a dream come true. I found my prince and we were going to live happily ever after." The longing look is replaced by sadness, regret. "And then life happened and we grew apart." She rubs my hand. "But at least we have you girls."

Her prince. Her happily ever after. She sounds just like me. Just last week, before I found out about the divorce, I was hoping Dylan was my prince and that maybe we'd have a happily ever after. But there's no such thing. If there were, my parents wouldn't have fallen out of love and ended up at the place they're at now.

I stand up. "I'm going to go to my room."

"You all right?" my mom asks.

"Yeah, I'm just tired."

"Okay, honey." She opens her laptop. "Anytime you want to talk, I'm here."

Back in my room, Kira calls. "Hey, can I come over?"

"Sure. Like right now?"

"Yeah. My brothers are driving me crazy. I'll be over in a minute."

When she arrives, she plops down on the chair next to my desk. "I love my brothers but I've about reached my limit with them. It's time to go back to school."

"I know what you mean. Once you go away to college, it's hard to go back and live at home. And the longer you're away, the harder it gets."

"Especially when you have a boyfriend." She sighs. "God, I miss Austin so much. I'm counting the days until I can see him again. I'm sure you feel the same way about Dylan."

I'm quiet as I pretend to smooth the comforter on my bed.

"Amber." Kira waits until I look at her. "You miss Dylan, right?"

"Yeah. Of course." I fake a smile.

She sits up straight. "What's going on? Did you guys have a fight?"

"No. Everything's great."

"Then what's the problem?"

"There's no problem. We're fine."

"Amber, I can tell when you're lying. So fess up."

I scoot to the end of the bed, dangling my feet off the side. "There's no such thing as fairy tales."

She looks confused. "Um, yeah. I kind of already knew that. What are you getting at?"

"There's no happily ever afters either." I circle my foot on the floor, my eyes following the movement. "And love is a joke. A cruel stupid joke meant to trick people into buying flowers and candy and engagement rings."

"Amber, just because your parents are divorcing doesn't mean love doesn't exist. I know you're upset but you've gotta stop thinking that way. It's not you. You're the most romantic person I know, with your love of old-fashioned romance. Romantic movies. Dating shows. Love letters. Love songs."

"Yeah, and it's shit. It's all lies. Love is temporary and when it goes away, you're left with a broken heart, anger, and resentment."

"That only happens to *some* people. Not everyone. *My* parents aren't like that. They still love each other."

I look at her. "When's the last time your parents went on a date? Or held hands? Or did something nice for each other?"

She shrugs. "Okay, fine, so they're not super romantic but they still love each other. If they didn't, they wouldn't be together."

"I'm not trying to pick on your parents. I'm just saying that love fades and eventually goes away. So why bother?"

"What are you saying? You're breaking up with Dylan?"

"Maybe," I mutter, my gaze falling to the floor.

"No." She gets up and stands in front of me. "You're not doing that, Amber. I won't let you. You and Dylan are great together. I'd even go so far as to say you two are in love, at least that's how it looks when I see you guys together. You're not giving that up just because you're upset about your parents."

"Why would I continue something that I know isn't going to end well?"

"You don't know how it's going to end, or if it'll end at all. For all you know, you could end up marrying him."

"And then years later, after a house and a couple kids, we'll decide we're no longer in love and get divorced. Or we'll stay together but live in a loveless marriage."

"If you're really thinking that way, then you need to get out of this house. Your parents are turning you into someone I don't even recognize. The Amber I know would never sound that hopeless. You've always been positive. The cheerleader. Always looking on the bright side."

"Yeah, well, when it comes to love, the bright side only lasts so long before it dims and eventually burns out."

"Amber, don't be like this." Kira sits down beside me. "And don't take your anger with your parents out on Dylan. He didn't do anything wrong. He's been a great boyfriend the entire time you guys have been dating." She goes to my desk and picks up an envelope. "And he's still writing you letters." She holds it up. "He writes you LETTERS, Amber. You know how much he must love you to keep doing that? Nobody writes letters, especially guys."

"I know," I say, feeling guilty at the thought of breaking up with him. "But I don't know if I can keep doing this." I close my eyes, then open them and look at her. "I love Dylan. I haven't told him that yet but I do. I love him, and I want us to keep dating, but right now, I feel like I can't be in a relationship. Like I shouldn't be because I'm not a hundred percent in. And that's not fair to Dylan."

Kira sets the letter down. "If you love him, you're not giving him up. I'm not even letting you consider it."

"It's not like this is going to last. We're too young and we have no idea what we're going to do with our lives."

"So figure it out together. That's what Austin and I are doing."

"You guys aren't planning the future."

"We don't have any definite plans but we talk about it. We love each other so we'll do what it takes to be together. You and Dylan need to do the same."

"I'm just not there yet."

"Were you there before you found out about your parents?"

"Yes, but that's when I was letting my dreamy romantic side take over. Dylan was my prince and we were going to live happily ever after. And you know what's weird? I was talking to my mom earlier and she said when she met my dad she thought the same thing. That my dad was her prince and they'd live happily ever after. And look what happened." I throw my hands up. "After years of being married, she eventually grew apart from my dad and they started fighting all the time. It's proof that the same thing could happen to me."

"You're overreacting. Just because it happened to your mom doesn't mean it'll happen to you."

It sounds logical but I find it hard to believe, especially when I think about how similar I am to my mom. I could easily see myself repeating her mistakes.

Kira glances up at the bulletin board I have over my desk. It's covered in photos from our childhood and other stuff I've collected over the years.

"I can't believe you still have that," she says, pointing to the remnants of a red balloon.

I shrug. "Guess I should throw it out. I don't need to keep it."

The balloon was from a summer trip to Lake Michigan back when I was a kid. We were on the beach and I saw this balloon coming right at me. I caught it and could tell there was something inside it. My dad popped the balloon for me and inside was a note written in kid handwriting. It was from a boy and said that whoever found the note would be his girl, if in fact a girl happened to find the note. If a boy found it, he was instructed to throw it out. Those weren't the exact words but that was the basic idea.

"Remember the day you found it?" Kira laughs. "You called me and told me all about it. Then when you got back to town, you ran to my house and showed me. Then you made me come here to your room so you could try on dresses. You had to find the perfect one."

I laugh. "I had to be prepared in case he showed up. Which he never did. Another fairy tale destroyed."

She shakes her head. "It wasn't a fairy tale. It was just a note. Do you still have it?"

"Yeah, it's in my jewelry box back at the apartment."

"That's sweet that you kept it. You shouldn't ever throw it away." Kira's phone dings and she checks it. "Crap. I totally forgot I have to take my brother to hockey practice." She gets up. "Sorry. I'll drop him off and come right back."

"Okay."

She races off. I go over to my desk and pick up Dylan's letter and take it back to my bed. I got it yesterday but didn't open it. I was saving it for today, because yesterday my dad was here fighting with my mom and I wasn't in the mood to read a romantic letter from Dylan. I'm still not in a romantic mood but I'm dying to read his letter. I love his letters.

My Dearest Amber,

Oh, how I've missed you since you've been away. My days just aren't the same without your beautiful smile and those sparkling blue eyes. I long to hold you in my arms again and dance the night away.

'Dance the night away' is code for sex, in case anyone ever finds and reads our letters, like my mom.

The letter continues. *When we're finally reunited, we shall dance for hours. Days! Weeks! Until our bodies collapse from exhaustion. And then we'll replenish with pizza from Patty's Pizza Palace, devouring it in our favorite booth, the booth where our friendship blossomed into what it is now. But until then, I shall await your return.*

Love, Dylan

I laugh because it's one of his overdramatic letters that I always find humorous. Sometimes he's more serious in his letters, but he went with humor for this one because he knows I could use a laugh.

What am I going to do with him? I love him. Want to be with him. But I'm afraid of what's to come.

Love doesn't last. My parents are proof of that. And if love doesn't last, then why keep pursuing it?

CHAPTER TWENTY-FIVE

DYLAN

Amber is coming back to Chicago today. She's been gone for three weeks but it feels more like three months. After all that time apart we need some couple time so I asked Austin if he and Kira could stay at his place tonight so Amber and I could have the apartment. I didn't want us staying at my house because Van has a new girl and she's over there all the time.

"Welcome home," I say as Amber gets out of her car. I'm in the parking lot of her apartment. I wanted to surprise her. Austin texted me when Amber dropped off Kira at his place so I'd know when Amber would be here.

"Dylan!" Her face lights up and she runs to me.

I hug her, lifting her off the ground and kissing her. "You miss me?" I smile as I set her down.

She answers by hugging me, her face pressed against my chest.

"Guess that's a yes." I kiss her head. "I missed you too." I pull away. "Let's go inside and I'll show you how much."

"I just need to grab my stuff." She goes around to the back of her car and pops the trunk.

"I got it." I take her suitcases and we walk to the door. I can't stop looking at her. She's so damn beautiful. Even with her hair in a messy ponytail and no makeup, she's beautiful.

"God, I feel like a mess," she says when we get inside. "I need to shower quick and change clothes."

"A shower sounds good," I say, setting her suitcases down.

She smiles. "You look pretty clean to me." Her arms go around my neck and she leans in, taking a deep inhale. I wore the cologne she loves. "You smell really good."

I lift her face up to mine. "I'm still dirty, at least my mind is, thinking about you and all the things I want to do to you." I press my warm lips to hers, then breathe over her mouth. "I've missed you so fucking much."

"I missed you too," she whispers, her eyes closed, lips parted.

I kiss her, slow and deep, and listen as she moans, the sound and the feel of her making me instantly hard, wanting her, needing her.

"Let's go," I say, leading her to the bedroom.

"But the shower," she says.

"Later. Right now I want you in bed." I want to feel her, touch her, kiss her all over, and I can't do that as easily in the shower. We'll do that later. We have all night.

"Dylan!" she cries out as she comes, her hands digging into my shoulders, her legs tightening around me. It only took a few minutes before she got there but it took everything in me to hold myself back. I was ready to come the moment I was inside her. That's how much I wanted her, how much I missed her.

"Fuck," I groan as my release hits me, my body shuddering from the force. It's always so intense with her, so powerful, unlike anything I've felt with anyone else.

After a moment of rest, I kiss her and feel her smile against my lips, her eyes still closed.

"I've missed that," she sighs.

"Which is why we're going to do it again." I kiss her neck. "Let's get in the shower."

"Let's just stay here a minute."

I hold her in my arms, gazing at the smile that's still on her face. I'm smiling too, having her here, back with me. I've missed her as my girlfriend but I've also missed her as my friend. She's become the person I go to when I need to talk or just want to hang out. Austin and Van are still there but I see them less now that I have Amber. And Austin is always with Kira.

"How was the trip?" I ask, running my hand up and down her back.

"Good. Kira and I blasted the radio and sang the whole way. I'm surprised I have a voice left."

"I didn't know you were a singer."

"I'm not. I'm horrible. I only do it when the radio's too loud for anyone to hear."

"Sing something for me."

I laugh. "No way. Never. You'd hear one verse and be out of here so fast."

"Sorry, but not even your supposedly bad singing would send me away. I want to be with you, no matter what." I kiss her forehead.

Her body tightens and I hear her swallow.

"Amber, is something wrong?"

"No." Her body relaxes again. "Just the thought of you hearing me sing made me cringe. I'm so bad."

"Speaking of singing, I still need to give you your gift."

"Is it a song?"

"Yeah, but I need to finish one last thing before you hear it."

"Are you going to play it at the bar next week?"

Vandyl's playing next Saturday at a bar downtown. It's a big deal because the bar is really popular and does a lot of promos on the radio. They're already promoting the concert next week.

"It's not ready to perform," I tell her. "Besides, I'm not sure I want to share it with anyone but you."

"Dylan, if you wrote it you should play it. You're really good at writing songs. Look how much people love *One Night*. People go to your concerts just to hear that song."

267

"That song's only good because of the person who inspired me to write it. If it hadn't been about you, it wouldn't be any good."

"That's not true. It'd still be good. You're a great songwriter."

I tickle her side. "How would you know? You've never heard any of my other songs."

She laughs and squirms from my tickling. "Then let me hear your other songs. Sing one right now."

Reaching around her waist, I lift her on top of me and look at her face, into those bright blue eyes. "I never finished them. *One Night* is the only song I ever finished and that's only because it came to me so easily." I kiss her. "You're my inspiration. As long as I'm with you, I have a feeling I'll be writing a lot more songs."

Her smile falls and her body tightens like it did earlier. Why does she keep doing that? Is it something I said?

Before I can ask her what's wrong, she pushes off me and gets up from the bed, standing beside it. "Shower time."

"That's it? I thought you wanted to lay here."

"I did, but now I want to shower." She turns around, her back to me, eyeing me over her shoulder. "You gonna join me or not?" she teases.

My eyes go to her perfect, round ass, then up the curve of her back. I move to the edge of the bed, sitting up, my hands landing on her narrow waist, then sliding down, following the lines of her curves. I kiss her lower back, my hands gripping her hips.

"Dylan," she whispers. "The shower."

"There's no rush," I tell her. "Just let me be with you."

She gets back in bed and I touch her, kiss her, make love to her. Because that's what it is. Love. I love Amber but I'm afraid to tell her. I've thought of writing it in a letter but I'd rather say it in person, see her reaction, and explain why I love her in case she doesn't believe me.

I'm just not ready to say it yet. It'll be the first time I've ever said it to a girl so it's a huge step, and I'm worried she may not feel the same way.

That night, as we lie in bed, I think about what it'd be like to have a future with Amber. Having her gone for weeks made me realize how much I miss her when she's not around. How much I'd miss her if we broke up and I never saw her again. That got me thinking about the future and I've been thinking about it ever since. My mind keeps telling me it's too soon to think about that but my heart keeps coming back to it. It knows what it wants and it wants Amber. But being with her means making some big decisions. Decisions that have to be made soon.

It's already January and in a few short months I'll be graduating. I have to figure out where I'll live and what I'll do for a job. I'd planned to leave Chicago and go wherever a job takes me, but doing that means saying goodbye to Amber, maybe for good. Long-distance relationships rarely work, and when she graduates next summer, she may not want to move to wherever I end up.

That leaves me wondering if I should just tell her how I feel. If I should tell her how much I love her and want to be with her. I've already hinted at having a future with her, several times, but every time I do, she gets quiet or changes the subject so I'm taking that to mean she doesn't feel the same way, or she's not ready to admit it.

So I guess for now, I'll keep quiet and maybe drop some more hints in the days and weeks ahead.

Unfortunately, that becomes hard to do because her schedule doesn't allow me to see her, or even talk to her. Monday morning when I call her before class she tells me she's too busy to talk, and I don't see her at the hospital because this semester, we'll only be working together for a couple hours on Friday mornings.

Monday night when I tell her I'm stopping over, she tells me I can't because she has some emergency project to work on.

I was hoping to spend the night with her but she turned me down, saying she needed to be up early the next morning.

I was thinking maybe she was avoiding me because I did or said something to make her mad, but she insisted she's just busy and that we'll see each other later in the week.

The next few days, I give her some space so she can catch up on all the things she needs to do. She told me she always gets stressed at the beginning of a new semester so I'm hoping that's all this is and she isn't purposely distancing herself from me. I don't know why she would. Sunday was great and nothing has happened since then that would give her reason to act differently.

By Thursday, I start to get concerned because the night before, she wouldn't talk to me for more than a few minutes, saying she had to study for a test she had the next morning. Normally, that wouldn't bother me but she sounded strange on the phone. Her voice was rushed and a little shaky. I asked her what was wrong and she said nothing, but I knew she was lying. I pushed her to tell me but she still wouldn't open up so I told her I was coming over but she told me not to because she really had to study.

This morning she texted me that she has to work at the restaurant during lunch. She fills in whenever they need her and today one of the waitresses was out sick so they called Amber. Desperate to see her, I decide to go there for lunch. I was already downtown to meet with the bar manager about Saturday night's concert and the restaurant where Amber works is just a few blocks away.

When I get there, I'm seated by a girl about my age with sleek dark hair and olive skin.

"I love your voice," she says, handing me a menu as she smiles at me. So she's a fan of the band. That explains why she's acting this way. She's been flirting with me since I walked in, her body brushing against mine as we weaved through the restaurant to my table.

"Thanks," I tell her, opening the menu.

"I heard you're playing on Saturday. It's been all over the radio."

"Yeah, it's kind of a big deal. We've never played there before." I glance up at her and see her still smiling, looking like she might ask me out. I know that look because I get it all the time from fans wanting to date the lead singer of Vandyl.

"So um..." She bites her lip. "Would you maybe want to get coffee some time?"

I look around and still don't see Amber. Maybe she didn't have to work after all. Maybe the other waitress showed up for her shift.

"Do you know if Amber's working?" I ask.

"Um, yeah, why? Are you guys friends?"

"I'm her boyfriend. I was hoping to surprise her. Is this one of her tables?"

"You're dating Amber?" She sounds shocked. Does Amber never talk about me?

"Yeah, we've been dating for months."

"Are you serious?" She looks behind her, which is where my eyes are because I just spotted Amber coming out of the kitchen.

The girl waves at her, getting her attention. Amber glances at the table and sees me and immediately smiles. It's the smile she only uses with me and I suddenly feel relieved, setting aside my suspicions that something was wrong between us. If there was, she wouldn't smile that way.

She's in her uniform, a tight black skirt and white button-up, her hair down and straight. She looks gorgeous and I notice all the male customers checking her out. All older businessmen, probably married with kids, yet still staring at the waitress. My girlfriend.

She comes up to the table. "Dylan, what are you doing here?"

"I came to see you." I get up and kiss her cheek, not wanting to give her a real kiss at work and risk getting her in trouble. "I had to come downtown to meet with the bar

271

manager. The place is just down the street so I thought I'd stop by to see you and have lunch."

Hostess girl hasn't left and says to Amber, "You didn't tell me you were dating a celebrity!"

"I talk about Dylan all the time," Amber says.

"Yeah, but you didn't say it was THAT Dylan, the lead singer of Vandyl."

She shrugs. "I guess I just didn't think to mention it."

"Are you crazy?" The girl turns to Amber. "If I were dating him, that'd be the first thing I'd tell people. You know how many girls want to date him?"

"I try not to think about that," she says, looking at me. "So did you check out the menu? I should get your order in. We're really busy. It might take a while."

"Oh, shit," the hostess says. "I've got people waiting." She hurries back to the hostess stand.

Amber motions to her. "That was Angela if she didn't already tell you. She's one of your biggest fans."

"Why didn't you tell her about me?"

"Because I don't like people thinking I'm only dating you because you're in the band." She gets her order pad out. "Did you decide what you want?"

Just like that, she turns business-like, as if I'm just some random customer.

"What's going on?" I ask.

"What do you mean?"

"Why are you acting like this?"

"Like what?" She checks behind her, then turns back to me. "Dylan, I don't have time to talk. All my tables are full and I'm already behind."

"Then I'm coming over tonight so we can talk."

"You can't. I have to work on a paper."

"So now it's a paper?" I sound angry. It's because I'm tired of this. I'm tired of her avoiding me and not telling me why.

"What's that supposed to mean?" she asks, also sounding angry.

"You've been giving me excuses all week. You won't even let me stay over. Why won't you let me see you?"

"I have a lot going on, okay? I can't spend every minute with you." She glances back at her other tables. "Are you going to order or not? I'm gonna get in trouble if I stand here all day."

"Just forget it." I drop my menu on the table and get up and leave. When I'm at the door, I look back and see that Amber's gone, probably back in the kitchen.

What the hell just happened? Was that our first fight? But why did we even have it? I went there to see her and she seemed happy to see me but then she just changed, acting like I wasn't her boyfriend but just some random guy who came in for lunch.

And she never wants to see me anymore, or even talk to me on the phone. Something is making her this way but she won't tell me what it is. I have to find out. I don't want this getting out of hand and leading to us breaking up.

I'm not losing her. I went all those months without her, thinking I'd lost her, and I did, but this time that's not going to happen. We have something good here and I'm not letting it go.

CHAPTER TWENTY-SIX

AMBER

It's Thursday night and I should be studying but instead I'm sitting on the couch watching TV because I can't study when my mind keeps wandering to Dylan. I hurt him today at lunch but I didn't mean to. He surprised me and I didn't know what to do. I've been trying to avoid him all week to give myself time to think about how, or if, we move forward.

On Sunday, I was ready to be all in, wanting a future with him. I loved that he showed up and surprised me at my apartment. I'd missed him, and when I saw him I couldn't believe how happy I felt. It proved to me how much I love him, and made me want to forget all my doubts about love and just be with him.

Then Monday came and my mom called and told me she'd hired a divorce attorney. My dad filed the papers, and according to my mom, he's trying to make her sell the house and move someplace smaller since it's only her and Britt living there. That made my mom even more angry with my dad and she spent a half hour telling me how much she hates him and doesn't know why she ever married him.

I didn't want to listen to her go on and on but I felt like she needed to get it out so I just waited until she was done. But listening to her talk that way about my dad, the man she used to love, really bothered me. I still don't understand how a relationship gets to that point, but knowing it can made me panic about my relationship with Dylan. So when he called me later and asked if he could come over, I made up an excuse for why he couldn't. I needed time to think about our relationship and where it was going.

And now, four days later, I'm still not sure what to do. When I saw Dylan at lunch, I felt that burst of happiness I feel every time I see him. But then I remembered that my mom used to feel the same way about my dad and I wondered if I'm just setting myself up for heartbreak. With my past relationships, I've never worried about that because I didn't love the guy. But I love Dylan, and I love the feelings that come with loving him. The happiness. The joy. The excitement. But if it's all just going to go away someday then why am I doing this?

There's a knock on the door.

"I'll get it," Kira says from the kitchen while I remain on the couch. "Dylan," I hear her say.

Shit. What is he doing here? I'm not ready to see him. I don't know what to say to him.

"Is Amber here?" he asks.

"Yeah, she's right over there," Kira says.

Traitor. She knows I'm avoiding him.

I sit up and see him coming over. "Hey, Dylan."

"Hey." He has a serious look on his face as he comes over and sits on the chair next to the couch. "Thought you were working on a paper."

"I was, but I wasn't getting very far so I thought I'd take a break."

"And you couldn't call me during this break?"

"Um, guys," Kira says from behind us. "I'm just gonna walk down to the corner and get a coffee. I'll be back later."

"You don't have to go," I tell her.

She eyes Dylan and me. "I really need a latte. See ya." She gets her coat and hurries out of the apartment.

"I'm sorry I didn't call you," I say to Dylan.

"You haven't called me all week. What's going on?"

"I've just been busy."

"You were busy before winter break and you still found time to call me. So what is it? Did I do something wrong?"

"No." I pull my feet up under me on the couch. "I just need time to think."

"Think about what?"

"Us."

"What about us?"

My eyes shift to the floor. "I need to figure out what we're doing and if we should...if we should continue."

"Okay, hold on." He gets up from the chair and sits beside me. He lifts my chin up so I'm forced to look at him. "Are you breaking up with me?"

"I...I don't know."

"What the hell?" His hand drops from my face. "Is this because of what happened at lunch? Are you mad at me for showing up there without telling you?"

"No. It's not that. I'm just confused. I don't know what I want right now."

"I thought you wanted *this*. Us. I thought things were going well."

"They are, but...who knows what will happen later?"

"*Later?* What are you talking about?"

"You're graduating in a few months. You'll take a job. Move away. And then what? We'll break up, so why are we doing this?"

I decide to use the future job excuse for why this will never work. It's a valid excuse and definitely something to be considered.

"I don't have a job and I don't know when I'll get one or where it'll be. And even if it ends up being out of town, that doesn't mean we'll break up."

"But there's a good chance we will. I'm just being realistic here."

"Well stop being realistic and think with your heart. Do you want to be with me or not?"

I don't answer.

"Amber, do you want to be with me or not?"

I still don't answer.

"Fuck," he mutters under his breath. "You don't want to be with me." He sounds so hurt it breaks my heart. "Why didn't you tell me this sooner?" He rubs his scruffy jaw. "Is this why you've been avoiding me all week? I don't understand. Sunday was great, and now you won't even talk to me? What happened? You just decided you don't like me?"

"No! Of course I like you!" I raise my voice, my emotion taking over. "That's not it."

"Then what is it? Is it because—"

"It's because I love you, dammit!" My hand flies over my mouth as I realize what I just said.

Dylan's stunned, his face a mix of shock and confusion. "You love me?"

All I can do is nod.

"You love me," he mutters to himself, like he can't believe it. And then he chuckles.

I swat his arm. "Why the hell are you laughing?"

"Because I was afraid to say this, thinking you'd tell me it was too soon and freak out and maybe even break up with me."

"What are you talking about? What were you afraid to say?"

He looks me in the eye. "That I love you." He picks up my hand and holds it. "That I haven't been able to stop thinking about you since the night we met. That I've never wanted anyone this much." He smiles. "But basically, that I love you."

He loves me. And I love him. So now what do I do? Apparently panic because that's what's happening.

I yank my hand from his and jump up from the couch. "I can't do this."

"Do what?"

"Be with you. It just...it just won't work."

His brows draw together in confusion. "Why not?"

"Because I love you!" I toss my hands up in frustration. "Weren't you listening?"

He laughs because my reasoning sounds ridiculous but I'm not kidding around.

"Amber, that's the craziest thing I've ever heard. You can't be with me because you love me?"

"Yes. And I know you don't understand it but I can't explain it."

"Well, you're gonna have to explain because I'm not accepting it." He leans back on the couch, spreading his arms out along the back cushions.

I sit down but say nothing.

"Amber. You better start talking or I'm going to kiss you."

"You're not kissing me." I tuck my legs into my chest, my arms wrapped around them.

"If you don't explain yourself, you're getting a kiss whether you like it or not."

"You wouldn't understand."

"Try me."

"It's complicated."

"I'm sure I'll be able to understand. I'm almost a college graduate." He smiles that damn smile that is annoyingly irresistible. He brings his arms down off the couch and slowly moves toward me. "Kiss or tell. You choose."

"Fine," I say.

He resumes his position, arms extended along the back of the couch.

I take a breath and simply say, "Love doesn't last."

"Says who?"

"Just look around. Couples are constantly breaking up. Almost everyone's divorced. The proof is out there, Dylan. Love doesn't last."

He nods, as if considering it. "And yet sometimes it does. My grandparents were married for fifty-two years before my grandmother died. And my parents have been married for twenty-five."

"That doesn't mean they're in love, or at least not as in love as they used to be. Love fades over time."

"I disagree. It changes, but that doesn't mean it's faded. My grandparents grew more in love every year. My grandfather, who is not romantic at all, used to get up early every morning to make my grandmother her favorite breakfast; two poached eggs and a piece of toast with strawberry jam. He made the jam himself because she didn't like the store bought kind. That may not be love to someone our age but to them it was."

The story makes me want to cry. I'm such a sucker for romantic stories, especially ones with old people.

"Then your grandparents were lucky," I say. "Most people aren't. Most people end up hating each other after years of being together."

He pauses a moment. "So this is about your parents. You're projecting their problems onto us."

"That is not what I'm doing," I insist.

"It's exactly what you're doing."

"You're wrong. I'm not projecting anything. I'm simply stating a fact that love doesn't last."

Ignoring my statement, he nods. "Seems to work out timing-wise. You got the news Christmas day and that's when you started acting differently. You weren't as open. You didn't call me as much."

"That had nothing to do with—"

"Sunday when you got back, things seemed back to normal. Even *better* than normal. But then Monday you started pushing me away again. So what happened Monday?"

I hesitate, not wanting to talk about it.

"Amber. Tell me."

I sigh. "My dad filed the paperwork for the divorce. My mom got the papers and called me and went on and on about how much she can't stand my dad."

"Which made you think the same thing would happen to us. That our love wouldn't last and eventually we'd hate each other."

"Maybe not hate but...." My voice trails off.

Why does he have to be so damn smart? He wasn't supposed to figure this out and now that he has, I know he won't understand.

"Dylan, I'm just not ready for a serious relationship."

"Too bad. You're already in one and I know you don't want it to end. You said you love me."

"I do, but that doesn't mean anything if it's all going to end."

He leans forward, his elbows resting on his knees. "Amber, don't take this the wrong way but your logic is totally fucked up. And not just this time, but back in May too. You left me back then because you thought dating me would ruin the memory of that night if we ever broke up. And now everything's going great but you're trying to end it because someday it may not be as great as it is now?" He shakes his head. "That's fucked up."

"It's not fucked up. It's realistic. Love is temporary. All the books and movies that tell you it's not, are lying."

"You don't need books and movies to tell you about love. It's right in front of you, everywhere you look. You're just choosing to only see your parents and their experience. And Amber, I'm sorry about your parents but you don't know the whole story. You don't know what got them to this point and you probably never will. That's between them, but I'm sure it involved more than just having busy lives and growing apart. Relationships are complicated and no two are the same, so trying to compare ours to theirs isn't fair."

"I'm not comparing them. I'm just proving a point that love doesn't last. My mom said she used to love my dad more than anything, so how does that feeling just go away?"

"I don't know, but it's not going to happen to us. We're not them."

"You really think we're going to last? Our relationship started with a one-night stand."

"Yeah? So?"

"Even if I still had faith in love, I wouldn't want the story of how we fell in love to begin with a one-night stand. That'd be like the worst love story ever."

"It wasn't just a one-night stand. We've talked about this, Amber, and we both agree that night was special. There was something about it, like it was meant to be. And we didn't just have sex that night. We talked. We connected. We felt something for each other."

"Yeah, well, it's still a terrible way to start a love story. It's not something I could ever tell my kids or my grandkids."

"Then we'll alter it to make it more G-rated. Our kids won't have to know the truth."

Kids? Now he's talking about kids? This conversation is not going where I thought it would. I was supposed to tell him we were taking a break, and then he'd get angry and walk out, which would give me more time to think about what to do. But instead, he's planning our future, and our future kids!

"We're not having kids," I tell him. "And we're not getting married. You're moving way too fast here."

"I'm not saying we'd do these things today or next year. But I *have* thought about a future with you."

I've done the same thing. I've imagined a future with Dylan. Marriage. A house. Kids. The whole thing. But that was before my family fell apart.

"I don't even think I want that stuff anymore," I say.

"What stuff?"

"Marriage. Kids."

"Are you kidding? Amber, you love kids. Every time we're out and you see little kids, you smile or go over and talk to them. And you love all that wedding stuff. You've got bridal magazines in your room."

"Because I like looking at the dresses. They're pretty."

"I'm just saying, I know you want that stuff so don't act like you don't. You're just upset because of what's happening to your parents."

"It's proof that love doesn't last. And I don't want to be hurt when it ends."

"It only ends if we say it ends." He cups my cheek and our eyes meet. "I really believe we were meant to meet that night back in May. I don't know if it was fate or what you want to call it but I felt something that night that I've never felt before. That's why I kissed you before I even told you my name. It's like I couldn't stop myself. I had to kiss you. And after I did, I didn't want to let you go. I knew there was something between us."

I felt the same way. Why did we feel that way? People hook up at parties all the time and don't feel that way. They just continue on with their lives and never think about the person again. So why was it different for Dylan and me?

"I just need some time," I tell Dylan. "But you're right. My parents' divorce is what caused me to push you away this week, but I'm serious when I say I just don't think love can last."

"Then let's prove that it can."

"And if it doesn't? Then we'll both end up hurt."

"That's part of life. And if this ends, we'll survive. But I don't think it will. I never thought I'd feel this way about someone, but then you walked into my life and I finally understood what they meant in all those love ballads. That's why I was able to write one myself. You have to experience it before you can write about it."

"Dylan." I take a breath. "I love you. I really do, but I still need some time. Can you just give me that?"

He stands up. "I'll give you time but I'm not letting this be the end. I'm not letting you throw this away."

He walks off and I catch up to him at the door.

"That's not what I—"

"And don't you dare run out on me." He turns to me, anger on his face. "You did it once and I forgave you, but I won't do it again. If you decide you don't want this, you owe me an explanation why. I won't accept lies, or excuses, or the silent treatment. I want the truth, and I want you to look me in the eye when you tell me."

He leaves and I'm left standing there feeling lost and confused. What am I doing? Why do I keep running away from him? I ran from him last May and now I'm doing it again. But why? Dylan is everything I said I wanted. He's sweet, romantic, kind, smart, talented, super hot. And he loves me. So why am I letting my fears drive me away from him?

"Hey." Kira comes in the door. "Is Dylan here?"

"No. He left."

We go over to the couch and sit down.

"So what happened?" Kira asks.

"I told him I needed some time to think."

"Think about what?"

"About whether I want to be with him."

"Amber, are you kidding me? You broke up with him?"

"I didn't break up with him. I just told him I needed some time."

"Which is the first step to breaking up. Why are you doing this? Because of your parents?"

"Because of a lot of reasons, but yes, the divorce is part of it. It's affecting me more than I thought it would."

"It'll get better. I promise. Right now it seems bad, but once your parents get everything settled, you won't feel like this."

"Maybe. Or maybe not. I just don't know. I've always had this romantic idea of love and what it should be, but I learned all that by watching movies and reading romance books. But when I think of real life, and look around at not just my parents but everyone else, all I see are couples who don't get along. People who claim to love each other but then go out of their way to hurt each other."

"Some people, not everyone."

"You hurt Austin and it almost destroyed your relationship."

She looks down. "But I didn't want to hurt him. I wanted to tell him the truth. I just couldn't. And now that we got through that, our relationship is even stronger."

It's true. She and Austin are much closer after their break-up but that isn't true for everyone.

"So what happens now?" she asks.

"He said he'll give me space but that he's not giving up on me. I'm not sure what that means in terms of us dating. I'll see him at work in the morning so we'll see how it goes."

"I know he said he's not giving up on you but he's not going to wait forever."

"I know."

She goes to her room, giving me time to think, but all my thinking just leads to more confusion. More doubts. Fear of making the wrong decision.

***

The next morning, I arrive at work and start on the new project, which is coming up with promo ideas for all the health fairs that will be taking place this spring.

Dylan shows up and sits across from me. "Hey, how's it going?"

His tone is different; friendly, but lacking the hint of flirtatiousness that he usually uses with me. And there's no flirtatious smile. It's as if we're nothing more than friends.

"Good. How are you?"

"All right." He starts up his computer. "So you're working on the health fairs today?"

"Yeah. The promo ideas. I started to make a list when I was here on Wednesday. Did you want to go over it?"

"I'm actually working on something else. Donna assigned you the promo ideas. I'm working on marketing materials for a medical conference."

"Oh. Why didn't you tell me that before?"

"Because you wouldn't talk to me all week."

"So Donna doesn't want us working on it together?"

"She assigned me a different intern to work with. I'm supposed to help train her."

I'd forgotten the other interns were starting this week. There are two others but I haven't met them yet.

"Who's the intern you're working with?"

"Carrie. She just texted me. Said she's making copies. She should be back in a minute."

Just then a girl walks in. She's tall with a curvy figure, but not at all fat. She's wearing a dark blue dress that fits close to her body and has long, dark, wavy hair. As she walks up to Dylan I smell her perfume. It smells expensive.

"Hey, Dylan." She smiles at him. "You just get here?"

"Yeah." He motions to me. "This is Amber. She's one of the other interns."

He doesn't mention I'm his girlfriend given the rule about co-workers not being allowed to date. But if we were, would he still leave off the girlfriend label? I guess technically I'm not his girlfriend if I've asked him for space.

"Hi, I'm Carrie." She shakes my hand then turns back to Dylan. "Ready to go in the conference room?"

"Yeah, just let me grab my stuff." He takes a folder from his desk and the two of them disappear in the room behind me.

Okay, this sucks. The guy I love is alone in a room with a girl who definitely wants him. She was totally flirting with him. And she's gorgeous. And just last night I told him we needed a break. So would he go out with her? Is my fear and uncertainty going to drive Dylan away from me?

I need to figure this out. And soon. Otherwise I'll lose Dylan for good.

CHAPTER TWENTY-SEVEN

AMBER

For the next hour I can't concentrate on work, my mind fixated on what's going on in that conference room. Why have they been in there so long? Maybe they aren't talking about work but about other things, trying to get to know each other. What if Carrie asks Dylan out? Would he say yes?

The door finally opens and the two of them walk out.

"Yeah, totally," he says, laughing about whatever they were talking about. It doesn't sound like something work related.

"So lunch at eleven thirty?" she asks.

"Sounds good. I'll meet you in the parking garage."

She walks out the door and Dylan returns to his desk. Meanwhile I'm stewing with jealousy, wondering what went on in that room and what's going on at lunch. I'm generally not a jealous person. In fact, I've never felt this jealous in my life. But I'm finding that being in love makes me very jealous.

"Where'd she go?" I ask Dylan.

"She has class and then she'll be back."

"You guys are working through lunch?"

"We're not working. We're just having lunch."

"Oh." I feel like I just got punched in the gut. Dylan's going out with another girl. I think I'm going to be sick. "I'll be right back," I say, getting up to go to the restroom. It's way down the hall and when I get there, I stand at the sink taking deep breaths as I wonder, for the millionth time, what the hell is wrong with me. My parents' divorce should not be affecting my relationship with Dylan like this, and yet I'm letting it happen. Why am I so afraid of love? I've always known it could lead to heartbreak but I was willing to take the risk. Now I don't know if I am.

I leave the restroom and find Dylan waiting for me in the hall. "You okay?"

"Yeah. I just wasn't feeling well for a minute but I'm fine now."

"You sure?"

I nod. "We should get back to work."

As we walk back, he says, "So about tonight. I made plans to go out. I assumed you wanted to be alone."

Hearing him say that makes me want to cry. I wish I could just stop this and be with him but I told both him and myself I needed to think this over so that's what I need to do. For Dylan and I to work, I need to get over my fear of a broken heart. I need to believe in love again. It's not fair for me to keep seeing him unless I can give him all my heart and commit to him the way he's committed to me.

"Yeah, okay," I say, my words rushed, my breathing shallow.

"Hey." He stops me in the hall, his hand on my arm. "You said this is what you wanted. I'm giving you time. Space."

"I know." I chew on my lip, tears stinging my eyes.

He lowers his voice. "This doesn't mean I don't love you. I'm just trying to give you what you asked for."

I nod, tears threatening to fall.

He turns back, like he's checking something, then grabs my hand and leads me to a door. He opens it and I see it's a supply closet. It's not the same one we were in before but it looks the same, with mops and brooms and bottles of cleaning solution.

"What are we doing here?"

He brings me into his arms and gives me a hug, which is exactly what I need right now. I relax into his arms and chest and take a moment to breathe.

"I'm sorry," I say. "I'm sorry I'm being this way. I don't know what's wrong with me. I honestly don't. I keep telling myself to stop feeling this way but then I can't."

"It's okay. I understand. It's tough seeing your parents split up. I've seen a lot of my friends go through it and it's never easy. Van's parents broke up a few years ago and he's still having a tough time with it. I think that's why he can't stay in a relationship. He says it's because he likes playing the field but I think it's really because he's afraid of relationships in general."

I pull back to look at him. "I didn't know Van's parents were divorced. How long ago?"

"When he was a senior in high school, so about four years? He was supposed to go away for college but he stayed here because his younger sisters couldn't handle the divorce. They were a mess. They went to counseling but Van didn't think that was enough. So he stayed here to help them get through it. That's how we ended up going to college together."

"He's a good big brother."

Dylan lets me go and steps back. "I know you're going through a really hard time right now but just remember that I'm more than your boyfriend. I'm also your friend. So if you need to talk or just need someone to listen, I'm here for you."

A tear slips down my cheek and I hug him. "I love you. And I promise you I'm trying to get past this. I really am."

"I know you are." He kisses my forehead.

The door swings open and we turn and see Mary standing there.

She gasps, pointing at us. "I knew you two had something going on! Don't think I'm not going to report this! It violates hospital rules."

Dylan and I let go of each other and Dylan calmly says to Mary, "I was just giving Amber a hug. She's going through a rough time right now and she's not feeling good."

"And what exactly is the problem?" Mary asks in a skeptic tone.

"I just found out my parents are getting a divorce," I say.

"Oh." Mary glances to the side and clears her throat. "I suppose that would be upsetting."

"My dad filed the papers this week and now my mom is really upset and it's just been hard. On my whole family."

Mary looks back at me. "I'm sorry to hear that." She straightens up. "Well, I'll leave you two be." And then she walks out.

"That was close," I say.

"We weren't doing anything."

"But she thought we were."

"And now she thinks we're not. I get the feeling she'll leave us alone from here on out. I think she actually felt bad just now."

"It felt weird to say it."

"To say your parents are divorcing?"

"Yeah. That's the first time I've said it to someone who isn't a close friend. For some reason, it made it more real. Like it's really happening. Does that make sense?"

"It does. Saying it out loud always makes it more real. When it's in your head, it's just a thought, but when you tell someone, it's out there. It can't be taken back. And that makes it more real."

I look at him. "Like when I said I love you."

He smiles. "Yeah. Kind of made it more real, right?"

"A lot more real."

"I feel the same way. It's one of the reasons I was afraid to tell you that. I wasn't sure if I wanted it to be real." He pauses. "You're not the only one afraid of this, Amber. I'm afraid of it not working out too. I'm afraid of getting hurt. I'm afraid you'll leave me like you did last time. But I'm willing to risk it to be with you. That's how much I love you."

Tears fall down my cheeks. "Stop it. You're making me cry." I wipe my face and take a deep breath. "We should

289

probably get out of here or Mary really *will* think we're doing something."

He goes to open the door but I stop him.

"Wait." I hold onto his arm.

"What?"

"What's the deal with um...Carrie? Are you two..." I don't finish, not wanting to say it.

"Going out?" When I don't answer, he chuckles. "No. We're just having lunch. But it's good to know you're jealous."

"So jealous I almost got sick. That's why I had to go to the restroom."

He lifts my face to his and looks me in the eye. "There's nothing to be jealous of. *You're* my girlfriend, not her. And I'd never cheat on you."

"I'm still your girlfriend?"

"Aren't you?"

"I want to be. I just wasn't sure if you were okay with that, given that we're kind of on a break."

"You're still my girlfriend. And it's not a break. It's just some time for reflection."

I smile. "Reflection. I like that. I'm reflecting."

"Just don't reflect too long. I miss you."

He gives me a kiss, then opens the door and we go back to the office. I feel better after our talk but I still need to figure things out in my head. I know I want Dylan. I just need to get to a place where I can give him my heart without worrying about the fallout that would occur should we ever break up.

That night, I really miss Dylan and want to be with him, but I resist calling him and instead sit in my room and make a list of all that I'm afraid of when it comes to him. And it turns out, everything on my list are things that happened to my parents. Falling out of love. Breaking up a family. And the pain and heartache of losing the one person you thought you'd have forever with.

The list confirms that it's the divorce that's holding me back from being with Dylan. My parents' divorce, and years of watching them fall out of love. I thought it might be more than that but it's not. It all comes back to my parents and what I witnessed all those years they grew apart. The fighting. The hurtful comments. The separate bedrooms. It all affected me more than I was willing to admit. I think that's also why I sought out the fairy tale for so many years. The dream of a happily ever after. I wanted the opposite of what my parents had.

I spend Friday night and all day Saturday thinking about this. I don't talk to Dylan, but Saturday night, I go with Kira to hear his concert. When he sings *One Night*, I start crying, which happens every time I hear it because I still feel terrible for hurting him that night last May. Other girls are crying too because Dylan sings that song with so much emotion. And hearing the emotion in his voice makes me even sadder because I know that emotion is real. The sadness I caused him when I left that night is still there.

After the concert I don't stick around but I do text Dylan and tell him he did a great job, as always. He texts me back and thanks me for coming but doesn't ask if he can come over. He's giving me space, like I asked, and I appreciate that. He really is the best, most understanding boyfriend I could ever ask for.

The week goes by and I don't see Dylan at all. We text a few times but that's it. He doesn't call or stop over and I'm starting to wonder if he's given up on me. If he's tired of my indecisiveness and wants someone who can commit to him. I want to be that someone, but right now I just can't. My emotions are too wrapped up in what's going on with my family, trying to accept the loss I feel over my parents splitting up. Trying to figure out why this happened. Why they fell out of love. I know it happens all the time, to everyone, but I'm finding it hard to accept with my parents because I still remember the years they were in love. Their love was real and strong and something I wanted for myself someday, so how did it just end?

Friday at work, Dylan isn't there but Carrie is and she sits at his desk, using his computer. She tells me Dylan had car trouble and probably won't be coming in. Given our lack of communication this week, I guess I'm not surprised Dylan didn't tell me he wouldn't be there, but it's still depressing that Carrie knew where my boyfriend was but I didn't.

On Saturday morning, my mom calls to check in. We haven't talked for a while because she's been so busy dealing with all the stuff you have to do when you get divorced. And I've avoided calling her because I don't want to hear her rant about how much she hates my dad.

"How are classes going?" she asks.

"Fine. How's everything going there?" I hold my breath, hoping she doesn't start in about my dad.

"It's been hard," she says, sounding sad. "But we'll make it through this. It'll just take some time to adjust."

"How's Britt doing?" I ask, but I already know she's not doing well. I talk to her every night and she cries almost every time.

"She's having a difficult time accepting it. I think she'd rather have your father and I together fighting than to have us apart, but then again, that's all she knows."

Britt's earliest memories were at a time when my parents were growing apart so she's used to their fighting. She doesn't remember the good years. She was too young.

"So how is Dylan?" she asks.

"We're kind of taking a break right now."

"Things aren't going well?"

"They are, I mean, they were, but I needed some time alone to deal with this. The divorce."

"Honey, I'm sorry. I hate what this is doing to you girls, but remember it's only temporary. When it's all over, things will get better."

"Maybe, but I'm still struggling with how this all happened, like when it started and why. I know that's between you and dad, but I'm having a hard time accepting this without

292

an explanation. You and Dad used to be so in love. I remember how he used to bring you gifts for no reason. How he used to always hold your hand and kiss you the second he got home from work. So how does that just end? Until I understand that, I don't know if I can keep dating Dylan."

"What does this have to do with Dylan?"

"I love him. I love him so much that I could see a future with him. But I'm afraid to be with him knowing we could end up like you and Dad. I don't want that. The fighting. The hate. I don't want that with Dylan. Even if it doesn't happen for years, I'm scared of the possibility and it's keeping me from being with him."

There. I said it. I was totally honest. I wasn't going to tell her that because I didn't want her feeling guilty about what the divorce is doing to me. She's already hurting enough and I didn't want to add even more hurt, but I really need an answer and she's the only one who can give it to me.

"If I tell you something," she says, "can you promise to keep it just between us? I don't want your sisters knowing this."

"Yes. I promise. I won't tell." I'm feeling nervous, wondering what she's going to say.

"I never wanted you girls to know this, but I also don't want what's happening to your father and me to affect your future relationships. I want you to be happy, and if Dylan is the boy for you, then I don't want anything to ruin that."

"So what are you saying?"

She sighs. "Years ago, back when your father was traveling a lot for work, I got lonely. There was a man. A man who worked at my office and we...well, we went out a few times, and one time, things went too far."

"You cheated on Dad?" My jaw practically drops to the floor. My mom is the last person in the world I would ever think would cheat.

"I didn't mean for it to happen," she says. "It was just one of those things that happened in a moment of weakness. Your father kept promising me he'd cut back on the travel but he didn't and it was making me angry. I worked full time and had to be a single mother and take care of the house. It was all too much. So when this other man paid attention to me, listened to me, offered to help in any way I needed, I felt cared for. Appreciated. Like someone finally understood what I was going through. It was wrong, and I knew it was wrong right after I did it but by then it was too late."

"How did Dad find out?"

"I told him. I couldn't live with the guilt so I told him and we ended up going to counseling. But it didn't help. Your father was too angry with me. He couldn't forgive me. And to get back at me he...."

"Cheated on you."

"He said it only happened once but I don't know if that's true. Honestly I think it went on for a couple months. Anyway, after that we discussed divorce but both decided to stay together for you girls. Looking back, that was probably a mistake but it was the decision that seemed right at the time."

I take a deep breath as I let this sink in. My mom cheated. And so did my dad. I never in a million years would've guessed that's what sparked all those years of fighting. I guess I don't know my parents as well as I thought I did.

"We tried to get back to the place we were at before," my mom says. "But we just couldn't do it. There was no trust left. No respect. And eventually, no love."

"If it hadn't happened, do you think you'd still be in love?"

"It's hard to say. I'd like to think we would, but other things could've happened to drive us apart. Your father and I were never good at communicating. Whenever I wanted to talk about serious issues he'd shut down, and that's hard on a relationship."

Dylan doesn't shut down. He's always open with his feelings. I'm more likely to shut down than he is, which is something I probably get from my dad.

"Amber," my mom says, her voice soft but stern. "Don't let the divorce affect your relationship with Dylan. I know it's easier to push him away until you've accepted this and dealt with it and feel like you're in a better place, but this is the time when you can really test your love for each other. If he's willing to stick by your side through something like this, then chances are you can get through most anything. So don't push him away. Let him be there for you. Let him show you how much he cares."

I nod, even though she can't see me.

"Your father and I had many good years. Just because things didn't work out doesn't mean I regret being with him. We had a love that I'll never have with anyone else and we have three beautiful daughters to prove it. So don't let this divorce discourage you from being in a relationship. Don't ever be afraid to love someone. Go into it with your heart open. That's the best advice I can give you, because when you love someone fully and completely and they love you back, it's the best feeling in the world." I hear noise, like she scooted her chair back. "Honey, I hate to rush off the phone but I have to take Britt to cheerleading practice. Can we talk later?"

"Yeah. But mom?"

"Yes, honey?"

"I'm sorry you have to go through this. I'm sorry things ended this way."

"I am too. I wish things could have gone differently. But we'll move on from this. I promise you, things will get better. I love you, honey."

"Love you, too. Bye, Mom."

She hangs up and I lie on my bed, feeling like a giant weight has been lifted off me. Like the dark clouds have parted and there's light again. My parents' infidelity explains why they fell out of love and I really needed to hear that, but that isn't the reason I'm feeling so much better right now. The reason I'm feeling better, more hopeful, is because my mom still believes in love.

After everything she's been through, I expected my mom to be bitter about love. To have closed her mind and heart off to the very idea of love. To discourage me from ever pursuing it. But instead, she told me to go for it. To love with everything I am, despite the risks of having my heart broken.

My mom loved my dad with all her heart and now her heart is broken. But despite that, she still wants her daughters to experience love. To take the risk and go out in the world and find someone to give our hearts to.

I already found that someone. And I'm ready to give him my heart, without hesitation or doubt or worry about what may be.

I go to my desk and take out a piece of paper and my special pen and begin writing. Writing to the person I'm giving my heart to. The guy I met last May who I was only supposed to be with for one night but ended up being the guy I want to spend my forever with.

I still have my doubts. I still have fears. But I'm taking my mom's advice. Open my heart. Love fully and completely. It's exactly what I've wanted to do but my uncertainty about the future wouldn't let me. But I'm letting those uncertainties go because I want to be with Dylan. He's the one I love. The one I want to be with. The one I want to give my heart to.

CHAPTER TWENTY-EIGHT

DYLAN

"I'm going out," Van says as he opens the door. "You want anything?"

"No, I'm good, but thanks." I focus on the basketball game on TV but hear Van laughing.

"Seriously, dude, is this ever going to end?"

"What?"

He comes back holding an envelope and drops it in my lap. "This letter shit. You guys are already dating. Why do you keep doing this?"

I smile. "Because it's romantic."

He rolls his eyes. "Whatever, man. See ya later."

After he leaves, I rip open the envelope. I haven't seen Amber in over a week. It's killing me not to see her but I want to give her space. I want her to come to me when she's ready and I'm hoping this letter is telling me she is.

Or she could be breaking up with me. Shit!

I unfold the sheet of paper. It's covered with scrolling letters written with her special pen.

Dear Dylan,

There once was a girl who believed in fairy tales because fairy tales were better than real life. Real life is full of sadness, disappointment, stories that don't end well.

So the girl chose to believe in fairy tales and waited for her prince. And she found him, in of all places, a frat house. Not exactly a castle but it would do. After their brief encounter, she ran away like Cinderella at the stroke of midnight.

The night they shared was magical but she feared the magic would disappear if they ever met again. But staying away from him wasn't possible. She had to see her prince again, and when she did, the magic was still there, sparkling all around her, even brighter than before.

Then something bad happened. Something that made her question magic and fairy tales and happy endings. A dark cloud hung over her and she shunned the prince, uncertain if she trusted the magic between them, or if it could last. But she still felt it, even without him there, because it was in her heart.

No matter how many dark clouds followed her, the lightness, the magic, remained in her heart because the magic she felt was love. True love for her prince. And then suddenly, the dark clouds parted and she saw the light again. Bright, powerful rays of light that made her feel happy and alive and desperate to see her prince again. But this time, she promised herself she would give him her heart, fulling and completely. And she hoped he would do the same, because he was, after all, her prince. She knew that now more than ever.

Throughout this journey, the girl discovered that happily ever afters don't really exist, but that love does, and love, although it has its ups and downs, leads to true happiness. So now, she wants her prince back, if he's willing to take her. She knows she hasn't made it easy on him, making him ride through the dark forest, chase her through the grassy meadow, wade through the rushing stream just to get to her.

But if he still wants her, she's waiting with open arms, and an open heart.

Love always, Amber

I smile. That might be her best letter ever.

My phone dings and I see it's a text from Amber. *Did you read it?*

Yes, I text back.

There's a knock on the door. I set the letter down and go to the door. When I open it I see Amber standing there in a light pink dress, her blond hair down around her shoulders, styled with soft curls. She looks like a princess, which I think is intentional.

"Hi," she says, looking hesitant. "I'm here to um..."

"Get your prince?"

She smiles. "Yeah. I rode on a horse and everything."

I chuckle as I glance at the driveway. "Your horse looks like a Ford Focus."

"It's the best I could do on short notice." She looks down, then back up. "So um, can I come in?"

"Yeah, sorry." I step aside. I was so busy staring at her I didn't realize she was still outside.

We go in the living room and she stands in front of me. "I don't really know what to say other than—"

"You already said it. The letter said it all." My arms go around her and I tug her into me. "It was a good letter. Better than your other ones."

She laughs. "Meaning my other ones were crap."

I shrug. "So you're not a writer. Not everyone is."

"At least I got my point across." She looks up at me with those bright blue eyes. "But I didn't get an answer."

"You didn't ask a question," I say, teasing her.

She tilts her head. "Will my prince come back to me?"

"He'd ride through the dark enchanted forest to be with you."

"So that's a yes?"

"It's a yes." I lean down and kiss her beautiful lips, the ones I've missed so damn much that once we start kissing I can't stop, until she slowly backs away.

"Let's go to your room."

After some much needed make-up sex, we go out and get something to eat. Then later that night, we go to Amber's apartment because Kira is spending the weekend with Austin.

We have sex again, then lie in her bed, her body resting against mine.

"We still don't have a good story," she says.

"What are you talking about?"

"Our story. The one we'll tell our grandkids."

So she finally sees a future with me. I smile at that.

"I told you, we'll make something up. Or we'll just tell them we met at a party. We'll leave out the one-night stand. Nobody needs to know about that."

She stretches her arms out and sighs happily. "I'm hungry. Want to go find something to eat?" She turns to me. "Oh! Would you make that egg thing again? That was really good."

"It was just scrambled eggs."

"It was still really good."

"If that's what you want, then yeah, I'll make it." I give her a kiss. "Let's go."

She gets out of bed and puts on her robe while I put on my jeans.

"What's that?" I ask, pointing to the bulletin board above her desk. There's something red hanging from it.

She goes over and looks at it, then laughs. "Kira must've taken it from my room back home and brought it here. She was probably hoping it'd restore my faith in love."

"What is it?"

"The remnants of a balloon I found when I was a kid. My family was on vacation at Lake Michigan and the balloon floated down to me when I was on the beach."

"Huh." I walk over to get a better look at it. It seems familiar. Oddly familiar. "Why'd you keep it?"

"Because I'm a hopeless romantic." She laughs again. "There was a message inside from some kid. I still have the note."

The note? My heart beats faster. There's no way. No freaking way.

"Is it back at your house?" I ask.

"No. I keep it in my jewelry box."

"Can I see it?"

She looks at me funny. "Um, okay." She goes to her dresser and opens her jewelry box and takes out a small scrap of paper.

Holy shit. That can't be it. How would that even be possible?

She starts to read the note. "To whoever—"

"Wait. Stop."

"Why?"

"To whoever finds this," I say, slowly walking toward her. "If you're a boy, throw it out. If you're a girl, it means we're meant to be together. When I'm old, I'll come find you and we'll get married. So don't marry anyone else. Just wait." I'm standing in front of Amber now. Her eyes are wide, her jaw dropped. She looks down at the note and we say the last line together, "I'll come find you."

"Oh my God." She drops the note as her hand flies over her mouth. "You were *him*? You were the little boy? How is that possible?"

"I went to camp that summer. It was just north of Chicago along Lake Michigan. One day they made us write notes and send them off in balloons. I don't even know why I wrote that. Everyone else wrote basic shit, like their name and where they're from. But when I sat down to write, it's the first thing that came to mind. And then I sent it off, never thinking it would make it to anyone."

"But it did," she says as her hand falls back by her side. "I can't believe this. I found your note. YOUR note, Dylan."

I smile. "I know. It's crazy."

"I waited for you. When I got home from the trip, I tried on every dress I had so I'd be all ready for when you arrived. But then you never came."

"I was only ten." I chuckle. "Didn't have any wheels back then, other than my bike, which I doubt would've made it to Michigan." I cup her cheek. "You really waited for me?"

She nods. "For weeks. Months. I didn't know who you were or what you looked like, but in my heart, I felt that if I ever saw you, I'd know it was you."

"And you did," I say, putting the pieces together. "That night at the party, we both felt something. We both felt like we'd met before even though we hadn't."

"But we *had* met, just not in person." She looks in my eyes. "I knew it was you. I didn't understand it at the time but now I do. I felt connected to you. Drawn to you. Because I knew you. I knew you from the note. I waited for you."

"And I found you." I wrap my hands around her face and kiss her.

She's the girl. Amber's the girl I wrote the note to. The girl I said I would marry. I found her.

If I ever doubted fate, I never will again. This is fate in all its wonderful glory. Fate brought Amber and me together. We were meant to go to that party that night. We were meant to meet. Meant to be together.

"You know what this means?" I ask, smiling at her.

"What?"

"Our story didn't start at that party. It started when I sent that balloon. When I was ten and you were nine. That's our story, Amber. That's the story we'll tell our kids, and our grandkids."

Her eyes widen and she smiles even more. "You're right! That's our story. And it's perfect. Better than perfect! It's amazing. Better than anything I could even make up."

"Let's go eat," I say taking her hand. "Then we're going to come back here and I'm going to make love to the girl who found the balloon."

She gives me a kiss. "I love you."

"I love you too."

What are the odds? I mean, seriously, it makes absolutely no sense for a balloon to make it all the way across Lake Michigan and land at the exact spot where Amber was standing on the beach.

It has to mean something. It has to mean we were meant to be together.

CHAPTER TWENTY-NINE

AMBER

Two weeks have passed since Dylan and I officially ended our break and found out about the balloon. I still can't believe it. I told the story to everyone I know and nobody else can believe it either. It seems too crazy to be true but that's what makes it so special. We're probably the only two people in the world ever brought together that way. It's a story unique to us. And it proves we were meant for each other.

"Are you nervous?" Kira asks as she sits beside me. We're at the bar where Vandyl is playing, seated at a table near the stage.

"A little," I say. "Okay, maybe a lot." I take a big gulp of the drink she brought me.

"Relax. You two are together so it's not like it was really a one-night stand."

She's referring to the fact that tonight Dylan will be singing his new song, *One Week*, for the first time, and he'll be singing it to me. And since it's a follow-up to *One Night*, soon everyone will know I'm the girl he wrote the song about.

A few days ago, Dylan sang *One Week* to me and I loved it. Just like *One Night*, the lyrics were rich in emotion and I cried when I heard it. Dylan was right when he said the best music is inspired by someone. The inspiration is what creates the emotion.

After Dylan played the song for me, I told him he had to perform it but he said he didn't want to. He said it was just for me, but I told him he had to play it for others because it's too beautiful not to share.

When he finally agreed to perform it, he asked if he could sing it to me from stage and I panicked. I didn't want people knowing I was the girl, but then I thought about it and decided it'd be okay because as Dylan and I have said all along, that night wasn't just a one-night stand. It wasn't just about sex. It was more than that. It's the night that brought us together. The night we realized there was something between us that we'd never felt with anyone else.

"I think I'll be okay," I say to Kira, swigging my whiskey sour.

I hear Dylan behind me. "Better slow down on those drinks." He sits next to me and gives me a kiss.

"Don't you need to be backstage?"

"We've got a couple minutes. You nervous?"

"A little, but I'll be fine."

He leans over and whispers in my ear, "I love you."

"I love you too." I kiss him, then back away and notice girls watching us, jealousy in their eyes. I'm still not used to all the attention he gets from girls.

"I've gotta go." Dylan gets up. "See you after the show."

He leaves, and a few minutes later, the guys appear on stage, girls screaming their names. Hearing girls yell for Dylan should make me jealous, and it used to, but now it doesn't because I know he's mine.

The guys play their regular set, saving Dylan's songs for last. Girls are screaming *One Night*, begging the band to play it, and when I hear the first notes, I get so nervous I feel like I might be sick. But then I see Dylan looking at me with those big brown eyes and I start to relax. Soon I get lost in the song, lost in the sound of his voice, and it isn't until the very end that I notice people staring at me.

Do they know? Do they know I'm the girl in the song? I can't tell. Some of them look like they know but others seem unsure.

I glance away from them and look back at the stage when I hear Dylan's voice through the speakers.

"We've got a surprise for you guys tonight," he says to the crowd. "It's a new song I wrote called *One Week*. It's a follow up to *One Night*. I hope you like it."

He plays the first notes and everyone quiets down. The lyrics describe how a letter showed up at his doorstep. How he knew it was from me before he even opened it. The song continues, describing that first week we were together, and the feelings we had when we saw each other again. The music is slow but has a lighter, more hopeful sound than *One Night*, which was dark and moody.

The chorus plays and I hear the girls next to me quietly humming along because the chorus is similar to *One Night*, which Dylan intentionally did to link the two songs together.

Dylan's eyes are on me as he sings the chorus. *One week. I was with her. One week. Couldn't get enough of her. One week. And she was mine. One week. I have her back.*

He looks out at the crowd as the song continues, glancing at me during certain parts.

At the very end, he focuses solely on me and walks off the stage to where I'm sitting.

One week, he sings, *and I have her back.* He stands in front of me and takes my hand as he sings the last line, *I have her back.*

He pulls me up from my chair and kisses me and the crowd goes crazy, clapping and yelling, "That's her!"

Our secret is out. Everyone knows Dylan and I shared a night together.

One night. A night we would never forget, and that we never thought would be anything more.

One night. That's all it was supposed to be.

One night. And yet it changed our lives.

One night. The night I met my prince.

One night. The start of my forever.